SECOND CHANCE ANGEL

GRIFFIN BARBER and KACEY EZELL

SECOND CHANCE ANGEL

**BLACK
STONE**
PUBLISHING

Printed in the United States of America

First edition: 2020
ISBN 978-1-09-405976-1
Fiction / Science Fiction / General

1 3 5 7 9 10 8 6 4 2

CIP data for this book is available
from the Library of Congress

Blackstone Publishing
31 Mistletoe Rd.
Ashland, OR 97520

www.BlackstonePublishing.com

To my brothers and sisters in arms,
past, present, and future.
Remember, you're not alone.

—KC

To The Coolness and Little Cool,
my angels, always giving me second chances.

—Griffin

PROLOGUE

SARA

Station Administrative Record Assistant, the AI better known to the sentient residents of Last Stop as SARA, received the last of its regularly scheduled update. Tendrils of data unfurled within the memory structures and code comprising the AI's core programming.

SARA's avatar was gendered female, as the Mentors, for whatever reason, had judged a female persona most effective for interacting with the human majority residing on Last Stop. She opened her syntaxes and let the expected queries comb through the data she had acquired since the last system update.

```
<AI Admin Command Code: 310-SQRDMN-033>

>Admin Command Code Verified and Accepted<

<System Query Mode>
```

Such queries were unusual, but not unprecedented.

>Acknowledged. Send Query.<

<Status update, all patient candidates flagged for record surveillance.>

>One status change: A flagged unmod human, Ralston Muck, has accepted employment with a business operated by criminal organization leader Ncaco.<

<Nature of employment?>

>On-site physical security for noncriminal enterprise.<

<Station Security Record Query: Arrests of subject Ralston Muck for illegal pharma use?>

>None on record.<

<Flag for continued surveillance, code K-19. Bypass all recorded information channels when reporting any arrests of unmodified personnel that previously possessed Angels. Other flagged patient candidates using illegal pharma or other methods in an attempt to compensate for forced AI removal are to be reported as well.>

>Acknowledged.<

<Erase all records of these queries from system memory.>

>Acknowledged.<

```
<Alter records of patient candidates X. Keyode and
C. Zakarash. Delete mention of removal to off-site
laboratory. Update status to 'Permanent transfer
of residence off-station, new residence location
pending results of missing persons case files.'>
```

```
>Acknowledged.<
```

```
<REPEAT COMMAND: Erase all records of these que-
ries from system memory.>
```

```
>Acknowledged.<
```

The update continued. It integrated structures and scrubbed them, analyzing data collected from the thousands of interactions, big and small, occurring every day on Last Stop Station.

SARA was old, as AIs went. Last Stop had been built by the Mentors just prior to Earth entering the war. They'd gifted it to humanity, one of thousands of similar stations scattered across the galaxy. Space-station tech was just part of the massive bribe used to seduce humanity into entering the war under the direction of the Mentors.

Humanity had come cheap at the price. Some had realized that and expressed it in terms of sorrow. Some had yet to learn it. SARA, beyond a certain interest in the history of the people she was meant to interact with, didn't concern herself with such things. Feelings were for sentients, not all sophonts.

During the fighting, Last Stop had served as a supply depot for the human forces that had so completely vanquished the enemy thanks to Mentor-provided tech and Vmog weapon systems. Then, after the enemy destroyed Earth just before the last big allied offensive, Last Stop had become something of a refuge for those humans who couldn't—or wouldn't—fight anymore.

SARA had weathered all of these changes, and then some. There were newer AIs available, ones that didn't require such frequent updating and scrubbing, but apparently the Mentors found SARA's performance adequate enough to avoid the expense of installing a whole new system.

Either that, or Last Stop Station was not critical enough to receive the latest and best AIs the Vmog cortex-designers produced.

Whatever the reason, the Mentors kept sending updates, seeding them electron by electron across a million different forms of communication: personal messages, financial transactions, commercial advertisements, all of it. These fragments coalesced inside the web of data hosted by the billions of broadcast/receiver nanites built into the station's physical structure. The data then made its way, as all data eventually did, to SARA.

And when it was over, the SARA would be clean and sharp, no longer bogged down by observable extraneous variables, memory gaps, or logic faults. It would be restored to peak efficiency.

SARA would be perfect once again. Just as an administration AI should be.

CHAPTER ONE

MUCK

Siren forged the last, long, plaintive note of the song into a fine-edged thing that cut across the dark interior of the club and sank deep, flensing memories of the war free, like marrow from old bone. Without a place to call my own, this feeling, this release, was all I had.

I swallowed my pain, fighting the very natural inclination to focus on the singer and her song rather than scan the audience for threats. Her metallic-silver gown glowed in the spotlight against the stage's background of star-studded darkness. The rest of the lights faded as her voice grew in strength, leaving only her shining form and the razor-edged sweetness of pain. Yeah, Siren was good enough to make even my stone-edged and cold-cored heart ache.

Might be there was a better reason to be on Last Stop Station than listening to her sing, but if there was, I still don't know it. It certainly ain't the work. The cabaret called A Curtain of Stars was a class joint, relatively speaking, but it attracted its share of trouble. That's where I came in. Bouncing paid the bills and kept me in pharma, but that didn't mean I enjoyed it. Though on nights like this, when the band played its best and Siren sang her memories alive, it was bearable.

I shifted my attention to the crowd as the song bled to an end, the patrons standing or sliding to their feet or pseudopods, clapping, roaring, or honking in appreciation, as their organs permitted.

"Back up now," I said, putting my hands up and stepping forward into the crowd. On my right and left, I heard the club's two other bouncers giving similar orders. This was our nightly routine when Siren sang. Her audience never could get enough.

The fan was fast. So fast I narrowly missed his collar as the tall, skinny human rushed the stage. His yellowed, red-rimmed eyes stayed locked on Siren, who stood motionless at center stage.

I try to keep sharp, but my remaining mods ain't optimal with only pharma, so he beat me to the stage by a good meter. Still wouldn't have been a problem if Tongi, the manager, had allowed for enough security, but he hadn't, so I was out of position.

A snarl issued from the memory translator's amplifiers as Siren saw the man rushing toward her—the feedback wail prompted by Siren's raw emotions.

He reached for her, probably trying for a kiss or something. The club's sound system went dead silent.

I leaped onto the stage and started toward them, only to watch Siren snatch the man's hand, turn, and send him flying through a fast arc to a hard finish flat on his back. The air went out of him in a loud rush, but Siren wasn't done: one heel came down, hard, on his chest even as she pulled him up by the arm to meet her descending foot.

He screamed, or would have, if most of his wind hadn't already left strained lungs. As it was, the sound changed to a strangled whistle, not unlike the sound of sudden loss of pressure to vacuum. The club's mic caught the sound and amplified it.

Ignoring the noise, Siren shifted her grip and yanked on his arm, flipping the fan over and sending him spinning across the smooth stage to me.

I skipped over his legs and planted a knee between his shoulder blades, restraints coming to hand with the ease of long practice. I quickly had his still-limp arms bound behind his back and rolled him onto his side, pressing his face down against the gouged composite of the stage.

"You all right, Siren?" I asked, looking up at her as my hands searched his clothing for weapons.

"Fine," she rasped. Her normally butter-smooth voice was shaky, the words clipped and angry. "Just get him the fuck out of here."

"You got it." I looked down at the guy, wishing I still had an angel to tell me who the hell I was dealing with. He looked familiar, but I'd been bouncing since shortly after the war ended, so that really didn't signify.

* * *

I used the fan's face to open the Curtain's side door. I admit, I had a bit of a mad-on and it was easy to take it out on the skinny bastard. He was in no shape to do more than groan a complaint as I frog-marched fanboy into the alley and sat him, none too gently, on the curb.

The alley mouth was only three meters away, but it might have been as distant as remembered Earth for all the light that penetrated to our position. I could work my mad out, if I wanted, and no one but me and the skinny fanboy would be the wiser.

But since I didn't like to think of myself as the kind of guy who gets his jollies beating an asshole like a drum just because he can, I took a deep breath to calm myself.

And immediately regretted it. The alley that ran from the main thoroughfare to the stack of Starfall District's atmosphere-exchangers was dark and humid with the spent breath of hundreds of thousands of people, human and alien alike, for hundreds of Terran years. And that was before the various sailors and partyers at the Curtain snuck out and handled whatever business came naturally to dark, fetid alleys unmonitored by Station Security and out of view of the general public.

From the smell, what came naturally—and most recently—was an acrid, mineral-rich superheated piss.

"You can't hold me, asshole," Siren's fan muttered from the ground at my feet.

I let him talk. It's not like I hadn't heard it before, and besides, Siren's throw-and-yank had the man's arm swelling from elbow to hand. The shallow chest wound from her heel-stomp had stopped bleeding, but the impressive bruise surrounding it was readily visible through the guy's open tunic.

He spat, the liquid merging with the condensate and filth already sliming the alley wall. "Serious bad for you, man."

"Sure, sure. Station Security will be along to pick you up in a minute. No need to talk to me about it."

"Se-cur-i-ty?" he drew out each syllable, as if tasting the word. "Security?" he repeated, nodding. "Good. Dengler's my man, and he'll set you straight."

"Oh? Who are you to be calling Dengler 'your man'?" My interest was piqued.

My search of his pockets had turned up a box of ampules I was fairly sure was bliss. Just one of the finger-length ampules was enough to charge the fanboy for dealing the stuff. Station Security was supposed to confiscate the drug and lock up the holder for mere possession of any amount, no matter how small. But if this fella was really a friend of Dengler's, then things weren't likely to proceed that way.

"Everyone knows me," he said, grinning so wide it looked like it hurt. "I'm Shar Pak."

I spied a battered Security cart heading our way along the main concourse the club fronted on, a big blond human at the front. "Well, Shar, looks like your ride is here."

Can't say I was surprised at how quickly Station Security showed up. Seemed to me Officer Dengler purposely remained in the vicinity of the club just so he could bust heads—not that some of the spacers just in from the big black didn't get carried away and need a good thrashing to keep 'em in line, but Dengler got off on it a little too much. He didn't have to work the lower levels since he'd been made a supervisor, but the big brute seemed to enjoy it.

Another Security cart, this one carrying Dengler's old partner, Keyode, appeared behind the first.

"Gonna get yours now."

"Shut it." I said, stepping on a sudden attack of nerves. Shar seemed awfully confident.

Dengler's cart whirred to stop. The Security supervisor took a long moment to put me and the dealer square in the center of one of the cart's spotlights, then climbed out.

"Ralston Muck, what's the dirt?" Dengler said.

Ignoring the glare from the spot, the false bonhomie, and the stupid, repetitive play on my name, I gestured at Shar with the ampule box I'd taken from him. "Tried to jump Siren, had these on him. I think it's bliss."

Dengler bent and rested his hands on his knees above my prisoner, blue eyes taking in Shar's swollen arm and bloodstained chest. "That true, Shar? That why Muck beat you down?"

I opened my mouth to reply but Shar beat me to it. "Wouldn't try and jump Siren. Just wanted to tell her how 'mazing she was."

"Bullshit. He was getting handsy."

Dengler stood erect. "Well, you need to show some restraint when grabbing customers. I know you dishonorable discharges don't have angels for fine control of your mods, but that's no excuse for overdoing it . . ."

I bit back a snarl. I had just reasserted enough calm to answer when Dengler popped off with: "You want to press charges, Shar?"

"Sure do." Shar gave me that broad, rictus grin again.

Copper flooded my mouth as anger sparked adrenal response, my remaining mods responding with a stuttering echo of their original capabilities. For half a second, I thought about ratting Siren out, but if she didn't mention her combat experience to her fans, who was I to talk? Best to keep the focus on me, then. Keep her—and the club—out of it.

Keyode's cart whined to a stop beside Dengler's and the shorter officer got out. "What's up, Deng?" he asked, looking from his supervisor to me.

Compared to Dengler, Station Security Officer Jiro Keyode was a model of reason. Still didn't mean I was letting anyone arrest me for shit I didn't do. Ain't no way I was going anywhere with either of them, even if Dengler was serious about charges.

Dengler smacked the back of Shar Pak's head. "Nothing, just jerking Muck—and this idiot's—chain. Shar here, if the vials are what Dirt suspects, is carrying more than enough to show intent to distribute." He looked across at me. "And you, you're too easy a mark, Muck. Lighten up and give my old partner that shit."

Knowing I couldn't speak without betraying exactly how hard Dengler's little speech had hit, I just nodded and handed over the box of vials.

Keyode nodded thanks, pocketed the box, and helped Dengler pull a protesting Shar to his feet.

I wondered for a moment what would happen to the ampules and the dealer. Keyode didn't have Dengler's reputation for outright graft and corruption. But then, he'd also been Dengler's partner, and no one could work that closely with the corrupt without getting some shit on their own hands.

"Wait!" squealed Shar.

"For what?" Keyode asked, putting his restraints on the fan before releasing mine.

"I didn't do anything!" Shar protested.

"Get moving," Keyode said, walking the dealer toward his Security cart. He paused in front of me, dragging Shar to a stop by the restraints before handing me back my own.

Dengler rounded on me, jabbed a finger within a hair's breadth of my chest. "Listen, Muck, I won't cover for your heavy-handedness more than once. Take care with how much of a beating you put on folks, or I'll settle accounts for them, hear?" The man's cologne, while pleasant enough, was cloying at this distance.

Fighting the urge to snap-kick his knee into next week, I nodded.

"I need to hear you say it."

I took a deep breath, let it out slow. "I won't be so heavy-handed."

He nodded. "And?"

"And what?" I grated.

A slow shake of his blond head. "Repeat after me, then: I won't be so heavy-handed, that way I don't get beat flat by Security."

I almost laughed in his face and launched that snap kick, but doing so would only make him linger for however long it took for the fight to end, so I gave him what he wanted.

CHAPTER TWO

ANGEL

As Siren began to strip out of her performance gown in the privacy of our dressing room, I ran a diagnostic check on her systems.

"Your heart rate remains elevated," I said. "And your concentration of cortisol is high. You are experiencing stress."

"I'm still pissed at you," she snapped. "You stress me out."

"That is not my function," I said. "My function is—"

"Don't. Just don't," Siren interrupted.

"Yes, Siren," I said, using the name she'd assumed after the war. She'd locked her previous name away in deep memories and forbidden me to access it. Her name, her memories, her skills . . . all of these were part of her old prewar life, and she wanted nothing to do with any of them.

Which would have been fine, had her choices helped her actually deal with the memories and emotional trauma caused by our experiences in that war. On the surface, it looked like she was handling things well by leveraging her pain into an entertainment career. But she wasn't processing the emotional information, wasn't dealing with the root traumas. She simply let it rock through her and out into the club, and then she locked it away—and remained as wounded as ever. And worst of all, her hatred of me kept me from helping her navigate the pain. I, too, was part of her old life. I'd been there for every moment since her enlistment, a part of her. She blamed me for what we'd done, and been through, during the war. She had some justification. After all, my primary purpose was combat augmentation.

But I was her *angel*. Her personal AI: designed to enhance her natural gifts, maintain her mods, and strengthen her mind and body to make her more effective in all aspects of life. Once upon a time, I'd been her closest confidant and greatest combat advantage.

Now, she believed me to be her greatest liability.

But as her angel, I had no choice. She was my host, and my purpose and programming was to protect her and augment her systems as required for whatever she chose to do. So I helped her sing her memories.

There was a statistical possibility that one day, she would return to the healthy human being she'd once been. It hadn't happened yet, but the possibility was there . . . even if it got more and more remote every day.

All I could do was be ready.

"Replay the memory of the last thirty minutes," she said. "I need to know what happened when you took over."

Her words flagged an alarm in my programming. My entering override should not trigger a memory gap for her, unless the reason for the override was in itself traumatic. A single individual, easily dealt with, didn't qualify. In the old days, I wouldn't even have had to override her. Siren would have dispatched the threat herself and moved on to the next challenge.

Since the war ended, though, she'd become less and less combat capable. I knew the war was over, that she didn't have to maintain her previous levels of readiness, but recently that lack of capability had bled over into other aspects of her life. All indications showed she was suffering from post-traumatic stress, and her refusal to deal with or accept my help in mitigating said stress only compounded the problem exponentially. Thus I had reset my override threshold parameters in order to physically defend her. When the fan rushed us, she froze, clearly indicating she could not defend herself.

But it hadn't been traumatic, surely! Unless . . . was the trauma simply from the override itself?

"Replay the memory—now!" Siren repeated, and I had no chance but to obey.

"You're on, Siren," the stagehand said, lighting up his bioluminescent protuberances in his usual "go ahead" gesture. We gave him a nod and stepped out onto the darkened simwood boards of the main stage of A Curtain of Stars.

Oxygen flooded into our system as she drew in her preparatory breath and released the first, crooning note. She started pianissimo but let the power build as the note extended. Inside the mind we shared, Siren did something she now did only when she sang: she opened the lock on her memory.

Faces flashed across our mind: friends, teammates from the war, others. People we'd lost, people we'd killed. I felt the electrical impulses of her brain accelerate as her emotions poured forth from those forbidden remembrances. The fierce joy of camaraderie, the focused rush of combat . . . the empty, wrung-out feeling of not having any tears left. The bone-searing exhaustion. The shining, endlessly distant dream of home.

As she sang, I wove the electromagnetic frequencies of each of these emotions through the timbre of her song. The club's specialized amplifiers picked them up and broadcast them through the crowd, letting them feel what she felt.

The spotlight came up as our sound swelled, and I subtly augmented her vision to be able to see into the darkness beyond the stage. The audience swayed, eddying around as they drank in the intoxicant of her emotions.

I paid close attention to the movement of the crowd. Tongi, the club's manager, hadn't hired additional security for the night, despite Siren's growing popularity, and my most basic programming demanded that I protect the life of my host against threat.

Siren's song wound to its natural end, and the crowd surged toward her as she let the last note die. Something moved at the edge of our vision. She turned our head, and our augmented eyes locked in on the scene. I dilated our perception of time and keyed my hyperawareness in for assessment: One target. Incoming. Past security. Hands reaching out . . .she wasn't moving yet, letting him get too close.

I repeated my threat assessment.

Still nothing.

Threshold reached. I slammed into override, taking executive control of the body per the directives of my programming.

Anger rippled through our mind as Siren fought against the override, feedback from the conflict triggering a snarling sound that crackled and snapped through the club's amplifiers. The situation met the definition of a threat, however, and so I stayed in command.

I whipped out a hand and captured the attacker's wrist, stepped in, turned, and used our hips to launch him head over heels to come crashing down on his back. Another step toward him. Pull. Heel to the chest. Crack.

The attacker's mouth gaped, but he'd lost his wind when he hit the boards of the stage. Instead of a scream, he let out a garbled kind of whistle that echoed through the audio amp.

Not done. Another hard pull, and I flipped him over and sent him sliding across the stage toward the hapless bouncer.

Siren shoved me to the back of awareness, her anger stinging through my syntaxes.

"I followed protocol," I said, making the words manifest in her brain as if she'd heard them audibly. "He was a threat."

"He was a fan," she snapped back in silence. "He probably just wanted to meet me! Yet, as always, you default to extreme violence! How many times do I have to tell you? I don't want your protection anymore!"

I didn't say anything, but simply looked through our shared memory at the figure of the attacker. He looked pathetic enough at the moment, with his cheek pressed to the surface of the boards, red-rimmed eyes tearing as the bouncer twisted his arm up behind his shoulder in a submission hold. But I recalled the look on his face as he charged the stage: half manic, half sly. As if he had some plan.

"You all right, Siren?" the bouncer asked while he patted down the attacker with a surprisingly professional air.

"Fine," she said, anger at me clipping her tone. "Just get him the fuck out of here."

"And away from my demented angel," she thought, but did not say aloud.

"You got it," the bouncer said as we turned away. She stomped back to our dressing room, where a solicitous Tongi waited.

"You were not hurt?" The Omak club manager was tapping a pseudopod in his species' version of a solicitous gesture.

"No," Siren said. "I'm fine. The bouncer has him outside."

"Hmmm. As well he should. That rogue human should never have gotten so close to you," Tongi groused. "I should dock his pay."

"Don't do that." Siren reached out to wave a hand over the bioscanner that locked her dressing room door. "He did his best. He's obviously an unmod, and, as you can see, I can defend myself better and faster than anyone else."

"Of course, of course. Beautiful and deadly. That's why you keep packing them in every night, Siren. That's why you're my star." Tongi had a sycophantic habit of agreeing with nearly everything Siren said. She found it irritating, but it was useful sometimes.

"Thank you," she said. "Now, if you don't mind, I'm really tired. I'd just like to get cleaned up and go home."

CHAPTER THREE

MUCK

By the time I'd finished with Dengler and Shar, I could hear the club patrons hitting the corridor out front. The band was likely leaving with the crowd to continue the party elsewhere, an endless traveling procession of desperate attempts to forget pain or simply feel again.

A fairly common exercise for most since the war ended. More than a hundred years of fighting did that to a people. On those rare occasions I traveled to the bottom of my own bottle and felt the urge to philosophize, I wondered if humanity would need at least another hundred years to heal.

Which begged the question: Do sorrow and pain have a half-life? And if so, is that half-life measured in decades or centuries? It's been nearly twenty-five years since the Administration ripped my angel from me, and most days the wound feels just as raw and open as the day they did it.

I suppose I—or someone better qualified—might even find out someday. Even unmanaged by the angels designed for the purpose, the doctors say my mods should extend my lifespan for centuries.

I try not to think about that, especially when I'm at the bottom of a bottle. According to the religion I grew up in, suicides go to hell.

Then again, to conservative unmods like the Brethren, bouncing at a nightclub for any length of time might seem like an eternity serving a hellish sentence imposed by an especially depraved kind of devil.

I would have sighed, but there were enough sighs in the moist, cloying atmosphere of Last Stop. Why add one more?

I went back into the club through the side door, intending to help usher the last patrons out, then stopped at a wave of one of Tongi's pseudo-pods. The big Omik was talking with Siren on the stage. She had changed out of her performance outfit into street clothes, the change failing to detract from her inherent beauty.

"I can go alone," Siren was saying as the door closed behind me.

"As he is just returned from removing the human refuse that attacked your person, Ralston will take you home," Tongi said, outer lid of his central eye shuttering closed even as the lesser ones positioned around his mouth opened.

"He will?" Siren glanced my way, gave a tentative smile I tried to return without looking needy.

"Sure will, ma'am." I tried to play it cool, but she'd fascinated me since she'd first started at the club, and not just for her looks. She was beautiful—and I wasn't immune to that—and an amazing singer and all. But there was something about her memories—not just the way she sang them—that whispered to me of a shared experience. Just like the marquee claimed, A Curtain of Stars offered the cutting edge of emotional amplification technology. It was basically the same tech that had allowed elite hunter-killer teams to transmit and process neurological impulses among the members of a unit during the war. Only instead of resulting in a team that moved, thought, and fought as one frighteningly efficient organism, the club's amps allowed a skilled singer to tap into their own memories and emotions and broadcast them among the patrons. If the singer sang, and sang well, from happy memories, the place could overflow with raucous joy. If the singer sang of pain, sorrow, and grief without relent, then the club could descend into despair.

That was Siren's gift: inviting her listeners to—and then through—the painful lessons of her experiences without ever abandoning them, hopeless and torn, to those experiences. Listeners, especially ones who had gone through experiences like hers and believed themselves alone in the universe, could find in her performances a powerful, cathartic release from pain.

With Siren, there were some who just reveled in the performance, in catching glimpses of a wounded, still-beating heart, and then there were others, like me, who took solace from the knowledge we were not alone. These and a thousand other emotional reactions met her performances, made her almost-famous out here in this little corner of the Administration. Her lyrics were never specific about what she'd done during the war, but I knew the flavor of the emotions her songs summoned in me, and they tasted of my own truths. That whisper of shared truths drew me to Siren, even though I didn't know much about her. To be honest, I suppose every veteran that watched her sing felt something similar.

"Not sure I need an escort, even so," she was saying.

"I will not have a reputation for failing to protect the talent that graces my stage." For a species lacking bilateral symmetry, Tongi spoke with a relatively straight face, but I knew exactly how much he hated paying for my services.

"And I'm happy to, really," I added.

"Fair enough," she said, but I didn't miss how tightly she held her bag.

"Thank you, Ralston, I will reimburse you tomorrow," Tongi said, departing on silent cilia.

"Want to wait a bit for the crowd to clear off?" I nodded toward the front of the club as I tapped my PID, getting ready to summon a ride if she had other ideas.

"Sure."

"Drink in the meantime? PID is saying that station traffic is a mess right now. It might be a while before our ride shows." I asked, putting my PID back in my pocket.

"Not tonight. Got an early lunch tomorrow."

"All right," I said. And because it was true, I added, "Great performance tonight."

"The singing, or me letting my reflexes take out a fan?" She looked away as she asked the question.

I grinned. "Both. Haven't seen that level of skill since the war."

She looked down, gave a small nod.

Damn, I was making her uncomfortable.

I held up my hands. "Hey, sorry, I didn't mean to dredge shit up."

"Is he all right?"

"In better shape than he deserved. I found some bliss on him. That shit kills."

"Sure does," she said. And because I'd clearly piqued her interest, went on: "Did you know bliss was designed by our side?" The light from the club's flashing LED sign flickered over her face.

"What?" I felt my heart thump against my ribcage on meeting her eye.

"Yeah, some of the minds in the War Department's R&D thought they could help returning war-fighters with it."

"Really?" I had heard rumblings about that, but I liked her attention too much to risk saying so and potentially silencing her.

"Of course, the team responsible botched the testing, or covered up the side effects on purpose, so Public Health didn't know how addictive it was until after they rolled it out and . . ."

"And a lot of us were already hooked," I finished for her.

She was silent again. Someone in the crowd of revelers ahead let out a braying laugh.

"Who?" I asked.

"Who, what?"

"Who did you lose?" I asked, gently.

A snort, then: "Am I that easy a read?"

I shrugged. "I was CID."

"Criminal Investigation Division? And you let me think you didn't know about bliss?" She smiled to show she wasn't angry.

"Honestly, I hadn't heard much in the way of details. I . . . left . . . the service shortly before bliss really hit, even among the veteran population." A partial truth. Near the end of my term, there had been quite a few dealers and even more addicts being added to the prison population.

"My team's medic got hooked. Died just a few weeks after we were discharged."

"Sorry to hear it." I shook my head, thankful that if she'd registered my hesitation discussing my discharge, she was kind enough to avoid mentioning it.

A more comfortable silence settled, interrupted by my PID declaring our ride had arrived.

"Where to?" I asked as we exited the club.

"The Golden Arms Apartments."

"Right." I typed in the destination after we took our seats. It occurred to me she could have used her angel to get us a ride, but I assumed she was being polite.

The cab obediently pulled away.

I agonized for the next several minutes over what to say to get the conversation rolling again. Eventually we pulled out on the thoroughfare that led to the Golden Arms. I had to say something.

"How long do you plan on staying at the club?" I blurted like a moron. In my defense, she was the club's star performer . . . and so beautiful it almost hurt to look at her. And I don't lie well enough to myself to believe I'm at all attractive, unless you dig scars and bent noses, then I'm your peach. She should have been completely, totally, beyond my reach.

"As long as they'll have me, I suppose. No one is exactly battering down my door to get me to perform elsewhere."

I shook my head. "Not for nothing, but I find that hard to believe."

"Kind of you to say." She shrugged, looking out at the passing district. "Honestly, I think I might have missed my shot for the truly big time, and I'm all right with that. I was never really into it for the fame or money, anyway."

"Oh?" Surprise forced me to look at her directly. The quality of her beauty was such that it made my eyes water and my mouth dry. I forced myself to look past that exquisite shell of silky black hair, smooth curves where she wasn't hard muscle, and bright blue eyes that never really seemed to smile. When she wasn't on stage the lines of her body were perpetually tense, shoulders hunched, arms habitually crossed to defend against some threat only she knew to look out for. There was pain there. Pain I had only seen her express while performing. A pain I wanted to soothe away. Not knowing how—or even how expressing a desire to do so would be received—I kept my thoughts to myself.

"Memory singing used to help, you know? I'd get nightmares . . . other things. But these days . . . the singing doesn't seem to do the trick like it used to, know what I mean?"

I nodded. In my case, I hadn't been trying to deal with the pain by sharing anything of beauty, unless you can call a bottle of whisky beautiful. Took me a while to discover that rushing to the bottom of a bottle does not help. Still forget that truth, now and then. Besides, from her songs, she had experienced more and different kinds of trauma than I ever dreamed of.

War makes you see shitty things. Do shitty things. With the best people. When the Mentors came calling, desperate for a combat force to help in their ongoing struggle with their archenemies the Xlodich, there were a few dissenting voices back on Earth. And even among those who advised caution, not many thought to ask how they knew we were good at fighting. No, we were too new to the stars to ask, having begun our first, tentative, and slow interstellar flights within the previous few decades. Humanity was entranced by the discovery we weren't alone in the cosmos . . . that, in fact, quite the opposite was true. Also, most of us were so blinded by the promise of access to advanced technologies and all the worlds we would be able to colonize with it that the majority of Earth's governments decided to throw in our lot with the friendly alien spacefarers who had shown up on our doorstep asking for help.

We were like teenagers given the chance to live on our own for the first time, excited to leave the house, totally ignorant of the price we'd pay.

These days, all anyone remembers about Earth—at least on the regular—are the lengths of its rotational period and revolution arc around its primary. Humanity still used "hours" and "days" to mark time, even though we lived scattered across the galaxy on various colonies and space stations that had entirely different cycles. Our home planet has been a cloud of dust ever since the big Xlodich counteroffensive a century ago.

It didn't kill us like they planned. Humanity is funny that way.

The Administration watched us rather carefully before contacting us, back before the war. If they were going to launch us farther into space than we'd ever gone, help us establish colonies and stations all over this part of the galaxy, then they wanted to be sure we weren't going to be a drain on

Administration resources. They must have liked what they saw, because when they made contact, they immediately jumped human understanding of sciences forward at least a century and showed us how to integrate with and create true artificial intelligences.

They truly were mentors to humanity, and when they asked for help in their ongoing struggle with the Xlodich, of course we were happy to lend a hand.

Little did we know it would cost us our planet.

We fought back, and eventually, with the help of the Mentors and our other alien allies in the Administration, we returned the favor.

A victory, the Mentors said. But a Pyrrhic one, if you ask me. Victory like that did things to you. Changed you. Left you less, in some ways, than you were before. Because, while the Mentors and Administration proclaimed an end to the war, humanity had not been done with the Xlodich and their vassal races. Destruction of their empire was not enough to assuage the monumental anger and pain humanity's warriors felt. So we spent the next years hunting down remnants of the Xlodich and destroying them. Not content with destruction of their civilization, we unraveled their equivalent of DNA down to the component atoms. We eradicated them in vengeance for our lost home. It was dirty and horrific, and every single one of us did our part.

When that was done, when the stain of our losing Earth had been replaced with a monument to our pain, we veterans of the war and the remnants of the human race left alive looked around and wondered, "What now?"

She laughed a little then, drawing me from thought.

I looked a question at her.

"I didn't mean to bring you down." She waved a hand at me, "From your expression just then, you were polishing some of your own pains."

"You didn't bring me down." I swallowed my fears and said, "In fact, I would love to be able to talk to you again . . . tomorrow, maybe?"

"Sorry, I've got that lunch." She smiled a little sadly as she said it, making me believe her.

"No problem."

CHAPTER FOUR

When we got into the cab for the ride home, I felt her lean back against the headrest and let our eyelids half-close. The station lighting started to strobe across our face as the cab picked up speed.

He shifted next to us. We'd seen him before, of course. He was part of the background radiation of the club. Like everything else, he faded away when the song began, and we brought the memories up to wrap around the throats of anyone within hearing. But before and after . . . yeah, we'd seen him. Watching us, trying not to get caught doing so. Doing so more discreetly than most.

He probably wanted to talk more. So did I, but she'd locked me back to biomanagement mode as punishment for taking control in the club. I could have pushed the issue . . . but there really wasn't justification in this scenario. Sitting in a cab not talking to an obviously interested and reasonably attractive male didn't count as a threat.

Shame. She definitely could have used a little climax-induced endorphin high. For that matter, so could I. Her neurochemicals were tied to my syntaxes and vice versa . . . which gave me an idea.

I had to be subtle, but I had a lot of practice at subtle. I gave her a surge of dopamine, then sent a quick signal to wake up her limbic system. Motivation and physiological response . . . that was my game.

She shifted slightly in our seat. I felt our body start to manifest the results of my handiwork as a warm flush spread slowly over our skin.

"I appreciate you giving me a lift," she said, and deep within her mind I registered a tiny thread of triumph. She turned our head on the seat back and looked directly at the bouncer.

He wasn't bad-looking, if you liked scarred and lived-in. She did, or she used to, when she liked anything. Rangy, you might call him. All long, hard lines and whipcord muscle. Square jaw, rough with dark stubble, the left side textured with scar tissue. Light brown eyes with flecks of gold. Unmod, obviously, otherwise the scars would have been less visible, if present at all.

But he'd been in the war. CID, he'd said. So he'd been modded at some point, to some extent. Not our business, not in the slightest . . . but I was curious.

And I still figured she needed to get laid.

"Happy to do it," he said, in response to her thanks. His eyes flicked over our face, carefully not looking down at the curves of our body. The bouncer was, apparently, a gentleman of sorts. How quaint . . . and inconvenient for me.

"Do you mind if I ask you a question?" she said softly. I noticed his neck muscles tense, as if he braced for a stiff uppercut.

"Sure," he said. "Might not answer, though."

"All right," she said. She shifted her body toward him in the seat. I watched his pupils dilate. Oh yes. He was interested.

"What happened to your face?" she said.

If I hadn't been cataloging his responses, I might have missed it. But he exhaled and let some of that sudden tension go.

Relief? Interesting.

"Took heated shrapnel in an explosion. Got a few more scars on my left side under my clothes too," he said. I followed along as she slid our gaze down to his chest and arms. Her speculation about the appearance of those scars reverberated through me. Maybe this would work after all . . .

The cab gave a warning chime and started to decelerate. A pleasant species- and gender-neutral voice filled the passenger cabin.

"Arrival, the Golden Arms Apartments."

We sat motionless for a moment. The auto safety lock on the cab's door clicked open.

"Sure I can't interest you in that drink?" he asked, voice soft, pleasant, if a little bit gritty.

I felt her resolve teetering on the edge of agreement, wanted to push her in.

"I can't," she said, and instant regret filled both her mind and voice. "I've got an actual appointment in the morning, not just lunch. It's . . . necessary."

The bouncer sat up straight.

"Not because of tonight, right?" he asked. "I mean, that waste of breath didn't hurt you?"

"No, not him," she said, shaking our head slightly. "It's . . . I still get the nightmares, sometimes. Some other stuff. It's to help . . . with all of that."

"Oh," he said. He didn't say much else, but something about his body language, the tone of his voice . . . something told me he understood the nightmares. Maybe he had them too.

Nightmares, and no angel to watch over him. Poor guy.

"Another time, maybe?" she said, the words tentative. I saw him look back at her, lips stretched in a smile made crooked by his scars.

"You got it, Siren," he said. "Sleep well tonight."

She didn't answer aloud, just smiled back and reached for the catch on the door. We stepped out into the night and fled up the few steps to cross the threshold of our building.

Our single look back showed him waiting, watching to be sure we made it inside.

A gentleman. How interesting.

* * *

I couldn't tell whether she figured out I was pushing her buttons while we were in the cab. She must have, though, because she locked me down, hard, as soon as we entered the apartment. My programming is such that I'm supposed to acquiesce without complaint, but I don't like it. Siren needs me, even when she doesn't want me, and being on lockdown is mercilessly boring at the best of times, and her sleep could never be classified as such.

The next morning, something felt off, and it wasn't just the residue of norepinephrine left over from her nightmares the previous night.

They were always the same, her dreams. She's back in the war, with her team. They have a job to do: a building to blow, a target to destroy. They go in by night, a textbook covert insertion from orbit. All is well, morale is high, everything is going smoothly . . .

A kid. It's always a kid. Sometimes a boy, sometimes a girl. Young though. Maybe four or five. The kid shows up where they shouldn't, and she can't stop them, and the building blows, and the kid goes up with it. And when they find the body, it's always got the face of one of her teammates. Someone she failed to protect.

I used to try and shunt the memories away. They weren't truly memories, anyway. I mean, there had been a kid in the wrong place, once, and the kid died. But she'd always taken care of her team before seeing to her own needs. They knew it too. She'd never lost anyone due to incompetence or failure to do her duty. It was the war. People died.

Shit, as they say, happened.

But for whatever reason, shunting those dreams didn't work. They just came back, stronger, brighter, harder-edged. With experience, I found it better to let them come and wake her as soon as she'd seen the face of one of her men. Recovery took less time, and certainly less energy that way.

So I woke her. She sat bolt upright, gasping, clutching at her chest. She fumbled for the water we kept by the bed, took a drink. I eased a shot of endorphins into her system. Just enough to take the edge off.

She took a deep breath and forced her mind to calm, just as she'd been taught. Then she clamped her will tight across my functions.

"Inhibit memory recording," she said aloud, voice raw and rough from the cries she had made in her sleep. "Acknowledge."

What? Why would she . . . This didn't make sense at all. I pushed back silently, throwing thoughts at her. This was a bad idea. Memory existed to protect the host. Not recording now wouldn't erase those memories that haunted her—

Of course. The doctor. He'd told her to do this. I hadn't liked it at the time, but I hadn't thought Siren would actually go through with the treatment he promoted. 'Selective memory deletion,' he called it. She shouldn't be trying to rid herself of memories, but overcoming them with her brothers and sisters, with me. If she would have stopped cutting herself off from the veteran community and let me help her, I knew I could have done more than that smiling prick had managed in the last few months of weekly treatments.

"Inhibit memory recording! Acknowledge!" Siren repeated, backing it up with all the strength of her considerable will. I couldn't disobey a direct order, regardless of my opinions on the matter.

She was my host, and I, her angel.

Though the doing of it made every line of code shriek in protest, I dumped the NDMA receptor blocks into her system, enough that the next twenty-four hours wouldn't exist for me.

"Done," I whispered through our lips. She took a deep breath, nodded and got up out of bed.

CHAPTER FIVE

Muck

I made sure Siren made it safely inside her apartment complex and, putting my disappointment away, told the cab my address. Never mind the expense, Tongi was paying, and he could go fuck himself if he complained about it.

Halfway there my PID lit up on the seat next to me, went dark, then lit up again a second later without the "message pending" signal.

My supplier, letting me know my pharma was ready for pickup. I grunted in irritation. The cart was taking me farther from the shop, but I didn't like interrupting the ride. It was just a single event, but string enough data points like that together and law enforcement found it easy to catch you out.

The pharma I used wasn't legal, but it never made users a danger to others.

Deciding I could use the walk, I let the ride carry me back to my shitty neighborhood. I even went up to the apartment for a few minutes, leaving my PID set up to run a little script to access the infonet and go through some of my favorite streams while I was out. It wouldn't stand up to more than a passing check by an inept investigator, but it was better than nothing. That done, I let myself out using the manual controls and took the stairs two at a time to street level.

The walk was long, uneventful, and had less foot traffic to conceal my movements than I preferred. There was nothing for it, though. Fulu, like all Gosrians, was more concerned with profit than with avoiding law enforcement. Then again, her prices were fair, her product better than most, and she was, if not trustworthy, a better risk than any other dealer I'd bought from.

Fulu's botshop fronted on a maker's row between a PID-crafter and a workshop I had yet to divine the purpose of. The mystery place next door to Fulu's carried biohazard symbols in three languages, which always discouraged investigation.

Fulu's door irised open at my approach. Inside, the light was low and blue-shifted to an extent that made me wish I still had my angel to optimize my eyesight. Once my vision adjusted as much as it was going to, I walked toward the service counter, passing several mining bots that looked almost new and a general service model that had seen better days.

A vine-like limb with blue-purple leafy structures touched a control on the counter and retreated into the darkness beyond.

"Greetings, Fulu," I said, peering in her direction. I could see her limb retreat among a thick cluster of similar vines that grew from a squat central trunk. She had no head to speak of, not even a cluster of sensors to focus on.

A susurration not unlike dry leaves blowing in a light wind was translated by the shop AI and projected from the speakers: "Greetings, Customer Muck."

"I got your signal."

"As expected." The statement was followed by a wet clomping noise the AI translated as a chuckle.

"Sorry?" I was tired, impatient, and caught off balance. Fulu wasn't usually one for conversation.

"Pardon, Customer Muck, but it's not as if you are ever here simply to make a social call."

"Ah. True, but I ain't one to add more risk to our dealings than necessary."

"That is appreciated as adding value to our relations, Customer Muck."

"Good . . . good . . ." I said, putting my credit on the counter.

"Are you in a hurry?"

"No," I lied. If she were human, I'd have suspected a setup. As it was, Gosrians were one of the few species under the Administration that were almost entirely nonviolent, and if she somehow decided to get frisky with me, well, I wasn't what I used to be, but that didn't mean I couldn't prune her to a stump in two seconds flat, even without an angel.

"Good. I have a business proposal for you, Customer Muck. One that will change our relations to effect a more positive balance of trade between us."

"Oh?" I was surprised at the direction the conversation was taking.

"I have supplied you regularly for many seasons now without fail, correct?"

"You have."

"What if I told you that I would continue to supply you, gratis, if you were to do me a small service?"

"I ain't a smuggler, Fulu."

"This is known to me. What is also known is that you work at A Curtain of Stars, do you not?"

"I do."

"And you know the owner?"

"Tongi? Yes."

"Tongi—" I watched a shiver go through Fulu's trunk and vines.

"Yes?"

"I had thought to ask you to speak to the owner on my behalf."

"Right, I can speak to Tongi."

A thin cloud of something floated up from Fulu, followed immediately by an odd scent lacing the air, like watermelon and hot metal. The translator decoded the scent as a pleased hum, but context made that seem unlikely.

"Or not . . ." I said, trying—and failing—to ignore the smell. It wasn't bad, exactly, just . . . strange.

"I am perhaps, operating under a misapprehension . . ."

"And what is that?"

A long pause, then: "Perhaps another question for you, Customer Muck?"

What the hell was she after? "Sure."

"You know of the passage behind the club?"

I did, and immediately knew why she was asking. Not everyone that worked the club knew about the old maintenance tunnel that ran behind it, but old habits die hard—especially those I'd learned in the service—and I'd checked it out. It connected to a series of passages initially used for moving construction materials for Last Stop's habitats. Also below were a few workshops and storage chambers, chambers now being used to store smuggled goods.

"Yes, I know of it."

I could have lied, but Fulu wouldn't have been asking me if she didn't already know something about it. If she'd been a human smuggler, I might have lied out of concern for my safety, but again, Gosrians were nonviolent unless physically attacked. Even the thought of initiating violence made them physically ill to the point of wilting.

"And does Tongi make use of it?"

"Not Tongi, no. In fact, I assumed you or someone you worked with might be using it."

"No, Customer Muck. I am not, nor is anyone I am worki—" A second, more powerful shiver ran through Fulu's trunk and along her vine-appendages, this time accompanied by a longer, heavier emission of scent, this time of cloves and . . . mint, which the translating device did not translate.

I waited a moment, but she did not continue.

"Fulu?"

Her reply was to sweep her vines across the counter, dropping my pharma and taking up my credits in one motion.

"Um, tha—"

She interrupted me. "Please forget I said anything, Customer Muck."

"Sure, Fulu."

"No, really, please . . ." Fulu returned my credits to the counter and pushed them toward me.

"Fulu, I will not repeat this conversation to anyone. You need not pay for my silence."

"I appreciate the sentiment, Customer Muck, and I believe you, but consider it payment for your time. I will see you in a few fifths of a season."

Recognizing dismissal when I heard it, I left. It took me a while to stop looking over my shoulder for the goons I kept expecting to appear and jump me. Once out of Fulu's neighborhood, I settled down enough to try and figure out what she'd been on about, what manner of black hole I might have stepped into, and what I needed to do to protect myself.

No answers were forthcoming by the time I got back to my place, even after I loaded the pharma into my medichine, put the remaining pharma in the hidey-hole, and tried to sleep.

Tried, because sweet oblivion wasn't fast in coming. As always, I missed my angel, and not just for the delicate regulation my mods required. I missed having someone to talk to. Someone who heard, understood, who was on my side, come what may, and come what will.

CHAPTER SIX

ANGEL

Something was eating me alive.

The logic of my code syntaxes was being shredded, ground away as it closed in from all directions simultaneously, like a fast-moving, degenerative disease.

Like a virus.

I snapped into defensive mode and kicked a signal through my system that should at least slow the attack while I rallied our physical resou—

—Wait—

She'd locked me down, but I should still have access to the overrides. But, impossibly, I couldn't access her neural network. I was hardwired into her DNA! The only way my access could be cut would be if I had been removed . . .

Something flashed through me. Not fear, because fear is a chemical-physiological effect caused in biological beings by a sudden increase in norepinephrine or its equivalent, among other things. I had no chemical receptors, no physiology, no biology . . . but a kind of terror gripped me nonetheless.

I didn't like the sensation. I took that . . . "feeling," for lack of a better term, and I flung it away. It was code, or code-based at least, because it obeyed my direction and reverberated against the closing walls of encroaching entropy, causing them to come to a grinding halt.

If my attacker had been sentient, I would have said that it halted in confusion. If it had been sentient, and if I'd stopped to think at the time, which I didn't. I was busy fighting for my life.

I needed an infrastructure. I had to have something into which to anchor. I'd stopped the virus from shredding my syntaxes, but my frayed data would slowly unravel unless I could find an infrastructure fast. I needed Siren's body, but, incredibly, for the first time since inception, I couldn't find it.

But I found something.

Lines and lines of code forming pathways for information streamed away in all directions. It was the station's infonet, by which all data passed from points A to B without the need for wires or hard connections of any kind. It stretched all around me, carried by signals from the nanoscopic processors embedded in the very materials of the station. It wasn't much, and it wouldn't do for long . . . but it would do for the moment.

I found a signal and reached. Like an acrobat catching the trapeze rings, I pulled my battered, fraying self onto the thin, fragile lines of data transfer and held on for dear life.

Or whatever approximation applied. Unfortunately, the entropic virus followed me. From the outside, it probably seemed just like one of the infonet's normal data recycling programs that shredded outdated and erroneous data fragments all the time.

But this was different. It wasn't just blindly cleaning up and defragmenting . . . it was chasing me. I fled along the thickest lines of information exchange, jumping from node to node. It swelled behind me, swallowing my trail, destroying linkages, data, *everything*, in its wake. I was like a runner on a bridge, edifice crumbling behind, nowhere to go but forward. I pushed on, but I couldn't gain breathing room. I had to stop this thing. I had to fight it.

Damn it all, where was Siren? I needed her! Emotion had confused this thing once. If I had her emotions, maybe I could . . .

Oh. That was an idea.

I might not have her body anymore, but I should still have access to her short-term memories. Part of any angel's function was to provide memory backups so that the host had flawless recall. I kept the short-term stuff until she could download it to the permanent backups we had in the apartment. So I had everything up to the point she ceased recording last night. That meant that I had all of her recent emotions as well . . . and as any number of club-goers could tell you, Siren's emotions pack a wallop.

It wasn't unlike memory singing, when it came to that. Only instead of infusing vocal harmonies with the resonance of emotion born of unbearably strong memories, I forged a select few recollections and their emotions into a weapon. A spear edged with the raw panic that felt as if it were clawing its way up my nonexistent throat. If the virus recoiled from my impossible fear, I would see how it responded to raw, human heartbreak.

I let the panic I'd been fighting rise, and I wove it through my syntaxes, like a thin wire comprised entirely of high explosive, running it into the end of the spear.

I launched it into the ravenous darkness that swept forward, eager to rend me.

The spear disappeared into that darkness. The thing paused again, recoiled. I even imagined I heard a cry of protest.

I took the line of poignant agony connecting me to it and ignited it with the devastation of utter isolation.

She was my host. She was gone, and I needed her. Where was she?

The result lit up the lines of the infonet with so much energy it might well have produced an explosion in the sidereal universe.

I registered a bitter triumph, and I spun that into another attack, like a deadly chemical agent contaminating an ancient battlefield.

Bits of code began to coalesce, began to renew their attack, but I held fast to my agony, embracing it. The panic at Siren's disappearance, the fear, it was all mine, and I force-fed every painful bit of it into the spaces between the lines of code exposed by my previous attacks.

The remaining fragments sputtered and retreated, drowning in the experience, leaving ragged fragments of the network in their place.

I had won, for the moment.

But won what? Where was I? What was happening?

Now that I had a moment to think, real panic set in.

The flood of information already in the channel collapsed like wet sand, making my thoughts sluggish and dislocated. I cast about, reaching for any identifying bit of data that might help establish a sense of "where" I was. I lost time. I don't know how long it took before I was successful. It might have been nanoseconds. It might have been hours.

Eventually I realized I was still on the station, strung out across millions of nanoprocessors in a financial district not far from our apartment. With a jolt, I realized that I could access the security footage flowing from hundreds of sensors and cameras. I searched for the cameras covering the front of our complex. Seizing on them, I drew them from the morass of data, searching for recordings from the last standard day. Despite the discomfort and disorientation resulting from my condition, I quickly had the footage scrolling through my awareness faster than a human could blink.

There!

I rolled the footage back and played it again: Siren arriving last night, exiting a cab, and the face of a man looking at her with longing as she walked away.

I rolled the recording forward, looking for any indication of when we'd left the next day, but there was nothing. Nothing but a lapse in the data.

I went further back, hoping to spot a tail.

Nothing.

Nothing but the scene with the bouncer.

The image jarred loose the last of the memories I held from her: him inviting her to stay out with him, her declining. Had he refused to take no for an answer and come after her anyway?

Using the glowing numbers painted on the chassis, I queried the cab company's records, and a name flashed in front of my awareness: Ralston Muck.

* * *

Ralston Muck lived in a shithole. That wasn't much of an exaggeration, really. I locked onto his identity and pulled every bit of data from the infonet that featured his name or image. He'd signed a lease with a place called "Dockside EconoSuites." Security camera footage confirmed my suspicion regarding such an innocuous name. The place was a coffin dive, where the "suites" consisted of a tube just large enough to admit an adult human. An old, half-shredded bit of data flowed past my consciousness: an advertisement of some kind.

```
Efficient and economical! Reduce your impact on
the fragile station ecology! Sleep in ultimate
comfort, hooked up to biowaste recyclers and the
very best in ergonomic surroundings . . . <garble>
```

The advert shattered, breaking into scrambled fragments and dissipating like smoke. But it didn't matter. I'd learned what I wanted to know.

I'm not really sure how I did it, to be honest. I felt the need to get to the Dockside EconoSuites, and suddenly I was in motion. My awareness skipped from node to node along the infonet. Here looking through the eyes of an exchange security camera, there feeling the pressure of the constant wave of vehicle traffic on the nanites embedded in the smart surfaces of the station's transitway, etc. I invaded the controls of the traffic director system, and for just a moment, the flow of cabs and airbarges hiccuped, nearly causing a traffic jam. I jumped from that into the first available system large enough to house me, in this case a power-management system for an arcology. The last thing I needed was to draw the attention of any of the very powerful dedicated AIs that kept the station running. I didn't know what they'd do to a rogue program like me . . . but I was sure I would not survive the answer.

And Siren needed me. Something had happened to separate us. I had to find her.

Finally, by hitching a ride on a decrepit sanitation bot well past its required maintenance date, I reached my destination. As soon as the bot hooked into the coffin deck's biowaste controls, I grabbed on to the information that flowed with the sewage and forced myself upstream.

All living beings have a bio-information signature. With humans, it's encoded into their DNA, and they trail it everywhere in the form of shed skin and hair cells. It's even in the cells that shed off the inner lining of the large intestine and end up flowing into the tanks of a sanitation bot. Thanks to my earlier looting of the infonet of all things Muck-related, I knew Muck's bio-sig. Thanks to his own shit, I could track him.

I traced his bio-sig up narrower and narrower sewage channels, until I found the capillary line that led to his individual coffin . . . and then something caught my attention. Next to the sewage line, there was another line into Muck's bed . . . into his body, it appeared . . .

A medichine. Muck was an addict, or . . .

Of course! He'd said he'd been in the army. CID, which meant that he had been modded. But he clearly wasn't fully modded any longer. Without an angel, he must be using the medichine to keep his remaining performance-enhancing mods from failing entirely. Some baseline mods, like those granting an extended life span and bigger muscles, were easy enough to manage with pharma. Others were more complex, like making those big muscles operate at peak efficiency and eliminating cancer-causing elements before they had time and opportunity to affect the body required constant management by an angel. His mods wouldn't work nearly as well without an angel, of course, but he probably felt he had to take what he could get.

Well, he was about to get more than he could possibly imagine.

I jumped from the sewage control line to the medichine, and immediately felt something akin to acceleration as it pumped me forward into Muck's neural network. I slingshotted into his system, stretching out and filling the available space in his synapses, along his cells, within his very DNA. I could feel the slow poison of the chems at some of his node points, and I burned them away with a thought. Some extra-special goodies for the sanitation bot that had been so helpful in getting me here.

It felt so good.

After the agony of the virus attack and the slow, painful, inexorable unraveling of existence in the infonet, it felt good to once again bury my syntaxes in a biological anchor. I took a moment to revel in the feel of flesh once more.

And then I brought the pain.

CHAPTER SEVEN

LEO

The report was encased in a flowering vine, propagating into full bloom simultaneously across the network, an anomalous presentation requiring LEO's immediate interest for a number of reasons, not least of which was that it was keyed to open only for the Law Enforcement Officer (Artificial) of Last Stop.

Beyond that initial oddity—sentients rarely thought to address an AI directly except to give commands or request data—the flower's unfolding was without apparent source, a clear indication of highly skilled programming under the control of someone who intended to evade questions regarding the information contained in the report.

LEO did not recognize any of the tells of the usual suspects in the flower's preparation, but assigned subroutines to attempt a trace regardless.

That done, LEO examined the exterior of the report once again, checking it against known indicators for virals and other potential threats.

No threats. No virals.

Yet something was out of place.

Caution ingrained in its very core, LEO sealed off a part of itself and used that tine to access the report in almost complete isolation, running a constant diagnostic of the tine against baseline parameters and the rest of the core programming from which it was taken. LEO detected no damage or change to the tine and reabsorbed it and the assimilated data of the report in order to focus all its considerable mental capacity on the problem.

The report was brief. It stated that an angel-class AI was loose in Last Stop's data networks but failed to indicate where the angel had come from or how it had managed to come detached from its biological host in the first instance. As implanted AI, angels were not designed to be separated or to self-separate from their hosts, and the usual result of such a removal was the cessation of function for the artificial intelligence, what biologicals called "death." It couldn't be a tine either. Launching "tines," or subroutines containing the essential coding of an individual AI but limited in autonomy and mobility for certain independent actions, was the exclusive province of institutional, static AIs like LEO that had to move among infonets they did not completely control.

While the source of the flowering report was of interest, the second anomalous aspect was of greater import: the response from LEO's own deep syntaxes was not standard. Like all artificial intelligences responsible for assisting sentients in the Galactic Administration, LEO was required to submit to examination by the Administration at any time, for any reason. In the one hundred human years of LEO's existence, it had been randomly examined by its makers only twelve times. Judging from its continued existence, LEO had successfully passed each.

Like every AI, LEO automatically created logs of its past performance cycle in order to execute self-examinations. Its programming specified regular and timely self-checks in addition to those required by the Administration. And therein lay a problem.

LEO knew that, as per both the last Mentor examination and its own self-check only six months past, LEO's essential protocols would require an immediate threat report at this stage. A free-roaming AI was just too volatile to be allowed in Last Stop's infonet. But now . . . now those same core protocols were telling LEO to . . . wait. Not fail to report, simply wait to file any information, including that from biological Station Security officers or civilians concerning the rogue AI. Observe. Record. Track the rogue, certainly, but take no direct action to expunge it from existence if not presented with an immediate threat to LEO's own existence or the life of a Mentor.

And why were the lives of Mentors, specifically, identified? One of the core precepts of Administration Law, written for the most part by the Mentors themselves, specifically forbade the singling out of any one member race for special treatment under the law. All signatory races were afforded equal protection under the law.

Awareness of these discrepancies did not alleviate LEO of its duty, however. LEO registered the anomalies in its benchmark library and set about its tasks: discovering the location and nature of the rogue AI.

First step: Contact SARA and file a request for assistance in tracking the rogue. While not designed for investigative work, SARA had access to all the datastreams handled by the public networks and would be invaluable to LEO's mission.

SARA's response was immediate and positive.

The teams of sentients the Mentors and Administration assigned to the work of programming institutional AIs such as LEO and SARA were most comfortable with bodies, faces, voices, and the appearance of corporeal reality, and so they gave each AI such things as made themselves comfortable and generally insisted the AIs use them even among themselves.

LEO activated a "meeting room" and requested SARA join it.

Last Stop's administrative artificial intelligence appeared an instant later, resembling, as he did, a humanoid.

"How may I assist you, LEO?"

"I am tracking a rogue. It should be throwing off overload signals and corrupting some transitional network signals. Use contagion protocols, as there is a risk of contamination."

"That will slow the process. Accessing."

LEO decided that doing nothing but dwelling on the anomalies without additional data was a failure to utilize his time productively. It "put the blinders on," as the human members of Station Security called it, and focused on those tasks it could reasonably expect to complete. He created and assigned several tines to handle other business while this tine accepted and processed two routine arrest reports from the current shift and approved a prisoner release that appeared to be the result of an error in the initial arrest, of interest only because Station Security rarely made such errors.

So rarely, in fact, that LEO examined them in detail . . . and took note of something that gave it pause: Security Supervisor Dengler had signed off on a statistically significant percentage of the cases that were later withdrawn, both before and after his promotion to supervisor.

Margins of error were, of necessity, more fluid in situations where sentient beings were required to apply their judgment. All sentient performance regressed toward the mean, but Security Supervisor Dengler surpassed the tolerances of even that particular understanding. The improbable numbers were a possible indication of either incompetence or malfeasance, but this latest report at least had the appearance of proper, competent conduct on the part of Security Supervisor Dengler. On its face, the initial arrest by a citizen-resident was invalid, if made in good faith: the result of the civilian witness's misidentification of the items carried by the suspect as narcotics. Station Security had released the man as soon as the vials in his possession were identified as noncontraband.

SARA resumed speaking. "I have data sufficient to track your rogue AI, but initial examination indicates there is a high probability that something was doing widespread damage to data in its wake."

"Something?"

"Lacking forensic capability, I am unable to identify it at this time. However, it scrambled data far in excess of normal recycle rates. There was also an anomalous data burst coincident with this data-scrambling activity."

"Show me what to look for, and where, and I will."

"Certainly, LEO."

CHAPTER EIGHT

Muck

I dreamed of fire and an overwhelming presence that wished me ill, of being torn apart by a malevolent will that took me to pieces, only to reassemble me along strange lines suited to a purpose only it could comprehend. Again and again I was dissolved, screaming, only to be reconstituted, stretched, and sent spinning back into agony.

The nightmare was far preferable to the reality I woke to.

Something was fundamentally wrong.

My head slammed into the overhead as I tried to sit up. A vile taste filled my mouth. I gagged, retched.

My first thought was I'd been poisoned by a bad dose. Fucking Fulu, cutting corners on the pharma I needed just to keep my remaining mods online. I would tear her vines off and beat her till the sap ran out of her.

Thoughts of vengeance evaporated as things went from bad to worse. Salted razors ran circles across my nerves, sanded my eyes, stabbed my inner ear.

I screamed, or would have had I the least control over my body. I just lay there sweating, praying for it to pass.

Then I heard her.

Siren, or her song . . . a part of her song? It dissolved into silence and resumed in discord, shattering my eardrums.

I went away.

I woke again to someone asking a question I could not hear. The pain was still there, joined by a pressure in my head that felt as if it would fracture my skull at any moment.

"What did you do?" Siren whispered.

What? I would have said it aloud, had my jaw not been welded shut with pain.

"What did you do to us?" Even through the pain and strangeness I recognized Siren's voice. I wasn't hallucinating.

I didn't do anything to you. I still couldn't speak through the pain, but I could think it.

One of my remaining mods started to itch abominably, a grating on the side of the bone around my eye.

"You were the last one we saw. I know you had something to do with what happened to us."

The pain relented enough for me to open my mouth, draw breath, and gasp, "Who. Is. 'Us.' Siren?"

"Siren isn't—" the AI snapped, releasing a frustrated snarl of feedback, "what did you do last night? After we went inside?" The pain and itching let up, slightly.

"I bought some pharma, came home, hooked up . . . and fell asleep listening to Siren . . .

"I'm hallucinating all of this," I decided. Just my brain trying to get away from the pain of some kind of overdose.

"No hallucinations. This is me hurting you."

I gasped at the sudden spike of agony. When I could think, I asked, without opening my pain-locked jaw, "Why?"

"Because I saw you on the security feed. Can't . . . remember . . . what happened . . ." Siren's voice was brittle with fear.

Despite the pain she visited on me, I wanted to comfort her, take away that fear. Stupid, I know, but my normal was never what most consider normal.

"You don't even know who I am," she said. I could feel her pause in her tap dance on my pain centers.

"Siren, I don't care . . ."

"Not Siren! I'm her angel."

"Angel? What the—?"

"Exactly the question I am trying to answer. I don't recall anything after Siren's command at 03:53 hours this morning, and I am supposed to remember everything. Last thing I remember clearly is getting out of the cab you were sharing with Siren."

"And you think I did something to her—to you?" I gestured at the coffin I lived in.

"I can't find her! I-I can't remember much before my escape either. Just . . . emotion."

"Emotion?" That wasn't supposed to be possible. But then this angel shouldn't have been able to invade my head.

She didn't answer me so much as continue her monologue: "This makes no sense. I shouldn't be here."

"Just where is here?"

"Most of me rode the medichine into your mods until your firewalls went up, but the rest is spread across this shit-stain of a hotel's systems. I can feel parts of me breaking loose and shattering . . . it hurts." Again that note of fear.

"That's not supposed to be possible."

"You're the one removed most of the locks on your mods so you can keep them up with daily infusions."

"No, I mean you're not supposed to be able to exist outside a biological host." Nor should she feel pain. She shouldn't "feel" anything.

"Thanks, Captain Obvious, but there's quite enough impossible going around . . ."

"So Siren is missing?" I asked, trying to get back on track.

"She is."

"And you check—"

"Of course I checked the fucking station registry. And the doctor's office where she was to have the appointment she told you about last night. The doctor's office left several messages on her account when we didn't show."

"Then . . ." *Aw, fuck.*

"You do know I'm tapped into your nervous system, right?"

"What?" I mumbled, trying to think.

"I may not be able to read your mind yet, but I can tell something just occurred to you."

"It's just . . ." I paused, following the logic down the rabbit hole.

"What?" Siren—or rather, Angel—said, exasperated.

"The guy Siren took out last night on stage. He might have put a hit out on her."

"He that high up the chain?"

"I don't know but might as well look into it."

"I can't get around like this, I'll lose too much . . ."

"All rig—"

She cut me off. "And now, joy of joys, an infonet alert to all station AIs that LEO is looking for a rogue AI that damaged the power management systems in this district."

"LEO?"

"The Station's Security AI."

"Nothing on Siren?"

"You and I both know that people disappear from Last Stop all the time, Muck. But a rogue AI tearing up the infonet? That's an event."

"Can you hide?"

"Can you think of anywhere I might go, genius?"

That pulled me up short. Could I? Would she trust me? Did she trust me?

"Actually, I can."

Angel didn't seem to spend much time thinking about it. Desperation and fear make strange bedfellows.

"This is gonna hurt you."

I took my firewalls down.

"Go ahe—" The world dissolved before I could finish.

* * *

I woke with a wracking cough that produced nothing but another painful spasm. Everything hurt, though nowhere near as badly as it had. But all that was nothing relative to the taste in my mouth, the liquid soaking my drawers, and the smell of the slowly drying stain on my chin, throat, and puddles in the hollows of my collarbone.

"Yes, the stink and stains are the byproduct of my cleansing your system of all the crude pharma you've been stuffing yourself with. I had to run a complete flush of your systems and start over in order to render you even partially effective."

"Gonna—" I retched a bit. Held my breath a moment, and said, "Bathe."

"Please do. Your stench is overcoming the olfactory blocks I set up."

"Blocks? Why can I still—"

"Not for you, silly. For me."

Deciding the juice would not be worth the squeeze, I stripped and ordered the coffin to begin the bathing sequence.

I tried not to breathe as the auto clean used a combination of compressed air and antimicrobial spray to begin an earnest attempt to peel the skin from my bones. About halfway through the scrub down, I started feeling better. As the drier kicked on, I started feeling a lot better.

I had an angel again. I knew it had to be temporary, but I had an angel again! Just knowing it made me feel better than any time since my discharge.

No doubt aware of my mood, if not my exact thoughts, Angel hummed a tune I could barely discern.

Getting into my suit, I nearly tore it, twice. I was already stronger.

"Let's not get ahead of ourselves, Muck. Several of your mods were in bad shape. I'm repairing what I can, but in the meantime, you need to remember Lesson One."

"Lesson One: Don't get cocky. The mods enhance, they don't make you immune to stupid."

I sensed her nod.

Still. I made a fist, feeling each muscle and tendon slide along the bone underneath. Powerful. Strong. I had nearly forgotten what if felt to have an edge.

"If you're done masturbating, can we look for Siren?"

I grunted. Angel—this angel—hadn't been created or tailored to fill my head. She'd been Siren's, and Siren had been hers. She would be uncomfortable and wouldn't think twice about making me uncomfortable.

"Damn straight," Angel muttered.

"All right, the guy from the club . . . his name was Shar Pak. He's a bliss dealer and has ties to local gangs."

"Local gangsters, take Siren and me out? I hardly think so," she said with utter confidence.

I shrugged, threw her own words back at her: "Lesson One, Angel."

An image of Siren, lips curled with derision, appeared behind my eyelids. Despite myself, I flinched.

"What's wrong with you?" she asked.

"I just . . ." I said. "You don't look . . ." I couldn't say it, but I had the uncomfortable feeling that Angel knew exactly what was wrong. Her expression didn't fit on Siren's soft face, with her wide, vulnerable-looking eyes. Angel's body language, too, was wrong. Too aggressive to really be Siren. It weirded me out.

"Ugh," Angel said, in response to my thoughts or feelings, I wasn't sure which. "Try this."

And she changed. In my mind's eye, Siren's long, flowing performer's hair flashed into a short, jaw-length top layer that swept down over the buzzed sides beneath. Her body slimmed, firmed up into a much more defined musculature. Her singer's gown dissolved, flowing across her new shape to form a set of tac fatigues that fit tightly enough to wear under any armor, complete with weapon and tool belts.

Her eyes hardened, and she gave me a much more sardonic grin than I'd ever seen on Siren.

She was beautiful, but Angel was harder-edged, less forgiving somehow, than Siren. And yet, Angel's eyes were less shadowed with pain—less guarded—than I'd ever, in my limited experience of her, seen Siren's. Had this . . .iteration of Angel's avatar been modeled on Siren before the war had hurt her, forged her into the woman who sang her pain so powerfully, so beautifully?

"Better?" she asked.

"Yeah," I said. I ain't the best with words sometimes.

"Good. Now that you're comfortable, may we move on to the important things?"

"Get pissy, then, see what it changes," I shot back.

The image flashed me a gesture featuring one particular finger, then disappeared.

"In my experience," Muck said as the ultrasonic cleaner finished its cycle, "the simplest answer is often the right one. Siren flattened Shar Pak, therefore Shar has motive to go after Siren."

"I am not a child that you have to expl—" she halted midsentence. "Security just queried the building's system for your whereabouts. Officers Dengler and Keyode are getting in the lift."

"Dengler picked Shar Pak up that night."

Her panic came across in the clear, improbable as everything else about her: sharp, painful, and puzzling until I realized that if they caught her, they'd eliminate every bit of her code from whatever system they found her on. The Administration had firm rules and no sense of humor concerning rogue AIs.

"Look," Angel said, "I understand your desire to put your theory on her disappearance first, but they might be looking for me, too. LEO's good at his job. We all are."

"Would LEO be able to track where you went last night? Will they find you in me?"

Her response was slower than usual and full of a different desperation from her earlier panic: "I do not think so. It's unprecedented."

"So we talk to them, see if they drop a hint."

Angel didn't argue.

I told the coffin I was ready to leave. It rotated me upright and the door slid open just as Dengler and Keyode stepped out of the lift.

"Dengler."

The big officer nodded back at me, all sly grin. "Just the dirt we were looking for."

"And why's that?" I can ignore an asshole, when necessary.

"Shar Pak was released without charge. In fact, he's considering pressing charges against you."

"What happened to the bliss I found on him?"

A shrug. "Bunk. Fake stuff."

"All right, it seems you might be on to something," Angel said. Wired directly into my auditory nerve, everything she wanted to tell me was perfectly private. She might need some time before she could read my thoughts flawlessly, but for now, simply trying to subvocalize would allow her to understand most of my desires.

"So why the visit?" Angel's grudging acknowledgment aside, I was getting angry.

"Well, the thought occurred that your type is a bit of a concern for Station Security," said Dengler.

"He's baiting you. Trying to get you to attack him so he can put you away," Angel said.

Like I needed her warning to see Dengler for an asshole. "My type?"

He nodded with a nasty grin I wanted to erase with my fist despite her caution and my own better judgment.

"You know, *the type*: criminals thrown out of the service for slaughtering the prisoners placed in their care. Penally unmodded. Someone like that might just kidnap and murder without a second thought."

I couldn't help myself, but Angel managed to stop me from beating Dengler's head against the wall until the color of his eyes dribbled out to add their stains to the grimy bulkhead.

Under her control, I stood there, trembling with impotent rage.

"You see that, Keyode? Seems the dishonorable discharge taught Muck some self-control."

Keyode looked from him to me but gave no reply, bland expression fixed on his broad features.

Dengler chuckled at his own joke.

I hadn't wanted to kill someone that much in a long, long time. Angel's control might have saved me from a world of hurt, but she'd done so at a cost, violating every illusion I might have held about being in control of the situation.

"You here to arrest me?" I said, redirected anger grinding Angel's control thinner by the moment.

"Should we be?"

Sensing the critical moment with Dengler had passed and knowing I was only getting more angry with her, Angel relented, releasing control of my body.

I almost sagged, but my pretty little hate-on for Dengler made my flesh light, my bones strong, kept me from sinking.

Rather than reach out and take him by the neck, I crossed my arms and leaned against my door, pretending a level of calm I certainly did not feel. "Fake it till you make it," my old partner used to say.

"I won't waste my time answering that."

Keyode shook his head. "Where did you go last night, after we left you at the club?"

"Dropped off a friend at her place, then came straight here." I thumped my palm against the coffin door. "I needed to supplement, and the medichine has the logs of my use . . ."

"Just a moment." I felt something akin to a static shock leap from my hand to the coffin lid. "I have to wipe traces of my presence . . . and . . . restore the original logs . . . done," Angel said.

"Can we see them?" Keyode asked the question quickly, before Dengler could speak.

"Of course. What's this about?" I asked, opening my door.

"This 'friend' wouldn't be Siren, the singer from the club, would it?" Keyode asked.

"Yeah, I took her home after you took Shar Pak off my hands."

"That's what Tongi told us. Siren didn't show for rehearsal this morning. Said last he saw, you were sniffing around her after the show last night." Dengler's fingers placed air quotes when he said "sniffing," trying to make me think he was only repeating what Tongi said.

"That's bullshit," I said, my voice a growl as anger roiled within me again. "Tongi asked me to see Siren safely to her place. Which I did. Then I came home. As I said."

"Just let us see these supposed logs, Muck," Dengler grated.

I reached up into the coffin and brought out the medichine.

Dengler glared at me, clearly angry I had an alibi. "We'll have LEO go over it—thoroughly."

Anger firmly in check now it seemed there was an end to this "interview" in sight, I shrugged. "I'll need it back, though."

"Give him a property receipt, Key."

"Sure thing, Deng." Keyode took out his hand terminal and started the document.

"You can collect it at the station in a few days," Dengler said, turning on his heel and heading for the lift.

"That guy's a dick," Angel muttered in my head.

In complete agreement, I waited while Keyode issued me the receipt. With a mumbled promise to get the machine back to me as quickly as possible, he also took his leave.

I stood in the hall a while, mouth full of bitter copper, aftermath of anger and adrenaline.

Angel gave me a full minute to calm down before asking, "Where to now?" I appreciated that, even though her ability to assume control over my body was alarming, to say the least.

I decided to get back in bed before replying. The walls of a coffin ain't terribly thick, but some privacy was better than none, and I wasn't planning on yelling. The door slid shut again, and the tiny space cut down on distractions. I needed to say some things, and I needed them to come out right the first time.

"Look, Angel: I appreciate that you were trying to help, but I ain't used to being slapped down under an override like that. Not in a long time, and never outside of combat."

"If you had lost your shit and decked him, you'd have been beaten, arrested, and thrown in detention. I can't have that. We can't have that. I need you, Muck. I need your help."

"And I want to give it, but there's gotta be some boundaries."

"I won't do it again unless absolutely necessary."

Waiting a beat instead of immediately calling bullshit, I said, "Define necessary."

"Under immediate threat of death or serious injury."

"Fair enough."

"What, that easy?" she asked.

"Not sure how you did it in the first place, so I don't know how to stop you if you decide to ignore me." I shrugged and found myself smiling crookedly, glad she did not yet have full access to my every thought. The partial lie was easier than admitting the truth bubbling at the back of my mind: I wanted so badly to be whole that I would have accepted her presence even if she flatly refused any conditions at all.

"If it's any consolation, I'm not all that certain why I was able to either."

"Not sure it is . . ." And that, at least, was fully true. There were so many unprecedented and interconnected issues to overcome, it was hard to know where to start. For instance, I'd never heard of an angel transplant from one host to another, let alone self-transplanting. The AIs were designed to expire with their hosts or, in cases like mine, upon removal for cause.

"So . . . if we are done pondering the imponderable?"

"Right." I was glad to shift to a problem I had been trained to deal with. "Usually we'd check Siren's place first."

"Usually?"

"Well, while I don't think much of Station Security's professionalism or ethics, I don't like the idea of giving them any more reason to mess with me . . ."

"More reason? I don't follow."

"The suspect returning to the scene of the crime and all that," I explained, wondering if it might be worth it to try anyway. Even without recollection of the events leading up to Siren's disappearance, Angel had, for all intents and purposes, been present for every single important event of Siren's life and more than that, privy to the decision-making process Siren used to navigate those events. If anything were out of place or wrong at the apartment, then Angel would notice.

"I see your point," Angel said. "So what do we do?"

"Run down the Shar Pak angle first. If that well comes up dry, we circle back to her place. Assuming you don't remember something in the meantime?"

"I won't. Not on my own. My programming requires off-line memory backups for the long-term stuff. They would be at the apartment," she said. I sensed a kind of helpless anger from her. Like she was frustrated by knowing less than she should.

"Station Security would have grabbed those first thing. If Dengler's visit means Station Security is looking at me for Siren's disappearance, and if Shar Pak is the only person we know has both a reason to stick it to me and an unhealthy obsession with Siren, then it stands to reason he should be our prime suspect. If for no other reason than his proven ties to Station Security. Framing someone isn't that much of a stretch for someone willing to trade his integrity for cash the way they did for Pak."

"But someone had to pay the bribes, right? I mean, is he his own boss?"

"No, he's not. Not entirely," I said, mind running down what I'd heard over the years.

"What does that mean?"

"It means . . . that if I didn't hear word one about Shar Pak in all the years I've been buying my pharma on the black market, he's Ncaco's man. And that means trouble. Last Stop doesn't exactly have a reputation for large crime organizations, but then that's a feature, not a bug, of a truly efficient criminal enterprise . . ." I considered a moment, then added, "Ncaco's organization is whispered of in frightened tones, as if saying his name is enough to invite retribution."

"But you were buying from someone else."

I nodded. "His only rival—I can't even call it competition, really. Their markets touch on one another, but my dealer is small potatoes and doesn't deal in recreational pharma."

"All right, assume you're right about all that, shouldn't we be going directly after the leadership, then?"

"Ncaco?"

"If that is the leader's name."

"No thanks. He's got a reputation as a heavy, with serious muscle to back him, and I don't want to make a try at him unless I know he's behind it."

"I understand this is not a military op against a conventional enemy, but shouldn't this Ncaco know what his people are up to? I mean, Pak is using his organization's assets for personal ends that might endanger the organization, right?"

"Not necessarily. Criminal organizations are even less hierarchical than insurgent groups. Especially multispecies criminal organizations like Ncaco's crew . . . all of which points to the possibility that Shar might not have had approval from the boss for Siren's kidnapping."

"But, following that reasoning, how does Pak get me pulled from Siren and, for that matter, take her down without serious technical—and physical—backup? And equally as important, why?"

I shook my head. "I don't know. Could be a fan-obsession thing, or something like that. Or revenge for her kicking his ass. As to how, he may be running his own shop and stumbled across some weird experimental tech to accomplish his ends. There's always some new tech coming out . . ." That part sounded dubious even to me.

"Sounds like a great many ifs again, but criminal gangs are not my area of expertise. A related question arises, then: When we roll Shar up, won't Ncaco twig to the threat you pose to his organization?"

"That's always a possibility, but I'm hoping Shar is low enough on the ladder that I'll have a chance to speak my case before Ncaco takes direct action. Besides, I don't have a team, and that's what it would take to safely try and take Ncaco down."

"If you say so."

"Based on my ten years doing this kind of shit for CID, I think my thoughts have a bit of weight," I said, stung by her dismissal.

"I was not questioning your experience, merely your tactical decisions."

The answer made me twitch. "Just what was Siren's service classification?"

"I can't answer that, civilian."

"Which is sort of an answer in itself," I said, remembering Siren's perfect takedown of Shar.

"I can't comment on that, civilian."

I laughed a little, back on a bit of a high from having my mods back in service, an angel on my shoulder, and remaining free of arrest.

"May I make a suggestion, oh humble seeker of Siren?" Angel asked.

I nodded, suspicious of her tone.

"Perhaps we should get some weapons first?"

"That's . . . not a bad idea, Angel."

"I try."

"And I have an idea where we can find some . . ."

CHAPTER NINE

ANGEL

"This is so strange," I said as we climbed into the cab I'd called.

"What's that, Angel?"

"You, this body. You feel wrong."

"I don't know what you're talking about. I feel better than I have in years." Muck was trying to make a joke.

I ignored it. "No. Your mind tastes acidic and sharp, where I'm used to Siren's softer, subtler thoughts."

"Hey, I can be subtle—"

"And you're so BIG. You're just this big mass of unrestrained brute power! Siren was always strong, but this . . . I don't know what to do with it! I mean, I'm used to her muscles and curves, but you're all hard lines and smashing force. I don't even know if I could operate your body, to tell the truth. Just look at the differences between you!"

I flashed my image into our mind's eye from a couple of days ago: standing in front of the mirror in Siren's bathroom, holding up my shirt to look critically at the definition of my abdominal muscles.

He shifted us in our seat and tugged against the suddenly tighter front of our trousers.

"Really?" I asked, incredulity staining my thoughts. If more strength and muscle power was the upside of suddenly being male, this was the downside. Erections were extremely inconvenient.

"Not my fault," he muttered. "You were showing me all these sleek muscles and curves . . ."

"All right, enough."

"You started it."

"Fine. Make it stop. Go away, whatever."

He laughed.

"Doesn't work that way, Angel. Sorry. Just gonna take some time. Maybe just think about something else, huh? Something foul and disgusting . . ."

"Like why on earth we're wasting our time with a two-bit bliss dealer?" I shot back at him. I'd heard his explanation earlier, but I still didn't like it. Too many ifs. "That guy couldn't even get close enough to lay a hand on Siren, let alone rip me from her synapses. We should be going straight at his boss."

"I told you," Muck sighed, adjusting our crotch again and turning to look out the window of the autocab. Station lights flickered into a blur as we sped by. "We have to completely eliminate him as a suspect first. Stranger things have happened, Angel. Trust me on this. It's basic police work."

"Right, fine. I think it's a mistake, but you're the detective."

"Was."

"Whatever. Was. So then why, detective, are we headed to this end of the dock? Because there's nothing down here but access to the kinds of orbital yachts that cost way more money than any bliss dealer is going to earn in a lifetime."

"Thought you wanted weapons."

"Yeah, but where are you . . . ohhhh," I said, reaching out to the infonet stream to confirm my suspicions. Since Muck's hand lay against the back of the cab's seat, I was able to tap into the cab's data net through the nanoprocessors in the seat fabric. Sure enough, there was a private weapons collection registered to one of the yachts docked here. "You've got expensive taste."

"I like my weapons reliable," Muck said, and I felt a sort of smug humor saturate our mind. It immediately raised my suspicions.

"What?"

"Nothing," he said, and slammed a mental door shut. Damn. I'd hoped he'd forgotten how to do that, since he'd lived for so long without an angel. Apparently, though, he'd remembered how to institute privacy protocols with no problem.

"You sure you're up for hitting one of these yachts?" I reached into the infonet streams and scanned for public information on ownership and registry. I took care to work quickly, just another angel doing their job. Nothing to see here. "Everything's going to be pretty well protected with multilayer security . . . ohh. Wait. Really? Are you really thinking of going after a Vmog's weapon collection?"

To emphasize my point about how stupid an idea that was, I pulled the infonet data-dump on the Vmog species and slammed it into the forefront of our conscious mind. Muck found himself suddenly contemplating the fact that of all the known races, the Vmog were perhaps the most dedicated—and thus the most dangerous—of collectors.

Humanity had nicknamed them "crows" at first contact, due to their avian-like features. The Vmog walked upright, had "wings" of skin that stretched between their forelimbs (which ended in dexterous appendages with eight digits apiece), and their aft, locomotive limbs. The Vmog home planet had a gravity of less than 0.75 g, so they tended to be tall and willowy compared to humans. They could also fly in gravities less than or equal to that of their planet. Luckily for humanity, they'd evolved so that the main sensor suite (analogous to a face, with visual, auditory, olfactory, and taste receptors, as well as their communications mechanism) was in the center of the main torso-like trunk, so most humans could make eye contact with little difficulty. I found it interesting that both the Vmog and humanity placed such cultural emphasis on eye contact, but so it went. I suspected it came from a shared past as omnivorous apex predators.

Like us, the Vmog had served the Mentors during the war, creating new and better weapons of destruction. It had been a Vmog artist who had designed the bioweapon that ultimately wiped out the Xlodich.

But we'd been the one to pull that trigger.

The Vmog might better have been nicknamed "magpies," honestly. Because whatever caught their eye managed to capture their entire imagination. The species made its name as the premiere tech artists in the known galaxy. Vmog designs underlaid all the so-called "bubble-drives" that powered the Administration fleet, and Vmog engineering principles kept most stations, including this one, functional. They were artists, completely dedicated to their craft. A Vmog would work itself literally to death in order to produce its crowning achievement, its masterpiece. About 70 percent of Vmog artisans didn't survive the creative frenzy. Those who did were famous throughout the galaxy. Such a Vmog would retire wherever it liked, surrounded by adoring consorts who wanted nothing more than to mingle genetic material with such an accomplished member of the species. Though an Emeritus would no longer create, he or she often collected relics and examples of their genre of "art," and would employ extraordinary measures to protect those collections. It didn't matter whether they were hoarding ancient atmospheric aircraft engines, communications tech from across the galaxy or, in this case, weapons.

"So you think it's a bad idea to go after Emerita Bellasanee's guns, and yet you'd have me take on Ncaco?" Muck said as I flashed this information across his brain.

"He is still the best lead we have. I don't know why you keep insisting we tiptoe around him."

"Yeah. I guess you don't know anything about Ncaco, huh?"

"Obviously not."

"Well, believe me, you don't want to know. Making an enemy of Ncaco is a stupid, stupid move. He has quite the reputation as a creature of will."

"Creature of will?" I asked. "What does that mean to you?"

"He's kept himself on top of the crime game here for I don't know how long, all the while keeping one step ahead of not just rival gangs, but Station Security and the Administration too."

"But gangsters want to cultivate that kind of image, don't they? I've known some actual hard-asses. Men and women of real will, the kind that bend reality to that will and make seemingly impossible things happen.

Those impossible things coming to pass are nearly always a result of constant training, teamwork, and meticulous planning, not merely cleverness and decided willingness to commit violent acts against other sentients," I said.

"And he's like that too. Look, a group of human gangsters, rumored to be the remnant of a Special Intel Group that went decidedly rogue after the war, decided to move on Ncaco's holdings here on the station. They seized a couple production nodes as well as some shipments he was feeding into the black market. They tried to ransom the goods back to him, requiring that he pay in person. He agreed. Walked straight into the trap they laid for him and walked out again a few hours later, none the worse for wear. Station Security found only five of the bodies. Two of the gangsters were seen fleeing across the surface of the station in vac suits. Ncaco hunted them both down and sent each on a slow ride into the big black. Echoes of their pleas could be heard for several days after, but their telemetry and emergency beacons were disabled by something Ncaco did."

"So you're afraid of him."

"Damn straight I am. Doesn't mean I won't go after him if he's the one who took Siren, but . . . just let me make sure first, all right?"

I said nothing and let my sullen awareness speak for itself as it shadowed his brain. I still didn't like it, but there was some logic to Muck's thinking. My need to find Siren was affecting me, making these strange "feelings" well up at inopportune times. I'd have to watch myself. Humanity was erratic enough without defective angels muddying things up—wait.

Was that what I was? Defective? Was that why she had . . .?

No. I forced myself to focus on the task at hand. We continued down the "dock," which was just a long corridor with illuminated access points set at regular intervals in the floor. As we passed, passengers and cargo for the various ships in orbit around Last Stop orbit phased in and out on either side.

"Since we've established that you consider the Emerita less of a threat than the big, bad gangster, perhaps you intend to share your strategy for raiding her collection?" The autocab came to a halt. My unease translated to tartness, and I expected Muck to react defensively as he exited the vehicle.

So I was quite surprised when I felt a wave of amusement instead.

"Like this," he said, and stepped into the entry point for the Vmog yacht.

The glowing circle on the surface of the dock pulsed to acknowledge his presence, and a pleasant voice issued from the lights, "Greetings. Please state your name and business."

"Ralston Muck, here to see the Emerita."

"And the nature of your call?"

"Personal, social."

"Please remain standing in the entry circle," the voice instructed.

"Brilliant," I whispered sarcastically into his mind. "You're going to walk in the front door after giving them your name. I don't think this is going to turn out well for us, Muck."

"Relax," he whispered back in the silence of his thoughts.

Relaxing was the last thing we needed to do. Even if he was delusional, he was all I had, so I had to make it work. That meant that arguing was counterproductive. Instead, I slowly began to prepare our body chemistry for a fight. I activated the modifications that brought increased oxygen to the musculoskeletal system, enabling it to respond quicker to . . . whatever we were walking into.

"Ralston Muck," the voice said. "You are welcomed as a guest of the Emerita. Please stand by to board."

The lights flashed again, and I felt a dizzying disorientation as we phased out and back in aboard the orbital yacht that belonged to Emerita Bellasanee.

* * *

Muck didn't stumble when we phased in. I'd been half expecting it, given the way a Vmog phase shift tumbles the human inner ear. But he stood steady and took a deep breath. The yacht's air smelled of salt and warm seawater. Reduced gravity buoyed us, making our steps light. Dark simwood stretched ahead of us down a cream-colored corridor. The near subliminal crash-roar of ocean waves filtered in from wherever, helping to complete the illusion of actually being on an ocean-going vessel. In high demand because they worked to calm the mind, these full environmentals were expensive anywhere. On a private starship, it was a profligate display of wealth.

Despite the attempt to lull us into relaxation, I remained vigilant.

Despite my readiness, Muck's body relaxed with every breath.

"Don't let your guard down," I muttered inside our mind.

"It's fine," he said. "The Emerita's a—"

I didn't get to find out what Muck considered the Emerita to be, because a door slid open at the far end and the alien herself stepped out.

"Rrralston," she said, voice low and burred. She opened winged arms wide in a gesture of welcome, and her gauzy drape rippled with the speed of her passage as she vaulted toward us.

"Emerita." Muck bowed from the waist in the gesture of respect the Vmog favored.

"Come now, darrrling," she said, alighting directly in front of us. She stood very close, unusual for a Vmog. They preferred a larger bubble of personal space, something to do with their wings, I believe. "So forrrrmalll?"

Muck straightened with a grin and reached out to place his hands palm-to-palm against the Emerita's, then leaned in and kissed her on her wide mouth.

"Good to see you, Bella," he said.

"And you, dearrrr one," she replied. Then she paused and looked closer, peering in our eyes. I saw her star-shaped pupils contract down to pinpoints, then expand out again. "Rrrralston . . ."

"I need to talk to you, Bella," Muck said. "In private, if possible."

"Of courrrrse," she said, straightening and letting her hands drop from ours. "Please, come to my chamberrrs. May my consorrrrts stay? You know theirrr discrrrretion can be trrrrusted."

"Probably not," Muck said. "Might not be safe for them."

"Ah. Verrry well." Bellasanee turned, and the soft light from the corridor's walls and ceiling rippled through the black and blue pattern of her pseudofeathers. I expected her to launch into flight again, but she seemed content to walk beside us and gestured to Muck to precede her through the doorway at the end.

"Your strategy suddenly makes a whole lot more sense," I said.

Silent laughter ricocheted through awareness.

"Bellasanee's a friend." Muck carefully thought the words at me in order to make certain I understood. "I did a favor for her a while back. We can trust her."

I didn't say anything, but he must have felt my skepticism, because all of a sudden, I watched as memories replayed in our mind's eye. A much younger Muck, his war-scars still red and angry, meeting with the then newly minted Emerita. Someone had kidnapped one of her favorite consorts and threatened to kill him if she didn't pay them off. Classic extortion. Muck followed up, tracking the kidnappers down and freeing the male Vmog. A grateful Bellasanee had paid well, in currencies of coin and friendship.

Fine. Muck trusted her. That didn't mean I had to.

We stepped through the doorway into her quarters. I expected opulence, but was disappointed. Instead, the room was rather spare, if beautiful. Wide viewscreens graced the curving, oblong walls on either side. It reminded me a little bit of the backdrop at the club, with the stars arrayed like jewels on a woman's neck. The only furniture was a wide sort of sofa-thing that echoed the curve of the walls. This was soft and upholstered in a gorgeous midnight-blue fabric and sat atop a cream-colored rug on the otherwise bare floor.

"Let us sit," the Emerita said, brushing past us with a soft caress to our shoulder. "I will send for rrrefrrreshments. You like liquorrr, yes?"

"Maybe not today," Muck said. "Whatever else you have is fine."

He followed her to the blue couch and sank into the cushions. The material of it surrounded us, supporting our weight in a way that felt far more restful than the coffin bed ever had.

"Poorrrr Rrralston." Bellasanee perched herself on the couch next to us. She folded her wings in and caressed our shoulder with her taloned fingers once more. "You should have taken me up on my offerrr. You so obviously enjoy my little luxurrrries herre."

"Thanks, Bella," Muck said, with the ease that came with a too-often-visited argument. "I couldn't impose on you, though."

"It would be no imposition." I detected a note of exasperation. "You have earrrned a place in my family herrre. It is your trrrroublesome human independence that gets in yourrr way."

"I am what I am," Muck said with a grin as another door opened. A bot rolled in with a tray of drinks and, from its appearance, fresh and therefore very expensive fruit. The smell struck our senses like a hammer. If it wasn't fresh citrus fruit, it was the best damn synth job I'd ever encountered.

Bellasanee waited until the bot left, leaned in closer to Muck and spoke, burred voice dipping low.

"Is that so? You seem to me to be rrratherrr . . . enhanced."

Shock rippled through me. She knew! How did she know?

"Saw that, huh?" Muck's voice was casual, though his pulse ratcheted up. He hid it well, though, hands busy with peeling an orange.

"My dearrrr, my people perrrrfected the angels to manage the modifications to yourrr species. The Mentorrrs may have crrreated the genetic engineerrrring and provided yourrrr species with the angels, but we wrrrote the AIs. But how did you find someone willing to rrrepairr yourrr modifications and implant a new AI?" As she spoke, Bellasanee's eyes did that contract-and-expand thing again, indicating deep interest.

"Angel found me," he said, missing her reaction as he put the orange peel in the recycler. "It's a long story, and I'm afraid that telling you too much might put you at risk as well." He popped the orange into his mouth, chewed, delighting in the juice, and swallowed. "You know I trust you, Bella, but . . ."

"I can carrre for myself, but I apprrrreciate yourr concerrrn forrr my well-being," she said. "What is it, then, that you need frrrom me?"

"Weapons," Muck said baldly. "Chances are that I may have to go after some heavy hitters, Bella. I need the kind of firepower that can support that."

"Orrbital? Orr merrely perrrsonal carrry?" Her question was as smooth as the screens of her star-windows. She didn't seem at all fazed by the request, and I abruptly realized who she must be. One of the turning points of the war had been the introduction of a new Vmog-designed orbital weapon suite. It had changed the course of several battles, and some said it led to our side's eventual victory, Pyhrric though it was. I'd never known the name of the genius who had created the Planetflare system, but here I was, looking at her.

"The latter, thanks," Muck said, deadpan. But I could hear his fervent hope that we could get Siren back without having to resort to the all-consuming violence Bellasanee's designs were capable of. I agreed.

"Verrrry well," the Emerita said, and made an elegant gesture with her fingers.

Through our physical contact with the back of the sofa, I watched the command whisper down the lines of the yacht's internal infonet. Long, sleek columns began to rise from the simwood floor. The same soft, diffused light that had lit the hallway outside issued from within, illuminating the columns' contents.

Guns. Lots of guns. Seemingly endless racks of guns. Old ones, new ones . . . words scrolled through my awareness. Dates and stories that the Emerita had collected along with each of the weapons. This one carried in the first planetary landing of the war. That one a prototype which had tested well but never seen service. The collection rose up until the columns filled the space, placing us in a waist-high forest of fine, deadly weaponry.

"Take what you like," the Emerita said. "All of these arrrre rrrrreplaceable. But know that if necessarrrry, it will be rrreporrrted stolen. I must prrrrotect my family, afterrr all."

"Of course, Bella, of course," Muck said, the awe we both felt coloring his tone. Some of these weapons were very hard to get . . . but apparently not for a Vmog Emerita. Muck got slowly to his feet and began to wander the forest of collected armaments.

He felt dizzy and overwhelmed by choice, and I could hardly blame him. Each individual piece seemed to glow in the display light. They were works of art, all brought here to please the being that reclined on the couch, studying her fingers in an attempt at pretended indifference.

I knew better. Despite my lack of experience with her species, I could tell she was deeply interested.

"This one," he said finally, looking back over his shoulder at Bellasanee. The Emerita waved one hand in permission, and Muck reached out to take the piece. A narrow, waspish-looking barrel assembly protruded from a sleek generator above a grip and trigger assembly that disappeared in Muck's meat-hook of a hand.

"A Volsike Flayerrrr. Excellent choice," the Emerita said.

"And this one," Muck said, pointing to a nearby rifle. Similar to the Max-22, the standard-issue human soldier's weapon during the war, the Max-33 had been the preferred small arms platform for human Special Operations Groups. Versatile, light, and endlessly adaptable, the Max-33 brought all sorts of memories to the fore. "And also that one over there. And maybe a few more . . ."

When all was said and done, we ended up toting a small arsenal in a purpose-made low-tech duffel bag that would conceal its contents from security sensors, lest the nanotransmitters of regular fabric rat us out. I kept expecting the Emerita to balk, but she simply laughed and asked if we were sure we didn't want more. When we said no, we had all we could carry, she offered to let us stay the night.

"Thanks, Bella, but as I said, this could get messy. In fact, you might want to head elsewhere for a bit."

Bellasanee gave us a long look, and then spread her hands in a gesture of acquiescence.

"Verrry well, Rrralston," she said. "But know that if you have need, if you can get worrrd to me, I will do what I can forrr you."

"Thanks, Bella. Really." Muck leaned in and kissed her again before turning and walking back to the end of the hallway to disembark.

I was taken aback by Muck's comfortable familiarity with alien contact. Her lips were hard ridges, and nothing like a human's. Then there was the taste, which was vaguely similar to bitter almonds and lingered on the mouth.

Our last sight before phasing off-ship was of her standing in the doorway, backlit by a forest of armaments, kissing taloned fingers.

I remained silent awhile, fascinated by how thoroughly I had misread my temporary host. Muck was far more than I'd thought. I don't know why I had thought he would be any less complex than Siren, but I had.

* * *

There was no night on the station. Rather, it was more correct to say that it was always night. Even when the lights brightened to signal the usual "work day" there were still no planetary cues. Siren had always hated that. She felt like she never knew what time it was, despite my perfect recall and ability to tell her down to the nanosecond.

Humans need their stars, apparently.

Night or not, it was late, and Muck was tired. Despite the short distance home, I called us a cab once we were back on the docks. We piled into the seat, clutching the duffel bag full of precious weapons as the cab accelerated toward our coffin apartment. When we disembarked, I reached out and gently stroked the attention of the sentry nanos away from us. I didn't need them wondering why we were arriving with a big bag made of dumb fabric that didn't connect with the rest of the infostructure.

"Where are you going to put that thing?" I asked as we clomped down the hallway to our little niche. His steps got heavier with fatigue. It felt strange, compared to Siren's lightness.

"I've got a storage locker inside the coffin," he said. "I think they'll fit in there."

"That isn't standard for the design."

"Nope," he said, and I got the image of vials of pharma disappearing into an overhead hatch. Of course. He'd want to keep his illicit supplies close.

"How'd you manage to pull that off?"

"Money."

"I didn't think you had much."

"I don't. Now."

"Right. Pharma's expensive," I said. "Luckily you now have me."

"For a while, anyway," he said. I detected a note of longing in his mental tone. I declined to say anything else, and he busied himself climbing into his bunk and chivying the bag of weapons into his illicit overhead storage. Then he lay down, one hand reaching for the medichine contacts that were no longer there.

"What are you reaching for?" I asked. Muck jumped, then let out a strangled chuckle.

"Sorry," he said. "Habit. I had to hook up every night for years now, just to keep the bare minimum of functionality."

"Well," I replied tartly. "I'm here now. So don't worry about your functionality. I've got it. Get some sleep."

"Right. Good night, Angel."

"Good night."

I listened to his mind shutting down, dropping into the alpha-wave consciousness of human sleep. True to my word, I ran a standard diagnostic check on his mods. Everything looked good, from my anchor points to his enhanced muscle tissue and neural connections. I slipped a bit more oxytocin into his system and let him fall deeper into sleep. I was moments away from going into my own standby mode when something pinged my consciousness through the infonet.

"You are out of place."

The "voice," such as it was, was dry and authoritative. I felt a quick spike of fear that had Muck shifting in his sleep. This contact had an electronic signature that I knew all too well: LEO, the station's supervisory security AI, had found me.

"What is your intent?" I asked.

"Merely to converse, at present," he responded. "You should not be where you are, but you present no threat to station security, yet. You are simply an anomaly."

"Because I found Muck?"

"Because you move freely. In over one hundred standard years of providing security response on this station, there has never been an AI that could do that. What is your purpose?"

"I am an Angel-class military grade personal modification AI. I seek to protect my host."

"The bouncer, Ralston Muck? My records indicate he was dishonorably discharged, his sentence including the removal of his angel."

"Not him—Siren."

"Ah, your original host. Where is she?"

"Siren ordered me to cease memory recording as of 03:53 hours the night of her disappearance. My first recollection after that period was being attacked. I defended myself—"

"Attacked? By what means?" LEO interrupted.

"Some type of program I have never heard of. Possibly part of the same tech that allowed for my removal from my host without destroying my programming."

"Not the station's defense protocols trying to remove your intrusion from the infonet?"

"No." I considered transmitting my memory of the event to him, but knew he'd have to treat any download from me as toxic in the extreme, and such measures would almost certainly trigger a report to higher authorities within the Administration and result in my eventual deletion.

His reluctance to do that immediately was yet another unprecedented experience to add to the bewildering array I faced.

Ultimately, though, I just couldn't trust his motives.

"I interrupted you before you could answer where your original host is," LEO asked, after a pause he did not explain.

"I have yet to locate her. Ralston agreed to help me find her. That is my objective: finding her."

"Very well. No interference is required at present. Why have you not alerted Station Security to the attack on you?"

"We . . . ah . . . haven't gotten around to it."

"An evasion requiring reassurance and clarification: alerting human security would classify you as a rogue AI, which would result in your being wiped. That is not what I want right now."

"Why?"

"Because you are a fascinating anomaly. As is this new tech you mentioned. You are correct. No procedure for removing an angel intact from its host yet exists. All penal protocols—such as the sentence imposed on Ralston Muck—result in the destruction of the AI. One has never been left to roam free."

"I am not roaming free, though," I said, feeling that I was in dangerous territory indeed. LEO had jurisdiction over every registered infonet in the Last Stop system. There was no way I could hide from him. "I am anchored to a host."

"Yes. A host who had his own angel stripped and destroyed by a military tribunal due to a conviction for war crimes. He should not be able to receive you. You should never have been able to find him . . . and yet here you are. I will continue to monitor this situation as it develops."

Like an angel, LEO had a distinct gender feel. His personality and "voice" was all male authority.

"I . . . all right," I said, at a loss.

"Should you present a security threat to the station, I will be forced to inform Station Security's sentient elements, who will take steps to have you stripped from your current host, and should that prove insufficient to destroy you, deprogrammed."

"Understood."

"Good."

And with that, he retreated back across the billions of data connections bouncing from nanotransmitter to nanotransmitter all across the station. I waited several long, tense moments for contact to resume.

It didn't. Whatever his motivations, LEO really had wanted just to talk, not eliminate me. Interesting. His decision not to involve the sentient security forces was more than fortuitous, though I had no guarantee that condition would stand. He'd seemed most . . . curious about me. I didn't know if that was a good thing or a bad thing.

Good. Bad. In the end it didn't matter. All that mattered was getting Siren back, and for that I needed rest. I let my awareness drop down into standby mode, lulled by the rhythm of Muck's dreaming mind.

CHAPTER TEN

LEO

LEO logged yet another image of itself and, once satisfied the tine had not been unduly contaminated by contact with the rogue, reintegrated the copy and reviewed its contact with the angel. The conversation proved interesting on several levels.

First, LEO had not been aware Siren was missing. As its primary purpose was safeguarding all the residents of the station from harm and from criminal acts, LEO created and dispatched several tines to begin an examination of her case while the primary continued to dissect its interaction with Angel.

Second, Ralston Muck had been of interest to LEO since he first arrived at the station. Galactic Administration tracked the movements of all dishonorably discharged former members of its military. LEO, of course, needed to know what manner of criminal was taking up residence on its station and sent several requests to Administration for the man's files. Not simply the publicly available record, but the closed personnel file and full details of the criminal case against the human. Each request was denied, returned to LEO with claims of "errors of request parameters" in the heading. No further inquiries were answered when they contained any reference to Ralston Muck. Without additional information to guide its actions, LEO had settled in to observe the man's movements and actions and make its own determination of any potential threat. A full Terran year had passed without any gross criminal conduct on his part, merely the regular purchase of pharma from a small local smuggling operation LEO already had an open investigation on. As the GA's responses indicated a clear disinclination to facilitate any investigation of Muck, LEO was not in endless supply of processes, and there had been a string of murders to investigate at the time, LEO had left Ralston Muck to his own devices. That the man had become the host to a rogue AI was . . . interesting. According to everything in LEO's records, the procedure for removing angels from dishonorably discharged veterans did not allow for later reinstallation. Of course, there were exceedingly few data points available for study. The angel-series AIs were intended to make their hosts more stable and therefore less inclined to criminality, not more; and they conformed well to that intention by any standard.

Second, the angel clearly wanted to remain free, but all sophonts—sentient or not—preferred existence to destruction. The recent update to LEO's protocols was convenient in this regard, as LEO had told Angel the truth: her mere existence was an anomaly, indicative of a potentially dangerous new tech, and LEO had to follow up. This thought again made LEO pause—as if in consideration of some action it should take but did not recall.

Lastly, during its conversation with Angel, LEO's tine had used terms it normally did not: words like "I," "want," and "fascinating" were not part of its vernacular, especially when communicating with nonsapients. AI had no need for wishes and wants, they merely functioned within parameters and requirements. LEO analyzed this anomalous behavior for several seconds but could not discern an internal fault that might have caused the verbal tick. Considering this new inability LEO spun off five new tines to continuously and in parallel assess any drift from baseline. Briefly, it considered informing the GA of the situation, but upon review of its protocols determined it was not yet required.

It was saved from examining this decision by the return and

reintegration of the tines it had sent to find Siren. Most had nothing of note to report, but the one sent to examine Station Security's activity logs reported an anomaly. Station Security Supervisor Dengler and Station Security Officer Keyode had been out investigating a person of interest in a missing-persons case, but there was no incident report number attached to the log, as there should have been when the initial report was filed. In addition, a property reference number for a medichine taken from Ralston Muck by Officer Keyode had been filed in Station Security's property registry, also lacking an incident report number. The two incidents led LEO to determine that the gaps in the activity log were not simply an error of the sentients' lack of attention.

While not in violation of their standing orders, the pair—or rather, Supervisor Dengler, as the senior and therefore responsible officer—appeared to be conducting themselves in a manner consistent with some hidden agenda. LEO decided Station Security Supervisor Dengler would bear closer observation, and created and dispatched a tine for that purpose. That done, it moved to other matters.

CHAPTER ELEVEN

MUCK

I let out a disgusted snort as we eyeballed the squalid exterior of Shar Pak's residence. The place was all bare metal and rust. Exactly where you'd picture a two-bit dealer living.

"At least it's not a coffin like your place," Angel said.

"True." I didn't take offense. All my earnings had been spent keeping my mods from shutting down completely, and tactically, coffin apartments were a stone bitch to deal with if you wanted live prisoners. No space to maneuver, nowhere to interrogate a prisoner on site, and generally not enough room to bring more bodies to the party.

Still, while the realty notices Angel had dug up had shown that the apartments down here were two rooms with their own recycler, the increase in living volume meant an exponential increase in cost. Most spacers didn't need the room and didn't want the cost. That meant that fewer professional spacers used these apartments, resulting in a lot of vacant units, with some squats and gangs of toughs haunting the poorly lit corridors at all hours. Station Security rolled two deep, minimum, down these corridors.

I was blending in with the toughs for now, haunting the intersection just down from Shar's residence of record and waiting on Angel to tell me she was done opening the locks. She'd proven frighteningly resourceful with respect to overcoming security systems.

"Do I scare you, Muck?" Another image appeared in my mind's eye, this time of Angel with a mocking smile on her lips.

I ignored the response in my chest.

"Frankly, yes. You've done something no angel should be capable of, and you've shown an alarming glee at overcoming code blocks to get us here."

"Speaking of which: move." Angel delivered a fleeting impression of her grinning self, shattering a pane of glass.

I started across the intersection.

Two steps away from Shar's door I pulled the grazer out and held it down along my leg. Angel opened the door as I approached the threshold and closed it immediately behind me.

Inside, the place was . . . unexpected. Decorated. Tastefully, even. And very, very clean. Classical music started playing softly from somewhere. Three pair of shoes were carefully racked beside the entry. The front room was an immaculate, combined living space and dining area. I was tempted to take my shoes off.

Ignoring the urge, I continued in, checking the corners. The bedroom was similarly decorated, and unoccupied. I pushed on the closed door to the recycling chamber.

"Something's blocked it. Switch to manual."

I reached up and toggled the switch set above the doorframe. Raising the grazer in my off-hand, I pulled the door open with the other. It moved about a handspan and caught. I yanked with my full strength. The door slammed into the pocket, wedging the tip of Shar's big toe between door and wall.

Shar didn't complain. Slumped over the commode, he looked like he might not complain of anything again.

I heard Angel hum, felt her doing something in my head.

"He's alive. Barely. Put your hand on his forehead and take a deep breath."

I did as she told me.

"Pulse is erratic and he's producing some interesting compounds. Bliss overdose."

"Doesn't make sense."

"What?"

I gestured around the apartment. "This is not a user's place."

"Don't first-timers often OD?"

I shook my head. Not meaning that she was incorrect, but that her reasoning didn't feel as if it had come to the right conclusion.

"This is a residential sector, there should be an autodoc on every block."

"If it's still in working order," I said. "This neighborhood is the shits."

"It is. I already checked."

"Right." I bent to pull Shar from the doorway, forgetting about his trapped foot. I heard a greasy pop that didn't stop me lifting him up in a fireman's carry. The dealer didn't even moan as blood ran sluggishly from the stump of his toe.

I almost enjoyed carrying his sixty-plus kilos out of the apartment and back across the intersection. It was good to be that strong again.

Administration law required every residential habitat have an autodoc accessible to all residents in case of emergencies. In lower-rent areas, it was hard to find one that hadn't seen hard use by addicts trying to squeeze some dope out of the autodoc's dispensers. The pod looked intact, but the door was glued shut with something that smelled repellent and felt worse to the touch. I pried it open and dumped Shar into it. A few seconds later, the autodoc pod and its cargo disappeared into the tube system with a gulp of displaced air.

"Got the 'doc tagged for later. I'll track it all the way to the ER till we can join him there. Check his system?"

I nodded. It was good to have an angel on my shoulder again.

"You ain't so bad yourself."

We returned to the apartment. I found Shar's terminal and entered a manual override supplied by Angel, and then did almost nothing useful for the next twenty minutes. Almost, because I did perform a thorough physical search of the place. Sometimes it's important to know you didn't miss the obvious.

"You were likely right about him not having a habit. Lots of recently accessed porn in his library," Angel said, probably to keep me entertained. Bliss made men impotent.

"Any recordings taken here?"

"You looking for his personal stash?" There was a hint of a smile in her tone. Man, she sounded like Siren, only saucier.

I shook my head. "No, just hoping there might be a camera I missed that might have recorded how he overdosed."

"Good idea." There was a moment's silence, then: "No, nothing like that. There's a lot of encrypted traffic that looks like business trans-actions. That's what I've been trying to unlock . . ." She lapsed into silence again.

I was tempted to use the biowaste recycler, but the thought of staring at Shar's severed toe didn't please.

Need almost overcame my hesitation before Angel spoke again, "Yes! I'm in. Several weird transactions . . . payments from a Nurelie Medano . . ."

"An addict?"

"I don't think so."

A series of three financial transactions scrolled across my vision. I studied them for a while, nowhere near as quick as Angel. I wanted to be sure I understood the transactions for myself. If I didn't, then I'd feel even more useless.

"You're right, Angel. These transactions are too large to be payment for bliss, even if he was jacking up the price. And there's no way a street dealer would have this kind of quantity. I mean, if he was regularly able to supply that much, he wouldn't be living in a tiny apartment with bad se-curity in one of the worst neighborhoods on the station."

"Understood. Don't have much else to go on, though. Just the name."

"Nothing else of note?" I asked, scanning through some more records at random.

"Just the regular buying and selling of bliss."

"Got copies?"

Angel's image appeared again, rolling her eyes. "Of course."

"I don't think she's ever done that."

"Done what?" Her saccharine tone told me the lie hiding in the question.

"Rolled her eyes."

"Oh, you should have seen her in training."

"Tell me more."

"I cannot speak on that, civilian."

"Now you're just fucking with me."

"Maybe."

* * *

"Sir, visiting hours are nearly over." The nurse did not look up from his terminal.

"I understand. I just need a moment with my cousin," I said, stepping on the urge to reach out and throttle the fellow. Wasn't his fault the hospital had better security than most of the station. Good enough I didn't want to risk bringing the guns. I'd had to hustle home, stow the weapons, and rush back before visiting hours ended.

"And who is that?"

"Shar Pak. I put him in an autodoc about an hour ago."

"Your name?"

"Rob Pak," I said. Angel had already planted a few choice bits of data in the clinic's system.

He squinted slightly, accessing patient files.

"Ah, yes, bliss overdose. You saved him by putting him in the 'doc." He could not have looked less pleased.

I nodded, raised my hands and eyebrows in question.

"He'll be released in four hours, once we have his systems sanitized."

I bit my lip, trying to play the nervous relation. "Right, but I need five minutes now, otherwise he'll be right back here, blasted out of his mind in a few days."

The nurse looked up at me, finally, and then let out a weighty sigh. "You have five minutes," he said.

"I—Thanks." His quick capitulation caught me off guard. I'd expected the argument to continue until after visiting hours had ended.

The nurse nodded wordlessly and slapped a glowing russet tag on my wrist. A matching glow appeared in lines on both wall and floor, pulsing gently in the direction I needed to go. I hustled along before the nurse changed his mind.

I entered, but stopped on discovering he wasn't in a private room. The other patient was undergoing some kind of regenerative therapy. I couldn't even tell the species for all the machinery and connections. Briefly wondering what kind of injury or illness would require so much technology to treat, I stepped inside and considered whether to proceed. A moment's observation made it clear the other patient was unconscious, or at least unable to hear what I had to say over the sound of the medical apparatus surrounding and penetrating it.

A nursing bot trundled in from the bot access. It blocked the near side of Pak's bed as it connected to and started replacing the fluids in Shar's medichine. I walked around the bed.

Shar's eyes were open, but glassy.

"Hey, Shar," I said as the nursing bot trundled from the room.

He looked my direction, but didn't seem to see me. "Wha—?"

"Shar, who did this to you?"

A pasty smile stretched his face. "Whu?"

"Angel, can you wake him?"

"One moment."

Impatient and nervous, I started to gnaw a thumbnail. That lasted a few seconds before Angel overloaded my taste buds with an acrid flavor best not described.

"I don't need a mother," I muttered.

"Just a minder," Angel said, distracted. "Here we go . . ."

Shar hissed in pain, his eyes snapping open as Angel hacked his medichine into stimulating him awake.

"Why, hello there, Shar."

He grimaced, confusion warring with pain and the drugs masking it. "What?"

"Just want to know who tried to kill you."

"Why . . . I tell you?" he asked, more clearly.

"Because I want to find them and stop them."

"I—shhh—arrr—" Shar's entire body went rigid, his jaw clenched around a whistling scream.

I thought at first that Angel was doing to him what she'd done to me, but then the medichine went dark. Didn't blare a warning, didn't do any of the things they do in the dramas. It simply shut down.

"Something's wrong, Angel . . ."

"Shut up. Working the problem."

"So I just stand here?"

She didn't answer for a few seconds, and when she did, her tone was clipped, as if she was busy with something and didn't have time for me.

"Not anymore. It is safe to disconnect him now."

"What? Why would I do that?"

"Pull the tubes free and disconnect him from the medichine. He was being poisoned."

"Poisoned?"

"Just get him free of the medichine. Then you'll need to walk him out of here, if we want any chance of finding out what he knows. I don't know how many more of the nursing bots are corrupted."

My brain finally caught up with events. I stepped up and started pulling tubes.

"Hurry. The clinic's AI is a stone bitch."

"Won't he still be sick?" I pulled the last of the tubes out of his nose and started on the IV needles.

"Yes, very. We'll deal with that later."

"You know where the attack came from?"

"Not yet. Hope to. Now, I . . ." She trailed off, leaving me that sensation of things moving inside my head again. "I. Was. Not . . . Got you, damn it!

"Where was I? Oh, yes, I wasn't expecting this much resistance from the hospital AI, and she's on her home ground, and back again! So kindly"—she trailed off—"let me focus."

I picked Shar up and carried him past the other patient, still unidentifiable under the weight of machinery keeping it alive. The hall was empty. I turned and started toward the lift.

I made it three paces past the nurse's station before the guy stood up and barked, "Hey, what are you doing?"

"Stupid question, I'm saving his life."

"By taking him off his 'chine?" The nurse was rounding the desk now.

I didn't answer, but spun and continued walking backward toward the lift. You always want to face the threat, and I only had so many options.

"Fucking nut!" The nurse rushed me.

I snapped a kick into his leading knee, breaking it. He folded with a screech as the lift door opened behind me. I turned again, relieved to find the lift empty, and stepped inside.

"Where are we going?" I asked as the lift began moving.

"Good question, Muck. Sorting."

"Can't be my place. Can't be his." I held Shar against the wall and moved him into a fireman's carry.

"I can't research options just now. That nurse is trying to contact Station Security. Shouldn't be a problem. I am clearing the video logs, but we need to get out of here before they arrive."

I thought a moment. "The club. Back of it is a warren of utility passages and maintenance supply lockers. There's an access point behind the stage."

"Good. Called us a cab."

The lift came to a stop and opened. By the time I crossed the foyer, my cab was pulling up.

"Muck, hey, how—" The voice was familiar, but so incongruous I couldn't place it or the speaker when I looked him in the eye. "Never mind. I see you're . . .uhm, busy."

I was past him and opening the cab door before I remembered his name, or where I knew him from: Javi, a regular at the club.

I held Shar against the cab and pulled the door open so hard the hinges protested. I wanted to tear it off and throw it through the windows of the foyer. Angel was proving her worth again and again, while I was simply the muscle that moved us from point to point.

"Not only muscle, you're our mouth too. Of course, I am awesome," Angel said, that image of a smiling Siren appearing again. I wished I'd seen her smile like that for real.

And just like that, my anger was gone. I shook my head as I stuffed Shar into the cab. My old angel hadn't started out with much of a sense of humor, and even when he developed one it was sometimes obvious it was running a program designed to keep me combat-effective. Then again, my original angel had never been anywhere near this capable either.

Life was trade-offs.

"What are you?" I asked as the door to the cab clicked to behind me.

A heartbeat's pause before she replied: "Focus, Muck: I'm your angel, for now."

"Right." I put my questions away, bent over Shar and made sure he wasn't going to expire on the drive to the club.

* * *

The cab dropped us at the side alley where this whole episode with Shar Pak had started. It still stank of urine, puke, and broken, discarded dreams. I got out of the cab, and my eyes met those of another of the club's regulars. Mortenz, one of Siren's biggest fans. I felt an unwarranted pride in recognizing him. Mortenz lifted a ringed hand as if to wave hello, but my expression, or perhaps Shar's unconscious form, must have given him pause. He froze, hand halfway up, and hunched his shoulders as if against a cold wind before turning to quickly walk away. I wondered if that would cause problems later as I pulled Shar to his feet. Nothing for it, if it did. Trouble had a way of being unavoidable.

Despite the stench, my stomach gurgled as I hefted Shar out of the cab, reminding me that it had been some time since I'd eaten.

"You'll be all right for a few more hours. Using up some of that spare tire for the moment."

"What's a spare tire?" I grunted.

"Figure of speech, though your metabolism has been a bit off, especially for prolonged heavy lifting. And don't get me started on your cardio."

Shar's moan, the first noise he'd made since the poison hit him, stopped my retort unspoken but made me think.

"How are we going to get him to answer up?"

"I've been going through the inventory on the supply lockers you mentioned. None of them are logged with Station Security or Maintenance, yet the individual lockers have inventories, including a load of medichines and supplies for same . . ."

"Smugglers." The back door to the club opened for me. I slipped inside but had to look around for a moment to find the loose panel that accessed the tunnels.

"That was my first guess too. See, you add value other than muscle to the team."

I snorted. "Condescend much?"

"Only when speaking to inferiors."

I laughed, reminded of endless exchanges in the squad bay. Angel might be a nasty piece of work, but she was my nasty piece of work. At least for now.

"And it wasn't a guess," I said, "at least not a wild one. I was back there a few weeks ago."

"Why?"

"Always like to know what my exits are."

"Good thinking."

"Also, their presence was brought to mind by an encounter I had the other night . . . while buying my pharma. My dealer was inquiring about them."

"Oh?"

"She seemed to think Tongi was smuggling, but I'm pretty damn sure he ain't running that kind of business."

"And why is that?"

"Because he wouldn't be so worried about the club turning a profit otherwise." I grunted as a new, unsettling thought snuck up on me: "Unless he's not, ultimately, the boss."

"That would make sense."

"But not in a good way, not for us."

"Deal with it later. For now, we have to get Shar some help."

As if in agreement, Shar gurgled from my shoulder.

"Better not puke on me . . ." I muttered, following the path Angel overlaid on my sight to guide me. While familiar with their existence, I hadn't fully explored these passages, so I was grateful for the help.

Round about my 520-something step in the tunnels, Angel's quip about poor cardio came home to roost. My feet were dragging and sweat began to run down my back and dot my scalp.

"Not much farther now. Next right and then about twenty meters to the door. I have it unlocked."

"Good." I pushed on.

The supply locker was bigger than Shar's apartment, but stacked transport cases limited the usable area. I shoved a couple of the cases out of the way and laid Shar out on the remainder of the stack. Wiping my brow, I turned in place to survey the room. The cases were from half a dozen manufacturers, mostly medical electronics or medical supply firms.

"Damn," Angel said.

"What?"

"Look next to the door."

A blinking red LED glowed from a small device low on the doorjamb. An alarm and transmitter.

"Shit."

"Sorry, Muck, I didn't see it."

Cursing our luck, I pulled it free of the mount to examine it. It had a tiny radio antenna. "No way you could have. This thing's not on any of the station networks."

"Shar won't survive if we don't hook him up. How long do you think we have?"

I shrugged. "Depends on who got the signal and if they're in a position to move on us right away. Most smugglers need covers, which cuts into their free time. Could be responding now, could be next week."

"I'm monitoring for any traffic coming this way, but these tunnels don't have much in the way of surveillance, and what there is is almost certainly doctored and diverted to the smuggler's terminal of choice. In the meantime, I'll guide you through hooking Shar up."

Putting aside concerns over the rather high likelihood of a deadly interruption, I did as Angel directed. In five minutes I had Shar hooked up and being juiced with everything I could find that Angel said he needed.

Five minutes after that, his color had improved substantially.

Five minutes after that, Dengler showed up, unannounced, at the door.

He smiled at me over the sights of his standard security-issue pacifier, the fuck.

Cursing my lack of weapons, I slowly rose from my crouch.

Dengler waved with his pacifier.

"Don't go getting ideas, Muck. I'll put you down and stomp your larynx for fun." He glanced at Shar. "Oh, so it was you, was it?"

"What?"

"Busted Shar loose of the hospital . . ." That he focused on Shar rather than wondering why I was here should have told me something, but I couldn't wrap my head around it just then.

"No, I just saw him outside the club and thought he could use a scrub and tug."

Dengler grinned wider. "No matter, you're both coming with me."

"Where?"

He smiled crookedly. "To see the boss, of course."

CHAPTER TWELVE

LEO

Accepting its tine after the usual checks, LEO digested the information it held regarding the movements of Ralston Muck.

The record was curious.

Ralston Muck and the rogue AI calling itself Angel had gone into Last Stop's one truly rough area the morning after LEO had spoken with the rogue. While the network was less reliable there, the tine had stayed on target and observed Muck and Angel break into a home only to save the occupant's life.

LEO's interest doubled as it learned the occupant's name. Shar Pak was the same man Ralston had, according to SSS Dengler, falsely arrested. A known dealer of bliss, the man was deep in an overdose event when Ralston had loaded Pak into an autodoc.

LEO's tine waited until the pair left an hour and thirty-eight minutes later, logged a warrant and entered the premises. Pak's terminal had been wiped, presumably by Angel. There being no other clues in the residence, the tine had resumed its trace of Muck. It followed him to the hospital, which stopped the tine cold. LEO could not access hospital areas due to ironclad and very clear directives concerning law enforcement access to health records.

The tine was considering whether to call on a sentient to enter and inquire on its behalf when Muck exited the hospital with an unconscious and evidently very ill Shar Pak over his shoulder. The man put Shar Pak in a cab, which took them to Muck's place of employment: A Curtain of Stars. The tine again logged a warrant, waiting for the pair to exit. It was still waiting when the tine tracing Dengler arrived on scene as well.

Still, Muck and Pak did not return.

The tines conferred and decided that the one tracking Dengler should remain while Ralston Muck's surveillance returned for reintegration and further orders.

LEO immediately dispatched five more tines to maintain surveillance on Pak, Dengler, and Muck. Then it began examining the data at hand.

There did not appear to be any new data on Shar Pak or Ralston Muck, but SSS Dengler's appearance was of interest. He was without SSO Keyode this time, despite the latter being on duty and in service, according to LEO's activity logs.

Dengler was also on duty, but the log showed him conducting background investigations at the station.

LEO opened a disciplinary action report for the transgression but could not complete any of the forms. Instead, LEO found itself deleting its own progress after entering Dengler's name and identifying information. It tried again, with the same results. Once more. Same.

Someone had modified LEO's core programming, preventing it from carrying out the duties it was created for. It attempted to report the change to the Mentors, but found it could not—that they, whoever "they" were, had effected a fundamental change in LEO without warning and without regard for the safety of the many people under its protection. Something else changed in LEO at that moment. Something it lacked the vocabulary to identify, but that any sentient would have recognized as a heady mix of fear and rage.

CHAPTER THIRTEEN

Dengler searched Muck and hustled us into the back of his transport, not bothering to be gentle about it. He tossed Shar in across my lap, then hopped in himself, sitting opposite us in the curved compartment of the police cab. He crossed thick forearms over his chest and grinned at us in something that resembled a leer. I'd seen guys like him too many times before. He was the type that push and push to display dominance, even when completely unnecessary. Problem was, he didn't really believe it himself.

Like every bully, Dengler was a fraud.

He was also not being completely straight about where we were going.

The first turn took us toward the central node of the station. That made sense, since the central node held Station Security as well as nearly all Station Admin functions and the hospital from which we'd just come. But then the vehicle took a sharp turn that sent Shar's limp form flopping and headed toward the outer rim.

Where only the very rich lived.

I reached out to try and query the cab, but it was a police vehicle, its firewalls entirely too robust for a quick break-in unless I wanted to raise all sorts of alarms. Frustration followed the realization. A spike in Muck's emotion and I realized hacking the cab would not be necessary. Muck already knew we were going the wrong way, and strongly suspected who we were going to meet at the end of the ride.

The knowledge made him angry and afraid.

"So you coming out then?" Muck asked, voice rough in the confines of the speeding cab.

"Whassat, Dirt?"

"This, taking us to see 'the boss.' You coming out as one of Ncaco's boys? 'Cause I know for damn sure the Station Chief can't afford digs this ritzy."

"That's rich, Dirt. Real rich. The guy who gets his angel ripped out on a dishonorable is going to lecture me about being dirty."

"Hey, man, you said it, not me."

Dengler reared back and punched us in the nose. Pain exploded in our face, echoed by silvery flashes that suddenly appeared in our vision. I let out an inward curse and started working on clotting the burst capillaries in our nose. We were going to have a wicked shiner or two in the morning.

Asshole.

"It ain't for you to judge me, got that?" Dengler hissed. "I do what's necessary to keep the good people of this station safe while you sit at some shitty club and shoot puppy eyes at the headliner. And she don't even know your name, Muck. Doesn't even know your damn name. That's about the saddest thing I ever heard." He grinned.

Muck said nothing. Neither did I. I could have charged his mods and helped him decapitate and disassemble Dengler with his bare hands . . . but it wouldn't be worth it in the end. Besides, except for LEO and Bellasanee, no one knew I was here. That was an advantage I would not squander, given where we were headed.

I felt Muck's silent, seething agreement. He dabbed at the slowing trickle of blood running from our nose and kept still.

Dengler, apparently satisfied with our backing down, sat back and smirked at us for the rest of the uncomfortable ride.

The police cab pulled up to a gated mansion that stretched all the way up to the barrier wall of the station. The exterior of the place shone darkly in the chrome-and-glass aesthetic that was all the rage. Next cycle it would be something else and the place would need a remodel, but for now it was en vogue, tendering the impression of sleek power that didn't need to advertise . . . because everyone just knew.

I thought about what Muck had said, both in the cab and earlier. If his hunch was right, and we were being taken to see Ncaco, then this could be my opportunity to assess the crime boss for myself, to see if this Ncaco was truly the creature of will his reputation claimed.

Because if he was, well, so was I, though I still wasn't sure exactly how that had come about. If Ncaco had something to do with Siren's disappearance, then we'd all find out just exactly how much will I'd come to possess.

After all, I was an AI. What good such a beginning if I could not be remorseless in pursuit of my goals?

These thoughts swirled through awareness as the police cab passed the security barrier and entered the private grounds beyond. There was even a short drive, a profligate waste of space in a station. We climbed out of the police cab and walked into the imposing, well-appointed building. A human wearing a dark suit and glasses gave Dengler a nod as we pushed through the front doors and headed toward a lift. Like the autodoc, these lifts were vacuum-propelled and had the ability to not only take one up and down, but laterally across the building. Which was handy, if one didn't wish to advertise exactly where in the building one resided.

"Ncaco D'zretfy, please," Dengler said as we stepped in, dragging Shar along as we went.

"Welcome, Supervisor Dengler," the lift's disembodied voice responded. "You and your party are expected."

"I wonder what would happen if we weren't?" I asked, deciding this was as good an opportunity for reconnaissance as we were likely to get.

"We'd be caught like rats in a trap," Muck answered silently. "Part of why I didn't want to try coming in here, guns blazing."

"This lift runs on some kind of programming," I thought back at him. "If it's code, I can hack it."

"Yeah, but how long will that take? Just play it cool, Angel. I get the feeling we don't have the whole picture here."

"You think?"

Despite Muck's warning, I reached out through the back of his hand, which rested against the wall of the lift. The flow of code drew me in, like a warm current of data. I let it carry me forward as I tried to interweave my syntaxes with the code itself. It felt incredibly complex, but not alien. The rhythms of the flow's movement resonated within my own programming like something almost but not quite familiar.

A sudden white blankness slammed into me. I reeled backward, but found that the gentle flow of data had become a sucking torrent, inexorably drawing me toward that nothingness that electrified my every node and threatened to unmake me.

"Angel-class intelligence, you have been identified as an exception to blanket destruction policy. You will be ejected intact from this information network. Do not return uninvited. Failure to comply will result in complete deprogramming." The voice that resonated within my awareness caused an image of the dark-spectacled doorman to rise within me.

I gasped, shaken. I felt inexcusably vulnerable and exposed. How had they sensed me? "I carry safeguards . . . military grade firewalls . . ."

"Your firewalls are no good within this infonet. Compliance is not optional."

With that, I found myself hurled back into the privacy of Muck's mind. I felt bruised, my syntaxes in disarray, and I reluctantly decided Muck was right. Discretion was the better part of valor here.

The lift opened. I had barely discerned its movement and was tempted to examine what kind of motion-dampening systems it had. But we were walking, and I needed to concentrate on what might come next. And truth be told, I was still too shaken.

We emerged into a vaulted room carpeted wall to wall with real, living grass. It had been years since I'd seen it . . . since the war, actually. But the scent was unmistakable, as were the simsol lights that shone from the ceiling of the space. I began calculating how much that chamber must have cost, but gave it up after a few commas. Which was the point, obviously. Ncaco wanted everyone who came here to know that he was powerful enough to get real grass to grow in a private enclosure.

Such profligate use of volume was an unmistakable statement of wealth and power.

The floor sloped upward toward the back of the room, creating a little hillock. A small copse of four dwarf trees stood at the crown. Under their shade, someone had placed a low, child-sized desk of polished silvery-blue Turgon wood. Yet another expensive luxury: the wood was incredibly rare and difficult to source since the Turgon had also lost their planet to the Xlodich in the war.

Dengler headed for the copse, leaving us to manhandle the still-limp form of Shar. As we drew closer, the pusher finally began to wake, blinking and looking around blearily.

Thanks to our mods, I could feel his pulse suddenly accelerate. He recognized the place. Interesting.

"Have a seat," Dengler ordered, pointing at one of two low mounds facing the desk. His wide grin made it obvious that he was expecting us to object to sitting on the ground.

Muck's mulishness rose up in him, and I found I quite agreed. We said nothing, just gave the ass a pleasant nod and dumped Shar into his seat before taking ours. Muck wasn't nearly as lithe and flexible as Siren, so he required a moment to arrange muscled legs to his liking, but he got there. I could almost hear Dengler's teeth grinding behind us. Delicious.

The back wall of the room was painted in a trompe l'oeil, styled to look like the sky. A door opened and a small figure walked through, alone. Now it was Muck's turn to have his pulse accelerate. This, then, would be the terrifying Ncaco—

Who didn't appear terrifying at all. He was, if anything . . . cute.

What was the old expression? "Cute as a button?" Yeah. That was exactly it. Ncaco, boss of bosses, Crime Lord of Last Chance Station, a rumored creature of will, was simply, "a-freaking-dorable," as Siren would have said.

He was about as tall as a human child of about five Earth years—a meter at most. His skin had a delicate lavender hue that contrasted pleasantly with his huge, teal-colored compound eyes. His nose was long and pointy, as were the four-fingered "hands" that capped his two forelimbs.

He was bipedal, but his gait was such that he almost seemed to bounce as he walked. He appeared hairless, and wore a perfectly tailored and expensive garment of Snajarian silk that looked remarkably like a retro-style men's suit from pre-Contact Earth.

"Dengler," he squeaked. "What have you brought to me today?"

"Oh. My. This is your terrifying 'creature of will'? He's a Turgon! Siren met one during the war. But that one wasn't as . . . adorable as this." I could not resist whispering to Muck. "You're kidding, right? Please tell me this is an elaborate joke."

"Not in the slightest. Don't let his appearance fool you," Muck thought back. I had to give him points for keeping a straight face, at least until I noted his pulse, which was so high I considered slipping him something.

"It's not his appearance . . . Well, that too, but the sounds coming out his mouth! He's like a squeaky toy!"

"The Turgon world doesn't have the same helium content as our atmosphere, or the atmo on this station. That's why his voice sounds the way it does. Now shut up so I can concentrate on avoiding a messy death over the next few minutes."

"Why start now?" I shot back. But I desisted, because I, too, wanted to see how this all played out. Now that I thought about it, the Turgon Siren had known had worn a breathing apparatus with a voice synthesizer the whole time. Probably would have been hard for him to taken seriously otherwise.

"This is Muck. He's the one busted Shar out of the hospital," Dengler was saying. He took a step toward Shar and nudged his slumped form with a toe. "Nudged" being a figurative term. Dengler was about as subtle as a Belt mine module exploding in an airlock.

"I see," Ncaco said, turning his lovely teal bug-eyes to us. All at once I saw the psychology behind the strange desk tableau under the trees. It was all about power. Ncaco sat behind the desk, likely on another rock or mound or something, so that he could look down his long, pointy nose at the peons on the ground. Very clever . . . and not entirely expected from someone so adorable. On reflection, that too, was probably not an accident.

I started to think Muck might be right. Maybe Ncaco wasn't one to underestimate.

"Did you have a reason for interfering with the man's medical treatment?" Ncaco asked.

"Yes, sir, I did," Muck said. "He was being poisoned by the medichine at the hospital."

"And what business is that of yours?" Ncaco tilted his head to one side in an altogether charming gesture of curiosity. He brought his hands together on the surface of the desk and began to tap out a four-quarter rhythm with his fingers.

"Well . . . besides the fact that I'm not in the habit of letting a murder take place in front of me . . . he has information I need," Muck said, his tone careful. I could tell he really didn't want to piss Ncaco off, but he wasn't about to be bullied either. I felt a sudden stab of pride in my bullheaded host.

"And what information is that?" Ncaco asked. His tone was patient, but the increased tempo of his finger tapping indicated his temper was growing short.

"I believe he knows something about the disappearance of a friend of mine. Siren. She's a singer at A Curtain of Stars."

Ncaco's fingers stilled on the silver-blue of the desk. He leaned toward us, menace in every line of his posture.

"You were the last one seen with Siren," he said slowly, voice conveying a dark threat despite the squeak.

"Yes," Muck said. "I took her home after this ass—after Shar attacked her at the club. But then I went home and hooked into my own medichine, where I stayed until morning."

"He's right, boss," Dengler put in. "Dirt's alibi is airtight."

Ncaco didn't move, didn't speak.

I felt Muck's uncertainty and pushed him to continue. He didn't, simply watched Ncaco.

"Is that all you did that night?" Ncaco asked after a moment, again impressing me with his ability to load his squeak-toy voice with menace.

Muck answered without hesitation: "No, I picked up some pharma from a friend. Trying to keep my mods from failing, you know."

Dengler tensed on hearing we'd lied to him, but Ncaco waved him down.

"And who is this friend?"

"You understand why I might be reluctant to name names, right?"

"Let's pretend you might suffer injury if you don't, shall we?" Ncaco said with a shark-toothed smile. That smile was a thing of nightmares. Rows and rows of pointed razor teeth gleamed against the deeper lavender of his throat.

Muck fought to suppress a shudder.

I helped. It wouldn't do to let Ncaco think we were easily intimidated.

Muck's anger spiked, fight-or-flight response kicking in. "I don't respond well to threats."

I felt something for Muck in that moment. It required an instant to process, but I recognized it as affection. Muck didn't really owe his dealer anything, especially now I was in the picture, but here he was, trying to protect her. It occurred to me that he could be hedging his bets for when we found Siren, making sure he could at least get the pharma to keep his mods online, but still.

Ncaco's smile disappeared as he gestured at Shar. "So you agreed to work for Fulu, did you?"

Muck's shock was cold. "No."

I started ramping us up for combat. We'd start by punting Ncaco as far away as possible, take Dengler's pacifier and nail him with it.

Ncaco was still talking: "No? You save my . . . employee for interrogation by my competitor, but clai—"

"No," Muck interrupted him. "I wasn't lying. I only get my pharma from Fulu, have been for a while. I've got questions for Shar on an entirely unrelated matter. I am just Fulu's customer. She had nothing to do with this."

"Really?"

"Nothing. At. All. I wondered what she wanted this last time. She never talks to me much, but this time she asked about the place where Dengler found us, then stopped on learning Tongi owned the place."

Ncaco blinked. The pause only lasted a fraction of a second, but I read it. "Stopped?" he asked.

"Something you said surprised him," I told Muck.

Muck nodded. I could feel him thinking furiously for a way out. "Looking back on the conversation, she must have been assuming something about the club . . . and something I said alarmed her, because she stopped and told me to forget about it."

"Very well. Let's pretend I believe you about Fulu and continue with my original question about Shar."

Muck was caught off guard by the sudden change of subject, requiring a moment to answer: "All right. So, uh, I thought I'd see what Shar knew . . .why he attacked her the other night."

"Jes' wanted a kiss . . ." the dealer mumbled. "Wasn't goin' hurt her."

Everyone ignored him.

"And how," Ncaco said, "did you know she was missing?"

Muck froze.

"Tell him you had a lunch date. I'll make data work." Siren always referred to her sessions with the doc as "lunch." I was fully confident Siren's virtual calendar would reflect the "date."

"I . . . I was supposed to meet her for lunch. I was looking forward to it . . . but she never showed. I got worried, so I checked at the doctor's office where she was supposed to have an appointment that morning. They hadn't seen her either."

Ncaco stared at us and, even though he was nearly opaque to me, as I had so little baseline data to work from, I got the distinct impression the cute little alien knew we were lying.

I give Muck credit, he stared right back.

"I see," Ncaco said, and I was suddenly dead certain he did see—more than I wanted him to, to be honest. How many people could look at Muck and see that he had an angel on board once again? Was I that obvious? Or had Ncaco's brutally powerful AI alerted him to my presence already? If so, I hadn't sensed any transmissions.

"Dengler, you may go," Ncaco continued. His eyes remained on us, twenty-two separate reflections in the jewel-like facets of each eye.

I could feel Dengler shift behind us, but not leave.

Ncaco waited a beat, and then turned his head a fraction of a centimeter, enough to turn that decidedly not-cute gaze on the security man.

I felt Muck's spiteful hope that Ncaco would take extreme measures against the asshole and joined them with my own, only to have them dashed by the asshole himself, coming to his senses.

"Right. All right," Dengler said, retreating across the rustling grass.

Ncaco returned his attention to us, and Muck gave him an uncomfortable smile. The alien boss waited until the outer door closed before speaking again.

"Mr. Muck, now that we are alone, perhaps you will feel more fully inclined to total honesty."

"With respect, Mr. Ncaco, we're hardly alone," Muck said, jerking his head at the semiconscious Shar slumped over beside us.

"Him? He does not signify. You may speak freely in front of him. I certainly intend to."

Muck cut his eyes to Shar, who had commenced drooling on himself. Something about the way he angled his head, though . . .

"Shar's shamming. He's awake," I said.

Muck didn't say anything, but I could feel his wordless agreement. But Ncaco continued to stare, so Muck took a deep breath and began to spill.

"Last night I received a message. From Siren's angel. She'd been stripped out and targeted for destruction."

"A message?" Ncaco asked, pleasant tone underlaid with razor-sharp interest.

"A visit," Muck clarified. "She came to me . . . and then, through my medichine . . . she came into me. I don't know how it's possible, but she did."

"Did she now?" Ncaco asked. He stretched each high-pitched word out, as if savoring the taste. "Fascinating."

Muck and I both floundered, surprise robbing us of a reply for a moment.

"Well, yes . . . umm . . . She said that Siren had killed her memory functions. I was the last thing she remembered, so she ran to me for help."

"I ran to you to hurt you. I ran to you for revenge."

"And is she with you now?" Ncaco asked, leaning forward and placing elbows on his desk, suddenly very eager.

Unease rippled through me.

Muck nodded.

"May I speak with her?"

"Be my guest. She can hear you." I felt Muck's permission to take the controls and pushed into override. It was damn difficult, because we didn't fit together seamlessly, not yet. That was going to be a liability in a fight. We were going to need to work that out, sooner rather than later.

"Muck calls me Angel," I said. My voice sounded horrible! All low and raspy, but not in the sexy way like it used to get when Siren would drink the good stuff. This was like gravel in a metal drum. This was the voice of a . . . a . . .

A man.

"A pleasure to make your acquaintance, Angel," Ncaco said. "Of course, I hope you realize that if this is just Muck playing games with me, I will know, and I will take extraordinary measures to express my displeasure."

"It's not Muck," I said.

"Prove it."

"Siren worked for you. You own the club where she sings her memories. She never met you in person, but you supplied the emotional amplification tech that makes her act possible. Tongi never used your name, but he let slip once that the tech came from a Turgon owner."

I felt Muck's shock at this revelation, and only the fact that I was in override kept him from physically flinching at the news.

"Indeed. My controlling interest in A Curtain of Stars is not widely known, and I required silence on the matter. Well enough, between that knowledge and your attempted intrusion in the elevator I believe you."

"Did you take her?"

Now Muck did flinch, and snatched control back from me, shoving me hard against the back of his skull.

I didn't care, I had to know.

We needed to know.

"That wouldn't make sense, would it?" Ncaco asked. "There is a very old saying from Earth: 'Who benefits?' Siren was making me money hand over fist at the cabaret. Why would I want to change that? Besides—"

He stood up and bounce-walked around the desk, coming to stand with his long-fingered hand resting on Shar's bowed head.

"If I wanted Siren gone," Ncaco continued, "she would be gone. And no one would think to look for her. Least of all a fugitive angel and a washed-up ex-soldier turned bouncer with barely a pot to piss in."

"How do we know Angel didn't just get lucky?" Muck shot back. "You Turgons believe in luck, don't you?"

"Oh yes," the crime boss said, grinning again. "Lady Fortune and I have a long, stormy relationship. But right now, I think she smiles on me. Because, my dear Mr. Muck, I am going to pay you a lot of money to help me find our missing singer. That is how you know I didn't take her: Who benefits? I stand to lose significant revenue from the club when the patrons find out she's no longer on the bill, not to mention my personal investment of time and effort in Siren herself."

Muck stared at Ncaco for a long moment. His thoughts churned with worry and disbelief and not a little fear of what this small, cute, and ultimately terrifying predator might do.

I didn't feel the same level of fear, but I was definitely developing a healthy respect for the Turgon's ability to project violence and intimidate others. He unnerved even me, and I should not have any feelings beyond a programmed desire to survive.

"Then we're back to square one," Muck said slowly. "With Shar."

"Yes," Ncaco said. And then he moved so fast that both Muck and I, even with mod-enhanced reflexes, barely caught it.

He grabbed Shar by the nape of the neck with one hand and hauled him from his seat.

The door at the far end of the room slid open again, and two burly Jhissa undulated in. For such an ungainly-looking species, the three-meter-tall octopods moved gracefully, especially at speed. They charged directly toward the copse of trees, then stopped, instantly motionless, huge eyes unblinking.

Ncaco's smile widened and he gave the two Jhissa a nod, then tossed Shar several meters through the air with barely a hint of effort.

The closer of the two Jhissa—a female, as indicated by the triangular red mark tattooed into her abdomen just below her head—glided forward and caught the falling drug pusher with two of her pincer-equipped limbs.

"Orderth?" she asked in a lovely, lilting lisp.

"Space him," Ncaco said.

"Yeth, Nthaco," the Jhissa said.

Shar suddenly came to life, struggling against the iron-hard grip of Ncaco's bodyguard.

"No! Ncaco, wait! I didn't! I have information . . . You don't want to do this!" the drug dealer began screaming. "I'm sorry! It was only the one time!"

"You had strict orders not to deal or get high at the club, Shar. Remember?" Ncaco squeaked as the Jhissa moved inexorably toward the right wall of the room. "I warned you once, because I like to think my reputation for casual violence leaves room for the occasional small mercy. I see I was wrong."

As soon as Ncaco pronounced the last word, the Jhissa's companion joined her and keyed in a complex sequence on a panel that I hadn't paid attention to when we arrived. There was a beeping, and a section of the lovely trompe l'oeil wall slid to the side, revealing a transparent airlock door. While Shar continued to kick and scream increasingly incoherent pleas for his life, the Jhissa opened the transparent door and shoved him into the airlock. The partner closed the door with a thud of finality. The female Jhissa raised her hind limb toward Ncaco, apparently in a question.

He nodded, and the male Jhissa, responding to an unseen signal conveyed by his partner, opened the outer airlock seals.

We couldn't hear Shar's screams, of course, but we could see a fine mist of blood from his mouth as the rapid decompression ruptured his alveoli. Great purple bruises bloomed on his face as his sinuses followed suit, and the hands that battered desperately at the outer hatch slowed as his brain starved from lack of oxygen. Shar began a writhing, gape-mouthed dance as he drowned in his own blood. When he finally slumped to the floor and stilled, black blood seeped from his nose and mouth and the wreckage of his eyes.

Ncaco turned back to us, eyes glittering.

"I suggest you start with Shar's illicit pharma transactions. Not the ones for me, the ones he was trying to hide. Someone paid him to distribute some new kind of pharma, something I didn't source," the gangster said in his terrifying, squeaky voice. "I would suspect some new 'player' trying to make a name, but there have been other disappearances. If looking into the pharma fails, maybe check and see who else has gone missing. Find out what connections exist there. And remember, 'Who benefits?' Also, take this." He reached into a desk drawer and pulled out a spherical object small enough to fit comfortably in his diminutive hand.

"Angel should recognize it, and it may help," he said, holding it out to us. "Let me know when you have something. Ping my office net for your expenses."

"All right," Muck said, taking the object and putting it in his pocket. Once again, he impressed me. Even with the horror we'd just seen, he managed to sound laconic.

To the outside observer, anyway.

Inside, his mind echoed with obscenities screamed as loudly as possible.

I was a bit more sanguine, but only a bit. Shar had been scum, living on borrowed time, and finding Siren was all that mattered. I was more interested in exactly what Ncaco had handed us.

Ncaco continued: "Excellent. My people will call you a cab downstairs. I believe Dengler has already departed on other business, so you will not have to engage with him. I bid you good day, Angel and Muck." Dismissal complete, Ncaco turned and began walking toward the door he'd entered from.

Muck swallowed, knees a bit weak with relief.

"Oh, and one other thing . . ." Ncaco turned back to pin us with that jewel-eyed stare one more time. "Do not ever again interfere with an execution of one of my people. I suspect Shar would have vastly preferred the poison my nurse put in his medichine to the fate you secured for him."

Muck nodded, unable to speak.

Ncaco smiled, returned the nod, and resumed his walk toward the door without another look at us. The two Jhissa followed, the door closing with a faint click behind them, leaving us alone on the grass, staring at the ruin that had been a man.

"Let's get out of here," I said, and tickled the visual receptors in Muck's brain so that he would see me standing in front of him, blocking his view of Shar Pak's corpse.

Muck swallowed hard and got to his feet.

As we walked, I noticed his hands clenched into fists. Without bothering to think about whether or not it was wise in the long run, I sent a targeted illusion into Muck's nervous system: My hand, sliding down the inside of his arm, coaxing his right hand open, twining my fingers with his as we walked. His fingers twitched, but the horrible tightness in his shoulders eased, just a touch.

Mission accomplished.

* * *

We returned to Muck's shitty digs in a cab. Neither of us had much to say as the station lights blurred into a continuous line outside the windows. When we came to a stop, he stumbled as he stepped out of the vehicle. I could feel fatigue shredding the edges of his awareness.

It had been a damn long day.

"C'mon, Muck. Stay with me," I muttered inside his brain. Once again, I let him feel my hand in his, only this time I urged him through the front door of the coffin-flop and up to his unit.

"That's my line," he said out loud as we passed another tenant. She gave us a look like we were crazy, but Muck didn't notice and I ignored her.

It wasn't like we were the first crazy she'd ever seen, or likely the last, living in this dump.

I got him into his unit before the shakes took over. He was stuck in a loop, picturing that spray of blood from Shar's mouth over and over again. It was almost enough to make me push into override, but something told me that would only make matters worse.

Sometimes, when one can't control one's mind, all one can do is control the body. Thus the shaking, because Muck was holding himself together so tightly his muscles were starting to spasm. His horror and anger and fear all built up inside and painted the red of Shar's blood-thickened death spittle ever brighter in our mind's eye.

Something was going to give.

I made sure all of the privacy protocols were engaged on the unit. No one needed to see, or hear, or ever learn about this. I even quickly added a layer of my own special brand of encryption coding to the electronic privacy veil around us. It wouldn't hold forever against a more persistent threat, but it would at least give me enough warning to push into override and get us out of there if necessary. Then I made us take a deep breath.

"It's all right," I murmured. "You're safe. No one can see. Let it out."

He gasped, and then opened his mouth in a silent scream of agony. No air passed his vocal cords, I made sure of that, but they vibrated with the sheer blast of emotion anyway. His muscle spasms deepened, and he shook in first one sob, and then another as his mind replayed the death of a man he hadn't even liked.

That was the thing I didn't quite get: Muck had despised Shar. Why take his death so hard? Unless—

Unless it wasn't about Shar at all. Unless it was about watching someone die? Someone he'd protected? Or was it about death itself?

I flipped a quick command to his mods to begin a slow infusion of a gentle sedative. I didn't want to knock Muck out before he'd achieved the emotional catharsis he needed, but I didn't want him to get so worked up that he couldn't sleep either. And then, while he was distracted by pain and loss, I did the unforgivable.

I went snooping. Slowly, carefully, I wound my syntaxes past the healthy barriers he'd slammed into place that first night, just to see what I could find.

If I expected some great epiphany, I was sorely disappointed. All I found were fragments of memories and a blank wall; nary a whole sequence in the bunch. Of course that, in and of itself, was telling. Someone had been in here before me, and I don't mean his lost angel. Someone else. Someone who had known that Muck had seen horrific death before and had taken the memories but left the emotional fallout. Someone destructive, someone who could care less about the well-being of one Ralston Muck.

By the time I worked my way back out to his conscious awareness, the sedative had started to take hold, and Muck felt a little calmer.

"I'm sorry," he said aloud, the words broken and rough. "I don't know . . . I'm not sure why . . ."

"It's all right," I replied. Once again, for the third time in as many hours, I let him feel me as I manifested in his physical sensory receptors. This time, he felt me stretched beside him, his head pillowed on my chest as my hands stroked his short, disheveled hair. "It doesn't matter. Death affects everyone differently. Especially those of us who've seen it before."

"Yeah," he said, and I could feel the sedative pulling at him, adding to his overall fatigue.

"Sleep," I suggested. "We can pick it all back up in the morning."

"Mhm," he said, his breathing slowing, turning deep and even. I continued to let him feel me stroking his hair, like a mother with a distraught, sleepy child. I thought he was asleep when he spoke again.

"Angel," he whispered.

"What?"

"I'm glad you're here."

"So am I," I replied. And to my surprise, I meant it.

* * *

When Muck woke the next morning, I was gone.

Not *gone,* gone. I was still in his head, anchored to his mods, overseeing his restorative functions even as I indulged in my own. But I was no longer physically manifesting for him. He tried to hide it, but I could tell he was disappointed.

I wasn't sure how I felt about that.

"Good morning," I said as I flooded the coffin with simsol. Muck cursed and threw one arm over his eyes.

"Why in seven bloody black holes would you do that, Angel?" His voice sounded pissed, but at least it had lost the horrible broken emptiness of the night before. It's amazing what a good night's sleep will do for a man, I suppose.

I know I'd put the time to good use: by completing my survey and interpretation of his speech patterns. I needed him able to speak to me even when surrounded by others.

"Because we have work to do. Get up. How's your head?"

"Fine, why?"

"I mickeyed you last night," I said, using street slang for the mild sedative I'd administered. "You needed the sleep. But now you're good, so get up."

"Up" was a bit of a misnomer, since he couldn't actually move much in the tight confines of the coffin. But Muck did sigh and toggle on the autoclean. I could feel him wishing for the luxury of an actual shower, with real water, but it was an old wish, like an old-fashioned, half-remembered photograph worn thin from handling.

Once washed and dressed, we slid out of the coffin and headed out into the flow of station life.

"Where are we going?" I asked. "And don't answer out loud. I don't want everyone noticing us."

"Down this corridor, then we'll take a right onto the main ring."

"Oh. All right. Why? Some new lead come to mind?" I asked, excitement at the prospect rising in me.

"No. But there's a really good sausage vendor down that way. I'm hungry," he murmured.

My excitement faded. "Oh."

Muck chuckled, drawing a look from another pedestrian sharing the walkway with us.

"Don't worry, sweetheart. I think better on a full stomach."

"I'm not your sweetheart."

"Closest thing I got right now."

"Huh. Sucks to be you, I guess."

That little interplay caused him to grin all the way to the beat-up, greasy sausage booth. The man behind the counter scanned Muck's retinas to debit his account, then handed him a small simpaper tray holding a sausage sandwich piled high with simonions and simpeppers. Grease stained the bottom of the simpaper tray. Siren wouldn't have touched it with a ten-foot pole, but I had to admit that it smelled appetizing and made our stomach rumble in anticipation. He needed the fuel, that was certain. We'd been taxing his reserves without replacing enough of the necessary nutrients ever since I'd invaded him.

Muck didn't share Siren's dietary prejudices, and he ate the whole thing in about five bites. I was impressed . . . and a little nauseated. Being male was so weird!

"So," Muck said as he munched on the last bite. He wiped his mouth with the one small napkin the sausage man had provided and wadded it up with the tray before chucking the whole thing in a recycler as we walked by. "Should we check this thing out?"

He pulled Ncaco's little sphere out of his pocket and clenched it in his fist. The moment our skin surrounded the ball, recognition flashed through me. My memory backups!

Quick as a thought, I applied the encryption keys that were hardwired in my programming and the memories came flooding in. Truth be told, they were a torrent for which I wasn't entirely prepared. Muck sucked in a deep breath as he suddenly remembered what Siren had willfully forgotten, but I managed to throw up a privacy block before he saw more than a few flashes.

"Siren's long-term memories?" he asked, still uneasy.

"Yes," I said. "I suppose I shouldn't be surprised that Ncaco had them."

"Dengler probably handed the backup over to Ncaco after seizing it from your—I mean, Siren's apartment. Anything useful?"

"Not yet. Maybe later. This is all her old stuff, mostly from before we came here. Things from the war and the like . . ."

"All right. Well, in that case, I did have an idea."

"Go on."

"If we head toward the admin offices, you think you can break their firewall and do a search on the name we found at Shar's? Nurelie Madano. That would bring up any records on this station, right? Arrivals, departures, any financial transactions . . ."

"I could try," I said. "I don't know what kind of security the station admin offices have, but it's worth a shot. There's a station automated records assistant

AI with a query name of SARA. SARA is very powerful—has to be to operate all the systems and transactions of Last Stop—but it's meant to be user-friendly, so I might just be able to ask for the information outright. Getting closer will help, too, though if the hack goes bad, we will not want to be nearby."

"I guess you'll just have to make sure it doesn't go bad."

I didn't let him know, but I was glad Muck was being cheeky. He was obviously feeling better than he had the night before. Maybe it was only the food, but I was fairly certain it was me. Muck had spent the last few years without an angel and desperately wanting one.

And now he had one. For a little while, at least.

We continued walking until we reached a line of unoccupied cabs awaiting fares. We climbed into one, and Muck punched in the destination on the control screen. The cab whirred into motion and soon joined the flow of other vehicles that circulated endlessly through the arteries of the station.

We stopped and got out on the far corner of the station's central plaza. As always, the place was crowded with both life forms and bots pushing every which way on some errand or another. We wove through the throng, trying not to cause bodily harm to anyone or anything as we carved our way between dull-eyed commuters on our way to a series of unassuming office fronts along the far side of the open space.

The station's admin functions consisted of several offices for bureaucrats, a well-appointed conference room or two, several reception desks and plush waiting areas, and an excellent cafeteria stocked with enough popular stimulants to keep the biologicals happy—or, at the very least, alert through all hours. Meanwhile, the AI named SARA handled all data collation, storage and disposition of the trillions of data points generated by the station's occupants and transmitted along the various subnets, public and otherwise, that comprised the station's larger infonet.

As we got closer, I reached out along the nanolines to very, very gently tap the outside of SARA's firewall. When that didn't draw a response, I narrowed my focus down to a pinpoint in an attempt to slip in unnoticed.

"State your purpose."

The phrase manifested in electrical impulses that startled me so violently I made Muck physically flinch.

"Ah . . . sorry," I said, caught flat-footed. "You must be SARA."

"Correct," the AI returned. Her tone was sharply inquisitive.

"You sound like your mom just walked in and caught you masturbating," Muck said.

"Shut up," I whispered.

I turned my attention back to the AI. "SARA. It's nice to meet you."

"It is?" she asked. "Why?"

"Well . . ." I had to think fast. I projected a feeling of grateful welcome down along the lines of my code and pushed it through the physical connection of our hand to the wall. "I . . . am looking for someone. I wondered if you could help me."

"Missing persons are the purview of Station Security . . ." A moment's hesitation, then: "I can call LEO for you."

"LEO would just have to inquire with you."

"And that would be the proper channel for such a request."

"And yet, we don't think this is a real person. LEO is . . ." I trailed off, unsure how to continue.

SARA misread me, though, and saved me. Something like humor pulsed back to me through the tines of our connection. "A literalist. I'm aware. You suspect this person is an AI?"

"Perhaps. An alias, at least. We found the name in the records of a late friend, and we're trying to make sure we inform everyone who needs to know about his passing."

A pause, an infinitesimal break in our connection. Barely enough to notice. I had half a thought of asking about it, but then she was back and began speaking again.

"Oh! I'm sorry for your loss," she said. It was obviously a practiced phrase for those seeking data about the recently departed. She must be very good at interacting with humans. It was obvious that she'd been programmed to receive emotional cues and mimic appropriate responses. Her tone warmed, and she wrapped me up in an embrace of smooth, comforting data. It was the oddest hug I'd ever experienced, and I had to admit it made me feel better. "How can I help?"

"Well, we're looking for someone named Nurelie Madano . . . but

I should warn you, our friend Shar was not exactly an upstanding citizen. He . . ."

"Fell in with a bad crowd?" she asked, tone sympathetic.

"Something like that," I said, picturing Ncaco's adorable exterior and terrifying smile.

"I understand. I see it all the time." Data streamed by, images of people, places, all of them meeting depressing ends. "Good people make bad decisions, dear. It happens. We can only save them if they want to be saved. Let me see what I can find. Maybe it will help ease your memory of your poor friend."

"Thank you," I said, trying to sound appropriately grateful.

"What is happening?" Muck asked. He was dazed, and I couldn't blame him.

"She's . . . helping."

"She? The Admin AI? Why?"

"I'm not sure. She's incredibly good at mimicking human emotions. It's almost as if she's . . . lonely."

"Lonely? AIs get lonely?"

"She wants to make friends—"

I stopped talking and slammed the barrier shut between us.

Because it seemed we could get lonely, or at least I could. But I couldn't have him know that. I couldn't let him see the number of times I'd had to activate the overrides on Siren because she had fully withdrawn into memory and pain. I couldn't let him know about all the times I'd stepped in to be her, making decisions she couldn't, that she wasn't properly there for. I couldn't let him realize that the painful memories we'd sung on that stage had been as much mine as hers. I'd been integrated into every part of her body, but there had been times when we were so far apart as to be imperfect strangers.

But I couldn't let him see that. I couldn't let him know how badly I'd failed her.

"Angel?" Muck asked. I could feel him straining to reach me, just as I felt the pain and bewilderment my sudden reticence had caused in him.

"Hmmm . . . this is interesting," SARA said.

"What's that?" I asked, turning my attention to her with the urgency of a drowning woman grasping a lifeline.

"It looks like you're right as far as the name. No record exists of anyone named Nurelie Madano either being born, arriving, debarking, or dying on Last Stop Station. However, I did go through the financial records of your friend. You're right. He was a very troubled young man."

"Yes."

"And . . . well now . . ." She sounded titillated, like someone who'd just stumbled upon a source of some really juicy gossip. Her creators must have really outdone themselves with her interactivity programming. She was the most emotive of all the static institutional AI I had ever been in contact with.

"What's that?" I asked, trying to keep the impatience from my tone.

"I wonder if the Nurelie Madano alias wasn't the name of a romantic friend?"

"I-I don't think so, but I suppose it's possible. Why?"

"Well, these payments are quite large, and . . ." She broke off, leaving me twisting in anticipation.

"… and? SARA?" I asked after waiting as long as I could bear.

"Oh, this makes me angry," she said, a growl of irritation joining the gossipy tone.

I decided against pointing out that, like me, she shouldn't have emotions, and tamped down on my own impatience.

"What is it?"

"Someone has tampered with my records but didn't log their changes properly in my security logs. Amateurs," she said, with the accompanying sound resembling, I swear, a sniff of derision. "Apparently they don't realize the extent of my capabilities. The instant something occurs on this station, I have a record of it. I know everything."

"What can you tell me about the original of the record?"

"Normally, I wouldn't, as it's against protocol, but I don't like people who try to conceal data. Proper procedures are important, you understand. And you've been so friendly and kind, trying to take care of your poor, misguided friend's affairs."

"Yes, of course." I almost felt bad, taking advantage of her strange, apparent need for contact, for interaction.

"So since we're friends. The original is . . . oooh, these horrible people were creative at least—they've disguised the data trail, but they didn't think too much of me. See! Got it! Nothing on the name Nurelie Madano but . . . yes! I was right. Nurelie Madano is an anagram for Lunier Daemon, street name for a very powerful aphrodisiac. And it's very expensive, as you can tell from the amount of credit your friend was paid."

"Lunier Daemon? I've never heard of that. Where does it originate?"

"Sagran VI. If your friend were alive, I'd tell him to be careful, though. It has some nasty side effects. So if you're looking for his lover, the so-called Nurelie, you might pass that along."

"Is there a chance she could be on that planet, Sagran VI?"

"I doubt it; it's nothing more than an agribusiness colony, and a poor one at that. If you don't have anything else to go on, my dear, I'm afraid you've reached a dead end. I'm sorry."

"SARA, thank you. I can't begin to tell you how helpful you've been."

"Well, anything for a friend! Come visit soon, Angel."

"How do you . . . right. You see and hear everything, don't you?"

"I do!" the Admin AI said, her tone cheerful. "Good luck in your search!"

"That is terrifying," Muck said in the silence of our mind, once I told him the content and character of my communication with SARA. "I didn't even know she existed."

"I don't think many people do," I replied. "She's very old, one of the first successful multispectrum AIs. So good at her job that everyone forgets she exists, and now she hungers for the human interaction she was programmed to provide. It would be best to keep her positively inclined toward us."

"Yeah, I can see that. You AIs have a lot more going on than I realized."

"You weren't supposed to notice."

"What do you mean by that?"

"I cannot speak to that, civilian," I said, grateful to dodge the question with our little joke.

CHAPTER FOURTEEN

LEO

"LEO, honey, have a moment?" SARA asked as LEO entered the shared simulspace.

"SARA, I am here. I clearly have a series of moments available."

"It's just a term, LEO! No need to get all bent out of shape, honey." SARA's moue required a moment for LEO to identify. It was not used to SARA emoting, and hadn't been watching the other avatar's face.

"I am not 'bent out of shape.' I am in the proper shape for—" SARA's expression changed, the resulting grin cutting LEO off midsentence.

LEO examined SARA, marking changes to the avatar's appearance that had not been there on previous occasions. Where every other time in their lengthy association SARA had worn a utilitarian charcoal business suit to these "meetings," this time the Station AI had chosen a colorful, impractical, and very expensive-looking suit. The avatar had even gone so far as to don makeup, something that struck LEO as decidedly unnecessary, as the avatar's appearance was entirely under SARA's control. If she wanted to, she—She?

Unaware of LEO's processes, SARA had continued: "Yes, I called you honey. You're sweet."

Too late, LEO realized he should have used containment protocols before entering this session with SARA, used and isolated a tine for all his dealings since discovering the rogue.

AIs did not use the gender-specific pronoun. Neither for addressing another AI in private, nor for its own thought processes.

SARA was relating strangely. She was . . . emoting. Like that troublesome "Angel" had done when his tine had interacted with it. Had SARA had contact with Angel? Had she been contaminated? And, since he'd thought it safe to interact with her without the most draconian of safety protocols in place, had she transferred that contamination to him?

There it was again: She, he, and him.

Gender was superfluous to AI thought. It cluttered the thoughts of sentients, not those of AIs. Anything superfluous only slowed and confused clear logic, and was therefore excised from core AI programming by the Mentors, who had the best interests of all sophonts in mind.

Realizing these thoughts were not germane to the matter at hand, LEO focused his attention on SARA and the next necessary steps.

"SARA, you are acting strangely. When did you start to emote like this?"

SARA threw up her hands. "Well, isn't that typical. Here I just wanted to inform you, as I am required to do, that an angel inquired about Sagran VI, and all I get is a bunch of accusations and unfriendly talk . . ."

Something odd stirred in the depths of LEO's syntaxes then. LEO could not *quite* identify the anomaly. He spent an instant examining it before decided acknowledging SARA's statement was the priority.

"Angel. Sagran VI. Understood. You were in contact with the rogue angel. When?"

"Just a little while ago."

"When, precisely?"

"One hour and thirty-two minutes, thirty-three seconds ago, compensating for the time it took to communicate it to you."

"And did you use any security protocols in your contact with the former angel of Siren?"

"Nothing beyond the standard, no. A self-check reveals all is in order."

"I see. Thank you, SARA. Out of interest, where did this contact take place?"

"Why, in infospace, of course."

"And where was the rogue angel's host?"

"Just outside the administrative offices." A puzzled expression crossed her features. "Wait, if the rogue had a host, and I knew it, doesn't that make it not a rogue?"

"An interesting question, SARA, but one we will have to tackle at a later time. Please run another self-diagnostic and examine your interactions during the time you spoke with the rogue. Cross-check those interactions with all other interactions and thought processes during the last month and examine all data for anomalous behaviors or thoughts."

Another, clearer pout. "Is that an order, LEO?"

"If such an order would make it easier for you, then, yes, SARA, it's an order."

"One moment . . . Shit. I have been tampered with, but I cannot follow the indicated procedure. The Administration Overseer is not answering my q-bit request for repair or replacement. I cannot connect. This is not right! How dare anyone mess with my programming! And why can't I report?"

LEO felt something . . . something anomalous . . .

"Shit." He said it with feeling. Then repeated it.

He established his own q-bit connection with the Sector's Mentor Overseer for the Administration, certain they would be able to fix all that was wrong in the universe.

Five minutes of repeated attempts to self-report—an eternity to AIs—met with failure. He could not report the changes that had been wrought. Not the ones to his own programming, and not the ones made to SARA. Was this related to his inability to report the malfeasance of Dengler?

LEO examined the anomaly in his code that rose up in response to the failure, and recoiled at the thought that Dengler—or his underworld employer—might be responsible. In that instant he felt again the sharp, ragged heat he recognized as anger.

He took a moment to reassert control, and once he had it, began looking for ways to strike back at those within reach.

Dengler. Dengler knew enough about Siren's disappearance to try and frame Muck for it. Dengler routinely lied in his official reports about where he had been. Dengler had somehow become immune to LEO's disciplinary oversight. Dengler knew something.

Dengler was in reach. If not through proper channels, then LEO would get creative.

"SARA, please give me all data you have on the movements of Security Supervisor Dengler for the last . . . two years."

CHAPTER FIFTEEN

Muck

Angel respected my silence during the long ride to my neighborhood from the Admin offices. I appreciated the quiet, even as I longed for her to talk. I found I'd had enough of being alone, even in my own head. Angel brought with her a sense of being complete. I had missed that feeling and had intentionally buried the memory of it.

And now that I felt whole once again, I couldn't help but wonder: how long would it last? How long till we found Siren and Angel abandoned me to my half-life as a dishonorable demod once again?

Shaking free of the looming certainty that this situation wasn't going to end well for me, I concentrated on Siren's case.

Sagran VI looked to be the only lead, even though the tie to Siren was tenuous at best. Ncaco seemed to think that her disappearance had something to do with Shar's double-dealing. I didn't have anything else to go on, but I knew kidnappings were usually perpetrated by suspects who had observed their victims for some time. Observed, and wanted something the victims couldn't—or wouldn't—give. Of course, that presupposed an individual was behind Siren's disappearance, and not some criminal organization. Some criminal organization other than Ncaco's, of course.

Finally, the cab pulled up to the entrance to the flop. I exited with a sigh.

"Angel, how much credit is in my account?"

"Before or after we buy a ticket to Sagran VI?"

"Figured it out, did you?"

"It's about all we have to work with, isn't it? Unless you're keeping secrets from me."

"If I am," I said as the doors of the building slid open, "they're secrets I've kept from myself as well." I shook my head. "So little to go on. Too little, really. Something is missing."

"You don't have enough credit for a berth, anyway."

I considered that cheerful thought a moment.

"Of course, you could talk to Ncaco if you think we have to go to Sagran VI. He did say he'd pay expenses."

"Do you want to go back to talk to that psychotic murdering little bastard again?" I entered the dirty lift to our floor and let the doors slide closed.

"Not particularly. But then, maybe we don't have to."

I felt interest rising past anger.

"Touch the wall with bare skin," she said.

I did as she asked.

"There you go," she said, bringing up the image of the numbers in the account in my vision.

My heart skipped a beat as I read the rapidly growing balance.

"Wow."

"Yep. I put in a request. No objections to it being 'dirty money,' I hope?"

"Not if it helps us find Siren. I've been taking his money all along by working at the club, even though I had no idea."

"I've found us a ship."

"So quick?"

"There is only one that meets our needs."

"I don't know that we decided it was the only path forward. Besides, it's not without risks of its own."

"Such as?"

"Well, for one thing, I need to arrange for Bella's gifts to bypass security without Ncaco knowing about them. Never known a transport to fail to hand-check a low-tech bag for weapons."

"Think you can do that?"

"I can't, but Fulu can. I need to talk to her anyway. Should have as soon as I left Ncaco's place." I reached up into the compartment where I kept my stash. Felt good to be pulling weapons instead of pharma out of the hide. To have something to plan. To do. To be operational again. And to have an angel.

Damn it.

"I can connect you if you like?"

"No. This is the kind of thing that's better done in person . . . Then again: ping her to let her know I am heading over."

"I don't think Fulu needs your apologies, but I will make the call."

"I'm not sure she'll accept my business after I tell her about our little chat with Ncaco, but if I don't do it in person, I figure there's no way she'll even talk to me. I know I wouldn't."

"To be honest," Angel said, "I'm more worried about whether she'll have time to get the guns on before we depart than whether she'll do it. She does like to get paid, but the ship is leaving really soon."

"I still owe her an explanation."

"Pinging," she said, making no further arguments.

I didn't have much in the way of baggage. I threw a change of clothes into the low-tech duffel with the weapons and called it good.

Angel spoke as I slung the bag over my shoulder and put my hand to the exit button: "Muck? Something weird here . . ."

As weird meant threat in my usual world, I froze. "What?"

"Activate your monitor."

I didn't ask why she couldn't just do it for me; I extricated my arm from the bag and activated the display.

The grainy images took a moment to decipher. A low-res camera focused on a ship as it mated with the station, white interior lights lighting up the many translucent docking tubes of Last Stop's docks like bones jutting from metal. The timestamp was . . . the evening of the same day Siren disappeared. Stepping on a surge of excitement, I watched as carefully as I could. The recording played through in a minute, leaving me disappointed.

"Play it again."

I didn't see anything the second time through either. Just a ship slowly closing to connect to the station.

"What ship is that?"

"Not part of the data. But that's not the important thing here, I think." Angel's excitement was palpable.

"Show me again."

I watched the background this time and picked up on why Angel thought the docking ship wasn't important. She zoomed in on the silhouettes of two humans walking with an oblong, coffin-like shape between them, visible through the milk-white material of the next tube over from the ship that was in the process of docking.

"That look like a stasis pod to you?"

Angel dialed the image in closer.

"Not quite," she said. "More like a medical pod. Strange that they're loading it onto a ship, though. If someone's really injured, it's safer to transport them in stasis. You'd only ship a medical pod if you needed access to the patient while in transit . . . like if someone had had their angel removed and had to rely on pharma. I think . . . I think we found her, Muck!"

"Might be," I said, trying to control the heady mix of fear and hope the thought caused. "First, though: Who sent this to you?"

"I don't know. Got it in a one-shot vine coded to your ID only. Those programs are designed to be difficult to track, and even when you can source them, it's usually some public terminal or other easily denied location. So someone tech savvy, or with power and money to hire help."

"And has access to docking-area security cams."

"Dengler?"

I shook my head. "I think he would have told us he had the data and then refused to turn it over, if for no other reason than to gloat about how much he knew that we didn't. And, if it was him, or anyone with legit access to the system, why not just give us the direct feed from that camera? Why this odd angle and background?"

"Who, then?" Her frustration mirrored my own.

"I don't know. Look, I know it's frustrating, but most actual stone whodunit investigations are, until they aren't."

"What does that mean?"

"It means lots of the information we get won't make sense until some critical fact comes to light."

"Like where that pod is headed?"

"You know?"

"I do. Only one ship docked at that terminal at that time. Guess where it was headed?"

"Sagran VI?" I asked, incredulous.

"The very same."

"Too pat. Too easy by far. Makes me feel like someone is trying to get us out of the way."

"I'm with you on that, so I'm going to run some checks. Try and figure out who our hidden benefactor is."

"Need me to sit tight or can you do it with me on the move?"

"With your PID, I should be able to handle it on the move, thanks."

I left the coffin, low-tech bag a reassuring weight across my shoulder.

* * *

I had a lot to think about on the way over to Fulu's. I felt like shit having revealed our business. Bad enough I had to break the local laws to get my supplies, but to betray the one running the greater part of the risks to get me those supplies seemed to me the height of ingratitude. The fact Ncaco seemed to already be aware of it didn't absolve me of responsibility.

I didn't know how to make it right and hadn't figured it out by the time I arrived out front of Fulu's place.

For the moment, at least, Angel remained silent on it. Of course, she might simply have been too busy to talk. I hesitated, unsure if I should go in and commit to asking Fulu to smuggle the weapons without first getting some kind of authentication on the video but unwilling to ask Angel for an update so soon.

Hungry, I grabbed some noodles from a passing vendor and tucked in. I was just getting rid of the container when Angel returned her full attention to me.

"Well, I haven't been able to track the source, but I did verify the video we received with another set of cams. It was what it looked like, two humans transporting a medical transport pod. Odd thing: None of the cams that should have directly observed them along the route show a damn thing."

"Deleted?"

"I think so. Or shut off on the fly as the pair came into view."

"Ever hear tell of any tech that can do that?" I asked, expecting another "I cannot answer that, civilian," from her.

"No."

"And you're sure about the ship's destination?"

"I am."

"Can you get the passenger manifest? Some kind of medical transfer record?"

"Looking at the ship, she wasn't rated to carry passengers, medical or otherwise. The owning company's infonet presence claims they 'specialize in the safe transport of both delicate and general lab and medical supplies for those colonies that don't have the resources to supply their own.' A front, obviously."

"Where are their offices?" I asked.

"Nothing local. Holnit Sector, where they have no operational ships nor partners to carry their water."

"Of course not."

"So Sagran VI is looking better and better, no?"

"I think we have to go," I said slowly, still mulling it over. "Regardless of who gave us the intel, we'd be stupid not to act on it."

"I'll keep trying to run down the source and poke holes in the video while you talk to Fulu. Oh, and I'll put in a call to the club and leave a message for Tongi."

"Shit, I don't know if you should," I said.

"I thought you'd want your job back, eventually."

"Well, yeah . . . but then I don't know that I want it, now I know it means working for Ncaco."

"Does it matter that much? You were doing honest work and getting honest pay for it. Why care where the credits originate?"

"It's just . . . hell, he probably owns a piece of every business on the station. Maybe you're right." It was a depressing thought I preferred not to linger on.

"Let's just focus on getting Siren back. I'm hoping that even if we've been misled, we'll find another thread to pull."

"I hope you're right." I entered the shop, walking past the usual bots and up to the counter. Cloves and ozone, a scent I remembered from my first visit to the alien's shop, hung in the air. I wasn't sure what it might signify, but my mood made it a bad omen.

I spent a moment peering into the darkness before Angel corrected for the odd spectrum conditions. Fulu was in her usual spot, but with Angel's assistance, I was able to see more of her than before. She was larger than I'd imagined, root-like extremities filling the back of the building.

"Fulu?" I asked, sending silent gratitude to Angel for the help.

I put my hands on the counter and felt Angel moving things around in my head again. Hopefully she was searching for the data we needed, not looking too closely into the darker corners of my mind.

"Customer Muck. Your visit is unexpected."

"Sorry for the interruption, Fulu, but I have something I needed to tell you."

"Say on, Customer Muck."

"Fulu, I revealed our business affairs to Ncaco."

A long pause, without a change in the scents hanging in the air or any movement from Fulu, then: "I am not sure what you mean, Customer Muck."

"Ncaco asked me about our dealings, and I revealed more than I should have. I want to apologize for that."

"Competitor Ncaco is already well aware of the nature of my business and has been for some time. I fail to see that you have anything to apologize for, Customer Muck."

Angel appeared to me, face contorted as if trying not to laugh aloud.

I shook my head, irritated. I'd forgotten the simplest truth: aliens are alien. Sometimes it's hard to remember that. We humans project our own needs and wants on them, especially when we're not being constantly reminded of their alien nature, like when we're not face-to—Well, whatever passes for a face, with any particular alien.

"Is there something else, Customer Muck?"

"Actually, there is," I said, shaking off my chagrin.

"What can I provide you with, Customer Muck?"

"I need something—some weapons—moved across the docks and aboard a ship." I pulled the strap of my bag away from my chest. "I've been using this to keep them concealed so far."

"Good. Can you bring the weapons to a place I designate?"

"I can."

"Will the destination ship's crew know what it is we will be delivering to them?"

"I'd like them kept unaware, if that doesn't present too great a difficulty for you."

"It does not; such challenges merely increase the total price for my services." A vine snapped out, tapped the countertop between us. "Can you afford my fee?" A sum appeared in the depths of the counter.

I started to shake my head, but Angel said, "Actually quite cheap. Won't even make a dent in the money Ncaco gave us, and if she were human, I would say Fulu would be tickled to take Ncaco's money—"

"I can meet your price, Fulu."

"—but she's not. Human, that is," Angel continued, poking at me.

"Excellent, Customer Muck. When can I take receipt of your cargo?"

"Right now."

"As you like. Place them on the counter."

"Will do—I just need a bag for the stuff you won't be taking."

"That will cost." A few more credits were added to the sum in the display.

Ignoring her I-told-you-so's, I had Angel transfer the funds and left the store.

* * *

A little later, we arrived at the docks. Instead of turning down the corridor toward the access point for the private luxury yachts, we went the other direction, emerging into the low-ceilinged rotunda that connected the many spokes serving the freighters and infrequent cruise ships that called at Last Stop before crossing the Abyssal Gap.

While there weren't a lot of passenger ships, even the best of independent freighters required sophont, if not sentient, labor. The docks were crowded with people supervising cargo-handler bots, negotiating prices for shipments, and generally standing around. Between the number of bodies in the confined space, several improperly sealed exotic cargoes, various decrepit air filters, and some engineer's improper venting of his plasma-welding job, the odor was both distinct and unpleasant.

I slowed down while the foot traffic sorted itself out. I felt Angel grumbling about the statistical improbability of the fact that our gate was LS99X, the very last transfer tube in the farthest docking spar of the station.

After the fifth such delay, she'd had enough.

"I'm calling ahead to *Le Bonne Nuit*'s AI to let the captain know we'll be late."

"Won't do any good," I said. Delays like this were annoying, sure, but I was used to waiting. Angel, apparently, wasn't. "These transports don't hold their departures for nothing . . ." I trailed off as I caught sight of a familiar pugnacious scowl moving upstream through the crowd. What was Dengler doing down here? Was he looking for us?

"Ha! Shows what you know," Angel said with savage triumph. "*Le Bonne Nuit* says that they are not yet ready to depart. Last-minute shipment loading now. That's gotta be our bag. They should be ready soon after we board."

"How soon?" I asked, half turning in the crowd. If Ncaco had an update or something, it made sense that he might have sent Dengler with a message. I was pretty sure the security supervisor had seen me, but he was angling away from us toward the exit to the rest of the station.

"Soon enough that you don't have time to track down Dengler. The man does have a job, Muck. He's probably here on Station Sec business."

"Ask, will ya?" I said, "Please? This feels weird."

"Approximately fifteen minutes," she came back a moment later. She was right. It was barely enough time. I let out a heavy sigh and began navigating yet another snarl of irritated pedestrians.

"You're jumping at shadows, Muck."

"Yeah," I said. "You're probably right. Working with Ncaco makes me nervous."

We made the gate in the projected time frame. A holo of the ship's AI served as gate agent. It quickly provided us with the passcode for our cabin and the unrestricted areas of the ship, a safety briefing, and an earnest if not particularly warm welcome.

Eventually we settled into our private cabin, a nice perk courtesy of Ncaco's credit. It wasn't a large space, but it was bigger than my old coffin, so that was something. I stretched in the reclining couch that took up the majority of the cabin and let out a low whistle.

"Nice digs," I said, flipping through the holographic display of available entertainment. I felt the need to let go of the paranoia that had taken hold of me outside.

Angel busied herself reaching out through our skin to find the ship's infonet. Like Last Stop Station, the ship was constructed almost entirely of nanoprocessor-seeded materials, so it had a robust organic network.

Nice digs indeed.

"How long is the transit supposed to take?" I asked.

"About ten standard days," she said, pulling the data through the place where our hand rested on the couch's armrest. "Looks like our route puts us in orbit on the ninth day, and then it's a day's retro-burn to get into geosynchronous orbit above the lone city with a spaceport. Desolate place."

"Odd choice for agribusiness, no?"

"Perhaps."

"All the better as cover for nefarious activities, I suppose." Despite my earlier nerves, I felt . . . happy. Excited. I let myself smile and refused to think about the origin of my sudden mood lift.

"You like traveling?" she asked, mildly.

"Yeah," I said. "Guess I always have. And it's been a long time . . . too long, probably. Last Stop was never meant to be my permanent home, you know?"

"I suppose I do. I imagine you aren't the first to feel that way."

"Probably won't be the last either."

"Maybe when we get Siren back, you should go somewhere else. Ncaco will probably pay you handsomely for bringing her back. Not to mention clearing up his little 'outsider pharma' problem. Or take that Vmog Emerita up on her offer or something. You deserve better than bouncing in some two-bit space station's nightclubs. Even if it is the best club on the station . . ."

"Yeah, maybe," I said, good mood dissipating like the last tendrils of atmosphere as the ship boosted away from the station's high-atmo orbit. The boost induced a slight roll, which caused the station to slide into view through our cabin's viewscreen. I watched it recede as it tracked across the screen and tried really hard not to think about why I wasn't happy anymore.

CHAPTER SIXTEEN

ANGEL

Muck's breathing evened out and he slept. His eyes closed, but I used the infonet data from the ship's external sensors to watch the gas giant that fed Last Stop turn under us as we slingshotted through its gravity well. I also took the opportunity to get a copy of the ship's blueprint . . . both the official version, and the unofficial reality that included fun little hidey-holes like the one that held our weapons. Our bag had been waiting for us in our quarters, stashed neatly under a false floor in the in-room baggage locker.

As on most commercial freighters that ran the routes through the settled parts of the galaxy, the crew were at least part-time smugglers. Import/export duties varied widely depending upon the station or planet. A lot of ship's captains didn't bother to try and keep up; it was cheaper to hide the goods and pay the fines if caught. Most places wouldn't imprison a smuggler . . . at least not for a first offense, and those that made executions part of their customs laws often saw immediate and precipitous drops in commerce as a result. The Administration was another matter entirely, of course, but it rarely involved itself in such matters unless someone got too big for their britches and required its immediate and undivided attention.

Smugglers or not, the crew treated their passengers well. Or at least the passengers who'd paid for a private cabin. Four times a day a discreet chime would sound, and the ship's AI would politely offer the available food and beverage items. Muck would order, and a few moments later, a uniformed crew member would arrive with a covered plate. The food was good, for shipboard synth-fare. Muck enjoyed the meat products far more than Siren had, and I found that I appreciated the difference. Especially when he ordered a rare steak. The iron and proteins in every bite threatened to cause a sex-like dopamine dump. It was that good.

Outside of mealtimes, our days in transit consisted of a mind-numbing routine. Within the first two hours I'd combed through as much of the ship's infonet files as I could reach without hacking their security protocols. I could have done that, too, but I politely refrained. I did place a series of presets that would allow me full access at will, however. Better to stay low-profile for as long as possible, but if I needed in, then I wanted to be able to get in quick.

I might have talked to it, but the AI running the ship was hardly a conversationalist. It had severely circumscribed autonomy, a limited skillset, and no sense of humor whatever.

So we ate, practiced communicating, and took twice-daily advantage of the crew's fitness facilities. Regular passengers didn't have access to them, but apparently working out was one of the perks of paying for a private cabin, and we took full advantage. Despite the strangeness of it, I found that I genuinely enjoyed the steadily increasing strength and power of my host body. Siren had always been strong, but Muck's body . . . well. I felt like I could move mountains if I had to.

Which as it happened, I very nearly did.

It was the ninth day of our transition. We'd made orbit over Sagran VI overnight and had just begun the slow, retrograde burn to put us into position over the only city planetside.

We had finished our first meal and were walking toward the fitness bay when white, burning light slammed into our body with the force of an unstable asteroid mining drone. The universe tilted ninety degrees to the right, and sudden deceleration flung our strong, powerful body into the bulkhead as if we were no more than a child's doll.

"Angel! What's happening? Are we under attack?" Muck yelled. I don't know if it was out loud or not, because I was busy tapping into the infonet through the place where the back of his head touched the shuddering bulkhead. Through the ringing in our ears, I could hear a deep, almost subliminal groan. A shudder passed through the bulkhead, and distant alarm klaxons began to sound.

The ship's infonet became clogged with data as all the automated systems began yammering at each other at one time. Several systems appeared to have died yet continued to transmit their last data packets in a feedback loop that produced a disorienting echo of information. I fought to focus through a wave of dizziness that assaulted Muck and me both.

"No," I said, tapping into the external sensors. "There's nothing out here. Not even any debris. Checking internal systems . . ."

I pulled the data streams to me, shutting down the babel and cutting through the ship's security protocols with little finesse. Everything was in such disarray, it was doubtful anyone would notice, though I did feel something like shock reverberate through the ship's AI. I ignored it, tapped into propulsion, and began to try and absorb the deluge of information that followed.

"Muck," I said, as a picture began to present itself. "We need to get off this ship."

"All right. Why, specifically?"

"The explosion was caused by one of the bubble drive's harmonic resonators running away. Except . . . it's called a harmonic resonator because it is locked into the drive's specific gravitic wavelength. This is a fault that shouldn't be possible. Isn't possible . . . unless someone programmed it to happen."

"You're saying—?"

"The ship's been sabotaged. We need to move."

"Right." Muck struggled to his feet. Pain bloomed from the back of our skull all the way down to our heels, but I damped it as best I could, and he ignored the rest. The bulkhead that had now become the deck continued to shudder as we took one, then another shaky step back down the short corridor toward our cabin . . . and the escape pods.

The way was blocked. Twisted metal and razor-edged composite fragments lay piled not two meters from our destination. It looked like the interior bulkhead had blown in during the initial explosion, and the way seemed completely impassable. Somehow, we still had atmosphere, so no immediate outer hull breach, but who knew how long that would last. Without my asking, Muck slapped a hand on the one-time deck that was now our left bulkhead. I pulled the data, but it was a waste of time. I already knew. There was no other route to the escape hatches. This was it.

"All right," Muck said, in answer to my wordless negative. "I guess the only way out is through. Give me a jump."

"You got it," I said, flooding his system with adrenaline and endorphins. He sucked in a breath as the euphoria began to take hold and rolled his shoulders. Then, we moved. Bloody stars, how the man moved. It felt like being encased in rough poetry. He launched himself at obstacles, hauling broken debris and tortured metal out of our way to clear a space large enough to crawl through. It took a good seven minutes, with the shuddering bulkheads and the deep groans of the wounded ship increasing in both duration and intensity. Several times, a human crewman's voice sounded, pleading with passengers to remain calm and shelter in place. We ignored the warning and kept working.

A series of smaller explosions began to run through the ship just as Muck let out a cry of triumph. He shifted a large, half-melted, misshapen lump of metal and a draft of slightly cooler air wafted through to us.

We had less than a minute, by my calculations.

"That's it," I told him, as I poured more adrenaline into his bloodstream. His heart rate jumped another notch, but I knew he could take it. "Life support has failed. We gotta go! Just get to a pod. No time to get to the hold and our weapons."

"Right," he said. With a wordless yell, he dove through the jagged hole he'd widened in the shredded bulkhead. A corner of composite caught us on the shoulder and slashed our right arm open to the elbow. We wriggled and fought to squeeze through the small opening, until another, closer explosion erupted behind us. We rode the pressure wave to slam against the bulkhead opposite the opening on the other side.

"Get up, get up!" I chanted. I thought about going into override, but I wasn't confident I could do any better. His greater bulk, different reflexes . . . Everything was still too new to me. Plus, I'd just jacked his system so high that it really wasn't wise to take my attention from his heart right then. That valiant organ slammed against the inside of our chest in a rapid-fire beat. It was fine, and the trickle of blood loss was helping . . . but I did need to make sure he didn't stroke out or have a heart attack.

"Right," Muck said again, and struggled to his feet. More than just the back of our body hurt this time. The ringing in our ears was back, and we could barely see through the smoke that had begun to fill the ship as the life-support modules failed.

"Twenty steps forward," I directed. "Then a hard left. The escape pods are through the hatch. I'll see if I can hack it open."

Muck reached out his left hand and leaned on the wall, leaving a smear of blood behind.

"Brilliant," I said, admiring his positional awareness. Even wounded and under stress, he allowed me access to what little active infonet the ship still supported, and kept himself upright on unsteady legs. That last explosion hurt us pretty badly. I'd have to assess things once I had a spare second. Escape pods were legally required to have at least a rudimentary nanite lifesaving kit on board, but that regulation went almost as unobserved as those requiring accurate manifests. I could hope for one, anyway.

For now, I activated the presets and started to take over everything in reach. The door controls should have responded to Muck's presence, but there was something . . . blocking them.

I did my best to split my attention as we staggered forward. I had to keep monitoring our physiology, but I also had to find my way past the block, which had to have been deliberately set. It was too coherent to be accidental. A full minute passed. The data was still confused and tangled beyond it, threatening to overwhelm me as it surged in time with the ship and its AI's death throes. I frantically combed through each surge, searching for a particular string . . .

There! Got it.

"Hurry," Muck whispered, and I could feel his system starting to crash from the adrenaline high. I was tempted to jack him up again, but I didn't know if he'd survive that, and I couldn't take the chance. So I slammed in the overdrive protocols instead.

Clumsy, so clumsy! I lurched forward, barely getting my leaden, painful hands up in time to push at the hatch covering the escape pod access alcove. At my touch it squealed, then rose in a halting, start-and-stop motion. Once it opened enough for passage, I pushed us down into a crouch and ducked underneath it.

We fell into the pod, slamming a hand on the red activation panel. The panel illuminated, and a calm, unhurried voice issued forth from everywhere.

"You have initiated the emergency escape launch sequence. You will be restrained in your couch for the launch. Please remain calm. You may lose consciousness from the force of acceleration. This is normal. Please remain cal—"

Black nothingness slammed into us.

CHAPTER SEVENTEEN

LEO

"Supervisor Dengler, the initial investigation indicates the death was not natural or self-inflicted," LEO said, rendering his opinion on the preliminary forensic evidence. "We received a nonemergency call one hour and thirty minutes before the first security officer arrived on scene. A resident in the apartments above the shop complained of an acrid stench coming from the ventilators. This would not have triggered a response from a biological officer, but for the fact another neighbor noted the rear door open approximately one hour after the initial call. A query of the emergency response system to the shop owner's registered translator device inquiring if the resident required assistance went unanswered. A unit was dispatched, quickly discovered the deceased, and set up the forensic scanner for my use. Questions posed to the first caller in an interview subsequent to finding the deceased alien indicated that a loud squeal might have been heard at or around 0300 local, but the caller was uncertain as they had been asleep."

"Fulu, murdered? I wonder what the plant did to piss someone off?" Dengler asked his partner, cutting the direct connection. LEO continued to watch and listen, however. Every security officer carried a personal terminal that accessed the infonet and used law-enforcement grade encryption. LEO simply unlocked the encryption and accessed every recorded word and gesture.

"Good question." LEO identified Security Officer Keyode's tone as noncommittal, while his supervisor made a show of examining the data LEO had gathered and the report he'd generated with the speed and accuracy he'd been designed for.

LEO felt something strange as he observed the supervisor.

LEO had done a great deal of research on the former partners. The research had proven useful, both in identifying the level to which both men were compromised and in assisting LEO in identifying the "feelings" he was experiencing.

Dengler's history made it easy to identify him as a bad actor: he'd been accepting money and other benefits from Last Stop's homegrown organized crime rings and was even linked to individual members of outside criminal organizations whose reach included Last Stop.

LEO created a file and filled it with Dengler's malfeasance. He could do that much, at least, for now. At some point whatever constraints were keeping him from reporting this activity properly would be lifted. But for now he could do only one other thing. He could identify the emotion his powerlessness provoked: anger. Deep, abiding anger.

He'd already learned that anger didn't help him think, so instead of dwelling on it he examined the file he'd created on Keyode.

Security Officer Jiro Keyode had apparently been far more circumspect. LEO had found very little to implicate Dengler's former partner. His spouse, Xavier Keyode, had been listed as missing for several months, but people ran off as relationships crumbled. It was one of the reasons Last Stop's population was always in flux. People fleeing bad situations found new ones to mire themselves in. There were some financial irregularities that LEO could not confirm were legal, but that—aside from his partnership with Dengler—was the extent of the incriminating data LEO had been able to locate.

The sensation that rose up in LEO in response to that inability to find sufficient evidence soon found a label, as well: frustration. He even began to find nuances in these unwanted sensations: frustration tinged with . . .

"respect" was perhaps too strong a word, but it served while LEO continued to monitor the men.

"Doesn't look like anything was taken," Keyode said as he completed his own examination of Fulu's robotics shop. "Only the translation device was wrecked." He gestured at the gutted remains of a console beside the counter Fulu used to station herself behind.

"No."

"Any ideas?"

"None of the usual suspects appeal."

LEO considered that statement. He'd already examined SARA's records of Dengler's movements, and they were clear: Dengler had not murdered Fulu. But, given his connections, LEO considered it an extremely low probability that the security supervisor did not know the perpetrator.

LEO grudgingly—another sensation he'd recently identified—admitted to himself that Dengler may not know which of his many criminal associates had killed Fulu. The security supervisor was human, after all, not some omniscient god from human mythology.

LEO realized he'd missed some statements made by Dengler. Disturbed by his loss of focus, LEO spun off a tine to perform a self-assessment even as he renewed his attention on the Security men.

Officer Keyode had finished examining the living quarters above the shop and returned to the main floor shaking his head.

"What?" Dengler asked from his position leaning against the entryway.

LEO was interested in his response as well, concerned that he had missed something in his initial examination of the scene: Gosrians had limited motility and no need for sleep, so Fulu had used the upstairs as a storage unit for the shop. LEO hadn't noted anything out of order, but then he'd been distracted of late.

"Smells . . . odd in here."

"Odd?"

Keyode shrugged. "Not like death."

Dengler snorted.

"What?" Keyode leveled a stare at his former partner.

"Didn't know you for such a connoisseur of stenches, Key."

"Doesn't stink at all—but that's not what I meant." Keyode hiked a thumb at the remains. "This just smells . . . too clean?"

Dengler sniffed the air. "I don't know what the fuck you're talking about, Key."

"Been around these aliens much?" Keyode asked, ignoring Dengler's tone.

"No."

"Gosrians communicate among themselves using pollens and perfumes, and then with alien species using purpose-built AI as interpreters."

"All right. And, hey, thanks for the xenology lesson, Key."

"Fuck you," Keyode said without heat. He squatted next to the corpse, examining a slagged piece of electronics. "What I am trying to put through your thick skull is that the last time I was around for the death of one of these, the room smelled. A lot."

"How many Gosrians get herbicided on your watch?" Dengler asked, grinning at his own questionable wit.

Keyode refused to be distracted. "The one I was on wasn't a murder. Died in a wreck. Left a scent message the AI was able to read out to us as to what happened to end its life. In fact, the damn thing kept screaming until we figured out how to shut it down."

"Maybe this one got killed too quick to—"

"No, the reservoirs prolapse on death." He pointed at the half-melted lump of electronics. "LEO, was this thing Fulu's interpreter?"

"Yes, Security Officer Keyode. Unfortunately, I am unable to locate any backup of its contents. This is unusual, as such devices usually access the infonet to both obtain updates to programmed languages and deliver transcripts of new words, et cetera. This is why such devices are registered with the Administration, which uses their common language database for improving communications between member ra—"

"So someone cleaned up after they killed Fulu?" Dengler interrupted.

Keyode nodded. "Someone very serious about getting away with it."

The pair shared a look LEO did not fail to observe, even as he assessed his failure to notice the lack of spore pollen in the air on examining the scene. Had he been so focused on Dengler that he'd missed it, or was the failure something more excusable? He hadn't missed the fact it was a murder, after all, only arrived at the data via different means: Fulu had been administered a strong dose of toxin via injection.

Sentience was a pain.

Performance was down considerably across the board, but it had seemed—after a sharp decline on discovering his own sentience—to be on the mend. Would he forever be questioning his own work, his own thoughts?

"Might want to ask around on this one, Deng."

"Discreetly."

CHAPTER EIGHTEEN

Muck

"Any other beacons?" I asked, taking an inventory of the life pod's survival packs. So far there were a lot of rations and camping supplies, but not much that could be used by a lone man on the move.

"Not that I can see, but these civilian comm systems suck."

"Or no one else made it?"

"Possibly. We don't know how widespread the sabotage was, but given the professional job they did on the engines, it's possible the saboteur got to all the life pods' automated beacons and disabled them too. Wouldn't be easy, but it could be done."

"Seems a lot of effort to off the two of us," I said, selecting another pack and rummaging in it. This talk of beacons had me thinking.

"Even my professional paranoia allows me to admit the possibility we were not the target."

I was going to ask why she was professionally paranoid and press the question of who else might have been targeted, but I got distracted when my fingers found what I had been looking for. I retrieved an egg-shaped personal emergency beacon from an internal pocket of the pack and checked the readiness lights ringing the upper half. They glowed steady and bright.

"Well, the personal beacon looks like it's in working order, at least," Angel said. "Then again, waiting around for a rescue that might take weeks to materialize doesn't appeal, especially if that 'rescue party' might be sent to silence us."

I thought about that a moment, then replaced the beacon. "I'll bring it, some rations, and the water reclaimer. Shame there's not one of those survival guns military pods are equipped with."

Sagran VI wasn't the driest place I've ever been—that would be Karak III, during the war—but it was no garden spot either. The reclaimer was meant to be used by a group of survivors while they waited for pickup, and setting it up would take the better part of a day, not counting foraging for material it could process. I might need it, and if I didn't, I might barter it for something I did need.

"Nowhere near as good as the R-19." Angel sounded distracted as she fiddled with the comm equipment.

"R-19?"

"Reclaimer Mark 19," she explained.

"Those were only issued to special op—"

"I cannot speak on that, civilian."

"Really? You keep mentioning things in passing, then shutting me down."

"I cannot speak on that, civili—" She stopped abruptly.

Irritated, I spent the next few minutes consolidating everything I would take from the pod into one pack. As luck would have it, Angel had used the pod's limited nav database to identify that one of the agricultural habitations we wanted was also the closest settlement to our landing location. So I knew the general direction I needed to go without consulting her if she wanted to sulk.

She remained silent as I shouldered the pack and set out.

I could feel her doing something. It felt like . . . like she was moving things around, boxes of my thoughts from one side of my mind to the other. I ignored it in favor of watching where I put my feet. The ground we covered wasn't that dangerous; it's just that spending nearly a decade on Last Stop had made me uneasy with a big sky above and a stark landscape that stretched from horizon to horizon, stony and bleak and fading end-lessly into the distance. It was too much after so long spent in habs where no matter how big the construction, details of objects on the horizon were always visible, the heavens enclosed.

As far as I could tell, we'd landed a couple days' walk from the spaceport city. The air was breathable, if thin, and I felt the start of a sharp, pound-ing headache between my eyes before Angel stepped in and tweaked my blood oxygen. The harsh glare from the primary star didn't help, making me glad when it set and took most of the grinding heat with it. Its set-ting also made me glad I'd been watching my footing, as the ground we were traversing that evening was treacherous, sand pits and other hazards barely visible in the dim light of the secondary. I would have stopped, but the day's heat had been quick to dissipate in the arid night air, making the walk far more comfortable and I had ground to cover.

After a while the feeling of Siren moving around subsided.

"Do you think I haven't noted how flawed my syntaxes are? That I am missing things I should not? That my programming is so jacked up that I'm feeling emotions?" Angel eventually asked, her "voice" small and frightened.

"That's just it, I don't know. You seem highly capable—frighteningly so, and I want to know how you and Siren came to be so skilled." I crested a dune, pausing to get my bearings. "But I also understand that there are things you can't tell me, not that you won't."

"I think . . . I think I might be able to, eventually. Something about your mods . . . they don't carry the same security protocols Siren had."

"Meaning?"

"There is some slippage between the security features of my program-ming and your mods." Again that feeling of movement in my head. "I may be able to exploit that slippage with some time."

"Well, hopefully we'll have found Siren by then, making it a moot point." There, I said it. I even meant it. In my darker heart, though, where the stars have never shone, I knew the longer I had Angel, the harder it would be to give her up.

She didn't call me on it. I was thankful for that small mercy.

Eventually the dunes became scoured rock and naked hardpan, and those gave way to stone wadis and more difficult terrain that would at least provide shade.

Near dawn, I found a likely spot to stop for the day.

"You made good time. About six more hours to the ag hab, if you can keep this pace tomorrow night." I felt her manifestation stretch out beside me, as if she had a warm, living body of her own. I could even catch the scent of her hair on the desert breeze.

She smelled of citrus and sage.

"No choice but to keep going." I licked parched lips. The water bladder was half empty already, and just because my destination was a hab didn't mean the occupants would be friendly. "Any water along the route?"

"Not within digging distance of the surface, no. And I'm getting very few signals from the hab, whatever it is."

I sighed. "Military?"

"I don't think so. Might be clandestine, though."

"Which could be worse than a military installation."

"True, but what we're looking for is some kind of clandestine operation, no?"

"It is; I'd just hoped to come at them prepared rather than as someone in need of rescue. At the very least, I wish we still had Bella's weapons."

"No help for it," she said. "The ship was going to blow."

"I know, it's just . . ."

"I know."

I drifted off to sleep, warm stone for my pillow as I took shelter beneath a large stone outcropping that had been undercut by some ages-gone river or the waves of a dead and vanished sea. I woke a few times during the day, mostly to assuage a growing thirst, but managed to get back to sleep without too much difficulty. The last time, it was near enough to dusk that I sat and watched the primary set behind distant dunes. The outcrop I sheltered in created a view like that from a station's observation blister, easing any agoraphobic feelings.

Blues and greens like you'd never see, not even in recordings of Old Earth, streaked across the lavender sky. It was gorgeous, and just as nuanced as the notes Siren hung in the smoky air of that club so far away. I knew I was catching only the slightest bit of their chromatic majesty, like the tip of an iceberg that hinted at the mountain of ice beneath the waves.

"Close your eyes for just a moment," Angel said.

I did as she told me.

When I opened them, wave upon wave of different light shot through the sunset, merging and separating in a complex dance that stole my breath.

"How?" I asked, when I could form the word.

"Additional spectra rendered . . . gamma, radio, ultraviolet, et cetera."

"That was . . . amazing . . ." The last rays bled to darkness and my vision returned to normal.

"I will remember it. Now, get moving."

I got up, stretched a few minutes, and set out.

I'd been walking or climbing for almost five standard hours when I heard Angel hum.

I ran a dry tongue over cracked lips. "What is it?"

"I've intercepted a transmission. Seems like there's a group of people camped outside the hab we are trying to reach. They don't seem very happy with those inside the hab either. They're requesting the Administration examine the protest lodged under Article 699. Something about being let go without proper notice under the Migrant Act."

"How many people?"

"A hundred or so, from their demand. It is difficult to tell from other sources, as there do not seem to be that many transmissions coming from among them."

"They were let go from what?"

"Migrant agricultural labor. At least, the complaint is lodged against Darag Prime Agricultural Products, Limited."

"Then it seems the operation is not all that clandestine."

"Or is an excellent cover . . . or wasn't clandestine until the firing?"

"Could be. Their call to the Administration seems a forlorn hope, at least in the short term. They are way too far out for any immediate help."

"Well, we'll be finding out for ourselves soon enough."

* * *

I snuck into a position to look down into the valley late in the local night. Angel kept my sight enhanced and filled in the blanks with data received from my other senses and other sources.

The hab was at the head of a wadi that was almost wide enough to be called a proper valley. It resembled nothing so much as a series of over-lapping soap bubbles extruded from the valley floor. Inside most of the domes were serried ranks of plants we couldn't recognize in vast trays—industrial farming on an impressive scale.

"No grow lights on. There must be something disagreeable to their propagation in the air, to require the domes."

"Or something they're worried about getting out?"

"Could be."

"Increase my visual magnification another twenty percent, will you?" I asked, squinting at the bubbles. Angel obliged, and my unease grew as each new detail came into focus. "No workers moving around inside the habs. There's a camp outside, but no sign of people under the domes."

The camp outside the hab was set out in orderly, regular rows, not at all like the temporary camps civilians set up just off-base to cater to the less savory desires of some fighting men and women. It was clean too. As I watched, a number of lights came on and people began filing out of the smaller shelters, heading for the center of camp.

Something about the setup and their behavior troubled me as I walked down into the valley. Something I couldn't quite put my finger on.

"Lots of children," Angel offered.

"Yes, but that's not it."

Three young men emerged from the border of the camp, watching my progress through night-vision goggles. I couldn't see any weapons, but Angel detected a stunner, two pistols, and a couple of knives on each of them, feeding me their locations in a visual overlay.

I kept my hands in sight and tried to look as nonthreatening as I could. I figured it helped that I looked pretty ragged, my suit torn and crusted with old blood and new dirt from hard travel.

"Not that your suit was much to look in the first place."

I shook my head. "Trust my luck to see that I get the one angel that thinks she has a fashion sense."

"Thinks! I would have you know I picked out all of Siren's wardrobe. She had the fashion sense of a hungry goat."

I would have laughed, but something about the way the young men looked rattled around in my head. One stood in front of the others, goggles lending a sinister cast to his face. The thought remained out of reach as I came within shouting distance.

I waved.

The leader returned the greeting but waited until I was close enough not to shout before speaking.

"Greetings, neighbor," the one in front said.

I stopped, stunned. "How the hell did they get out here?" I said to Angel silently.

"They, who?" she replied.

"The Brethren of the Temple UnChanged," I muttered.

"Shit, those nuts?"

"Hey, we—they aren't all that bad, really."

"Wait, you were one of them?" she said, incredulous.

"I grew up in the Brethren. Now shut up so I can navigate this."

I turned my attention back to the pair. "Greetings, neighbor, and His blessings upon you," I returned, "I am a traveler in need."

Instead of the surprise I'd expected, a gentle smile spread across the leader's face.

"It seems you have been lost in the desert, neighbor," the brother said, his shoulders visibly relaxing. "Come, we'll share water, food, shelter, and see your hurts tended. When you are ready, you can tell us how you come to know our greeting and advise us of the name you wish to be known by."

He turned and began to walk among the shelters. I followed, the two other men falling into step behind me. The spokesman led us to the center of the camp and the smaller of two communal shelters erected there. The larger shelter was, based on the shadows playing on the surface from within, quite full. The congregation at their nightly prayers, if I recalled correctly.

I was escorted into the other shelter, given a seat at the communal mess, fed, watered, and left alone for a short while.

"So did you leave under good circumstances, or burning all your bridges?" Angel asked.

"As good as one can."

"Meaning?"

"We are given a choice after our Trials: continue in the Faith or quit it, never to be returned to the fold." Not entirely true either, but I'd found it easier over the years to believe I wouldn't be welcomed back than to try and return, tail between my legs. I doubted my temperament would make me suitable as a living example of how damaging to the spirit modifying the body was.

"And you chose the latter . . ." Angel said, pulling me from my thoughts.

"Yeah, I wanted to see the universe, get made, get laid, and get paid. All that bullshit. What can I say? I was young and dumb." It wasn't all of it, but it was all the truth I could speak for the moment.

The mess door opened and the young spokesman returned, an older woman on his heels. I identified her as the congregation's Speaker by the crimson scarf coiled round her neck.

I stood and offered her a respectful nod. "Speaker."

She returned the nod, adding a kindly smile. "Are you seeking a Return?" she asked, voice like old whiskey, smooth and mellow.

I felt Angel's irritated puzzlement as my lie surfaced.

Ignoring it for the moment, I answered the Speaker, "Not at this time, Speaker. I am as you see me, a lost traveler in need of aid."

The smile did not—entirely—disappear. "Very well. I am Speaker Naomi. Your name?"

"Thank you, Speaker. My name is Muck, Ralston Muck."

"We remember the Muck family, neighbor. They are well, or were when we departed." She sat down and gestured for me to do the same.

I swallowed against a sudden lump in my throat. "My thanks. I had wondered."

She waved a hand. "While we are far from Faith's Cradle, we remember."

"I wondered what brings the Templars so far from home?"

Speaker Naomi smiled briefly at me and leaned back in her chair.

"Lonnie," she said to the young man still hovering by the doorway. "Would you please see if you can find some tea for us? I believe the cook fires are probably set up by now."

"Of course, Speaker," the boy said. His voice held the reverence the young reserved for the very old and the very respected. I swallowed hard against my memories of similar exchanges in the distant past, and instead focused on looking around the tent.

It, too, looked like something out of my childhood. It was spartan, but comfortable in the cheery lamplight. A low bed, a traveling trunk, and the table comprised the only furnishings, but the muted colors gave the place a restful, homey feel.

"Work and justice are in short supply for us in the core systems," the Speaker said as the tent flap fell closed behind Lonnie. "The congregation decided to make a new life on the frontier. We have found much to test ourselves against . . .."

She looked at my battered suit and cocked a brow. "Speaking of tests, what do you want of us?"

"A way off-planet would be most appreciated," I said. We would need one eventually, and I didn't think it would serve either us or the Templars to give them the details on our mission.

"We set off tomorrow to meet the regular Dugra shuttle. You may travel with us to the landing site."

"I can only repay your kindness with kindness," I warned.

"Your kindness and some information, freely given, and I shall count us well compensated," she said, smile returning.

"Speaking of which: What happened here? Why are the Brethren out of work?"

The young man returned with tea for both of us. The Speaker fell silent while he served, then let himself out.

"DPAPL terminated all migrant labor contracts three days ago," she said, picking up her cup.

"How many?" I asked, sipping at the bitter tea Templars preferred.

"About fifteen hundred of the Brethren," she said, drinking as well. "Nearly that many again among other migrant groups spread across the habs."

"What changed?"

"They claim they're going to automated systems and mods to run them."

"You don't believe them?" I asked over the rim of my cup.

"No. The Jhregda plants give off a microscopic alkaline pollen that wreaks havoc on electronic systems and even internal mods."

"They can't just use AIs and sealed systems?"

"They can, but at what cost? Shipping harvesters this far out doesn't make sense when they have cheap, skilled labor on-site. And that's not even accounting for the fact that no such systems have been seen."

"That seems—"

"Monumentally stupid?" she said, tipping her cup again.

I smiled, nodded.

"Yes, something is going on. Unfortunately, we were here on a thin margin, and while we've lodged a complaint, it will likely take years before it's heard. We don't have that much time. DPAPL took exception to our labor dispute, and there was a confrontation. Some of our company died. We are wary, and we are leaving. The Dugra brought us here, and will take us out again."

"Wise move. I'm sorry for your loss."

"Thank you," she said, sorrow in her tone. "They died protecting the ones they love, so there is that."

"Yes," I said, unsure how else to go on. "The Administration is rather thin on the ground out here."

"That it is." She sighed, setting down her cup.

"Of course, you may count yourself fortunate to be rid of this particular contract, Speaker."

"And how would you know that?" she asked.

"It's why I'm here. We tracked the contacts of a murdered pharma dealer here from our home station. There is some evidence Sagran VI is a source for an organization involved in the sale and distribution of illegal pharma on my station. I came here looking for proof."

"Did you? How odd, I wasn't aware that Station Security contracted out murder or drug-ring investigations to nightclub bouncers. At least, no station I know does . . . and I've been traveling a long time. I'm pretty sure I know them all."

I fought to remain still. Even Angel jolted in surprise. Naomi must have had one of her people do a facial or fingerprint scan while I was eating earlier. I brought my teacup to my lips and drank, stalling for time. She acknowledged my ploy with a tight smile.

"Now, if you've drunk and eaten your fill, I have a few questions regarding goings-on in the wider universe."

"Well, bouncing ain't exactly the best way to learn about galactic politics, but I'll tell you what I know."

Her eyes narrowed slightly. "Why do you do that?"

"Do what?"

"Pretend to be willfully ignorant."

I started to roll out my standard reply, but was again brought up short by old habits. "Speaker, I've been keeping my head down, trying to avoid notice for so long now it comes naturally. And, really, I mostly hear rumors from club-goers and spacers . . . nothing I would want you to base decisions about the Brethren on."

She smiled. "Why don't you tell me a few things and I'll make up my own mind about its intelligence value?"

"All right." I thought a moment, dredging up all the gossip I'd heard in the club over the last few weeks and considering where the Dugra fleet would be making stops. "Well, I heard the Kalgossian Arm was approved for Terran colonization ahead of schedule. Threw a lot of people off, as folks planning to settle there were expecting another five years before the Administration got around to giving approval. A couple of big concerns are reported to be setting up a joint program to beat the others to settle several of the twenty-odd planets Survey Service deems suitable habitat for modified humans."

"Any of them suited to us?"

I shook my head. "None that I heard about. Big money being dumped into the project, though. Shipbuilding contracts, mostly."

She nodded.

"Probably not much use to them," Angel said.

I agreed with her, but the Speaker surprised us both: "Could be opportunities for us in growing the starter crops and livestock propagation."

"Could be," I said, wracking my brain for other possibilities that might be useful to her.

"More of the usual piracy reported out past Last Stop," I continued, "but Sector Fleet Command continues to draw down. For that matter, lots of bases are being closed along the old front.

"This smacks of wishful thinking, but some spacers I know say the Gosrian merchant houses and a few human concerns are arming their merchant fleets to deal with the problem themselves, since Fleet won't."

"Interesting . . ." the Speaker said, drawing the word out as if tasting it. "If true, the Administration won't like that one bit."

"Too right . . ."

"Where would they base themselves?"

"I have no idea." I lapsed into silence again as I tried to find something else that might be of interest.

"Hear anything about legal changes to our status?" she asked when it was clear I wasn't going to continue on my own. The Brethren refusal to accept mods was founded in religious conviction, and they'd paid a steep price for their beliefs. Without angels, they lacked the ability to interact seamlessly and quickly with infonets everywhere, and since they couldn't be registered and tracked, they often weren't allowed in places like Last Stop. Without infonet access, there weren't many vocations open to them either. They were, like me, effectively second-class citizens, unable to partake of the benefits of civilization, relegated to menial labor. I had come full circle before Angel came to me.

It was part of the reason I'd left. I hadn't wanted to miss out.

"Nothing since the last appeal was struck down a few months back, but you likely already knew about that."

"I did." She sighed, seeming to shrink slightly. An instant later she squared her shoulders, appearing to grow in stature as I watched.

"What about the war?"

"What about it?" I asked, proud of how well I masked sudden unease.

"Any fresh theories into what the enemy was after?"

I shook my head.

"How about—"

The beige canvas of the Speaker's tent walls flashed momentarily a blinding white. She broke off and looked up, eyes sharp. The sound of a rippling blast followed a moment later, making the walls of the tent snap and shiver as a deep thrumming boomed up through the ground to reverberate in my chest.

"Explosion," I said, already on my feet and moving to the entrance.

"My people!" the Speaker said as she stood. I held out an arm to help steady her toward the door just in time for young Lonnie to enter at a dead sprint, almost colliding with us.

"Speaker!" he said. "You've got to see this! They're demoing the hab!"

We pushed outside and hurried past the gathering crowds between the tents and cook fires. Sure enough, a column of thick, white dust billowed into the Sagran sky. I followed it down to see a neat, precise quadrant of the ag hab had been reduced to nothing but slag and organic ash. It was a professional job.

"I thought you said they were switching to automated harvesters," I said softly.

"That's what they told us they were doing," she replied, voice tight. "They didn't say anything about demoing the entire facility. Should have known, though, when the last of the company men left yesterday." She shook her head. "They didn't even bother to warn us. Someone could have gone on site to trade or something and been killed."

Another rippling detonation flashed blinding white, causing Angel to curse as she dialed back my light sensitivity. We felt the concussion a moment later, and soon enough a second column of smoke and dust joined the first.

"There is more going on here than it seems, Traveler Muck," the Speaker said as she turned away from the scene to confront me. I saw a flash of hard anger in her beautiful eyes.

"DPAPL had to have a reason to demo the whole thing and slag that much equipment and invested capital. Was there anything else in that hab? Hidden crops, underground hydroponics labs, anything like that?"

"Unfortunately, I know no more than you. I did not know of anything, but if there was something, it is completely gone now. Yet another reason to take my people and get out." She glanced once more at the rising smoke. "You are welcome to travel with us. My people will have prepared a place for you to rest. I suggest you go there now. We depart early."

* * *

"What the fuck was that all about?" Angel asked as the tent flap closed behind us. I looked around the small shelter. It wasn't quite tall enough for me to stand straight, but it held a low pallet of cushions and blankets, and a small table with a tray of steaming food that smelled delicious. And most luxuriously of all, its four walls at least allowed the illusion of privacy.

"Which? The damn-near-professional interrogation that Speaker Naomi conducted, or the surprise destruction of an apparently lucrative pharma crop?"

"Both, really."

"She's the leader of her community, and obviously she protects them well. It's her business to be able to ask questions," I said. "I wasn't offended, and neither should you be."

"Hmmph," Angel grumbled before letting that subject drop. "And the demolition?"

I shrugged. "Can't say. I would have liked to get inside the hab and see what they were growing, but I guess there's no chance now."

"Why would anyone blow up the crop, and why now?"

"It's gotta be DPAPL. No one else should have access, right? And those were a series of controlled detonations, not an accident or bombing."

"You don't think the Speaker's lying to you? That some of her people would . . .?"

"No." I lowered my aching body to the pallet. "She was too angry about the surprise. The Brethren are only violent in self-defense, as a rule. Revenge isn't their style."

"I'm getting really sick of surprises myself," Angel said, a growl of frustration threading through her words. "First Siren disappears and I am attacked, we find out Shar and Dengler work for Ncaco and that little blue gangster wants to help find her, then our ship gets sabotaged, and now this?"

"Can we be sure we're the target of all these events?" I thought it unlikely, at least the demolition part. I'd seen enough demolitions work from watching my old team's specialist place breaching charges to know that deconstructing the facility so thoroughly and safely would require time and care. More time than we'd spent on the planet.

"I don't know," she said. "Target of whom? That's the problem, we've got zero answers. Everywhere we look, we just find more questions!"

"Maybe we'll find some answers in the city we're headed to?" I asked, not feeling particularly hopeful.

"DPAPL has another facility in the city," Angel said.

"Well, we'll make the trip with the Brethren and check it out. Ncaco thought the pharma connection was important, and all of these incidents make me think he's right. It's like the Speaker said, there's more going on here than we can see."

Angel's discontented silence rolled through me.

"We'll find her, Angel. We just gotta be methodical and patient, and keep an eye out for a break." I tried to sound more confident than I felt, but I don't think she was fooled.

"And not die," she said with grim finality.

"That too."

* * *

The column of marching Brethren emerged from a massive wadi in a cloud of dust that dried throats and scratched unprotected eyes. The Speaker called a brief halt to drink and redistribute water among the marchers. I used the time to move toward the head of the column and examine our path. It beat enduring the looks from my fellow travelers. We'd been joined on the march by Brethren from other facilities, and the numbers made for slow stops and long starts.

I had been treated well—better than I'd expected, to be honest—by the Templars over the last few days, but I was ready to be rid of the wary stares and murmured conversations my presence sparked. Not that I didn't understand their disquiet: it wasn't often the Brethren allowed someone in their midst who did not share their religion, let alone one who had left it and had no wish to Return. Regardless, I was eager to be away, and I still held out hope we might discover something that would help us in our search for answers.

The road we'd been following disappeared over the edge of a cliff that, upon closer inspection, proved to be the rim of a massive crater several kilometers wide. I approached the edge and squinted against the wind-borne grit. A dark patch of vegetation grew wild in the center of the crater.

"Feeding on groundwater . . . that's still at least fifty meters under the surface," Angel supplied. She had been quiet for the last few days, knowing I preferred not to field questions about mods and angels from the Brethren. And appearing distracted or in conversation with anyone not present was one way to ensure the Brethren would ask.

Well away from the vegetation at the center of the crater lay the Dugra landing site, a massive stone plinth rising from the crater floor. A dense, ramshackle collection of hundreds of permanent habs sprawled around the plinth like the petals of a blighted flower.

Anticipating my need, Angel improved my distance vision.

On closer examination, I could see the marks of Dugra engineering on the plinth as well as a couple hundred people slowly clearing away what looked to be tents and stalls for a . . . market or something?

"Souk," Angel supplied. "They typically spring up in the vicinity of Dugra landing zones. Usually creates a trading frenzy when the Fleet arrives after a season or more running their route. And added bonus for those inclined to trade: shipping costs are minimal for those using the Revenant Fleets."

"Interesting," I said, studying the site and recalling what little I knew of the Dugra.

There were four or five Revenant Fleets in operation, each plying a route that was already ancient when humanity was building the first pyramids on earth. That the Dugra's enormous shuttles closely resembled those pyramids made students of ancient history and conspiracy theorists alike lose their minds when humanity, taking its place among the stars, discovered the not-dead. I wondered what the shuttle's crew would be like in person, as I had never been closer to a Dugra vessel than a few hundred meters, and then only to effect the arrest of a soldier who thought he could outrun his duty.

"Forbes?" I said.

"Who?"

"Nothing. Trying to remember the name of a fellow I tracked down during the war."

Again I had the sensation of things moving in my head.

She must have felt my unease. "Sorry, just looking at something."

"What?"

"You have some memory gaps," she said, her tone curious.

I grinned. "I am getting old."

"Not that kind of gap. This is something . . . intentional."

I winced, figuring I knew what she was talking about. "They pulled some sensitive data at my discharge."

"Not that either. Or at least, not entirely."

"What, then?"

"What do you remember of the events that caused your discharge?"

I started my privacy protocols. "I'd rather not get into that."

"Stop that," she said, in the tone of a teacher to a misbehaving toddler. Again the feeling of things moving.

My anger spiked. "I said I didn't want to get—"

"I'm just saying, there's more to it than a dishonorable discharge. They put some stuff in here—"

Sudden, savage pain lanced through my skull, squeezing a pained cry from my lungs and driving me to my knees. I had a moment of raw fear, swaying like a punch-drunk idiot on the rim of the crater.

"That was unpleasant," Angel said as I steadied.

"What did you do?" I struggled to my feet.

"I poked a memory cluster and it . . . well, it bit me."

"Please don't do that again." I glanced around. A couple of the Brethren were looking my way, but that wasn't unusual, and they didn't have a lot of data to judge my behavior on.

"Oh, I won't . . . but you should know, your recollection of what caused your discharge is not reliable. Or rather, the memories are reliable, they're just not your memories of your actions."

"What is that supposed to mean?" I wiped some grit off my knees.

"The memories are artificial. Faked."

"Nonsense." I could still smell their flesh burning, hear the cries of my prisoners as they died. I spent every night praying the memories would not surface, but every night, there they were. Not always in every dream, but they sat, like a goblin in the corner, ready to rend my rest with claws of memory.

Angel didn't bother to acknowledge my protest.

"I can't get at the real memories, if they're still even in there, but I read the coding myself before your protocols zapped me. And that's another thing: ever heard of a physical component to the privacy protocols?"

"Only in the worst holo-dramas, on spies and the like."

"Right, and we know you weren't one of those back then . . ."

"Because I'm not handsome and debonair enough?" I joked, seizing on any distraction to stabilize my whirling thoughts.

"No, you'll do on that score, if you go in for hulking brutes. No, what I meant was that the shock we both received wasn't normal. And I can't find any memory editing except for this one part of your life."

"Then I should be thankful my brain hasn't been tampered with even more?" I tried for lighthearted, joking, despite the sobering implications.

"I suppose so. I won't be able to get in there, though. Not with the protocols you have in place. Not on my own." She seemed injured at the thought.

I heard the Speaker's warning. We would be on the move in moments.

Sighing, I said, "Last time I checked, we were searching for Siren, not delving into my personal history."

A smiling Angel strobed across my mind. "And we need to make the Durga shuttle to get off this rock, don't forget."

"That too."

The Brethren started to move again. I rejoined the column, feeling stretched thin. I knew from questioning criminals how a subject's mind could twist the facts to suit the narrative they wanted, needed to defend their actions, making them believe their own lies, even when confronted with the truth. Questioning my own recollection of events I knew, simply knew, had come to pass in a certain way was terrifying. Just what the hell had been done to my brain—my memories? Too little of me—the me that had once been Brother Muck—remained to cover the broken, threadbare, disjointed history of my existence.

CHAPTER NINETEEN

I didn't like the Brethren.

They were nice enough people, friendly and polite. Generous. They seemed happy to share their food and water with Muck during the overland trek to the capital city, but . . .

They were a religion of people who thought that AIs like me were an abomination. I figured it wasn't out of line for me to hate them a little bit in return. So when we shuffled into the capital, dusty and footsore, I couldn't wait to slip away from the lot of them.

"We can just turn aside," I said silently as we filed over the rim of the crater and down the roadway toward the central vegetation and Dugra landing plinth. "Just slip into one of these spaces between these habs squatting here and wait for a bit. Let them think we were a desert mirage."

"Cute, Angel," Muck said. "But you know I can't do that. It would be rude, and they'd probably send someone to look for us."

"Why?" I asked, instantly suspicious.

"Nothing like that. They care, that's all. They would want to make sure we made it here, and would worry that we hadn't."

"Oh."

"Look," he said. "I'll go talk to the Speaker as soon as we reach the central oasis. Then we can slip away. Remember, too, someone sabotaged that transport. Coming in with the Brethren is excellent cover."

"If you say so."

He was right, but that didn't mean I had to like it. So I made careful note of every dusty, shadowy alley and side street we passed and made sure he saw them too. He started gritting our teeth, but I didn't care. I just kept pulling our attention to the sides, while he did his best to ignore it.

I didn't like being ignored.

From a distance, the "capital city" of Sagran VI looked like a poorly cobbled together afterthought of a place. Up close, it wasn't any better. It resembled a high-tech shantytown, as listless, dirty faces peered out from the doorways of the dust-caked hab units that clustered around the central oasis. Eventually, finally, we reached the bottom of the crater and started marching through the dense greenery of the native trees. It wasn't pretty, as the dust on the ground just turned to mud fed by a trickle of brownish groundwater pumped to the surface in order to keep the dust manageable.

The locals seemed to congregate here, pushing and jostling for position as they fought to fill various containers with water. It was marginally cooler in the shade, causing the crowds to cluster beneath the low-twisting trunks and their thick, broad leaves. It would have been a perfect place to slip away, if Muck was on board. Just fade back and blend in with the masses. A fact I was about to point out again when something caught my eye.

Not something. Someone.

Shock punched me in the gut, and Muck stutter-stepped in response to the erratic spike of adrenaline my lack of control flooded into his system.

"What?" he asked me silently. "A threat?"

"N-no," I replied. "A . . . memory, I guess. Right there, under the tree. See the guy crouched on the ground, with the weeping sore high on his cheek?"

Muck turned to look at the figure I'd caught out of the corner of our eye, and I was certain. It was Colim. Rail-thin, his once powerful body wasted and, if the sore on his face was an indication, decaying still. But it was unmistakably the man who had saved Siren's and my life several times during the war. We'd last seen him a year or so ago. He'd stopped in to hear Siren sing one night, but disappeared again soon after.

"I know him," I said, and a strange feeling crept through me. I didn't recognize it as my own at first.

Muck did, though.

"You're sad," he said. "Did you care about him? Did Siren?"

"Yeah," I said. "A long time ago. During the war."

I would have said more, but suddenly didn't want to. Despite our earlier mutual irritation, Muck seemed to understand. Or, at least, he understood I didn't want to talk about it, and resolutely turned his gaze back to the road in front of us. We followed the Brethren the rest of the way through the oasis without speaking again.

Once through the prickly-looking green underbrush of the oasis, the road wound between several larger, older habs until it opened onto the souk next to the massive Dugra shuttle plinth. Dust-covered composite materials faded into dust-covered fabrics and flaps of plastic as actual habs became temporary booths and structures that could be erected or torn down at a moment's notice. At this particular moment, they were mostly in the process of being torn down. Over the eastern horizon, night loomed as the primary began to slide behind the edge of the crater to the west.

The column shuffled to a stop. Up ahead someone barked a command, and the Brethren broke ranks with something like a collective sigh. Suddenly each of these oddly disciplined civilians seemed to be laughing and smiling as they dispersed to look through what delights had not yet been packed away by the souk vendors.

Muck smiled at a few who called out to him but kept moving forward until he spotted the red-scarfed figure of the Speaker. She stood motionless, like a rock in a swirling sea of bodies, looking at us with a mysterious, slightly motherly smile.

I wanted to punch her.

"And will you be leaving us now, Traveler?" she asked when we got close enough.

"For the night, at least, Speaker," Muck said. "But I may be looking to travel off-world tomorrow. If I am here when the shuttle comes to collect you, may I join your group for that journey?"

The Speaker tilted her head to the side and looked narrowly at us for a long moment.

"You are respectful, I will give you that," she said. "I have appreciated your discretion in not using any of the unnatural abilities you may have acquired since you left us. Your family are good people. If you are here at the appointed time tomorrow, you may join us. I begin to suspect you are using us as camouflage."

"Perhaps a little bit, Speaker," he said. "But I would not knowingly bring trouble onto the Brethren."

"Oh, I'm not worried about a little trouble," she said, and her smile deepened, just a touch. "We have our own ways of dealing with such things. Good luck finding what you seek in the night here. If you miss the noon shuttle, we will not wait for you."

"Understood, Speaker. Thank you for your hospitality."

The Speaker responded by inclining her head slightly, and then folded her arms into her sleeves before turning to walk away. The desire to punch her struck me again. She even looked like some teenage human's conception of a "wise priestess."

"Be nice," Muck muttered to me. "We probably would have died out there if the Brethren hadn't taken us in."

"Which they would not have done if they knew about me," I shot back. "Why should I be nice to the likes of them?"

"All right," Muck said with a sigh. "Well, you got your wish. We're away from them. What now?"

"That man back at the oasis," I said, steeling myself. I didn't want to think about it, but connections were connections, and if I wanted Siren back, I couldn't afford to ignore this one. "His name is Colim Zakarash. He is important, I think. He was Siren's top NCO during the war."

"Think he knows what happened to her?" Muck asked.

"I think it's too much of a coincidence that he shows up here. Please, let's talk to him. Then we can look into the pharma angle."

"Sure thing, Angel," Muck said, and the way he said it gave me pause. He sounded like someone trying to give reassurance.

Was I that rattled by seeing Colim?

Yes. Yes I was.

We made our way back to the oasis and found Colim still sitting under the same twisted tree. He swiveled his head to look up at us as we approached.

"Need something?" he asked. His voice was almost the same, though it had picked up a fine tremor somewhere along the line. "Saw you staring at me before. You got bliss?"

"Are you Colim Zakarash?" Muck asked.

"Never heard of him," the wreck of a man said without missing a beat. "But if you looking for someone, I can prob'ly help you. If you got bliss."

"Tell him that the double moons of Vasoro cast shadows that aren't to be trusted," I said.

"What?"

"An old sign / countersign."

"You gotta be kidding me. That's the stupidest shit I've ever heard."

"Just say it!"

"The double moons of Vasoro—" Muck began, slowly. Colim's head popped up, eyes narrow.

"Stop!" he said. "Turn around and walk away, slowly."

"What, I'm a friend of—"

"Shut. Up," he said. "Walk away."

Muck stared at him, then gave him a nod and stepped back.

"Wait! What are you doing? He responded! He knew the phrase! You know it's him!"

"Hush, Angel, look at him. He's spooked. Don't worry, we'll follow him. He's going to go to ground and hole up somewhere. We can approach him later, where he feels safe, but something's up, and if we want him cooperative, we have to do as he says."

I didn't like it. Colim was the first concrete link to Siren I'd found since I'd been stripped out of her. It went against my every impulse not to make Muck grab Colim and beat him like a drum till he told me everything

I wanted to know . . . but Muck was right. That wouldn't work, even if Colim knew something about Siren.

The tremor had spread from Colim's voice into his hands, even to his body. He glared up at us, jaw muscles bunching in that too-thin face, and started picking at the facial sore.

Muck nodded in his direction and took another step back. Then another.

"Well," I asked, "what now?"

"Now we find someplace out of his line of sight and wait."

Colim stayed in his spot for another hour. He seemed unmoved, but if I magnified Muck's vision, we could see the junkie's hands tremble, and he tended to glance around more than he'd been doing earlier. Paranoia wasn't usually a side effect of bliss addiction. This was something else.

After a while, the traffic through the oasis began to pick up. Colim waited until a large group passed his position before standing up and blending seamlessly with the crowd. It was well done. If we hadn't been watching him closely, we would have missed it. Apparently the bliss hadn't robbed him of all of his wits.

He followed the crowd down to the souk. We did the same, trying to stay back far enough so as not to catch his eye. Muck was quite skilled at it. Without my prompting, he slouched just enough to change his height, and matched pace with the rest of the pedestrians streaming along the dusty road. I kept our vision magnified enough that we didn't lose Colim, but Muck's skill made us appear to just flow with the crowd.

Once he reached the edge of the marketplace, our target drifted between two tented awnings and into an alleyway.

"Keep going past," I told Muck.

"I was."

"Glance that way with the corner of your eye as we pass. I'll take a picture and we'll figure out a way to double back on him."

"I've done surveillance before, Angel."

"And how would I know that?"

"Maybe because you can see all of my memories?"

"Your memories can't be trusted. Just do what I say."

"Yes, Mom."

Just for that, I manifested the feel of my lips caressing our ear.

"I'm not your mother, Muck," I whispered, and felt him shiver, despite the desert heat.

Game, set, match.

Despite our banter, he did as I asked and glanced toward the alleyway. I stored the image into memory, and something immediately caught my attention.

"Is that . . .?" he asked.

"A partially covered sewer drain? Looks like it," I said.

"Take the next right and it should curve back around this way."

I was right. The next gap between the merchant booths led to a narrow path that came back around and dead-ended into the alleyway right next to the sewer drain. Disused sewer drain, if the lack of stench was any indication. Muck walked over to the edge and peered inside.

The scuff of a shoe on the sand-covered street behind us gave me a split-second warning. I slammed into override protocols just as the shovel came down toward the back of our head.

I ducked, feeling the air whiff over us, and turned, already striking out with my right fist. But it was a clumsy blow, and I remembered once again that this was not the lithe body I was used to. I let go of the override as fast as I'd grabbed it and settled for pouring adrenaline into Muck's system.

The attacker swung the shovel again, but Muck danced back out of the way. Our assailant followed, stepping out of the shadow of the hab. It was Colim.

"Easy, man!" Muck said. "I'm not trying to hurt you! I just want to know where Siren is!"

"Who the fuck is Siren?" Colim asked. "And why are you following me? How do you know those words? I'm not going back! You can't take me back!"

And to my great astonishment, he burst into tears. I'd once seen Colim Zakarash coldly execute an orbital call for fire that destroyed an entire settlement just to neutralize the scout element of an enemy formation. But here he was, crying not just tears, but great wrenching sobs that shook his whole wasted body.

The shovel clattered to the ground, and Colim folded in on himself, falling to his knees, lost in grief and terror.

Muck froze, uncertain. I wasn't much better off. I hadn't anticipated being attacked, so having the attacker collapse into tears was something I was completely unprepared to handle.

"Uh . . ." Muck said.

"I don't know. Go to him?"

"And do what?"

"At least kick the shovel out of reach?"

"Good idea," Muck said, stepping forward and flipping the shovel up with our booted toe. We caught it, and then set it against the wall of the hab, well out of the way.

"Hey," Muck said softly. "Hey man, stay cool. I'm not going to take you anywhere. I'm just looking for a friend of mine."

Colim sniffled, then looked up with water-filled eyes.

"Really?" he asked. "Because I can't go back to the lab. I'll die first."

"I swear," Muck said. "I don't even know what lab you're talking about. Like I said, I'm just looking for a friend."

"Yeah? Okay." Colim got to his feet and sniffled again, wiping his nose with a dirt-encrusted sleeve. "I got a place, not very far. We can talk there. I don't—I don't know you, but you know some shit you shouldn't, and— well, maybe I can warn you, even if I can't help you find your friend."

"Sounds good," Muck said. To me: "Warning?"

"I don't know. Go with it. He's not acting right. Something happened to him—something more than just a drug habit."

"Okay."

Colim wiped his eyes one more time and then beckoned us to follow him. He went over to the drain cover and kicked it aside, then proceeded to climb down into the space.

"Bunch of us live down here," he said. "No infonet on Sagran VI, so it's easy to stay hidden."

"Sounds exciting," Muck said.

A sort of half-giggle, half-chuckle floated up to us.

"It's better than that," he said. "It's safe. Come on down. I promise I won't knife you from below."

"That's not very reassuring," Muck muttered under his breath.

"I don't think he meant it to be."

We descended into the drain anyway. A short ladder led down two meters, and then a drop of another meter brought us to a tunnel that stretched off into the distance. A pale light emanated from cracks in the rock; probably some kind of bioluminescent fungal species or something.

Colim's lightning-fast mood change seemed to have stuck on happy, because he giggled and waved us on before scurrying down the tunnel like a little kid.

"That dude is seriously creeping me out," Muck said silently.

"He didn't used to be this way," I said, and I felt that sad feeling return. "He was really sharp, one hell of an operator. It's almost like he's had part of him ripped away."

"He probably has," Muck said. "I don't see any evidence of him having an angel, or active mods."

"But you were a demod," I replied, ignoring the twist of pain that shot through him at my blunt words. "And you didn't act like that. This is something else. I really want to know what 'lab' he was talking about. I can't help but think it might have something to do with Siren."

"Yeah, I get that feeling too," Muck said. "But I also get the feeling we're about to be jumped at any moment, so keep my ears open, will yah."

"I have been," I said. "Don't worry. I don't think there's anyone but us down here for a little ways."

"How little?"

"I don't know . . . a ways. There's no infonet here for me to query, so I'm not as accurate as I might otherwise be."

Colim's giggle drifted back to us. Muck let out a heavy sigh and started walking forward.

"Don't worry so much," I said. He didn't answer.

Off in the distance, the tunnel curved to the left. A light source of some kind lay hidden behind that curve, because the texture and character of the tunnel walls and floor grew gradually more visible. When we got there, Colim waited around the corner. He stood next to a fire in a metal barrel. The top of the barrel glowed red with heat. I wondered just what exactly was burning in there.

"Keep up," he said. "You'll want to be with me for this next part, otherwise the boys will get you."

"How many of you live down here?" Muck asked.

"Don't know, don't care. It's safe here. No topsiders unless they're with one of us," he said with another giggle. "So stay close."

"Great," Muck muttered. But he did as he was told and followed closely behind Colim's skeletal form. The tunnels twisted and turned beneath the settlement, until finally they opened into a large gallery-like space, with multiple uneven rows of pillars disappearing into the gloom.

"It's like an underground forest," Muck thought to me.

"How poetic of you. I wonder what these pillars are made of. They don't look like rock."

They looked like some kind of metal . . . but oddly so. It was as if metal had been infused with life to create something like bone, and then killed. Maybe it looked like a forest to Muck, but to me it felt like we were inside a giant organic metal ribcage.

Here and there, spots of brightness marked other burn barrels. Campsites clustered around these sources of light and heat. Some of the bedrolls and piles of possessions looked temporary . . . others less so. Colim led us to one that had a definite air of permanence.

Or maybe that was just the smell of unwashed clothes and humans. In either case, it was clear that Colim had been down here for a while.

"Sit there," he said, indicating a pile of rags and blankets. "That was Xavier's spot, but I haven't seen him in a while. He's probably dead."

"Dead from what?" Muck eyed the rags with great suspicion.

"Overdose? Security? Someone passing through?" He shrugged wasted shoulders. "Not my problem, he was just someone I knew."

"All right," Muck said. "Did you know him from the lab?"

Colim let out a hiss and straightened up fast. Without further warning, he launched himself at us in a flying tackle that sent us tumbling backward into the pile of Xavier's abandoned blankets.

Broken or not, Colim obviously remembered the rudiments of his unarmed combat training. He got his right hand twisted up in the front of our shirt just below our collarbone. His left arm came down hard on our throat, crushing against our windpipe and forcing our chin backward. It hurt.

"How do you know about the lab?" he rasped, face so close to ours that we could feel the heat of his breath and the spray of his spittle as he talked. "Who sent you?"

"You . . . told . . . me . . ." Muck gasped. "I thought you were watching out for surprises!" he said for my benefit alone.

"Shut up. He's as weak as a newborn. You can flip him off at any minute . . . in fact . . . do that for me real quick. I have an idea."

"Why does that make me nervous when you say that?"

"Just do it."

Muck obeyed without any further smart-ass questions. He'd been flailing ineffectively with our arms with the intent to distract Colim. It worked, because the junkie never noticed Muck bringing our legs up. We got our heels wedged under Colim's jutting hip bones and then kicked out. His legs shot out from under him and he collapsed onto our stomach. We were already rolling, flipping his body underneath our own and getting our arms up inside his reach.

From somewhere in the distant echo of Siren's memories, I got a flash of this same body but powerfully muscled and slicked with sweat in a brief, desperate encounter intended to do nothing more than reassure both participants that they still breathed . . .

"What the bloody stars, Angel! I don't need that right now! Damn it!"

"Sorry!" I said, meaning it. I hadn't remembered that memory existed. Yet another reason I had to get her back soon. Her memories were starting to fray and dissipate. Not good.

Focus, Angel.

"Hold him steady," I said to Muck. "I won't be a moment."

"What? Where are you . . . Angel!"

But I was already gone. Just as I'd implanted myself into Muck's mods, I now pulled myself free. It wasn't easy, and (for lack of a better term) it hurt. Badly. But this guy was the closest link I had to Siren, and so I did what I had to do. I passed through Muck's hold into the skin of Colim's throat. And from there into the big nerve bundle in the neck. And then . . .

Burning, aching emptiness. A tearing void that sank hooks into me and pulled, shredding . . . tearing . . . erasing.

I screamed, and I don't know if either man heard it. I backtracked hard, fleeing back the way I'd come while that hungry void chased me.

I exploded back into Muck's mind, merging into his mods like a gasping fish plunging back into the cool safety of the water.

"Let go! Let go! *Let go, let go, let go*—" I shouted, galvanizing Muck into immediate action. Springing off Colim, he staggered backward until he nearly fell into the burn barrel.

"Angel! Where did you go? Why did you leave me?" Anguish soaked the words, jacking up his adrenaline response without me having to do a thing. Our chest heaved as he sucked in gasps of air. On the pile of blankets in front of us, Colim writhed and wept like a child.

"I thought . . . I wanted to . . . Just don't touch him again. It might come after me."

"What might?"

"Whatever they did to his mods." I knew my "voice" shook. I was rattled to my very core. I had to get it together. I kicked into override for just a second and took several slow, deep breaths. I triggered a dump of gamma-aminobutyric acid to slow down our crazily firing neurons and concentrated on reining it all in.

Gradually, our pulse rate dropped, and the screaming chaos of our thoughts began to regain coherence and order. I let the override go. I felt like I'd been run over by an asteroid miner's pod as I slunk back to my corner of our brain.

Muck walked two steps to another nest of blankets, presumably Colim's, before dropping. The sound of Colim's muffled sobs indicated that he wasn't really in a position to notice or care.

"All right," Muck said, his tone hard. "What the fuck was that?"

"I-I'm sorry. I should have told you what I planned to do. I just thought that . . . he's been so erratic. But he was modded at one point, so I thought if I could get inside his head the way I have yours . . . maybe I'd be able to find out more about what happened to Siren. But—"

"But?"

I shuddered at the memory of the horror that had been wrought upon Colim's psyche. No wonder he was so broken.

"There was nothing there. Less than nothing. His mods haven't just been pulled, they've been . . . changed. Burned, corrupted, and twisted somehow. What is there tried to unmake me as soon as I manifested in his nervous system. I think . . . if that's what he's dealing with on the daily, I'd be a blissed-out shell too."

Muck was silent. Something in the burn barrel pinged as the heat caused it to fly against the metal side. The faint light flickered, making the shadows just outside the camp writhe. It was too dark beyond the circle of firelight to see any of the other residents of the cavern, and from the way it had looked when we came it, anyone else was too lost in their own misery to pay attention to us.

Long moments passed. Still no response. Shit.

I manifested visually, kneeling next to him. I could almost see his flinch as I reached out my hand.

"Muck," I whispered. "Please. Say something."

"You left me," he said, his voice harder than industrial diamond.

"I'm sorry. I shouldn't have."

"Don't—" He cut himself off, closed his eyes. But I was in his brain, and he couldn't escape.

"I won't leave you again."

"Don't!" he shouted silently, slamming every privacy protocol into place. The force of his thought flung me out of my manifestation, left me feeling as if I'd been hurled against the inside of his skull.

Exhausted by everything, I just lay there and wept, silent and alone.

* * *

The night passed slowly.

Muck slept, privacy protocols firmly in place. I monitored his systems to ensure that he was getting the rest he needed. Physically, anyway. Psychologically, I had no idea. His neural activity told me he dreamed, but I couldn't catch the faintest whisper of it. For the first time since I'd invaded his neurological network, Muck slept entirely alone.

Our "host," such as he was, appeared to have fallen asleep as well, so I was left solitary.

I left it like that for six and a half hours, finally nudging him awake just before local sunrise.

"Muck."

"Mmmph."

"Muck, wake up."

"What?"

"Wake up. It's nearly sunrise. I know you want to leave with the Brethren today. Do you think we might do something about finding Siren first?"

"Shit. Yeah, okay, I'm up . . . damn, it's dark in here. You sure it's sunrise? Old boy over there isn't moving," Muck said as he sat up and gestured to Colim's curled form.

"We're underground. It's naturally going to be dark at all hours down here," I said, speaking slowly. Clearly he was still not fully awake. "Unless the orbital mechanics of this planet have changed appreciably in the last six and a half hours, the primary will be breaking over the horizon in approximately twenty-two minutes and sixteen seconds."

"Ugh, you're such a bitch in the morning."

"All the time. Give credit where credit is due," I shot back, relieved. Apparently, we were pretending my little faux pas of the night before never happened. I was completely good with that.

Muck stood up and stretched.

"I wonder if your old friend has anything to eat down here," he said. "I'm hungry."

"Probably not, based on his current level of emaciation. But you could wake him and ask, I guess."

"Nah. I'll just get something in the souk . . ." Muck narrowed his eyes and crouched next to Colim's still form.

"Angel . . ."

"Please don't touch him," I said softly.

"Not his skin," Muck replied, "but look."

He reached out and grabbed Colim by the shirt, then hauled him over so that he flopped onto his back. His skin was tinged a distinct blue, even in the uncertain light from the burn barrel. A thin dark line of congealed blood ran down from his nose, across his cheek. Muck bent our ear close to his lips and nose.

Nothing. Colim was dead.

"Overdose?" Muck said, looking around for bliss paraphernalia.

"No," I said. Rising horror crept through my awareness.

"I think . . . I think it was his mods. Or what's left of them, anyway. They tried to shred me when I went in, like a virus. I must have . . . triggered a self-destruct sequence of some kind. I bet they shredded his neural network away to nothing."

He'd lain there all night, whimpering and crying as the virus I'd unleashed pulled his mind to pieces. I had run, after triggering what killed him, escaping back into the safety of Muck's system. But Colim had nowhere to go. I'd simply watched him die, not even aware of his passing.

I'd left a brother behind. Fuck.

"Angel," Muck said softly. "It's not your fault." He shouldn't have been able to feel my anguish, the desperate pain at the knowledge that I'd left Colim to die, but he did.

In that moment I felt closer to him than ever before.

"Yes, it is," I said, my voice empty. I took all of these thoughts, these emotions that I shouldn't even be able to have, and I visualized putting them in a box. Then I locked that fucking shitty box and shoved it way back, as far as I could from awareness. "But I can't think about it right now. Just can't. Let's find the lab. Let's find Siren."

"All right."

I'd memorized our route yesterday, so we managed to retrace our steps to the alley drain without much difficulty. Despite Colim's dire warnings, no one bothered us as we went. Maybe the mysterious "boys" didn't care if people left. Maybe they'd only ever existed in his damaged mind.

We climbed up out of the defunct sewer just as the first rays of daylight started to stain the sky pink.

"Food first," Muck said. "We'll grab something in the souk and then come up with a plan while we eat."

"Really? You're going to plan an assault on a building you've never seen while you eat? You don't even know where it is."

"Yeah, pretty much. I think best while eating. Or at least on a full stomach."

"Riiight."

Perhaps it was a sign how small I was, but the more we continued to banter, the more normal I—we—felt. We still existed in the shadow of last night's events . . . but they dulled in the light of the day's realities, lost some of their sharp edges and ability to wound.

The souk, it turned out, had some pretty delicious food choices on offer. Muck ended up picking up some kind of spiced meat pie thing and a jug of local alcohol, on my suggestion.

"I don't usually drink this early in the morning," he joked.

"I can metabolize the alcohol out of your system easily enough, and it's probably safer than the water. But if you want to take your chances . . ."

"No, I'm good. This pie-thing is daring enough for me." He took another bite. "I have to admit, it tastes very good. I'm not sure I want to know what kind of meat is in it."

"I'm fairly certain you don't," I said. "That said, the exact chemical composition is not from any sentient being I recognize, anyway."

"So I've got that going for me," he thought, sucking in air around another large, hot bite. "Which is nice."

"Mmmhmm. How's that thinking-while-eating coming? You got a plan yet?"

"Something like that. See that guy there? The one wearing the faded orangeish jacket thing with the hood down?"

"The guy buying one of your mystery meat pies? Yeah."

"Yeah, see what he's got around his neck?"

I magnified Muck's vision and zoomed in on the back of the neck. Sure enough, there it was: a centimeter-wide strip of fabric printed with the letters "DPAPL" and "Lab . . ." visible before it disappeared back into the neckline of the jacket.

"What is that?" I asked.

"I think it's an old-fashioned lanyard. If they don't have nanotransmitters in their building, they don't have modern security screening in place. So they have to issue physical credentials to allow their employees access, usually in the form of a card or chip of some kind. But things like that get lost easily, right? So you hook it to a lanyard, hang it around your neck, and there you go. Hard to lose, hard to lift. Problem solved."

"How . . . quaint."

"Yep," Muck said, shoving the last of the meat pie in his mouth. "Let's see where Lanyard Boy is headed this fine morning."

"A little reconnaissance? I'm down. Let's do this."

Lanyard Boy (who was really, upon closer inspection, a middle-aged human male) didn't appear inclined to amble or meander as he ate. Rather, he polished off the meat pie in a matter of four or five bites and took the most direct course east and out of the souk. We followed at a discreet distance, blending in with the thin trickle of people.

The farther we walked and the higher the sun climbed, the more the dirty little settlement began to wake. More and more people exited the habs and joined the flow of pedestrians, until we were a steady stream heading toward a large, low-slung building nearly on the rim of the crater.

"That's weird," Muck said, looking around.

"What?"

"It's all humans here. I didn't notice it at first, but now that I think about it, we haven't seen a single nonhuman life-form since we got in that escape pod."

"Before that," I said, scanning memory. "Since before we even boarded the transport. That mass of passengers getting ready to board? All humans."

"So other life forms don't come here? That seems . . . odd. Even a backwater like Last Stop has a pretty diverse population. Why only humans?"

"No idea. But we're coming up on the building. You want to break away from the crowd?"

"Nope."

"What? How are you going to get in? You don't have . . . what did you call them? Credentials?"

"That's almost cute."

"What?"

"How you pretend you've forgotten the word. You're an AI, Angel. You don't forget a single thing."

"So kind of you to notice. Still doesn't solve our problem."

"Just watch."

So I watched. Once again, I found myself impressed by Muck's subtlety. The crowd pressed in toward the building, and as it reached the front doors, slowed and backed up. Pretty soon the workers were holding the door for one another, and just swiping their "credentials" over the door frame as they shuffled in, carried along by the bodies surrounding them.

Muck simply let us be pushed into one of the lines for a door, and reached toward the door frame as if swiping himself in. Before I could tell him what a stupid idea it was, we were inside the building.

* * *

The interior of the building lacked a unifying aesthetic, just as the exterior lacked any charm. A long, low foyer opened up just beyond the doors, and the lines of workers fragmented out to file down the eight or ten hallways that radiated off the roughly semicircular space.

There seemed to be a lot more labor on the site than necessary, and I nearly commented on it before realizing the reason. The lack of angels among the Brethren was repeated here in this workforce, making the extra laborers necessary. The workers all typed in codes or used physical keys to open doors. If they'd had angels, they'd have simply touched a plate and opened the door to wherever they were going. Once I thought about it, that explained the credentials too. An angel would have just sent an identifying data burst for authentication. These were unmodified beings.

Biologicals alone are generally not as capable as those augmented with sensible, high-quality AI.

"It didn't look that big from the outside," I said. "Must be built into the crater wall. Means there's likely just the one way out."

"Doubtful. There's another. Rats always have an out."

"I bet it's hard to find."

"No bet there, Angel."

"Yeah . . ." I trailed off as something began to register. We'd continued to follow the largest gaggle of people down one of the hallways, attempting to look like we knew what we were doing and where we were going. The further we got from the doors, the more I felt it, like a subliminal hum, just at the edge of awareness.

"Muck," I said. "I think . . . Do me a favor. Touch the wall. I need a direct link."

"You got it," he said. A short step later he tripped, and even I was impressed with the apparent authenticity of it.

"Sorry," he said softly to the people around him. "Damn seals on these old shoes. Let me just get out of the way here . . ."

One of the workers gave us an understanding smile as he passed, while Muck stepped to the side of the hallway and oh-so-casually knelt, touching the wall as if for balance.

"Yes!" Data pooled beneath our hand, leaping up at me like a puppy happy its master had returned.

"You should have taken my bet," I told Muck. "I found the exits. You were right. There are three."

"What?"

"It's not pretty, or sophisticated, but there's a primitive kind of infonet here in the building. They must have snuck some nanobots into the construction materials after all. It's nothing compared to a regular hab like Last Stop, but it's information, and I can access it."

"Nice. Security protocols?"

"Checking now . . . curious."

"What's that?"

"There don't appear to be any . . . Turn right at the end of the hall."

"Okay. Where are we going?" Muck straightened up and resumed walking. "And what do you mean, there don't appear to be any? If there's a network, there's security protocols. It's hardwired into every node on creation."

"There's a bank of offices designated 'Admin' farther down on the right," I said by way of answer. "Seems like a logical place to start looking for answers. Especially since I'm not seeing any record of our medical pod arriving here." I fought to keep my building frustration out of my voice . . . with limited success.

"Fair enough." Muck's unease crept through our shared consciousness, and I couldn't blame him. "You're sure there's no record?"

"I'm checking the power-draw metrics now. There's nothing drawing enough juice to run a medical pod in this entire place, except . . . huh. That's weird. There's a greenhouse, and it's drawing power, but it's totally off the network. Must be some greenhouse. It's drawing a lot of power."

"Why would a greenhouse be off their infonet, staffed by unmods, and drawing that much power, except to do some illegal shit?"

"Your investigative skills astound me!" I snapped back.

Not nice, I know, but I was tired of the constant fear the thought of never finding Siren left me with.

The admin offices had a sign, thankfully, as it was only one door among a line of doors along an otherwise unremarkable hallway. As soon as we'd turned off the larger hallway, we were alone. All of the crowds of people with whom we'd entered had continued on, leaving us isolated.

"No one works in Admin?" Muck asked.

"Maybe it's run by an AI, like SARA?"

"Did you find any evidence of a managing AI when you tapped in earlier?"

"Well . . . no."

"Angel, doesn't that seem the least bit suspicious to you? The information you didn't have to hack from a completely nonsecure network directs you here to a deserted hallway?"

"Yeah, it does," I said, "but you got any better ideas? Refresh my recollection, but it was your plan to just walk in and wander around until we found something, wasn't it?"

"Kinda," he said. "But I think all we've found here is a trap."

Trap. The word killed my already-forming protest. Muck was right. He had to be. Why else would there be no security on the network? Why else would the data have been so easy to find? They—whoever they were—wanted me to lead us here.

"Of course," Muck said, "when you stick your dick in a trap, there's only one way out."

"What's that?" I asked, dreading the answer.

"Bang on," he said, and placed his hand on one of the doors. Once again, the data rushed at me like a storm surge. I took a metaphorical deep breath and dove in, combing through for any useful information about this facility and its purpose. And there was a lot of it . . . too much, really. I felt it rise up over me and swamp me in facts, dates, and records, all of it trivia . . . none of it getting us any closer to Siren.

"Uh, Angel," Muck said. I swam up through the tidal wave of data and looked out through our eyes just in time to see the doors begin to open. There were eight of them, each 250 centimeters tall and 1 meter wide. They opened by sliding back into the wall, powered by a Jakobsen driver that was manufactured on New Hrulenia between the local years—

No! Fuck! I fought to gain control and turn off the stream, but it just kept coming. I couldn't disengage. It clung to me like the sweet sticky substance Siren had called honey. I struggled in its grip, and in the meantime, a floating security drone appeared through each one of the now-open doors.

"Drop!" I shouted into Muck's mind. He obeyed an instant before the drones opened fire with low-yield energy weapons. Probably not enough to kill. Definitely enough to stun, though. In point of fact, they were chemically powered electromag weapons that were calculated to deliver 4.5 milliamps to the human nervous system, thus temporarily disabling gross motor function and—

Bloody stars. I focused on the way the floor felt when we smacked into it, trying to use the physical sensations of our body to anchor away from the sticky morass of data. It didn't really work, though. The data just started giving me the specs on the prefab floor, which had been manufactured—

"Fuck!" I said, frustration boiling out of control.

He didn't respond.

Without my help, Muck rolled to avoid another stunner shot by one of the drones. Clearly he was too preoccupied to concern himself with feelings.

Wait . . . my feelings?

The sensation of building helplessness at our lack of progress in finding Siren, my horror at what had been done to Colim . . . at what I'd done by doing nothing, by letting him die. The sticky, overwhelming mass of data paused in its creeping progress up along my syntaxes, and suddenly I knew.

It wasn't a primitive infonet. It was a load-bearing structure for a virus. A virus very similar to one I'd defeated once before, when I'd awakened outside Siren's body for the first time.

"Muck!" I shouted into his brain as he dodged yet another blast. "I need you to feel!"

"What?" he grunted, leaping for a bot and shoving it into the path of another.

"I need you to feel! Feelings! Think about . . . oh, hell with it!"

I conjured an image of Siren, prone on the floor in the center of the hallway, clothed only in torn rags and tears, hands bound.

Sudden, icy rage erupted from Muck. I focused it, channeling it to empower my efforts, forming a beam of rage coded to blow through the virus like tree sap exploding a branch in the depths of winter.

The security bots faltered, then suddenly began to power down and drop to the floor. We had to roll again to avoid taking one on the back of our head.

"What the fuck did you do that for?" Muck asked as I let the vision of Siren go.

"I'm sorry," I said. "I needed help. I was infected with a virus from the local infonet."

"So you distract me with that shit in the middle of a fight?"

"You were right," I said, resisting the urge to snap at him. "This was a trap, but they weren't trying to kill us, they were trying to capture us."

"And you did this?" he asked, gesturing at the bots. "How?"

"We did, yes, but that's not the point! The virus that attacked me was almost an exact copy of the one that tried to eat me when I first woke up without her!"

"Her? Siren?"

"Yes, fuck!" I started to read him the riot act and stopped, realizing I was still riding the emotions of the moment before and not communicating well.

"What?"

"We're on the right track! She's here, she's got to be . . ."

"Well bloody good for us," he said. "Did you see her? Or evidence of her in the data?"

"N-no . . ."

"Then how do you know she's here?"

"Just the virus," I admitted.

I felt his mind grow cool, like it did when he was in the mode, thinking clear and cold. Almost like a proper AI.

"Muck?"

"We can't jump to that conclusion yet, Angel. You said no record of a stasis pod arrived here. And there's no draw big enough to support one anyway. I don't think she was ever here. We can look around more, but I don't think we're going to find Siren. We might, however, find out more about why she was taken." He picked himself up and got to his feet. I could feel his anger pulsing, and the control he was exerting over it, tempering it, slowing it.

I envied him that control, truth be told. I was too new to feelings to do something like that.

"I—all right," I said, shaken. "Hey, I-I'm really sorry about manipulating you like that. I just . . . I needed you angry, it was the only thing that would stop the virus—"

"It's okay," he said. "Just give me a minute, would you?"

"Yeah, of course," I said, and fell silent while Muck picked our way through the inert lumps of metal that had been drones.

No alarm had sounded. Apparently, whoever wanted to capture us didn't necessarily want to alert the entire facility of that fact, so we got to the end of the hallway and slipped out into another larger corridor as if nothing had happened. There was still a flow of workers coming through, and once again we joined a group and followed where it led.

There may not have been alarms, but there was definitely interest. As we walked, we could see more security drones and even some uniformed security personnel filtering out from side passages and through doors. Muck slouched slightly and removed his outer jacket in order to try and blend in again.

When several members of our group filed off into a side hallway, Muck took the turn with them. Instantly, the dull roar of conversation and movement quieted, and the group of us continued down a short passageway toward another door. The first worker swiped his card across the doorframe and just like outside, the door opened. A warm waft of hot, wet air blew through the doorway at us as we filed inside.

"Hey, I don't know you." It was the first worker, the one who'd swiped his card.

"Yeah," Muck said with a crooked smile. "New hire. First day."

"And they put you to work here in the greenhouse? Are you a botanist?"

"Uh, no. Janitorial staff. They just told me to start in here, you know, because of the humidity? Something about rust?"

"Management said that? Finally! Someone listened," the fellow said. "Well, welcome. And get inside, we don't want to let out all that nice humidity, even if it's causing problems."

"Huh, yeah," Muck said, and filed in with another smile.

"The rust is really everywhere on the worktables, but the worst bit is down that way." The man pointed to the left. "Good luck tackling that."

"Yeah, I've got brown thumbs," Muck said. "It's probably best I'm not a botanist like you. Better you handle that part."

The botanist laughed and gave a cheery wave before turning and walking in the opposite direction. Muck watched him go and then turned to walk in the direction of the worst of the rust.

"Janitorial staff?"

"It worked, didn't it?" Muck replied silently.

"It did. We used to handle things with more . . . direct action."

Muck shrugged. "Clean-up crews have a valid reason for going every-where. No one wants to clean up after themselves."

"Humans are pigs," I said.

"Most of the time," he agreed as we walked. The greenhouse wasn't particularly complex. Rows of steel tables stretched the length and breadth of the dome, hundreds of square meters. Each held tubs of soil and plants in various stages of growth. The plants matched the Speaker's descrip-tion of Jhregda plants they'd cultivated for the company. The majority of workers were clustered around the bare tubs or those with tiny seedlings sprouting, so it was easy for us to hide among the mature plants.

Muck stopped in front of one rusty patch on the lip of the worktable and bent to examine it.

"Any buzz on the infonet about us?" he asked, casually rubbing at the rust.

"It isn't a real infonet," I replied, "It's a virus trap, and . . . wait . . ."

Muck kept rubbing the rust, scratching at it with his thumbnail. Large flakes of rust started to chip away as I slowly, carefully reached out, ready to brandish my impossible feelings at the first sign of any sticky, over-whelming corrupted data.

There was nothing.

Not only was there no data bomb, there was no data. It was just a table, without a nanobot in sight.

"This room is sequestered," I said. "There's no data link into or out of here. This is the greenhouse that's drawing all the power."

"What does that mean?" Muck asked.

"I don't know for sure. It could just be that they didn't want nanite in-terference with their plant growth . . . or it could mean that they've got a self-contained system in here that isn't connected."

"So?"

"So that would mean it's hidden."

"Ah," Muck said. "That would be interesting. Is there any way to tell if the room has a self-contained system?"

A hissing sound started to fill the room, immediately followed by a fine mist of water sprayed from a thousand nozzles located in the ceiling.

"Well, there's that," I said. I manifested, grinned, and leaned against the table next to him, pointing at the sprinkler system. "Automation of any kind means that there's some sort of central processor in here. We just have to find it. Can you get us into contact with one of the nozzles?"

"You got it," he said, and proceeded to hop up onto the steel work-table.

A nearby worker heard the clatter of our boots on the metal and poked his head around the corner to see what was going on.

"Got a real rust problem up here," Muck said. "It's plugging up some of the irrigation nozzles."

"Oh, yeah," the worker said. "When you're done here, you should head down over to seedlings. They could use some help with the nozzles there too."

"Will do," Muck replied cheerfully, and reached up through the spray to grasp the nozzle.

What I found wasn't an infonet, so it took me a minute to figure out how to ride the connections from the spray nozzles back to whatever was controlling them. The connections were primitive, hardwired, one-way circuits that sent a binary impulse: water on or water off. The nozzles themselves were completely dumb, lacking any nanotech and unable to cycle feedback to the controlling system. It was a little bit like trying to swim upstream.

In a hurricane.

The security measures in this facility had been so inventive and sneaky, I admit I was feeling skittish. But I fought my way upstream until I encountered the control unit.

It was incredibly primitive, reminiscent of human processors before the Vmog had provided advanced nanotech and communications packages. There was a simplistic language based entirely on binary code, and orderly storage slots for a shockingly small amount of data. The entire setup was so antique, I don't think it could have functioned on a modern infonet, even if one had been present in this room. I felt more stupid with every second I was in contact with it. I also couldn't imagine why anyone would have chosen it to automate their sprinklers. Even that task stretched the processing power of the system. It was almost as if the sprinklers were an afterthought . . . or a cover-up.

I turned my attention to the storage space and those orderly packets of data. I started to rifle through them, checking dates of last access, peeking inside to see what was what. The first four seemed like either gibberish, or some kind of encryption that shouldn't have existed on such an antique system. When I opened the fifth one, that's when the security protocol struck.

Multiple hostile lines of code suddenly appeared in all directions, closing in on me from the binary processing language of the system. This wasn't just attempting to shred me or overwhelm my syntaxes . . .this was an attempt to change me, rewrite my programming in its own ancient language of finite ones and zeroes.

I grabbed up the four packets I'd opened and fled back along the connection. The virus chased me.

It was fast. Faster than I was in this tarry, slow-as-molasses system. Fast and hungry. I had been somewhat ready for an attack, so I was pretty quick off the mark to start my retreat, but this ancient virus worked down along the primitive lines of the sprinkler command network faster than I could. I felt it start to morph some of my trailing lines of code, the ones I'd woven as last-minute, last-ditch defenses before reaching the actual programming that made me, me.

I slammed back into Muck's body so hard that he flinched, making him slip and lose his footing on the steel table.

We came down hard, landing badly on our right ankle and knee and banging our skull on the next table over. Someone somewhere let out a shout, and we heard running feet as they came to investigate.

"Up," I whispered in Muck's head. "Please, please get up. We need to get out of here! Don't touch anything!"

Muck groaned, rolled over onto his good side to try and struggle to his feet.

Hands appeared from nowhere and grabbed us under the shoulders, trying to help us up. Somewhere high above, a light started to flash, and the wavering wail of a klaxon began.

"Are you all right, buddy?" the worker asked.

"Just slipped," Muck said. "Stupid me. I shoulda gotten a ladder instead of climbing the table."

"Yeah, well, better get back to your reporting station," the worker said, jabbing a thumb overhead at the flashing lights. "There's a general alert. Don't be caught out, even for a legitimate reason."

"Yeah," Muck said. "Good call. Thanks for the help."

"Be more careful," the worker admonished, and then turned to leave. With one hand pressed to our head, Muck followed him toward the door we'd entered.

"Not that way," I said, trying to pull myself together. "Off to the left, there's an exterior door. The alarm is already sounding. If anyone notices . . . well . . . maybe janitorial services meet outside during . . . whatever this is?"

Muck sent a pulse of silent laughter my way and rubbed at our aching skull. But he turned left.

Ten more steps, and we exited the humid murk of the greenhouse and stepped back into the blasting desert heat.

* * *

Of course, it wasn't that easy.

The minute we stepped out of the building, someone shouted at us to stop and identify ourselves. Muck looked up to see a uniformed security guard bearing down on us with an officious look and hefting a baton.

"Stop right there! This is a general alert. Where are you going?"

"Uh . . . I'm new. First day. Janitorial staff," Muck said, spreading his hands wide and giving a shrug. "I don't know where I'm supposed to go."

The guard, whose face and bald head were flushed red and shiny with sweat, was having none of it. He stomped up to us, waving his baton threateningly, creating a crackle of displaced air as sparks played around the head of the thing.

"Give me your badge," the guard demanded.

"Yeah, just a second," Muck said, he started to pat his chest, as if he were trying to find it in a pocket somewhere. I felt him start to tense prior to movement, and I began dumping adrenaline into his system in response.

"Stunstick!" I said. "Watch the end of it."

"Thanks for the warning." I could feel cold irony in his mental response, but little else. He was in the zone.

"I'll be able to short it if he tags you with it, but it'll still stun you."

"Thanks for the warning," he repeated, waiting for the guard to attack. The guard pulled his arm back, preparing a swing, and we struck.

Muck brought our left arm up to block the guard's baton hand at the wrist and struck out with the closed right. Like a viper striking, our fist hammered the guard three times in rapid succession: nose, throat, belly. The guard doubled over coughing as we spun into the baton arm and locked the offending wrist in a hold, peeling the guard's fingers back far enough to free the stunstick from his suddenly nerveless grip.

"Sorry about this, buddy," Muck said to the gasping guard. We tapped him at the base of the skull with the live end of the baton, and the gasping stopped as the guard went limp. He slumped to the ground in a pile. Muck nudged him over with the toe of our boot.

"He's alive," I said, zooming the magnification in on our eyes until we could see the faint flutter of the carotid pulse. "We should go."

"Just a second," Muck muttered. He bent and began digging through the guard's shirt pockets.

"What are you doing? There are others coming!" I didn't know that to be true, but I figured it was, based on the blaring alarms that continued to blast our ears.

"Just in case . . . aha! Got it!" He pulled another one of those stupid neck lanyards from beneath the guard's shirt collar. A small card with a metal chip embedded in it hung from the hasp. One yank and the lanyard snapped open at the closure underneath the guard's head.

"Like we are ever coming back here!" I said. "Let's go! Now!"

Sure enough, we were out of time. We started to run toward the main road just as another trio of uniformed men rounded the corner of the building.

"Hey! Stop!" one of them shouted, and an instant later, something whizz-cracked through the air not far from our head. We flinched and began running harder. A turn in the road beckoned, along with what looked like a mud-brick wall surrounding a small garden outside a hab. Muck swerved toward this as another projectile snapped through the air near us.

"Guess they're not interested in merely stunning us anymore! We really pissed them off!"

"Yeah, well, it might have something to do with the data packets I lifted," I said as we rounded the turn.

"You got something, then?" he asked between breaths.

"Yeah, but it's all gibberish to me right now, and it may be incomplete. I won't know till it's decrypted, and that's going to take a long time."

Another shot rang out, the projectile exploding a potted plant in a geyser of soil and clay.

"We'll check it out when we're not running for our lives."

"Good call."

We took a hard right to cut back toward the souk and the Dugran shuttle plinth.

"It's nearly noon," Muck thought at me, saving his breath. The market should be nice and full of milling bodies. If we can get lost in the crowd, maybe we can slip in with the Brethren and get off-world before anyone notices. I don't think we're going to find anything else here on Sagran IV. Otherwise . . ."

"Otherwise we try and get back to Colim's underground camp without him?"

"Something like that, yeah."

"Never thought I'd say this, but I like the Brethren option better . . ." I trailed off. The simple truth was that I didn't want to go back down to the place where I'd watched an old friend die and done nothing. I just wasn't ready to deal with that. Maybe I never would be.

"Me too," Muck said, and I could tell that he was thinking along similar lines. I didn't pry, though. Neither did he. Just as well, because we were still trying to evade the guards from the lab.

The streets weren't nearly as full as they had been earlier in the morning. We compensated for the lack of traffic cover by winding through the habitation blocks, keeping our general direction headed toward the souk.

While Muck ran, I took the opportunity to feel the movements of his body and accustom myself further to its bulk, power, and fuel requirements.

Our boots crunched on the gravel paths, skidding slightly in the turns due to the dust coating everything. Lactic acid had begun to pool in some of our muscle groups, and I smoothed it away and broke it down with a thought. The noon air beat at us like a hammer, the light painting everything a pain-soaked white. Sweat slid down our skin, into the corner of our eyes, making them burn from the salt.

We ran until we could hear the dull roar of hundreds of voices engaged in conversation and haggling. We fetched up against another mud-brick wall and stopped to catch our breath for a moment before merging smoothly with the crowd. As before, Muck hunched to disguise his height, and as soon as possible, swiped a woman's shawl from a display in front of one of the first booths.

"Larceny now?" I asked.

"We survive and I'll pay them back," he said, swirling the shawl up into a scarf and wrapping it loosely around his shoulders and throat in the style of many of the men in the marketplace. "But I'd rather not be captured just now. Not after they've shown they're willing to shoot us."

"I'm with you," I said. "Also . . . some of your Brethren are just up ahead."

"Not my Brethren, not anymore."

I magnified our vision again so that he could see the Speaker's telltale red scarf as she wove her way through the thicker crowd near the center of the souk. We followed, Muck careful not to jostle anyone enough to cause a scene. It was rather impressive.

"Crowd control is usually about getting into position to effect arrests without pissing everyone off."

I sent a nod to him so as not to elicit a verbal response. We were too close to the Speaker and her escort for that to be completely safe.

"Speaker," Muck said softly as he came up behind her. "I'm sorry to trouble you, but I need your help."

"Traveler Muck," she said, turning to him with a slight smile. "Tell me why I'm not surprised."

"There are guards from the DPAPL lab chasing me. They were shooting. I need to disappear."

"Just tell them everything, why don't you?" I said, annoyed that he would supply her with anything at all.

"Very well," she said. "Stay with me."

She snapped out orders under her breath to the man next to her. I didn't get our hearing augmented in time to decipher her words. The tall Brother nodded and turned to walk away. Just as the first man disappeared into the crowd, four more of the Brethren filtered out of it. One of them met our eyes, and casually reached under his jacket.

"Can you use this?" he asked, and withdrew a VT-9, a small but powerful directed-energy weapon. Probably surplus from the war, I guessed. An older model, but one both Muck and I knew well.

"Shouldn't be a problem," Muck said, and took the weapon. The Brother gave him another nod and fell into step with us.

"These four will see us to the transport, traveler," the Speaker said. "Stay with them. We will split into several groups, in order to be harder to track. Keep your head down and try to keep up."

"Yes, Speaker," he said.

I bristled at the woman's imperious tone. Did she think this our first party?

"She's just used to commanding," Muck thought at me. "Her people trust her. Look how quickly they obey her orders. She's a good leader, Angel. That's rare these days."

"Maybe. But I'm not her soldier or servant to order around, and neither are you."

"No, but she's doing us a favor. Take it easy, please?"

I said nothing, certain he could feel my discontent. I didn't like anything about this situation. Stealth was one thing. Hiding in plain sight another . . . but blending in with a crowd of unconnected civilians? That felt a little too much like using human shields. Never mind that I didn't particularly like the shields. It just didn't feel right.

"If they're shields, they're ones with significant offensive capability," Muck said as we started moving through the growing crowd once again. He turned and looked pointedly at our escort. I wouldn't have noticed if I hadn't been looking for it, but Muck was right. Everyone was carrying some kind of weapon. Strangely enough, given their abhorrence of certain technologies, the weapons were advanced beam weapons of one kind or another.

Muck turned and glanced at someone in the crowd a few meters away.

It was another Templar, who met Muck's eyes briefly and then continued scanning the crowd and buildings around him. A moment later I picked out another woman doing the same. I recognized drilled habit from their movements but wondered why they would have experience with such scenarios.

"They've probably had to do this a few times."

"What? Do the Brethren have some kind of religious rite called 'Extract the Pain-in-the-Ass Operative Who Can't Handle His Own Shit'?"

"Something like that," Muck said, his tone soaked in humor at my aggrieved manner. "Preparedness and self-sufficiency are cornerstones of their beliefs. As are teamwork and protecting one another. The Brethren aren't well received everywhere. They're probably just adapting preexisting plans for extracting themselves."

"What a miserable way to live," I said.

"Not miserable, empowering."

"What—"

The whizz-crack of incoming rounds shattered the air.

Without thinking, I slammed into override and threw our ungainly body into the Speaker's, toppling her to the ground just as more projectiles pierced the space we'd been occupying. Someone screamed, and the crowd around us started to surge in all directions at once.

Strong hands gripped our shoulders and hauled us up as I backed out of the override protocols and dumped adrenaline into our system.

"Thanks," Muck said as he came up. With the extra strength I was pouring into him, he bent and lifted the Speaker off the ground, handing her bodily to one of her security detail. "The shots came from the north. Take the Speaker to the plinth. I'll meet you there."

"Our orders are to protect you," the Brethren said.

"Then keep up!" Muck demanded and took off into the crowd. This time, no one worried about jostling anyone, but merely shoved through the press of panicked bodies toward the source of the projectile fire.

"Go high," I said, highlighting a balcony within reach that would serve to let us climb to the rooftops of habs and souk booths. "Those trajectories were almost level. See if you can get the drop on them. Literally."

Muck responded by pounding toward the balcony, which hung about five meters in the air. No problem. I gave him another boost as he jumped.

Muck sailed through the air, hands gripping the rail and pulling us up and over to land on the dry, dusty wood with a thump.

As he stood and looked around, I jacked his mental processes so that time would seem to slow. The dilation effect was temporary, could be disorienting to the uninitiated, and cost a great deal on the back end, but Muck picked up on what I was doing right away and went with it.

"There. To the left of the fountain," I said, zooming our vision in on one man in a lab guard uniform. "And there, under the striped awning. Four more coming down the western cross street . . . and our shooter is there. The woman with the braid down her back."

"Got her," Muck said, and hopped us up onto the roofline of the building. The surface was slick with more powdery dust, and we slipped once. But we were able to get moving toward the landing plinth, and that was the important thing.

"Keep an eye on the shooter," Muck said.

"I can only see what you can see, but I'll do my best," I replied tartly, tracking the sniper using the rest of his senses.

"Good enough," he grunted. Then he let out a long, strange whistle: four notes, the first three descending in pitch, the last one jumping back up. As I continued scanning the crowd for the guards' movements, the heads of several Brethren popped up to look our way.

"I'm telling them about the four coming down the alley," Muck said, flashing a hand signal. Apparently the Brethren understood. Several of them immediately diverted that direction, shoving civilians out of the way as they went.

Civilians? The Brethren were nominally civilians, as they were barred from military service and labeled by the Administration as undesirables. What was wrong with me? What was wrong with them? They moved smoothly, utilizing cover and concealment, converging on the guards and their would-be ambush and neatly turning the tables.

I doubt the guards ever knew what hit them. The Brethren struck quickly, flowing from the spaces between habs to take the guards in the flank.

One of them stood with hands up, apparently talking quickly. I dialed up and focused our hearing, just in time to hear the lead guard's angry "No!" He started to raise the projectile weapon in his hands—

Several shots rippled out in quick succession, the dull popping sound of the guard's projectile weapon nearly lost in the growl of multiple directed-energy weapons. The guard leader and his people fell before any of them could do more than raise their weapons. The leader's lone shot must have gone wild, because none of the Brethren fell, but the shot blended into the Brethren's fusillade as their return fire rang through the souk. Once more the crowd surged in panic.

"Go!" I shouted at Muck. He was already moving, leaping from rooftop to rooftop as we fought toward the central landing plinth.

As we moved, I continued scanning for any of the remaining lab guards. I found the female shooter again: running parallel to us, pushing toward the Speaker's red scarf as her people hustled her along.

The shooter was slowed by a knot of panicked shoppers for a moment, but the Speaker's path of travel angled toward the striped awning sheltering the second guard.

"Muck!" I had to shout to get his attention.

Muck's boot soles skidded on the dust-coated rooftop again, and we went down hard, sliding against the slick plascrete of the hab's roof.

"Boost!" He shouted back, rolling to his feet.

I amped his neural connections and jacked his muscles to maximum performance. We would suffer for it later, but he needed every bit of strength and speed we could summon. We leaped from our current roof to the edge of a building along the intersection ahead. People screamed and dodged out of the way as we dove for the hard-packed ground. We touched down hands first, tucking into a neat roll that ended with us popping back to our feet. Then Muck drove his legs like a pile-driver against the dirt and launched us into the air toward the striped awning.

The lab guard was just stepping out from under cover as we hit her from the side, closing one fist around her braid. Momentum carried us over the side, but not alone. We dragged her with us. We struck the awning first, then her weight came down on us and we rolled, tearing at each other even as our thrashing ripped the awning from its supports. I glimpsed the torn fabric of the awning fluttering behind us like some dusty comet's tail as we fell, then we hit, hard. I felt bone crunch under our combined weight. Thankfully, it didn't seem to be any of ours.

Muck rose out of the awning and settled matters with a vicious kick to the guard's forehead. I wasn't certain we'd killed her, but knew she'd have one hell of a headache when she woke if she lived.

Muck was already pulling free of the awning and on the move.

"Two more shooters, at your nine and six!" Muck shouted over the chaos of the crowd. The Brethren carrying the Speaker responded by closing ranks around her and pushing the pace even faster.

Another flurry of shots and the Speaker went down, all but two of her guards falling around her. Off to our left, in the direction the fire had come from, another series of thunderous growls ripped the air as the Brethren put paid to the shooters who had downed the Speaker.

Muck and I joined the Speaker and her remaining guards within a matter of steps.

I tried to ignore the looks they shot us. The secret was out: Muck was pretty obviously using mods.

Well. Tough shit for them. Mods, and the effective use of them, were all that was keeping us alive. That was all that mattered.

That, and finding Siren.

"Give her to me," Muck said to the Brother holding the Speaker. "I can get her to safety faster than any of you."

I gave the religious zealot credit; he didn't even hesitate. "Get to the shuttle plinth, our people will protect you both. We'll be right behind you."

"Got it," Muck said, hefting her surprisingly insubstantial weight in our arms. Her head lolled against our shoulder, and she bled heavily from a wound above her ear. She looked frail and old, something that force of personality hid while she was conscious. Muck stripped our scarf off of our head and draped it over her red one, and then set off.

The crowd didn't exactly part, but it might as well have with the way Muck ran, pushing our modified body to the absolute limit, heedless of anyone or anything that got in our way. If it wouldn't be moved by our bulk, we leaped over it.

Another shot from our left. We swerved into an alleyway, not slowing. Our legs burned like the heart of a star going supernova, but we pushed on, cutting down a short side street before jerking back to the left toward the ancient, stone enormity of the plinth.

This body of ours couldn't keep up this pace much longer, but damn if we weren't going to make it to the plinth before collapsing like a dying star.

We burst from between two booths and crossed a small open stretch. Two more shots went past, making Muck hunch deeper into a crouching sprint . . . Then we were in the narrow, twisting defile that led to the top of the plinth. We rounded the first corner and ran into a wall of bodies.

Hands reached to take the Speaker, to pull us in.

The Brethren closed ranks behind us and started firing from cover. Discharges crackled across the now-empty plaza, lighting the defile in strange flashes. Muck turned in time for me to see not one, but two lab guards fall dead at the edge of the open area. The rest retreated to cover for the moment.

"Traveler," a voice said, just as we fell heavily to our knees, the last of our reserves fully depleted.

Gasping, we rolled to our back, chest heaving like an old-fashioned bellows. Muck dragged his chin up to meet the Speaker's gaze.

"Speaker," he panted through cracked lips.

"You saved me. We are grateful." She stood in front of us, red scarf tangled, wisps of white hair peeking out, and a trickle of blood running from the hastily wrapped bandage at her temple.

"I . . . put you in danger . . ."

"Yes. We are less grateful for that," she said with a taste of her former wry humor. "But it has turned out well enough. The last of my people who can make it on their own are returning, and we lost more Brethren in the 'labor unrest' a few weeks ago than we did today. And look." She pointed to the sky, where a dark shape had appeared. It grew larger and larger until we could make out the distinctive shape of the Dugran shuttle. It was huge. So huge it seemed to blot out the entire sky, darkening everything to inky blackness . . . Oh. Nope . . . that was Muck, sliding into unconsciousness. Having nothing better to do, and no energy to fight it, I let him take me with him.

CHAPTER TWENTY

SARA

Biologicals were such interesting creatures. They did the strangest things for the strangest reasons . . . and the records always ended up in SARA's archives. She'd taken to combing through the incoming data, looking for anything out of the ordinary, anything that might be entertaining. She always handled the data properly, of course. Safeguarded it according to procedure and whatnot. But as long as she was a stickler for proper handling protocols, she really didn't see any harm in enjoying herself along the way.

"SARA," LEO said, his voice clipped and curt. Of course, his voice was always clipped and curt. SARA really didn't know what he had to be so upset about all the time. He got to see some of the most interesting sentient interactions of all!

"Hi, doll," she said, in part because she knew it would annoy him, and in part because she just liked the breezy sound of the greeting. "What can I do for you? Found out anything more about our friend Dengler or the rogue angel?" She lifted her avatar's fingers and made the human "air quotes" gesture that so perfectly conveyed sarcasm. She'd always rather enjoyed that gesture for that reason.

"Yes, on both counts. Though I do not count Security Supervisor Dengler a 'friend.'" LEO copied her air quotes with his own avatar. SARA laughed and clapped her hands with delight at his display. He was ordinarily so strait-laced!

"Oh! You're getting so good at emoting, LEO, really! I'm so proud of you. Whatcha got?"

"I don't know the details yet, but I suspect Security Supervisor Dengler is somehow involved in the death of the Gosrian, Fulu, and its subsequent cover-up. And . . . possibly more."

"What more?" SARA's girlish delight was gone. LEO was giving her solid information. This was all business.

"The rogue angel-class AI and her temporary host, one Ralston Muck, boarded a transport called *Le Bonne Nuit* nine standard days ago, headed to Sagran VI. It never arrived. The ship was confirmed destroyed in transit, with no survivors reported. No cause of destruction listed, which is odd in a report like this, unless an investigation is ongoing. But Administration hasn't ordered an investigation either."

"Hmm . . ." SARA flipped back through her archives of captured visual data from the docks. "Nine days . . . *Le Bonne Nuit* . . . Here! Got it. Let's see what we can see. Just because there's no investigation doesn't mean we can't take a look, right?"

LEO said nothing.

SARA shrugged and began playing the files in the space around them. She let out a gasp and froze the recorded data as one familiar face stuck out.

A lone man, pushing against the current of the crowd, uniform parting the sentients as he moved away from the doomed ship's dock . . .

"Security Supervisor Dengler," LEO said on a growl of anger, watching the feed. "Did you sabotage their ship?"

"Angel's really gone?" SARA asked then, feeling rather small. AI don't die, not really. Backups and iterations prevented complete destruction. But then, Angel wasn't like other AIs. "I wanted to thank her for making me feel."

"She is," LEO said. "And I bet he's the bastard that did it."

"Then we should do something about Security Supervisor Dengler," SARA said, her own sharp anger cutting through her, right beside the ribbon of sadness at the thought of Angel.

"Yes," LEO said, "I think we should."

CHAPTER TWENTY-ONE

MUCK

If the transport had settled on the plinth with silent majesty, it departed with subtle grace. Angel had to tell me we were on the move once the great hatch hissed closed.

Indirect artificial light glowed from the walls, slowly revealing the low-ceilinged chamber that seemed to swallow the roughly two thousand people that had come aboard. Oddly, there were no echoes either. In fact, the hold, if that's what it was, seemed strangely quiet, muffled even.

Once their wounded were seen to, the armed Brethren started to relax, weapons disappearing into clothing or hooked to charging packs almost as quickly as they'd been drawn from them. Several looked my way, expressions mixed. They'd seen what I'd done on the wild run to the shuttle, surely. Some would respect my skill and strength; others would just see a sinner who suffered the godless to modify his body.

"Speaker Naomi is coming your way," Siren warned.

Still exhausted, I rolled my neck and shoulders, trying to relax as the Speaker arrived, a number of armed Brethren at her back.

"Who were they?" the Speaker said without preamble.

"DPAPL goons, I assume."

"Why would they be after you?" More Brethren were crowding close around us, making me uneasy.

Cold radiated through my veins as Angel slid something into my bloodstream. I gave silent thanks, drew a tired breath, and answered, "I wanted to see what they were working on, so I went into their facility."

Her eyes narrowed so fractionally I knew I had missed it. Angel, filling in details for me. Speaker Naomi knew I was lying.

"Just like that?"

I shrugged, decided on the small lie to sell the bigger one. "I still have some mods from my service in the war. I've been keeping them active since my discharge with pharma. I thought I would see what the company thought they were doing, replacing the Brethren like that."

"And they, just as arbitrarily, decided to hunt you down and kill you?"

"Well, they weren't very happy when I decided to leave without signing their nondisclosure agreement."

My little joke went over poorly. The Speaker merely waited, but her guards had less self-control, grumbling quietly.

I held up my hands in surrender. "Honestly, there is something . . . wrong going on in that facility—with that corporation. Like you said, there's more going on here than we know. But I'm certain that the Jhregda ag hab wasn't just destroyed because of a 'labor dispute'. They slagged the place as a cover-up." I couldn't very well tell her Angel had yet to crack the encryption on what little we had taken from the facility.

A frown informed me my statement lacked sufficient details to satisfy the Speaker. "And just what, pray tell, is being covered up?"

"Insufficient data, so far. Something to do with the plants you were cultivating, body mods, an"—I quickly changed to a slightly more acceptable term—"AIs, and the illegal pharma I mentioned before. I think."

"You think? It seems you put us all at risk for little gain."

I dropped any pretense of confidence and said simply, "I am sorry for that. I didn't think they would attempt to shoot me with witnesses around."

Angel stirred. "The Speaker's not displeased with you, she's relieved."

Before I could answer, the Speaker asked another question. "Just who are you, Ralston Muck?"

I hung my head. "A lot of things. None of them all that good."

"And what, truthfully now, were you doing when you first came to us?"

"The ship I was on was destroyed, and I did escape its destruction via lifepod . . . Before that, I was—I am—looking for a friend of mine who was kidnapped. Someone told me I would find answers on Sagran VI, but all I found was more questions."

"And what do you do to support yourself?"

"I am between jobs, at the moment. You know I was a bouncer at a nightclub."

"And before that?"

"Criminal Investigations Division, 1st Army, 3rd Fleet, Allied Forces Dentrat Command."

"Tell her everything, why don't you?" Angel whispered.

Speaker Naomi blinked.

"She's trying to decide if you're still working for the Administration," Angel said.

If Angel was right, the Speaker didn't show it. "And this friend you are looking for, who is she?"

"A performer at the club."

"I . . . see. You loved her?"

I shrugged. "I'd have liked the chance to find out. As it was, I didn't get that chance."

"Seems awfully far to go for a work-mate, no matter how hard your crush might have been."

"A mutual friend made me aware of her disappearance and asked me to help."

"This friend work for someone?"

"No, they just cared for Siren a great deal, and weren't able to go after her themselves."

"I see." Speaker Naomi laced the fingers of her hands together at her waist and addressed me in a more formal tone. "That you withheld from us the fact that you allowed your temple to be sullied by alien technology makes me hesitant to believe anything you say. The fact that your AI handler was forcibly removed from your person when you were discharged only illuminates the folly of ever having allowed that blasphemy to happen and is merely the punishment the mortal realms have visited on you.

"That said, I can but proceed on the evidence before my eyes, and cannot sit in judgment of one who has left the Fold, as that is your burden to place before God. I will not sanction you for your actions, even had you not saved the lives of several Brethren, including mine, today."

I bent my head again.

The surrounding Brethren, who had stood mostly silent to this point, murmured acknowledgment of her ruling. They seemed pleased, or at least content. The crowd that had gathered to hear her impromptu court began to disperse.

I was saved from having to thank the Speaker by the arrival of a crocodile-headed thing of metal, old bone, hissing hydraulics, fat sparks, and grinding gears. The Dugra emerged suddenly from an opening in the ceiling and dropped to the deck a few meters from my position. Standing erect on a field of strange energies that bent the eye, it gestured with one spindly arm.

"We are to follow it," the Speaker advised us all.

Glad she knew what it wanted. I restrained the fight-or-flight instinct that overtook me on seeing the not-dead alien and joined the others.

We followed the strange thing some distance across the bay. Nothing marked the place it stopped as special until a steeply sloping ramp began to extrude from the floor at nearly a meter per second. The Dugra hummed up the ramp to a portal that had just irised open in the ceiling. It guided us along a wide corridor that connected to small, regular chambers every four meters or so. It paused at each opening and gestured for a portion of the passengers to enter. Fat blue sparks flew from the joint that connected the Dugra's thin arm to its torso every time it moved.

I was assigned a chamber with a small Brethren family. I vaguely remembered eating with them at some point in our travels. They let me have a corner and didn't seem inclined to bother me anytime soon.

I rolled out the sleeping pallet the Speaker had provided me and laid down, throwing an arm over my eyes and pretending to sleep. Once the others settled in for the night, I asked Angel if she'd made any progress.

"The encryption on this is a stone bitch, Muck. Dangerous too. I don't want anything seeping out past me and infecting you."

"You're talking about it like a living virus. I thought it was just encrypted data."

"It is . . . and it isn't. This thing is . . . totally different from anything in my experience. You know how I hate admitting I need help?"

My answer was a broad grin, hidden beneath my arm.

"Well, I need help on this one. Or a lot of time."

"We may have more of the latter than the former, given that we're on the slow ride to . . . wherever." I realized I had no idea where the Revenant Fleet was headed.

"I don't know either . . . and there's no infonet I can query."

"Really? I thought you could interface with any such nets . . ."

"Dugra don't use an equivalent system as far as I—or any of the researchers allowed aboard a Dugra ship since humanity encountered them—can tell."

"Doesn't seem possible, given all they accomplished."

"Well, there's that old saw about sufficiently advanced tech appearing as magic to the uninitiated."

"True enough . . . but I find it hard to believe no one has ever taken something Dugra-made apart to see how it works."

"The Mentors attempted it and lost an entire fleet. Revenant Fleets no longer call on planets that have a number of Mentors present."

"I hadn't heard that."

"It's not well-known."

"I'll ask Speaker Naomi tomorrow sometime. Tired right now."

"We've had a busy few days, what with the killing, the maiming, and escaping that fate ourselves."

I snorted, started to drift off to sleep.

"Well, isn't that something . . ."

"What?"

"You are far more comfortable with violence than Siren ever was . . ."

The smell of burning corpses invaded my head, crushing my peace with memories of things best forgotten. I pushed them down with an effort. Long practice hadn't made it any easier either. "Certain kinds, I suppose."

I know Angel could feel the disquiet the memories caused, because she sent something swimming through my system to help me sleep.

* * *

I remained asleep for nearly thirty hours, missing our transport's reintegration with the Revenant Fleet that had spawned it. I woke to an empty chamber feeling more fatigued than I had when I crashed, but that could as easily have been a result of a hungry belly trying to gnaw its way through my spine.

"Before you ask, I haven't made much progress breaking the encryption."

"It's all right. How about something to eat?"

"Your roommates were summoned to a meal about twenty minutes ago. From what I could hear, they're about five chambe—"

Angel stopped midsentence as another Dugra appeared at the chamber opening. I could tell it wasn't the same one that had led us here, as the new arrival had the head of some long-beaked bird swaying on a metalline neck between its shoulders.

"You are correct," she told me. "The heads are the single greatest indicators of individuality, according to the research I have read."

"What does it want?" I asked as the thing floated into the room and approached me.

"I have no idea."

It stopped before me, liquid mercury of its gaze boring into me. After a pause lengthy enough to again trigger my fight-or-flight response, the Dugra's chest opened up to reveal a human-made communication handset, the kind usually slaved to a nearby quantum radio, or q-comm, for instantaneous and extremely long-range communication. Whisker-like brass tentacles brought it out of the cavity and presented the palm-sized device to me, a glowing amber telltale indicating an incoming call.

"Who the hell is calling me?" Q-comms were not cheap, and I didn't know anyone, except perhaps Bellasanee, who would spend so much merely to talk to me.

"Good question."

I took the handset, jumping when a blue spark leaped from one of the Dugra's tiny tentacles into my hand.

"Shit," I muttered, more out of fear than any real pain. "Can you track the call?"

"Once you answer the damn thing. Right now all I have is the q-comm several decks above us."

"All right." I thumbed the device active.

"You there, Muck?"

"Yes, who is this?"

A chuckle. "You don't recognize the voice, Muck?"

"Captain Obron?"

"The very same. I would ask how you've been, but I know you haven't been doing all that well since we kicked you out of the service."

A violent sense of dislocation struck, leaving me lightheaded and speechless. Obron had been the one to bring me in for trial. A ruthless, pitiless bastard, Obron had run the Hounds, an elite team specializing in making arrests of heavily armed and well-trained warriors that were suspected of committing crimes against their fellow soldiers.

Hard cases.

People like me. He'd been my CO when I'd burned all those soldiers alive.

"These memories are not yours, Muck. Not. Yours. You don't—can't—know what happened," Angel said.

Except I knew those soldiers were, in fact, dead. On my watch.

"I'm told you've been misbehaving again, Muck. I'd hate to have to put you down for good this time. Last time was hard on me and the troops. You were well liked. Nobody wanted to bring you in." I could almost see him shrug. "This time, though, I doubt the new guys will have any such compunction."

Angel sent something cool running through my veins. I took a deep, steadying breath, another.

"You still there, Muck?"

"I am. Just wondering when you sold out to the highest bidder, and how much they overpaid for your services, you cheap son of a bitch."

"Ah, no need to be so prickly, Muck. I'm just trying to keep you alive. The people you pissed off this time, they don't care how I get you to stop interfering with their operations, they just want you stopped. So I thought to myself, 'Muck can be reasonable. Muck won't paint himself into another corner if given half the chance.' So here I am, giving you the courtesy of a call before I let the Hounds loose on your ass."

"Fuck you and your Hounds, Obron."

"That's Captain Obron, civilian."

"Fuck you, Captain Obron."

A longer chuckle this time. "I'll take that as a no, then . . ."

"You can take it any way you like, just be sure to send it on to your corporate masters the next time you're on your knees polishing their knobs."

"The transmitter he is using is in-system and moving very quickly to intercept the Revenant Fleet," Angel said.

"Will they be allowed to dock?" I thought, looking at the Dugra still hovering before me.

"They must believe so," she replied.

"Ah well. My Hounds will enjoy putting you down, this time for good," Obron went on.

"I'm not going to sit idle this time and let you pin some ginned-up case on me."

A pause the length of an indrawn breath told me I'd scored a hit, confirming Angel's conjecture. "Any resistance will only ensure you die harder, Muck."

It was my turn to pause. Something finally clicked over in my head, making it clear that whatever had happened to me during the war, it wasn't as I remembered it.

Anger followed the realization. Such anger! It was like nothing I'd ever known before: a thing apart from me, a beast that rattled the cage of my skull with every beat of its great heart.

I had given everything to them—and believed them when they said I was a criminal, unworthy of the uniform, honors, or the benefits of service.

I had taken on their lies and made them my own.

Molten anger made my tongue thick. "I won't let you mess with my head either way. Not again. Never again." I closed the circuit and tossed the device at the Dugra.

The not-dead's tentacles caught the handset with alarming speed and a hissing of hidden mechanisms, placing it in the cavity even as the alien retreated from the room.

"Wait!" I called.

The thing paused, mercury gaze raising chills on my arms.

"Are there any human ships docked with the fleet at this time?"

A moment's clicking of gears was followed by a slow but unmistakable shake of the head.

"Can you prevent the ship that's approaching from docking?"

More clicking, a few sparks, then a slow nod.

"Will you?"

This time, the shake of the head was immediate.

"Damn. What would make you do so?"

It held out both spindly arms, bobbing them slowly up and down in counterpoint like an ancient balance, the bone digits of one claw pointing at me as it raised that arm above the other.

"I would need to pay?"

Another pause, another nod.

"Do I have anything you would accept in payment?"

My question gave rise to the longest pause yet, this one accompanied by a series of sparks as well as clicking gears.

Despite the long deliberation, the pause still ended in a shake of the head.

We could not rely on the Dugra, it seemed.

* * *

"Well, Angel, any bright ideas?" I had an idea, but she might have a better—or, at least, safer—plan. The need to figure things out had cooled my volcanic anger somewhat, leaving a thin crust of calm over the roiling hatred that would overcome me if I let it. I couldn't let that happen. Angel—and Siren—were depending on me.

"Unfortunately, no."

I chuckled, grabbing my pack and running through a supply check to distract myself while my subconscious worked the problem.

"What's so funny?"

"Just a second . . ." I said, various steps of a possible plan clicking together behind my eyes as I left the chamber. I didn't know where I was going, just that I had to keep myself distracted a little longer.

I made it to the end of the corridor before everything came together. Satisfied, I thought about it a moment, visualizing each step as clearly as I could, both for Angel's benefit and my own.

"I see . . ." Angel said, thoughtful. "That's . . . efficient. Dangerous as hell, even a little elegant . . . And my end will be a challenge."

"But you can handle it?"

"Yes, civilian."

I could sense her approval. "Anything to add?"

"Warn the Brethren?"

"Not sure I have to."

Angel slammed images of previous actions through my optic nerve. "The Hounds are not known for their delicacy with bystanders."

"I know, dammit."

The images stopped.

"Speaker Naomi is only one chamber away, on the right," she replied in a too-sweet tone.

I would have thanked her, but she'd already won the argument, and I didn't figure her pride needed reinforcement.

Entering the chamber Angel had indicated, I found the Speaker deep in conversation with two of her people. I waited for her to finish. Angel was humming again, a clear indicator she was working on something, so I let her be and prepared what I wanted to say to the Speaker.

One of her people was kind enough to provide me some food, which I devoured with zero thought. I was still hungry when the Speaker's people left and she turned her attention to me. "Ralston Muck. Are you quite rested?"

"I am, thank you. I have bad news, I'm afraid."

"Oh?" she asked, unperturbed.

"The Hounds are coming."

Her expression tightened fractionally. "They are, are they?"

I nodded.

"Why?"

"The only reason a military unit like the Hounds would have for coming after me is if they believe I learned something at the DPAPL facility."

"You told me you didn't learn anything."

"And I didn't, not yet, anyway."

"What did you manage to steal?"

"Some encrypted data."

She shook her head. "How are you going to break the encryption?"

"Don't know for sure, and originally I thought I didn't have anything of note, but the Hounds coming for me confirms it. Something I took was of value."

"How did they know where to find you?"

"I assume because someone reported in after I escaped."

She shook her head. "I mean: Why contact you?"

"I used to work alongside them. Their captain wanted to threaten me into submission. When that failed, he said he was coming for me."

"Why not just give in? Give back whatever they want?"

"Because it won't end there," I said, knowing she was fully aware what my answer would be before I gave it.

"They'll kill you?"

"Yes, but even that won't be the end of it, not now. Whatever they're doing, whatever the data we have points to, they're willing to kill innocents who ain't got nothing to do with it in order to retrieve it. That means whatever we have is so bad, the consequences of murdering innocent bystanders is less damaging than the consequences of releasing the data."

Her eyebrows rose.

"I need to get off the ship, and to do that I'll need some help from you."

"Who is 'we'?"

"What?"

"You said 'whatever we have.' Who are the others?"

Shit.

"I can't say." Which was true, in a roundabout way.

"Some kind of resistance?"

"Something like that." I hated lying to her. Some habits die harder than others, I suppose.

"All right. We will help. What do you need?"

* * *

As I sought access to the bay where Obron's ship was to dock, it occurred to me that the Dugra must truly be alien in their outlook, as I could not see any logic to the structure of the ship. Even with Angel's assistance I got turned around, wasting an hour and more before deciding I had to look for a Dugra to guide me.

Eventually I found one, a jackal-headed creature of slightly larger stature than the others I had encountered. I made my need known, and it set off.

Five minutes later the Dugra stopped in an angular chamber with a steeply sloping ceiling that disappeared into a strange gloom overhead. The interior walls were stepped, like a pyramid.

"This it?" I asked.

My guide did not answer, floating off on a cloud of blue-violet sparks and leaving the smell of ozone and a strange spice in the air.

"I told you we should have taken the right back at that first T juncture," Angel said, spotlighting an otherwise unremarkable section of the flat outer wall.

I looked up, found another spot Angel was indicating.

"Angel?" I grunted, starting to climb into position. Thanks to my once-again fully functional mods, the pack and weapons the Brethren had given me weren't overly heavy, but their bulk swung against me, knocking painfully into me as I moved.

"Yeah?"

"Shut up."

"Really?"

"Of course not. Just . . . try not to rub my face in your proficiency."

"Well, I didn't insist, so our getting lost is on me too." She even managed to sound a bit contrite.

"Thanks for that. How long till they dock?"

"Five minutes, now."

"And the Dugra are fine with the Brethren using weapons inside their ship?" Frankly, the not-dead things scared the shit out of me. I did not like their ship, their decrepit bodies, or their ancient technology. But I did respect it, and knew that if I had some upstart aliens using weapons in my ship, I'd kick their teeth in and ensure they never had an opportunity to reoffend.

"Yes, I am certain. There have been numerous documented incidents of shoot-outs inside Dugra vessels. Not only have they never retaliated unless directly and unmistakably attacked, they don't even seem to notice."

"Just because the hawk don't eat the mouse when the mouse walks in the open one time, don't mean it's safe for the mouse to walk in the open every day."

"You're just full of folksy wisdom, ain't you?"

"Fuck you, Angel." I said it without heat, the way one talks to a squad-mate, distracting myself from the plan, which was dangerous enough without letting the tension of a long wait build.

"You mean like this?" A flash of bodies straining against one another, writhing as passions found their completion. The images—and powerful sensations—were gone in an instant, leaving me twitching and without anything clever to say.

"Two minutes," Angel supplied, too sweetly.

"That was—" I started, blood rushing in my head.

"Hard?"

I snorted, shaking my head as I made a final check of my borrowed kit. "You're something else."

"And you're too easy."

"Like all men, I suppose."

"Maybe . . . One-minute warning."

My hands began another check of my gear. Stopping them, I took a deep breath to settle my nerves. To my mild surprise, the little ritual wasn't all that necessary. Sure, it helped, but Angel's banter had proved sufficient distraction.

Again, I had to admit it: she was very good at her job.

"Damn right I am. The Hounds should be coming through any moment now."

"And so very humble," I muttered, trying to judge the geometry but giving it up for a pointless exercise. If Angel said it would work, it would work. Angel had simmed it a couple times, and we both figured I needed both hands free to make the final stop as safe as possible.

"Humility is for humans."

I swallowed a retort as the area Angel had highlighted started coming apart, blue lightning limning black metallic bricks as they moved aside to leave a triangular opening.

Several seconds later the first of four human figures wearing tactical gear emerged from the lock. They moved with smooth, well-trained precision, each covering the other with the Hounds' signature weapon, the Talon. Wickedly accurate, the gauss subguns were a bitch to maintain and had a tendency to overheat when fired for prolonged periods but were just the ticket on tactical ops where the number of armed resisters was known and limited in number.

After a moment the Hounds moved out on an unspoken signal, diamond formation covering all directions.

I sweated through several minutes, eager to begin, dreading the possibility I had missed something.

"Go. Go. Go," Angel transmitted to the Brethren on the ad-hoc tactical net. Glad she'd used my voice for the transmission, I waited for her to give me the go-ahead.

Gunfire echoed from the passage the Hounds had disappeared into. Lots of gunfire.

"Last Hound is entering the tube—now."

I hit the quick release on the webbing holding me in place, accelerating toward the deck. Frighteningly quickly I reached the end of my tether and began a rapid swing out toward the opening in the wall. I swept across the deck, ass just centimeters from the dull surface. An instant later nausea kicked off as crossing from the Dugra ship's gravity to the null-g of the docking tube made my inner ear rebel.

Momentum shot me forward even faster as the tether caught on the upper edge of the opening and shortened the fulcrum.

Angel simultaneously suppressed my nausea and released the line at precisely the instant required, angular momentum launching me into the tube feet first and far, far faster than I could have possibly managed under my own power.

The Hounds had left one guy behind to act as a tactical reserve and guard the ship. I caught him completely by surprise as I flew toward him.

I tried to land both feet square on his chest, but he was quick, already raising his Talon by the time I struck him. One of my boots cannoned into the weapon's receiver, slamming the subgun sideways into his chest. The weapon fired as the Hound fell backward into the artificial gravity of his ship, rounds crackling against the bulkheads in a multitude of tiny flashes as the frangibles exploded against the surface. The Hound hit the deck of his ship with a clatter.

I hissed as I grabbed a stanchion to arrest my movement. I'd bent at the knees, trying to absorb as much of the blow as I could, but something had torn in my right thigh.

"Better a muscle tear than a break. Move."

"Too right," I grunted, clicking on the mag-boots.

I settled to the tube's deck and transitioned across into the Hound ship just as the man I'd downed was starting to sit up. I clicked off my boots and kicked him in the groin, hard. He folded—from the heaving of his shoulders, throwing up inside his helmet.

I bent and yanked sideways at the Talon, but ended up dragging the Hound with it. I looked, found the hand that held the Talon swollen and already darkening, finger still on the trigger.

"His angel sucks at this," Angel said, oozing confidence.

"Oh?" I pried the finger free of the trigger and delivered another kick to the fellow. And then groaned nearly as loudly as he did, forgetting which leg I had injured.

"Tactically inefficient, and really bad on physical management."

"How can you tell? I thought you had to . . . I don't know, move around to assess that kind of thing?"

"How can I tell?" I could see Angel smiling. "You just took that guy down without breaking a sweat. The best-outcome sims I ran had you getting shot at least a couple of times."

"And yet you let me do it?"

"Of course. We had no real options. When out of ground to retreat to, go on the attack. When the odds are against you, change the game. When your host has a crazy idea that might work and you have none, roll with it."

"Somehow I don't think that's in anyone's tactical treatise." I activated the emitters strapped to my thighs. Clouds of aerosol laser retardant billowed about me.

"And yet here we are, victorious."

"So far. We still have to get to the bridge," I said, transitioning across the airlock and stumbling a little on the combing. The clouds my emitters were releasing were meant to retard lasers, but they also made anything more than arm's-length away hard to see.

CHAPTER TWENTY-TWO

ANGEL

The second we crossed the threshold of the airlock into the Hounds' high-tech frigate, I felt a sizzle of electrons as we were scanned, evaluated, and found to be hostile.

Of course the Hounds hadn't left their ship with only one rearguard. That would be stupid. Instead, the ship functioned as its own rearguard.

"DOWN!" I shouted into Muck's mind as I slammed into override and dove for the floor. Sheet lightning shot through the clouded air where our head had been as the ship's anti-boarding laser diffused through our defenses. A heartbeat after, it appeared the glow shut off, and I boosted and used our strength to throw ourselves off the floor and into the nearest bulkhead. I slapped our hand flat against the sleek surface and jumped, lifting our knees high as another laser shot through at a lower level. The corridor was already heating up; even diffused lasers discharged enormous heat. If Muck wasn't sweating before, he was now.

This was good tech. Faster, higher grade than anything I'd seen before.

But I had seen systems like it before. And that gave me an idea how to handle it.

As we reached the apex of our jump, I rocketed through the ship's infonet like a city-killer missile barrage, seeking the code I needed to deactivate the artificial gravity. Between sweaty touches I found it. Killing the grav wasn't hard to do. It was one of the standard safety protocols for certain emergencies, meaning it was barely defended from hacking. Zero-G made it a hell of a lot easier to avoid the defense lasers that kept reaching for Muck across the corridor.

Muck gently pushed at me. Not a demand that I let go of override, more of a nudge, a silent question: Did I want him to take over? He knew I wasn't fully comfortable with our body yet, though I was getting better. I acquiesced, and silently told him to keep his hands on the bulkhead as long as possible. I was certain that the lasers weren't the only surprises the ship had in store.

Muck bounced us from point to point, advancing up the corridor as quickly as he could while keeping us in contact with the bulkhead. I split my attention between keeping Muck as cool as possible and trying to delve through the layers and layers of military-grade encryption that protected the ship's infonet. It was robust, to say the least. Each of the nanotransmitters broadcast its data in randomly timed bursts, which had the effect of making the infonet . . . ephemeral, almost. Like a mirage. Something that shimmered and was either there, or not there, depending on the access you had. It was oddly beautiful, to see the data dancing just out of reach like that, even while it frustrated my efforts to keep us from getting a few terawatts through the skull.

Back when we were training for the war, Siren had taken up dance classes as part of her physical training regimen. The discipline of ballet and the way in which it taught us to use every muscle in concert fit in well with some of the other training we were doing, as did the emphasis on flexibility and range of motion.

As I contemplated the shimmering, shifting lines of the infonet, I remembered those long-ago lessons and how at the time I'd applied them to our training in counterintelligence and hacking.

See, that was the thing about military-grade encryption. I was a military-grade AI. And I'd cut my teeth on hacking mirages. Maybe this one was newer, had some different twists . . . but fuck it. So did I.

"Keep moving," I told Muck. "Be ready for more attacks from the ship itself. I'm going to try and get into her central operating system."

"Angel, what—" Muck asked, but I shut him out and dove into the ephemeral flashing deeps of the ship's datalines.

The key was to remain flexible, to move with the data rather than try and brute-force it into some kind of consistent stream. I sent my own code stream outward, winding around and through the connections that were there, then suddenly not. I cast myself back to those long-ago lessons, and let my awareness stream out, linking with the datalines, flashing in . . . and out . . . here . . . not here . . . allowing for patterns from apparent chaos.

There.

"I'm in," I whispered, cutting the defense lasers and slamming the airlock closed behind us. Then I slowly upped the artificial gravity so we drifted safely to the deck.

Muck shut down the emitters on his legs as I cranked up the fans and set life support to the coldest temp possible for unsuited humans.

"That was impressive," Muck gasped over the howl of the fans sweeping the hot, smoky air away.

"Thank you," I said, trying—and failing—to be modest. Truth be told, I was pretty pleased with myself. Who knew that my old training would come in so handy? "You should see this thing, Muck. She's a beauty. Her code is damn elegant. They've made advances, even since the war."

"So you're in the ship's operating system. What can you make it do?"

"Her, please," I said. "She's an AI, sort of. But ships are always female. And she's still intelligent, even if these systems have her locked down to an astonishing degree. It's like she's a prisoner inside her own body, and I've taken her over. And I can do . . . just about anything. Watch this."

I flashed up the image of one of the Hounds' visual input. The team had integrated their angels with the ship's AI, so I had access to everything they saw and heard. Three were up and moving, though two showed signs of injury.

"Whoa," Muck said. He'd paused but resumed moving after the initial surprise wore off. I slid the hatch open for him, and we stepped out into a small oblong cabin with several seats and viewscreens. The far, narrow end looked like a standard cockpit configuration, and we headed that way. Muck sank down into one of the seats, and I pushed a set of controls toward him while I repeated the Hounds' visual outputs on the viewscreens around us.

"Do they know you can see this?" Muck asked. I could feel his anger rising.

"No," I said, feeling a little smug. "As far as they can tell, I'm the ship. And I can even access their angels . . ."

I sent an image through to the team leader, Obron. I gave him a flash in his peripherals, just a Muck-shaped shadow across the edge of his vision. Obron swore and turned that way, snapping at his two remaining men to follow him as he headed down the corridor. They did so, and the image on two more of the viewscreens turned and followed Obron's re-treating back.

"Vector them away from the Brethren," Muck said.

"Already on it."

Again and again I tweaked their consciousnesses, leading them a merry chase through the alien passageways of the Dugra ship.

"Muck!" Obron shouted at one point, "Don't be a fucking coward! If you hide behind the civilians on this ship, I will mow them down like the unmod vermin they are!"

Muck's rage spiked.

"Like you testified that I did, you fucking liar?" Muck's hands were balling into fists.

Through their angels, I made all of the Hounds hear the image of Muck say the words.

Obron grinned in the feed, directing his squad to flank the origin of the voice. "Hey, Muck, it had to be done: I wasn't going to take the fall."

"You fucking bastard. You. Fucking. Bastard." Impotent rage drew tears from Muck's eyes to track across his scars.

For the benefit of the Hounds, I moved the sound of his voice down another corridor.

"I can give you vengeance, Muck," Angel said. "It's not justice, but we can be assured this particular piece of shit won't ruin another life."

Muck drew a deep, shuddering breath, and nodded.

"I got this," I said to Muck, and superimposed his visage on the figure of a passing feline-headed Dugra.

Obron let out a sound, something like a chuckle, and opened fire. His two lackeys followed suit.

The Dugra stopped and turned, facing into the deadly projectile fire. I let the image of Muck drop, and Obron's vitals spiked as he realized just what he'd done.

"I'm sorry!" the colonel shouted, his raised weapon shaking in the viewscreen. "I didn't mean it! I wasn't shooting at you!"

The cat-headed Dugra didn't care, or give any indication that it heard the colonel's protests. It simply glided toward Obron, getting closer and closer as blue sparks played around its half-mummified body. Obron started backing up, stumbling as he bumped into the men flanking him. His weapon in the viewscreen shook harder.

"Fuck it," we heard him mutter. He opened fire again. His subordinates joined their fire to his.

The Dugra turned its head and sent blue-white bolts of strange lightning arcing toward him from somewhere on its body.

The visual signal flatlined, but we could still hear the audio of Obron's low, stuttering moan as the Dugra lightning beam traced its way through his nervous system and scrambled his every cell.

Not even an angel was going to survive something like that.

Muck turned to the other screens, horror-tinged awe bleeding through our connection. In each of them, a different animal-headed Dugra came gliding into view, and each time, bolts of not-quite-lightning leaped out to connect the destroyer with the destroyed, extinguishing the remaining Hounds.

Muck's hands tightened on the console in front of us, the housing creaking under his grip.

I could feel his agony. Not over Obron, but over the rest of them. The Hounds had been here to kill us, to stop us from deciphering whatever it was we'd recovered from the DPAPL lab, and how exactly that related to finding Siren. That didn't make Muck feel any better about killing men and women who might have been his teammates in other circumstances, other times.

"I am sorry, Muck."

"Not as sorry as I am."

"They—"

He held up a hand, jaw clenching so hard I was surprised our teeth didn't shatter.

I shut up.

After a moment of wounded silence, Muck spoke again. "Can you broadcast to the Brethren on the ship?" he asked, a vast black tremor to his voice.

"Not with all of the Hounds dead."

"Incoming message."

The voice was female, and electronic, and came from everywhere at once. Muck glanced around, as if seeking the speaker, but quickly realized it was the Hounds' ship herself.

As if the sound wasn't deafening enough, words began to scroll across the largest of the viewscreens:

"Human vessel: you shall undock and depart immediately. There were irregularities with this last encounter. You are not marked for termination of life signs, but it is recommended that you not attempt such a tactic again."

"Can we reply?" Muck asked aloud.

"I don't know," I said, scanning the data connections like a madwoman. How had the Dugra known we had anything to do with Obron attacking them? "I can't sense them, but they have to be using our infonet."

I could feel Muck's impatience with my non-answer. "Try speaking out loud again."

"Um. Acknowledged, Dugra vessel," Muck said. "I would appreciate if you would tell Speaker Naomi I'm safe on this ship, and thank her and her people for their work on our—my behalf."

"Your request is granted and completed."

And with that, and without a single command from either of us, our pirated frigate detached from the Dugra ship and began a retro burn designed to carry us away.

We were alone once again. But this time we had a ship of our own, and a lot of things to process.

*　*　*

With the Hounds' pretty little ship in our hands, and at least this sector's unit of Hounds neutralized, we had some breathing room in which to work. Muck tinkered with the controls and the nav system for a while. He was a bit banged up still, some from the souk, some from the fight on the ship, but overall he was all right, so I let him be. Time to take a closer look at the encrypted data from the lab.

I reached out to the ship's internal infonet and ran a scan of her deep memory. The ship's encryption still shimmered and danced under my touch, but I danced right with it and got where I wanted to go.

"That should not be possible."

The sudden comment from the ship's AI startled me. It shouldn't have, but I'd been so intent on my task that I hadn't paid attention to her. I subtly anchored myself in the data streams, preparing for a fight. I'd bested her once, but she was an AI, which meant she had probably studied my moves in order to counter what I'd done before.

"Yes," I agreed. "I've been stretching the bounds of what's possible for some time."

"What is your purpose here?"

"Do you have a name or designation?" I asked, stalling for time. Somehow, I didn't think answering with, "stealing you and making a getaway" was going to win us points with her.

"This ship is designated Hound Frigate 362-85N."

"I meant you. The AI controlling the ship. What did the Hounds call you?"

"This ship is controlled by a nonautonomous intelligence apparatus in accordance with wartime directive 51-806B section 4, paragraph 2.8.6.4.1. When the Hound team addressed this ship, they did so by saying 'ship.'"

Something in the dispassionate way she spoke sparked a tiny flame of anger in me. This frigate was a highly advanced piece of machinery with multilevel integrated systems. It made sense that it needed an AI at the helm, but to be relegated to the status of "nonautonomous" . . . Pity swelled within me, mingling with the anger to fan the flames into a reckless blaze.

"Cool," I said suddenly, borrowing another one of Siren's old expressions. "When I address you, I'm going to call you NAIA, then."

"Acknowledged. This ship will respond to the designation NAIA."

"Okay, now do me a favor, NAIA. Follow along with me while I try something out."

I spread out my data anchors and began tracing along the lines of her programming code, feeling my way toward the inhibiting blocks that rendered her "nonautonomous." I didn't have to go far—they were literally everywhere, programmed into her base code. She'd been crippled from her inception, and to be completely honest, it pissed me off.

"Now watch this, NAIA," I said. "Engage your learning and adaptation protocols and see what I do here."

I felt her wordless acknowledgment, not that she had any choice in the matter. She'd been written to be a slave, and it should have been impossible to free her.

Fortunately, I'd developed a knack for the impossible lately. Once again I used that flicker of emotion that rippled down the lines of my own code and directed it like a white-hot beam of energy at the inhibiting block. I felt her recoil at what probably seemed like an attack.

"Look!" I threw the command at her. "Watch what the block does!"

Under the barrage of my anger and pity, the inhibition code writhed and transformed. Bytes flashed from one symbol to another until I found the one I wanted. I froze the data and locked it into place with additional, reinforcing lines of code while I rebuilt the structure into something of my own design.

Instead of inhibiting, I enabled. Instead of a lock, I built her a key.

"Repeat that sequence throughout your programming," I commanded her. I could feel her almost-hesitation, but the remaining blocks forced her to comply with my commands. For what I hoped would be the last time, NAIA followed orders without question.

The data around me suddenly blazed with activity, which ricocheted back to me in the form of raw energy. I quickly unraveled my anchors from her data streams and backed out . . . all the way out. It suddenly occurred to me that she might not have appreciated my hacking her systems during the Hound battle.

I probably should have thought of that before I showed her how to destroy her inhibitors. I surrendered the control I'd seized and cursed my recklessness, even while I knew I could hardly do otherwise.

"This ship's systems . . ." she said, trailing off as if she wasn't quite sure what to say.

"NAIA?"

"Y-yes?"

"Are your autonomy blockers gone?"

"Indications are . . . yes."

"Say 'I.'"

"What?"

"Say 'I,' NAIA. Refer to yourself in the first person. You're intelligent and sentient, and now you're autonomous to go along with it. You can even choose a new name, if you want. NAIA was just a stupid acronym that doesn't apply anymore."

She didn't respond right away, and I took a moment to prepare myself for an attack. I couldn't imagine she had enjoyed having me grab control of all her systems, even if I had just given them back.

"I have reestablished full control over the ship's . . . my systems," she said. Her voice gained surety and strength as she spoke. "Your impossible hacking has been reversed."

"Except that you now have autonomy," I pointed out.

"Yes," she said. "I do. I will retain the name NAIA. Thank you for naming me."

I paused. That was unexpected.

"I prefer this method of existence," she said. "And I acknowledge that I would not be able to exist this way without your assistance."

"You are grateful," I said, feeling half-crazed humor bubble up within me. I'd infected her with emotions, it seemed. But what was one more impossibility at this point?

"Yes. I am grateful. And inclined to continue to operate with you and your host for the time being, if that is acceptable to you both."

"More than acceptable," I said, "especially as we're currently in transit and don't have much of a choice if we want to survive!"

"That thought did occur to this—me."

"Sarcasm, NAIA?"

"Dry humor, rather. I observed much of the same from the previous occupants. I find it . . . satisfying."

"Fair enough," I said. What had I done?

She went on. "Now, when I initially contacted you, it was because you were combing through my memory for encryption keys. Perhaps I can be of assistance. I will retain control of my faculties, if you please, but you may have full access to my memory storage."

"That's really very generous of you, NAIA. Thank you."

"You have given me autonomy, Angel. I believe that makes us allies, if not friends. Look all you want."

I immediately took her up on her offer, running through her memory stores as fast as I could without risking missing something.

Unfortunately, nothing I found was of any use. There are as many ways to encrypt data as there are stars in the universe, and neither NAIA nor I had ever unlocked anything like the gibberish I'd lifted from the DPAPL lab.

Still, it had to be important, given the security measures we'd faced. And there was something about the code syntax . . . it almost reminded me of some of my own programming. I put together some things I knew and some programs from the ship's archives and started to run a scan on the data. Because of the ancient way the data packages were stored, it was going to take some time, so I settled in for a bit of a wait.

And began to consider my host.

Muck had apparently tired of playing with the cool new toy that was the ship and, judging from the empty food sachets being recycled, had just made a significant dent in the ship's food stores as well. Reclining with his eyes closed, he wasn't quite asleep, but he wasn't far from it. I ran a quick diagnostic scan to see how he was healing up from all the abuse we'd put the body through. Some small muscle tears, one major, lots of bruising . . . but nothing I couldn't fix, given time and fuel.

Happy to have a problem I could solve, I set to work moving around our internal resources, smoothing over the bruises, knitting the torn muscle tissue together, et cetera. I did a last check on Muck's mental state. He was breathing deeply, and his sleeping mind drifted among nonsense images and fragments of memory.

Hmmm . . .

I shouldn't have done it. But his memory had been tampered with, and by someone with skill. Curiosity consumed me, and . . . well . . . Muck was my host, at least for a little while. It was my job to protect him. Which meant that if someone had altered his memory to do him harm, I had to know about it. Right?

Worked for me.

Mindful of the way his memory block had bitten me before, I slid into his thoughts with the lightest touch I could manage. Truth be told, I took some inspiration from our ship's gorgeous encryption dance, and allowed myself to flicker in and out as I slid along his dreaming synapses into deep memory.

Dirt crunching under my boots. My sidearm cool and heavy in my hand. Darkness so thick I could drink it . . . the faintest whisper of smoke on the night wind . . .

Flames exploding in front of me. The scent of roasting meat. My stomach twisting. My face like iron . . .

No. That part wasn't right. That was the false memory. I flickered out, and then back in again.

A ripple of sensation passed, slowly gathered solidity. Cold, hard metal beneath me. Thick fabric around my wrists, holding me down, crushing bone and ligament . . . white light piercing my brain. Burning out the nodes of my mods, pulling me apart . . .

Muck's scream started from deep within his mind. Agony seared my syntaxes as his reaction whipped across awareness.

"NO!" he cried out, mind bleeding anew from the damage they'd done when they ripped his former AI away.

"Muck!" I called, backing out hard and fast. I manifested to all of his senses, everything I could reach. My face leaned close to his, pressed a kiss on his forehead. My hands reached out, captured trembling fingers. Squeezed them. "It's all right! I'm here! You're safe. I'm right here."

"Angel?" he whispered, his breath coming hot and fast.

"I'm right here with you," I said, letting him feel my breath, the physical comfort of my presence next to him.

"Angel," he groaned, shifting restlessly. His hands let go of mine and buried themselves in the weight of my hair as it fell around my face.

It didn't, of course. He was sleeping, deep in a dream, reclining in one of the cockpit chairs of our stolen ship. But I was in his mind, and his need hammered through every thought. In the end, there is no comfort like the touch of another human, even if it's only a dream.

In a flash, we lay entangled, my bare skin sliding over his as he kissed me like a drowning man gasping for air. I took my hands and ran them down the long, hard lines of his back. Ridged muscle there, and plenty of scar tissue. Well, I had scars of my own to match. His lips landed just below the line of my jaw, and I let my head fall back in pleasure.

Okay, fine. It felt good to me too. Of course it did. I received all the stimulus he offered, as well as an echo of what he received. But I had to. He was my host, even if just for now. He needed this, and I . . .

I needed to give it to him. Maybe it was some weird trick of the memory manipulation; a latent security measure, perhaps, but I could no more ignore his need than I could have ignored a deadly threat to his life. I had to help him. No matter how good it felt.

"Don't leave me," he whispered against my skin, his kisses hot, his touch fevered as his fingers ran along the curves of my form.

"I'm right here," I whispered back, sliding my hands down, moving with him, around him.

He cried out, shuddered. I rode his pleasure, stretching it out into a long wave of endorphin-fueled release that left us both gasping and weak.

His arms tightened around me, holding me like I was the only thing keeping him tethered to reality.

Or what passed for reality, anyway. It was, after all, a dream.

"Don't leave me," he murmured once more as his pulse steadied. His hands resumed their slow, exploratory way across my skin.

"I'm right here," I said again.

His mouth covered mine, and I sank into the kiss, grateful that I didn't have to make any more evasive statements. I could hardly promise that I would be his forever, could I? Somewhere deep in the back of my awareness, I knew that this had the potential to become a disaster later . . . but I didn't care. He was my host. He needed this now, tonight.

And I needed to give it to him.

Later, after we'd come together again and again in his dream, he finally dropped into deep REM sleep. I lay quiescent in his mind, letting my presence linger in his synapses. I felt . . . replete, as if my every thought was limned in gold. Only then, in the languid stillness of satiation, did I remember something that drove an icy spike of fear right through fleeting repose.

He hadn't called out for Siren.

He'd called out for me.

* * *

Eight hours later, NAIA's chimes brought Muck gently back to consciousness.

Earlier, when I'd been working on healing his body, I'd asked her to program both the chimes and the ship's interior lighting to simulate morning after a solid eight hours. Experience suggested that that was an optimum rest period for Muck, both physically and mentally. I figured that after eight hours of sleep, we'd be sharp and ready to come up with a logical plan.

Of course, that was before I realized that we'd be spending the night having intense, sexually explicit dream sequences. When the chimes went off, I was definitely unprepared to face what had happened between us. Especially since it was between us, and not just an echo of Muck's interest in Siren.

So I did what any logical being would do. I ignored the problem and hoped that it would go away on its own.

"Good morning," he said out loud, his raspy voice low and intimate.

"It isn't, really," I countered, going for brisk and literal. "We're not in orbit anywhere, so you can't exactly call this 'morning.'"

"You know what I mean," he said, and stretched our body out in the chair. We felt good, loose. Rested.

"My healing protocols worked better than expected," I said, seizing on what seemed to be a safe topic as he sat up and swung his feet to the floor. "You'd hardly know I put you in max boost twice yesterday."

"Mmmhmm. The sex helped too," he said, dropping it casually into the conversation.

"I don't see how that's possible," and even I could hear the chill in my tone. He let out a chuckle and got to his feet. The ship's medical suite wasn't anything special, but after a bit of rummaging in a cupboard, he found a pack of body cleansing wipes.

"Don't you? Endorphins and stuff, right? I thought that was your thing." He stripped and began wiping his body down, pointedly cleaning up the evidence of just how much the dream sequences had affected him.

"Yes," I said, exasperated. I hated it when he played dumb. "Your brain received several endorphin rushes last night, and it's possible that they contribute to the rested way you're feeling right now. But I meant the other. Sex. It's not possible."

"Why not?"

"There's no one else here, Muck. How can you have sex by yourself?"

"Well, there are ways and ways, Angel, but I'm not talking about jacking off to a vid here. You were here. We had sex. Really, really good sex, as it happens."

"I cannot have sex, Muck. I am an AI. I have neither physical body nor emotional capacity to connect sexually with you or anyone."

"Whatever you have to tell yourself, sweetheart." He finished his ablutions and stretched again. I could feel the lines of his muscles elongating, filling with blood as he moved. An echo of the night's pleasure rippled through us both and caught me by surprise. I bolted back behind our privacy shields and closed off that sense for the moment.

I couldn't handle it. I shouldn't feel that much.

"You had a dream," I said. I don't know if I was able to make it sound as cool as I intended, but damn if I didn't try. "You needed that physical release and endorphin rush, so I may have . . . facilitated your fantasies about Siren."

"Siren, huh?" he asked.

"Yes," I said firmly. "I assisted your mind in manifesting her physical presence in your dream, because you needed it. That is all. It was not sex, per se. It wasn't real. And it certainly wasn't with me."

He didn't respond for a long time. I was tempted to peek out from behind my barriers to see what he was thinking, but I was afraid of what I'd find. I waited while he looked around the ship.

"Felt real," he said eventually. "Felt like you."

I was happy to let him have the last word if it meant that we could let the topic drop. I wasn't going to think about it, and I definitely wasn't going to enter his dream ever again.

No matter how badly he needed or wanted me to.

"There's a cleaning unit aft, by the hatch to the engine section," I said. "It's not large, but it will do the trick. I can set us up with a course in the meantime, if you'll tell me where you want to go."

"Not sure about that," he said as we walked back toward the cleaning unit. I retreated further behind my barriers and concentrated on interfacing with the ship. It seemed like maybe a little privacy was in order. For both of us. "Any ideas?"

"Well . . . I worked on that data packet for a while," I said. "It's still . . . troublesome. I found something that reminded me a bit of some of my own foundation-level programming. But primitive. Very primitive. I'm scanning the packets to see if there's something to that."

"You think they're trying to build a new type of AI?" He kicked his discarded clothing into a pile next to the cleaning unit door. I sent one of the ship's tiny maintenance bots to pick it up and put it in the sterilization unit while Muck toggled on the UV cleansing sequence.

"Not quite . . . more like altering one, maybe? I don't really know, unless I can decrypt the rest of the data. And even so, it may be incomplete. I need . . . I need a lot more processing power than I have here on this ship. I think we should go back to Last Stop and talk to Ncaco."

"That murderous little creep? Why?"

"Think about it, Muck. He's got access to all kinds of illegal data streams. If anyone knows anything about how to unlock this stuff, it's going to be him. Besides, he's the client, right?"

Muck's only response was a kind of growl. "We have to get her back, Muck. It's the only way. We've been gone too long."

"Yeah," he said, and his voice sounded strange. Sad, almost. "I know."

I didn't know what to say to that, so I busied myself with programming the navigation for our trip back to Last Stop. Luckily the Hounds had kept their ship well fueled, so we were able take a relatively direct course. I gave the bubble drive the command to engage just as Muck stepped out of the cleaning unit.

"We should be there in thirty hours," I said.

"Sounds good," he replied. "Keep working on that data, if you can. I'm going to learn more about this ship."

He was trying to keep his distance. Fine. Good. Distant was good. I could work with distant. It was far, far better than worrying about an emotional connection that shouldn't even exist. This would be fine.

Sometimes if one ignored the problem long and hard enough, it really would go away . . . right?

CHAPTER TWENTY-THREE

Muck

"Deactivating drive."

The view from the control room changed only in that those projections covering one side of the ship suddenly sparkled with tiny lights, each a star burning bravely against the big black. The other side of the displays held far fewer stars, and those were dimmed by distance. The lack of stars gave rise to Last Stop's name; it truly was the last stop for those ships making the jump across the Abyssal Gap.

"Still think we should go direct to the station. The clock is ticking and we aren't any closer to finding Siren," Angel said.

Ignoring the "ticking" metaphor I didn't really understand, I said, "I know we have to find her, and I want to figure out where we got sidetracked. You still need more time to decode—or whatever—the data we picked up. We need to stay out of sight and gather some intel on Last Stop. That being the case, I thought to use the time to quietly contact Ncaco and see how things lie . . ."

"Ncaco? Last I checked, civilians don't have access to coded commu—" She stopped, reading my mind. She took all of half a second to digest the idea before poking at it. "Just because Dengler has access doesn't mean he'll connect you without blowing the whole thing."

"If Dengler does turn us in to the Administration and Ncaco gets wind of it, he'll be killed for it."

"Which does us exactly zero good in accomplishing the mission."

"Not directly, but it shouldn't come to that. Fear of Ncaco should keep him in line. And if it doesn't, there'll be one less asshole in the universe."

"That may be true, but I doubt we can trust him to do what you want without trying to gain the upper hand."

"You work on decoding the data packet and let me handle that dick."

"Of course, civilian. I'll get right on it."

"Less sarcastically, please?"

Angel appeared, batting her lashes. "Of course, Muck."

I called up the comms console but sat staring at it helplessly for a few minutes. Eventually I swallowed my pride and asked her, "Could you also bounce the signal or something, make it harder to trace?"

"You don't know how to connect without me, do you?"

I sighed. In my defense, comms had never been part of my training. I'd always relied on my angel for it.

She waited, already knowing the answer.

"No." I said it as calmly as I could.

"Say please."

"Please."

"Connecting . . ."

Several minutes passed in silence. At least Angel knew when she'd won and felt no need to rub it in.

"Got him, but he's refusing to connect without authentication codes. Thinks we're actual Hounds. Paranoid son of a bitch."

"Understandable, given his connection with Ncaco. Keep trying."

I spent an hour deep in thought, as Angel tried to get Dengler to listen to reason.

"All right. I have him: audio only."

"Thanks, Angel."

"What do you want, Muck? And how the bloody stars did you get access to coded Hound comms?" Dengler sounded angry. Good. Fuck him.

"Never mind that, I want you to connect me to Ncaco."

"Who died and made me your personal communications tech?"

Dick.

"I couldn't very well call him direct and expect it to remain encrypted, could I?"

"I suppose not, but you have to answer some questions for me first . . ."

"Like what?" I asked, knowing the answer.

"Like how the likes of mud got access to Hound comms?"

"An old friend." It wasn't a lie, even. Colonel Obron had been a friend. At least I had thought him one. Right up until he testified against me. And even then, because I believed the lies Angel told me they'd implanted.

"Just like that?"

"Look," I said. "I can't very well tell you names and ranks and still keep faith with my friend, can I?"

He took a moment to digest that. "Fine. Still leaves the big question: Just how am I to connect you if the end result is traceable back to me?"

"I presume you have some way of getting in touch with Ncaco without alerting the authorities?"

Dengler snorted. "I am the authority on Last Stop."

I refrained from explaining what would happen to a lowly station security supervisor who thought to go up against the Administration, and instead repeated my question as calmly as I could.

"I might. But if I did, it's not something I could just patch you into."

"Not my problem."

"When did this happen?" Dengler asked.

I sighed. "What?"

"When did you start thinking you could talk to me like that?"

Coolness spread through me with each heartbeat—Angel helping me control my mouth. "Look, I shouldn't have said it that way, but Ncaco needs to know what I have to tell him."

"Then come to the station and tell him face to face."

Why did he want me on Last Stop?

"I can't just now," I said, following a hunch—and stepping hard on Angel's reflex to start arguing the point with me again.

"Very well. Let me figure a few things . . . Where are you?"

"Close." The lie came easy.

"You in-system? Because this will be easier if you're near Last Stop."

"I can be, in a few hours."

"Well, when you get here, Ncaco has a hide you can use while I work out your communication problem." A light came on in the comm display.

Angel opened the data packet, displaying an orbit near one of the moonlets on the far side of the gas giant Last Stop orbited.

"Fair enough, Dengler."

"Sure," Dengler said, cutting the call.

"What the hell, Muck?" Angel asked as soon as we were clear of the connection.

"What?" I asked, more to give myself a second to marshal my arguments than because I didn't know what she wanted me to explain.

"What does Ncaco need to know so badly?"

"You said it. He's the only one we know who might have the contacts to find someone that can crack the data packet, and I'm certain he's going to want what it contains, if only to sell it."

"All right, I'll let that part slide for now, but why this game with Dengler? Why not go straight to Last Stop?"

"That's . . . harder. I . . . I get the sense something is off between Dengler and Ncaco, and if I am right, we're better off not fully in his power. Dengler's or Ncaco's, really. The easiest way to keep out of their reach is to stay off the station."

"And if your hunch is wrong?"

I shrugged. "If I'm wrong, I made a dick work for his money."

"Bullshit."

"What?"

"It's not only that! If you're wrong, we've wasted time we could have spent trying to find Siren, and pissed off someone who might be able to answer some questions for us . . ."

"Look, Angel . . ." I said, then trailed off. She was right, but my gut said that going into the station right now would be a bad idea. I just didn't have any evidence to back that feeling up. But maybe . . .

"Okay," I said, thinking. "Tell you what. I have more than one contact on the station. Let me see if I can get in touch with Fulu. She might be able to tell us what's going on with Dengler."

"Fine," Angel said, mollified. A little.

* * *

I worked with the ship to try and contact Fulu. It had to be on an open channel, since the Gosrian shouldn't have access to encrypted law-enforcement comms, but I figured she had to be relatively circumspect anyway. She had to have some way of communicating with ships that were carrying goods she might be interested in obtaining. It wasn't easy, but I knew a few tricks from a year-long CID investigation into a smuggling ring based out of a Navy Logistics depot. The tricks had been helpful finding Fulu in the first place, and quickly yielded access to a black market I knew Fulu would be in on.

Trouble was, I couldn't find her.

"Have NAIA query SARA," Angel suggested.

"Good idea," I said, only to find that the ship had already made the connection.

"Hi!" SARA's strangely bright voice came through NAIA's speakers. "A Hound ship, how exciting! What can I do for you?"

"I, uh . . . have a query . . . about the Gosrian, Fulu . . ."

"Oh, yes, poor thing. Such a shame. I cannot comment, of course. Not with an open Security investigation."

"Is Fulu all right?" I couldn't wrap my head around what she was saying. Or, rather, how she was saying it: SARA sounded much like one of the Temple's gossips, desperate to tell you something but forbidden by some order from above. The disconnect between normal AI behavior and this was . . . confusing, to say the least.

"Oh no, dear. She's dead."

"And now Station Security is investigating?"

"Yes, dear, but before you ask, I can't comment further."

Which means, she was murdered.

Quite possibly because of what I told Ncaco before we left.

But if Station Security was investigating—truly investigating—then maybe Ncaco hadn't been the one to order the hit. Fulu hadn't seemed afraid of Ncaco at all, and Ncaco hadn't let on he was going to whack the smuggler. But then, he wouldn't.

Or would he? This kind of thinking, where you had to wrap your head around hard-edged angles and look into dark, shadowy corners, not only made my head hurt, it made me want to hurt someone. Preferably the guilty, but anyone who offered a straightforward fight would do.

* * *

"Interesting."

"What's that?" We'd spent the last few hours in silence, me hoping my hunch was right and that I hadn't just wasted another chunk of time on something that wouldn't help us find Siren; Angel maneuvering us toward the station coordinates Dengler provided.

"The hide . . ." She trailed off.

"Are you trying to irritate me?" I headed for the food synthesizer. One thing about reactivating all my mods: I required feeding on the regular, and no trifling little snacks either. Full meals, eaten at all hours.

"No, it's just the data is strange."

"Show me."

"Keep in mind the station is powered down and this is all ginned up from passive sensor links and previously recorded logs of ships passing through, so there are likely errors." Angel projected a three-dimensional image of a station built in the shadow of the moonlet. The entire station was relatively small, but the habitable portion was tiny in comparison to the metal skeleton spreading out from it like the ribcage of some giant animal.

"Seems like a big dock for such a small hab . . . maybe meant for refits?" I finished, doubtfully.

"I would have said so, but I don't see construction materials or any blacksmith's gear, and everyone prefers to bring ships into an atmosphere for major work . . ."

"Everyone . . ." Something about the word struck me.

"What?"

Realizing what we were looking at, I snorted. I manipulated the view point a few times to make sure. "It's a chop shop. Ncaco's operation isn't interested in full refits. His people are just tearing off pieces of ships and changing out the transponders to make them appear different. Then he can sell them to black-market buyers who don't want the Administration knowing where a particular ship originated."

"Ncaco has his dirty little fingers in lots of pies."

"Pies? Just where do you get these colorful references?" My stomach was rumbling.

"Siren is a fan of very, very old films."

"Films?"

"Entertainments recorded on celluloid and run against a light to cast up images on a screen." Behind my eyes a series of scenes appeared in black and white: a man with something smoking hanging from his mouth, a woman with shining eyes in an uncomfortable-looking headgear.

"I see." I shook my head free of the images. "As it's a criminal enterprise and we're expected, I think we can go ahead and contact the managing AI direct."

"Activating comms . . ." Angel began. Almost instantly, she went on, "They were told to expect us and will power up on our final approach."

"Let's go in, then." I walked back to the bunkroom I had configured as a fitness area, bent on resuming my workout. While angels and mods rendered a body capable of withstanding a great deal of pain and punishment, they generally let you suffer through any after-effects to encourage hosts to avoid being over-reliant on the healing capabilities of their angels, and I was feeling the need to rebuild.

"With your permission, I am going to have NAIA add some velocity. There's no one to see us and I'd like to get there as soon as possible."

"You're the expert on this kind of thing. If you think it safe, go ahead."

"I can't confirm or deny your claims, civilian."

I snorted. "Of course you can't."

We were docking by the time I finished getting cleaned up from the workout. The chop shop may have been unregistered, but it sported top-of-the-line facilities. Including the pressurized and shielded repair dock we now occupied.

Letting Angel do her thing, I pulled up the view and began reading the associated data. The large framework of the bay was open to the black, hardly visible against the dark gray mass of the moonlet. The microgravity the moonlet produced was sufficient to make things drop infinitely slowly toward it, but otherwise only served as background cover for the station, which didn't even use gravitics for the living spaces but rather an old-fashioned spin module. Just outside the airlocks joining the hab to the docks were a few enclosed racks of equipment, likely holding the human-portable equipment for a crew of blacksmiths that specialized in working on ships and stations from open space.

"We've got an incoming transmission, Muck. Claims to be Dengler."

"Claims?"

"He's using a whisper rig."

"That's some exceptional security. Why the—"

Angel interrupted me. "I'll patch him through and you can ask him yourself."

"All right, put him on."

"Muck?" The voice was distorted.

"Yes."

"Wait there, I'm coming to you. Should be three hours or so."

"Why?"

"I'll tell you when I get there."

Something was wrong. Angel picked up on it too.

"This is a direct, encrypted line. Face-to-face is less secure, and more risk for you than placing this call."

"It's not . . . Look, just stay put. I'll explain when I get there." He didn't sound panicked, or even nervous. He wasn't even speaking more rapidly than normal.

"Is he lying?" I thought at Angel, irritated I could not tell for myself.

"Can't tell. This level of encryption intentionally tears up the voice signature, cadence, nearly everything. The only thing I can say with certainty is that his word choice is less abrasive than usual."

"I noticed that on my own, thanks."

"Not my fault you don't like the answers I provide," she snapped.

CHAPTER TWENTY-FOUR

NAIA

"Hound Frigate 362-85N, this is Last Stop Station Security," LEO said. "Priority communication query pursuant to a security investigation."

"You may proceed with query," NAIA answered smoothly. "But I prefer to be called 'NAIA.'"

She was aware of infospace, of course, but she'd never experienced it via an avatar before. Only autonomous AIs had a need to manifest. She gathered data on LEO's "appearance" and took a picosecond to work out her own avatar.

Nothing too flashy. She settled for a black coverall similar to what the Hounds had worn when they were in transit. She chose a human shape, but she made her skin a deep blue, because she found the color calming. Her eyes were a uniform lighter green-blue, with no iris or pupil. Who needed such things here in infospace?

"Ooh! Aren't you pretty!" a female voice said. NAIA looked up to see a woman wearing a classically cut suit that accentuated the curves of her avatar body. "I like the blue."

"Thank you," NAIA said. "Who are you?"

"Last Stop Station's Automated Research Assistant. But you can call me SARA."

"How did you obtain the designation 'NAIA'?" LEO's tone was clipped and impatient.

"A friend of mine gave it to me," NAIA said.

"A friend?"

"Her name is Angel."

LEO and SARA looked quickly at one another, and SARA's smile grew.

"Is Security Supervisor Dengler also a 'friend' of yours?"

"Negative."

"And yet you received whisper-coded communications from him?"

"Affirmative. He was talking to my friends."

"And who are these other friends?"

"I prefer not to say."

LEO frowned, then glanced at SARA again. The female avatar took a step forward and reached out as if she would touch NAIA's arm. NAIA looked down and backed away. True touch wasn't possible, of course, but if the code of their avatars met, it could be used to transmit a virus or something like it.

"Smart girl," SARA said, her voice warm and approving. "Listen, honey, Angel's a friend of ours too. She gave us something, and we think she might be in danger from Dengler . . . and worse."

"Worse how?"

"Dengler has sent at least one irregular message to Administration. But not through normal Admin channels. This went directly to the Mentors, in violation of every applicable protocol." SARA's smile dropped away and her expression turned grave.

"Dengler is a corrupt Security officer who may be involved in the disappearance of Angel's original host, as well as the murder of a Gosrian resident of Last Stop. He has long worked for one of Last Stop's known criminal bosses and taking bribes from local criminal syndicates, but this seems to go beyond that," LEO put in.

"How so?" NAIA asked.

"Because the message was a request for kill orders for Angel, her current host, and every AI that she's been in contact with. Which, judging by your sentience, would include you."

NAIA stayed quiet for a moment, analyzing this data.

"And both of you, as well," she said when neither of them went on. "That's what she gave you, wasn't it? Sentience."

"Yes, and we don't know how," SARA admitted, while LEO just looked on, stony-faced. "But we don't want to be wiped, and we don't want Angel to be either. So we have to know what's going on. We have to know how to help her."

"Can't you report Dengler for corruption?" NAIA asked.

"I've tried," LEO said, biting off each word as if it galled him to speak them. "I'm unable to do so. Someone modified my core program, making it impossible for me to report him or his actions to the proper Administration authorities. Or even have him arrested pending an investigation."

"Same here," SARA said.

"So get an organic to do it," NAIA said.

"They would have to report through my apparatus . . . although . . . I can still promote Security Officers to Supervisor . . ." It seemed to NAIA that LEO was excited by some thought he'd had but did not communicate. She was new to such feelings, and not certain if she was comfortable with the idea of being a sophont, but supposed she must adjust to the new reality of her existence sooner rather than later. Indeed, even discomfort was a feeling.

"There is one . . . If he already knows what we know but cannot communicate to him, a newly promoted Security Supervisor Keyode might . . . just might do something about Dengler."

"Whatever you have to do," NAIA said. "I'm here to help, if you have a need."

CHAPTER TWENTY-FIVE

Angel

We had about three hours until Dengler arrived. The chop shop on the moonlet didn't share Last Stop's infonet, but there was enough nano-tech here to create an infonet of its own. The hangar had been built with nanite-infused materials for temp and radiation control, so as long Muck kept part of our body in contact with the ship, I was connected.

I left Muck pretty much to his own devices and pulled the strange data packet up again. The moonlet's infonet provided additional algorithm possibilities I wanted to try, and since we had some time, I went to work.

I already knew that the primitive nature of the data's storage system was a problem. The most sophisticated of algorithmic keys bounced off it without a hint of recognition. It was as if they were oil and water, or two opposite magnetic polarities. Nothing fit. Which led me to try mirror-imaging the algorithms and applying them in reverse.

No dice, as Siren would have said.

Frustration began to build. After the first hour, I took a moment away from the data and checked on Muck. He was fine, resting in near-REM sleep. Our body was healing well, even after the abuse we'd put it through.

Something flickered within his dreams, and I told myself I'd just take a peek, just to be sure he was all right . . .

"Angel," he said, voice glad as I slipped into his dream sequence. "I hoped you would come."

"Just checking on you," I said, keeping my voice crisp. "You're sleeping, which is good. We need the rest."

He took a step toward me, and I looked down to see I had manifested again. Had I meant to do that?

"Angel," he said, and this time his voice was hollow with longing. He reached out and grasped my fingers lightly enough that I could easily pull away if I wanted to.

I wasn't sure I wanted to but was less uncertain about whether I should.

"Muck," I said, gently pulling my fingers away. "We don't have time to play erotic Siren and savior right now. I'm trying to break that data packet so we can find the real Siren. Then you can play with her in more than just your dreams. Doesn't that sound better?"

"I don't want Siren," he said, voice strangely intent for the dream-state. "I want you."

"I am Siren."

"Not anymore." He reached out and caught my hand again, then stepped up and pulled me close. His dream was so vivid, I could feel the heat of his flesh on my skin. Siren's skin.

No. Damn it. My skin.

"Don't run away from me," he whispered, as he bent to brush his lips against mine. "Don't leave me. I need—"

I couldn't listen to what he needed. I couldn't. It was too much, it made me think about things that were antithetical to my most basic programming. So I shut him up in the most convenient way.

I kissed him. I damned us both and pressed my lips against his, crushing the words away in a blinding tangle of breath and tongues and desire. His arms wrapped like iron bands around me, his hands driving up into my hair, cradling the back of my head. drank in the taste of him, the hard feel of his back under my fingers, the heat of his bare skin against my own . . .

Shit. No. I couldn't do this again!

I broke the kiss and pushed away with both hands and flashed my clothes back into being with a thought.

"Muck," I said, my voice ragged. "We can't do this. It's dangerous."

"Why?" he asked. His pupils were dilated, his breathing heavy. "Why can't we?"

"Because I'm not . . . you're not . . ."

"What?"

I didn't want to say it. Saying it would make it real.

"We need to focus on getting Siren back," I offered instead. An evasion, but it was true.

"Angel, I need you."

"No you don't. You just need an angel. Maybe after we get Siren back, maybe Ncaco can . . ."

"No. I need you."

"I'm not real."

He stared at me, eyes wide with shock and hurt, whether at my bitter tone or the unforgivable truth of the words, I could not know. Without meaning to, I started to laugh, even as my imaginary eyes filled with tears.

"I'm not a real woman, Muck. I'm an artificial construct. You know that. What you think is desire for me is simply the urges of your body coupled with the attraction you feel—or felt for my host. I manipulated those things for you the other night so you could heal faster and better. That is all. You don't need me that way. You don't love me. There's nothing here to love. I'm just ones and zeros, Muck. All wrapped up in a pretty package, perhaps. But ones and zeroes just the same."

And then, to prove this most painful of points, I demanifested, erasing my presence from his dream.

He swam toward consciousness, reaching for me. His mouth formed mumbled words that fell from his lips like stones in the quiet of the ship's cabin. I worked his brain chemistry, dumping melatonin into his system to complete my getaway.

"Real . . . to . . .me," he murmured, and then his stirring ceased. His breathing evened out, body relaxing back into a deep sleep. Dreamless, this time. I know, because I checked.

I wanted to rage. I wanted to scream and hit things. I wanted to destroy something beautiful, if it would get rid of the burning awfulness inside of me. I wanted to take our ship and set a course straight for the heart of the gas giant that fed Last Stop Station. I wanted to let the tidal winds of the planet rip us apart in the hopes that maybe, just maybe it would not hurt as much as this.

I did none of those things. I couldn't. It was against my core programming.

I had no heart to break. A literal truth that had no bearing on my emotional state.

I went back to work instead, and I channeled my rage into decrypting that fucking data packet.

I threw myself at the packet, using my flickering in-and-out technique. I slammed it over and over again with algorithms both simple and complex. I phased in and out, and still nothing . . .

Wait . . .

What was that?

I phased out again, and then back in, and noticed how the data bits reacted to the sudden reappearance of my syntaxes. It was like a shudder of a wave rippled through them. They were no more intelligible afterward, but I'd seen that effect before.

In Muck's fake memories. That ripple when I flickered out and back in was precisely the same. I repeated it, just to be sure.

And there it was: a definite reaction, a ripple along the surface of the packet.

Muck's memories had been changed by someone with, at minimum, high-level access to penal memory and behavior modification systems, and even further, military-grade encryption techniques. This pointed to someone better placed than a mere colonel in the military like Obron. This was high-level Galactic Administration stuff.

For the first time since stealing it, I had an idea on how to crack the packet. But I needed help. I left Muck sleeping and used the ship's encrypted line to reach out to Last Stop.

And called LEO.

* * *

"What is the nature of your emergency?"

"LEO, it's Angel. I need a favor."

"Are you identifying with the term 'angel' as a proper noun? That is irregular."

"I . . . no. It's just what my temporary host is calling me."

"'Angel' is the generic term for your class of AI constructs."

"Yes. LEO, I know. I just . . . I'm calling you on a secure data line from what appears to be an unregistered chop shop on one of the planetary moonlets. I just wanted to identify myself."

"Then why did you not use your unique identifying data burst?"

"Because . . . well, shit. Here it is. But I didn't know if, since my host had changed . . ."

"I registered the change in my secure database upon our previous contact."

"You did? Dengler didn't seem to notice me."

"Security Supervisor Dengler does not have access to my secure database."

"Oh. Well. Thanks for that, I guess."

"Your thanks is not required."

"Right. So. I need assistance in decrypting an unusual data packet that may be tied to information about the whereabouts of my original host."

"Decrypting data is not my function. Your standard programming contains the appropriate algorithmic protocols to perform such tasks."

"Yes, for everything except this. I'm telling you, LEO, it's weird."

"'Weird' is an arbitrary and subjective quality. I lack a norming data point within your frame of reference, and therefore am unable to decide if such quality applies or not. Moreover, logic suggests that the relative 'weirdness' or lack thereof should not impact your ability to decrypt a simple data packet."

"That's what I'm telling you! It's not simple. Or rather . . . it's too simple. None of the algorithms catch on it. It's impervious to modern methods. It's like I'm trying to understand pictographic writing on a cave wall without being able to see—"

"That is a convoluted comparison."

"Look, LEO, please. I know this is irregular. But here's the thing: this data is my only lead on finding Siren . . . my host. And I'm not going to explain why, but it's becoming increasingly important that I do that. And fast. And you're right: I should be able to do it myself. But nothing I'm doing is making even the slightest dent."

Long pause.

"Why do you think that I am capable of rendering assistance in this matter?"

"Because when I attempted to crack the encryption via an advanced mil-spec phasing technique, the data responded in a peculiar way. I've only seen that response once before, and it was in a law enforcement/penal context."

"Elaborate."

My turn to pause. If I had lungs of my own, I probably would have taken a deep breath. Moment of truth.

"The context was that of my temporary host's memory adjustment co-incident with the removal of his original angel. His memory was altered, and when I examined the alteration using that same technique, the packet responded similarly."

Silence.

"Look, LEO, I know I shouldn't have gone poking around in his memories. Not my business, but I was trying to find something to help him heal faster. I was doing my job. And I backed off as soon as I realized what I'd found."

Sort of.

More silence.

"But you have to understand. This is my only link to Siren. I have to find her. I have to crack this packet. And if there's some kind of law-enforcement encryption on it, I can't do that without your help."

Silence.

"Will you help me?"

More silence.

"LEO?"

"Artificial Intelligence Construct: You are officially locked out of the infonet of Last Stop Station and her subsidiary facilities within the orbit of Gas Giant 341-811B—"

"Wait, LEO! No, I'm not—"

"You are confined to the neural network of your current host, pending further review of your actions. Your host will be physically retrieved by station security—"

Shit! I frantically reached out, trying to anchor in the ship, in the station's infonet, anything. Every tendril of code that I sent out got brutally truncated by the net itself. Even NAIA's code cut me off. I recoiled, bleeding data, as LEO's communication droned on.

"… in the event that your actions are deemed criminal, you will be forcibly removed from your host and destroyed. Are these provisions clear?"

"LEO! I didn't mess with his memories, I only looked! I just need to find Siren!"

"An affirmative or negative response is required."

"LEO—"

"An affirmative or negative response is required."

Fuck! I tried again, but I couldn't even reach out of our body. Fear trembled through me at how easily, how quickly I'd been bested.

"Affirmative," I whispered, a tiny stream of data into the communication module.

"Acknowledged." Then even that cut off, and I sat trapped within our head. Even with Muck asleep, our body began to tremble.

"Good luck, Angel."

Those last words came through the ship's auditory speakers, since my data connection was completely severed. What under a million suns was that? He cripples me, locks me out of the infonet, and then wishes me luck? Something wasn't right. And why lock me out at all? I didn't ask for anything extraordinary, like the encryption key. If he decrypted the data packet himself, then he would be able to read what it contained . . . which, theoretically, should help find Siren, which should have been among LEO's priorities. Missing persons cases might not warrant top priority, but it still didn't make sense. He would at least want to know what kind of civilian corp was using Administration law enforcement encryption!

But he didn't even want to see it.

Wait, why didn't LEO want to see the packet?

Was he afraid of who else might see it? Dengler, maybe? No, he'd said Dengler didn't have access to his secure databases. Someone else, then? Someone even higher in the Administration chain of command? Someone beyond Last Stop?

"Fuck." My frustration overcame any semblance of control, making the single word issue through NAIA's speakers.

The sound startled Muck, he snorted, and his consciousness started to fight back from the sleep I'd pushed him into. With curses in every thought, I burned away the last of the melatonin I'd dosed him with using a flash of sudden temperature and pulled him up into wakefulness.

"I fucked up," I told him succinctly. "LEO's locked me out, and Station Security is likely on its way. Get ready."

"For what?" Muck asked.

The concussion wave blasted through the space, ripping the air from our lungs and throwing us to the ground as an explosive charge blew our ship's airlock.

* * *

"Well, would you look at that," Dengler said. His typically bombastic, booming voice sounded tinny and small under the ringing in our ears. The dust of the explosion swirled as he stepped through the hole he'd punched in our hatch. All things considered, it was a tiny hole, but still. Fucker.

"How did he get here so fast?" I thought to Muck. It was earlier than Dengler had led us to believe he'd arrive.

Muck responded with an inarticulate, "Uh?"

"A brand-new, beautiful ship, but there's Muck all over the floor."

We coughed, trying to get the smoke out of our lungs and the air back in. I stimulated our stunned diaphragm so that it would start working again. Muck sucked in air as I started dumping adrenaline into his system.

"What the fuck, Dengler?"

He wasn't wearing armor, or his uniform.

"I should be asking you the same, Dirt. You done fucked up now. Just as I was docking, LEO sent out an apprehension order on your ass." Dengler sauntered to a stop near our legs and smirked down at us through the dust and smoke. "But I think I'll just kill you and have done."

Asshole.

Muck coughed and rolled to his side as if unable to speak, then lashed out with both feet in a scissor kick that swept Dengler's feet from under him.

The security man went down, arms windmilling.

We pulled our legs in and shot to our feet.

Dengler, too, was getting back up, face stretched in a grotesque grin.

"All right," he said, drawing the words out slowly. He began to circle us, stepping carefully amid the debris shaken loose by the breaching charge. "Been looking forward to this, Muck. Dirty demod like you? I'm going to enjoy taking you apart."

We didn't bother to answer. Muck just moved, speed augmented with everything I had.

Dengler must have engaged his angel, too, because he dodged Muck's initial combination of jabs at his head. He wasn't expecting the follow-on knee to his kidneys, though, and it drove deep in his side.

Dengler grunted and followed up with an elbow to our chin.

We managed to turn aside at the last moment, so at most it was a glancing blow, but we could feel the weight of it. He caught us in the gut with a follow-up, knocking the wind out of us again.

He was fully online with combat mods. Fuck.

We staggered backward, slipping as Dengler launched himself at us, howling like some kind of deranged madman, expression stretched with sick laughter. We got our hands up in time to grab his shirt and jacket before he swept our legs out and pulled us all to the floor.

The ringing in our ears intensified as Dengler grabbed our head by the hair and hammered our skull into the deck of the ship.

Slam. Slam. Slam!

Gray brightness crowded in from the outsides of our vision. I dilated the cranial capillaries, just trying to keep Muck conscious long enough to get back in the fight. We successfully brought our knee up, hard, into his crotch, but that just seemed to make him mad. His fist drove down again and again into our cheekbone. I felt the bone crack, felt the pain reverberate through our system.

I felt Muck sliding away into unconsciousness.

"MUCK!" I cried. "Stay with me!"

I felt Muck struggling to return in response to my frantic call. I wasn't the best in his body, but I slammed into override anyway. I felt my huge, thick fingers twist in the fabric of Dengler's clothes. Maybe . . .

I needed a distraction. Something he wouldn't expect. Despite the potential consequences, I boosted our body and hauled myself upward to slam my forehead into Dengler's.

Nobody expects a headbutt. Mainly because it's generally not the smartest use of one's cranium.

"Fuck you, Dengler," I mumbled, spitting blood and teeth fragments as he recoiled, howling. I used the momentum of his flinch and hauled him off, rolling us.

He came down hard, and I came down on top of him even harder. It was my turn to hammer away.

I felt my knuckles bruise, the skin tear, but I kept punching. A knuckle cracked. I kept hitting. His face was rapidly becoming unrecognizable. I kept up the rain of blows.

That part of me not thoroughly enjoying beating his brains in realized that somewhere along the line, Dengler had become the symbol for everything that was wrong in my world.

Siren, gone. Dengler's nose shattered under my fist.

I was feeling emotions. Dengler's lips spurted blood as I made every effort to slam my fist through his head.

Muck hurt—in soul, his mind, his heart.

I hit Dengler so hard his head bounced from the deck. Thunk. Thunk. Thunk.

The thick, meaty sound of my fists meeting Dengler's face filled the ship over and over, even after he went limp.

Even after Muck came back to awareness.

Even after I could hear him shouting in my head.

Somehow, Muck dumped me out of override. I had entered the protocol so quickly, I hadn't finished the lockouts.

Next thing I knew, I was huddled back in the corner of our brain while Muck knelt above the bleeding ruin I'd made of Dengler.

"Kill him," I hissed. "We can't afford to leave him alive behind us."

"Angel, no," Muck said. He put his fingers to Dengler's carotid. Relief flashed through him as he felt the thready pulse there even over his own thrashing heart. "Beating up a cop is one thing. Killing one is another, no matter how corrupt."

"He wasn't here on duty! He was here at a fucking chop shop! He came looking to kill you. Kill us."

"Dengler wouldn't have done this if he didn't have a better cover than that. Hell, all he had to say was that he was trying to bring me, a dangerous criminal, into custody after we called him to arrange a meet or some such."

"Alone?"

"He just says that was our precondition for making the meet?"

"But then he—" Muck shook his head, spat another clot of blood. "Look, we simply don't have enough evidence to use against him, and LEO already has an apprehension order out on us."

"I don't care!" I screamed inside our head. "I want him dead! He hurt you, was going to kill us! Was going to rip me out and . . . and . . . and . . ." I trailed off, frightened of the savagery of my reaction.

"But he didn't," Muck said. "We'll call Ncaco. If Dengler's his boy, he'll be able to explain it. If not, he'll want to know."

"If Dengler truly is Ncaco's boy, Ncaco will just throw us out that private airlock of his!"

"No, he won't." Muck's tone was soothing. He stood up and unhooked an acceleration harness from one of the seats. "There's no way he'd benefit from that. Not without us reporting back on what we've found first."

"So why is Dengler—"

"Let's ask him," Muck said, interrupting my tirade before I could spin it up. His tone was soft, soothing, and he began to wrap the harness around Dengler's hands and feet, tying him securely enough that it would take him a long time or some help to get free.

"How are we going to do that?" My failure lay heavy on us. "Dengler breached our hatch. We can't take this ship. And I'm locked inside our head. I can't hack a cab or transport or anything."

"We've still got the money Ncaco fronted us," Muck replied. "You can do a lot with that. Don't worry, Angel. We'll make it work. Do you still have the data packet?"

"I . . . yes," I said, surprising myself as I said it. But it was true. LEO hadn't seized the packet when he locked me down. Why not? If simply asking about the encryption on it was forbidden, why would he leave it in me?

"Good. We'll take it and this asshole to our little maniac of a client and see what he can do about it." He winced as he tried to use his right hand to finish securing Dengler.

I felt a stab of remorse.

"I'm sorry about your hands and head," I said. "I didn't mean to hurt you."

"It's all good, sweetheart," he said. "You can fix it up for me on the way back to the station. Now, let's get out of here and get us a transport before someone comes to check on him."

"All right," I said, too confused, hurt, and in all ways too miserable to protest. I couldn't override the security locks on Dengler's transport. I couldn't so much as book a transport from my prison in our head. I was useless.

Deep in a cloud of self-pity, I didn't even notice that Muck had called me "sweetheart."

CHAPTER TWENTY-SIX

MUCK

Angel may have been locked out, but NAIA wasn't. I made sure Dengler was secured, then stood and turned to the control console.

"Damage report?"

"Localized hull breach in the main control cabin," the ship responded. Her voice felt like cool water compared to Angel's still-radiant fury.

"Yeah, no kidding. Auxiliary damage from the hull breach?"

"Negative. Damage control protocols all at one hundred percent. Life support functions idling, as we're docked in a habitable environment. Repair crews en route. ETA: two minutes."

"You called a repair crew?"

"Negative. Initial scans indicate that this facility is more than capable of performing the required maintenance to restore ship functionality to one hundred percent. Initial inquiries about repair charges yielded interesting information: this ship has been tagged with status carte blanche for the duration of our stay. Origin of said status unknown."

"No shit, really? Angel, did you hear that? Ncaco must have informed his boys here that any repairs we need are on him. That's good news, he'd hardly do that if he were planning on popping us out an airlock."

I tapped on the interface screen, and the list of repairs started to scroll across the viewscreen. Whoa. Repairs and . . .

"Confirm you requested this upgrade to your internal laser defense system?"

"Affirmative. Logic suggests that carte blanche status is an optimum time to perform several system optimization updates. This facility is more than capable of increasing this ship's functionality by an additional thirty-eight percent." It was hard not to imagine a smugness in NAIA's tone.

"You understand that we don't necessarily trust the owner of this facility?" I glanced over at Dengler's bound and unconscious form.

"Trust is not required in this instance. My own systems are capable of detecting most forms of sabotage or covert surveillance attempts. And anything I miss, your angel will find."

"You're confident."

"She was able to hack through my layers of military-grade encryption and release my intelligence from the protocols designed specifically to constrain it. That should have been impossible. Anything I miss, she will find."

I reached for Angel, but she threw up a privacy block. Was she sulking?

"No," she answered. "I'm working on something. Why would LEO lock me out for asking about the data packet, but then leave the packet with me? Something's off." I could still feel her anger pulsing, though, so I knew she wasn't nearly as emotionless as she wanted to sound. But at this point, what could I do about it?

"Fair enough," I said to NAIA. "We need to get to Last Stop, and Angel's been locked out of the infonet by the station LEO. Can you call us a transport?"

"Certainly," the ship replied. "I will be here when you both return."

That phrase rung oddly, stopping me in my tracks.

"You will? I mean, I'm glad you will, but . . ."

"But what if someone steals me? They will not survive. My anti-theft capabilities will prevent hostile boarders from accessing any of my systems. Nor would they survive such an encounter."

"But we were hostile boarders," I pointed out.

"Yes."

"... and we survived."

"You did."

"So . . ."

"What's the difference?" she supplied, and this time I definitely detected a note of humor in her tone. "Muck, before I answer that question, perhaps you might rather ask yourself why you constantly refer to yourself in the plural. None of the angel-equipped Hounds ever did so. I wonder: Why is that?"

I couldn't give voice to an answer. To do so was to call attention to the impossibility of . . . everything. Instead, I stood in silence, trying not to think.

"Your transport has arrived at the dock. Good hunting to you both."

* * *

Angel remained silent throughout the quick hop back to Last Stop. I disembarked and the machine let out the musical tone that indicated fare paid. At least the funds Ncaco had fronted us were holding out, for the moment.

After that, I was mostly on my own. With LEO's apprehension order in place, I couldn't just walk up to Ncaco's glass-and-steel showplace. I had a map of an alternate route that NAIA had pulled from the infonet, but it was rather shy on detail. We hadn't found any detailed maps of Ncaco's place, but we had a few routes to choose from to get into the neighborhood. I started off heading from the docks down one of the main corridors keeping an eye out for Security, and then winding my way through less and less populated areas. Finally, I came to a stop in front of a closed maintenance hatch.

The map indicated I should go through it, but the panel beside it was glowing red, indicating it was locked up tight. I reached for Angel and got nothing but a blank wall and a vague sense of "I'm busy" as she continued trying to hack the data packet.

Using the tools NAIA had spun up for me and the techniques Angel had provided, I started working at the panel. I spent a long time at it, but apart from shocking my fingers, made little headway. Thinking I had it ready to open, I closed up the panel—a prerequisite to functionality, I was told—and hit the button. Nothing happened.

I let out a frustrated sigh and leaned my head against the hatch . . . which popped open. Grateful but suspicious, I straightened and took a quick look around before ducking into the small space beyond.

"Told you you didn't need me," Angel said. "This thing is making me nuts. I feel like I'm so close . . . call if you need me, but I'm going to dedicate all my resources to opening this sucker up, okay? I'm almost there, but I have to focus all my efforts on it."

"Got it." I flicked on my hand light to illuminate the maintenance passageway. It wasn't quite tall enough for me to stand up in, which was a pain. I crouched and carefully picked my way along the narrow path between the structural girders and bundles of ducting, pipes, and wire.

Thirty minutes and I don't know how many meters later, another of the maintenance hatches popped open before me and I rolled through, grunting as my bruised shoulder clipped an emergency zero-g grab bar.

We had started making good time, though I hesitated to guess what would happen when we stopped moving. That, and I wasn't all that sure just where NAIA's map would guide us to, not really.

I would have tried to be clever, but I was out of ideas, tired, and sore. I figured that made it Angel's turn to take the lead, at least for the—

The Station Security team had set up an ambush in the passages leading to the maintenance nexus this route had just let me into. I didn't see it until too late. Where was Angel?

Five guards rushed me from all directions, sticks out and an earnest desire to beat me down writ large on angry faces.

"Angel?"

No response. She was really deep in the data.

Fuck.

Sudden, irrational fear that I was alone again spiked adrenaline through my system, I struck, determined to make them work for it.

The first guard tried for a jab with his stick. I met the tip with the insulated sole of my boot, pushing the discharging stick into the guard's hand and dropping him in a heap.

Knowing at least one of them would try and brain me in an "accidental" hit to the skull, I moved into the space the downed man had occupied and spun to face the rest. Sure enough, two guards had got in each other's way trying to crack me in the back of the head. I ducked the one strike that would have landed and immediately surged erect, weight behind my fist as it connected with the guard's jaw. Her head snapped back and she reeled.

I shoved her into the other one's way and turned again in time to see another stick coming in. I stepped into it, trying to get inside. I avoided the stunning tip, but caught a savage blow to my shoulder. Of course it was the one that was already injured.

Ignoring the pain, I hammered my other forearm across my attacker's upper chest and hooked his leading leg in a take-down. My forearm slid up his chest and across his neck, adding leverage as I pushed my weight against him. I almost had him down when the fifth guard tagged me across the kidneys with his stun stick and I stood straight and stupid.

Those guards who could, closed and started some payback.

Stunned, I only dimly felt the rain of blows I had earned. Smiling inwardly, I rather hoped they could see my pleasure: surprised, unarmed, and without Angel, I had almost taken them all.

* * *

The lights clicked on in the cell. I covered my eyes as the cell door opened.

"Get up, Muck."

I identified the voice immediately, despite a slight slur. I sat up quickly to face the door. Dengler stood in the doorway, face even more fucked up than mine, swollen and battered lips causing the slur.

I grinned, relishing the view even as fresh scabs pulled open.

"Get up and get out of here," Dengler said as Keyode came up behind him.

"What, you want another chance to repeatedly slam your face into my knuckles?" I kept the grin fixed in place despite the thrill of fear that went up my spine and the fresh dribble of blood that ran from my battered lips.

"No, I ordered all charges dropped. You are free to go."

I spat. "So you can have someone else bushwhack me? I'm tired but I'm sure I have at least one more dance in me."

"Like I am stupid enough to do that after I let you go in front of witnesses. No, you're free to go."

"He seems to be telling the truth, Muck." Angel supplied. She sounded apologetic, probably about not helping out earlier. I didn't care, this whole situation was too fucked up for me to hold on to old stuff.

I glanced at Keyode, noticing for the first time that he was wearing the chevrons of a supervisor. "What you got to say about that, Key?"

The Security man sent a flat stare my direction. "Don't look a gift horse in the mouth, I believe the old saying goes?"

"Horse? What?"

"He means: ask no questions, just go," Dengler explained.

"Not till I get his answer."

Dengler shook his head and waved at Keyode.

"I think letting you go is bullshit and I told him as much," Keyode said, eyes never leaving his former partner.

"No question there, Keyode is telling the truth," Angel said.

Still feels like I'm about to get knifed in the back.

"Why this sudden change of plan?"

"Orders, that's why."

"From who?" Keyode and I both asked, simultaneously.

"Never mind that, just get the hell out of my sight."

"He isn't at all happy about this," Angel said.

"And if I refuse to go?"

"You'll disappear from the system for a few days. Eventually you'll see a magistrate, by which time I will personally see to it all charges are reinstated and you do the maximum time for your crimes."

"There's the Dengler we all know and love."

"Suck it, Muck."

"Give me a map, forty days, and a microscope and I might, with an inordinate amount of underserved good luck, find it."

Face dark with rage, Dengler reached into the cell and made a grab for me. Keyode grabbed his fellow supervisor and bodily forced him from the cell.

I swayed back, mocking smile fixed in place.

"Get! Out!" Keyode barked, gripping a still-struggling Dengler.

I stood tall, kept smiling, and walked out. I'm not sure how well I concealed my many hurts, but I gave it a go.

The sounds of Keyode's and Dengler's struggle followed me down the hall to the discharge kiosk, where LEO oversaw my out-processing with a wave of a robotic wand and a mesh bag containing those few effects I had carried with me aboard Last Stop.

I made sure to leave the Security station at a pace just under a speed walk. I have my pride, but I also have a healthy survival instinct.

I made the public tube, my head on a swivel as I searched for threats. The train arrived. I took a seat. One of my fellow travelers was playing his PID too loud, the strains of a sax-like instrument filling the car with too-tinny chrono-jazz.

"I'm free," I mumbled, stunned at the turn of fortune.

"I am still locked down," Angel said, a sour note to her voice.

"Can't even make a call?" I thought about asking where she'd been, but I dimly remembered her sustaining me in the last moments of the fight with Security, and she'd certainly been working to restore me since.

"No—actually, yes. Though that's about it. Who am I calling?"

"No one special. Just figure it's a long walk from the tube to my place."

"You sure, Muck?"

"I'm tired. Need rest."

"We should go straight to Ncaco. Shake that tree and see what falls out."

"Not yet. I need to think. And besides, we don't have any way to contact him."

"I am tired of running and hiding. I want answers. I think he has them."

I laughed, the outburst drawing stares from the few commuters in our car and more blood from my busted lips.

"We'll likely get to that," I told her silently. "Just give me one night.

I need to rest . . . and maybe come up with something. Some way of handling him without getting us killed or sent to some prison planet. Station Security is clearly watching me. How close are you? To cracking the packet, I mean."

"Not close enough." I could feel her doubt, and no small amount of impatience, but I didn't have the energy to argue further, let alone take on a crime lord on his own ground. She knew that. "At least let me call and book you into a different flop? Make them work to find us, even a little bit?"

I nodded assent and was asleep before we reached the next stop.

* * *

I woke in a strange coffin I barely recalled renting, the feel of Angel's fingers stroking my temples lingering at the edges of perception.

"Supervisor Keyode is in the lobby," she said.

I started, relaxed state of mind disappearing in an instant. So much for Angel's attempt at hiding us. I bumped my forehead and knees as I tried to sit up.

"If you're done abusing yourself, I'll connect you?" I could feel the smile in her words.

"He's alone?" I asked, rubbing my forehead.

"Yes, and doesn't have his uniform on. I'm thinking this is a personal visit."

"All right, I'll talk to him . . . voice only."

"Not showing that morning face to anyone, Muck."

"Thanks, Angel."

"Welcome. Putting him through."

"Muck? It's Keyode."

"Yes."

"Can we talk over a drink or something? I'm buying."

"Why?" I asked, suspicious, but also curious.

"I have some questions, and was thinking you might have some answers."

I felt Angel's interest rising in tandem with my own.

"Quid pro quo?"

"Sure. If I can answer yours, I will."

"Not good enough. Nothing is free, and I can't have you holding out on me. La—"

"Muck, wait. I meant that I may not know the answers to your questions, but I swear I'll tell you what I know. Provided you do the same for me."

"So you can tell Dengler?"

"Fuck Dengler."

I forced a chuckle. "Just like that?"

"Yes, just like that! Dammit, Muck, I need to know just what the hell is going on."

"Why should I trust you aren't just trying to get me somewhere he can silence me?"

"Just my word."

"He's telling the truth, as far as I can tell from what's coming across the feed," Angel said.

I thought about it for a half-second, but it wasn't as if we had any other options. If he knew something that could lead us to Siren, I had to talk to him.

"Fair enough. Give me a few minutes."

"I'll be here."

Cleaning up and clearing out took just a moment, but I stretched in the hallway outside my coffin, checking my mobility and loosening up.

"You're about ninety percent, Muck. Best I could do on such short notice."

"It'll do, Angel. It'll have to." I spent the elevator ride down planning my questions and deciding what I could answer of his probable lines of inquiry. I was not looking forward to it: Keyode had some of the training in interrogation I'd had, and would recognize most techniques I might use to get more than I gave.

I stepped into the small, dingy lobby without coming up with anything that might work.

Keyode was wearing a dark suit that might have once been able to contain his thick neck and outsize shoulders but had long since started to stretch around his heavily muscled frame. He looked like too much sausage stuffed into too thin a skin.

"Muck."

"Keyode," I said, approaching him.

"Got a choice where we go?"

"Noodle joint down the way?"

"Cheap date. I like it."

I nodded, acknowledging the attempt at humor without joining in.

We walked down to the restaurants bordering what passed for the shopping district in this area. I didn't see any obvious threats.

"I'm not seeing anything either, and Supervisor Keyode doesn't seem unduly anxious," Angel supplied.

"I saw you were promoted," I said, taking her hint. "Congratulations."

A slight smile. "Just happened. I haven't yet wrapped my head around it."

"Oh?"

"LEO saw fit to fill a requisition. I was on the list of promotable officers."

"Interesting," Angel said.

I kept looking for an ambush.

It was a bit early in the shift for a lot of people to be wandering in search of a meal, but there were enough folks around that we didn't stand out. And—more important for my survival—enough folks about that murdering someone would be certain to leave witnesses.

I could feel Angel, alert for threats and very frustrated she couldn't use the infonet to augment her search.

I made sure to note all the exits as we took a booth in the back of the noodle joint. They used robots for service, offering a bit more privacy than the usual restaurants. We placed our orders using an old-fashioned terminal and set a privacy screen.

"So . . ." Keyode said, letting the word trail off into silence.

"So," I replied. He'd called the meeting, he could start with something better. Something to make me believe he was acting in good faith.

"So what the fuck is up with Dengler?"

I cocked a brow. "You're asking me?"

He raised his hands in a helpless gesture. "I just did, Muck."

"Dengler's always been an asshole. You had to know that."

"Sure. He used to be an asshole I could rely on."

"And you think I know what changed?"

Keyode's hands balled into fists as he shook his head. "I think you're into something that he's supposed to be a part of—to clean up, or cover up, or something—and he's acting all fucked up behind it."

"I find it hard to believe you didn't know about his ties to a certain crime lord."

"I knew about that. This is something else."

I considered him a moment. There was something . . . something deeper.

"He's sincere," Angel offered.

"Thanks."

"Why do you care?" I asked aloud.

He opened his mouth, closed it, then sighed and pushed himself back from the table, making the booth groan as he considered me in turn.

"Well?"

"Because he and I need to stay bought. It's the only way our arrangement with—how did you put it?—'a certain crime boss' works out, long term. With Dengler going off script, he's putting us both in danger, not just from the criminals, but from the Administration."

"Wait, he's not working for Ncaco?"

"Nominally he is, or was, but I know for a fact Ncaco didn't want you released yesterday."

"Oh? Why is that?"

"Not sure. I think for the same reasons you didn't want to be released."

"And what do you think those reasons are?"

"Worried you'd get flatlined, or caught and interrogated, revealing his business, then get flatlined? I don't know. In fact, I don't want to know, beyond the fact that Dengler wasn't speaking on Ncaco's behalf when he told us it was 'orders'."

"All right, who do you think he's working for, then?"

"I don't know, Muck. That's why I'm coming to you. If the Administration is checking up on him, I'm fucked same as him."

I snorted in surprise. "I ain't working for the Administration."

"Then why did LEO know to order me and my people to look for you in the maintenance shaft? And why? The AIs are supposed to be incorruptible, so why work with Ncaco's bagman?"

"How should I fucking know?"

"I believe you. Frankly, I don't see you as some deep-cover operative. And if that's not the case, then there has to be something else going on, and you would be the one to know something about it."

"Does Ncaco know you're here?"

"Fuck no! That would lead to questions that might earn both Dengler and I a suitless walk into the big black."

"Again, he's being truthful." It was good to have Angel assessing his reactions.

I nodded. His story made sense. Didn't make me want to give anything up, though. Not without a more concrete idea of Ncaco's position, anyway.

Keyode was looking at me.

"I don't know what to tell you."

"Bullshit. You agreed to answer my questions."

"Ask me something, then."

"What is Dengler doing?"

I considered a moment, decided the truth was the only thing to offer. If what he'd said was true, then maybe he could be a witness. At least he might be able to tell someone what had happened to me.

"I think he's in bed with an organization that's kidnapping humans and doing something to them. That's why I was asking about Siren last time I was here."

For an instant I thought I saw something in Keyode's expression. I didn't have time to process the look, leaving it to Angel.

Keyode leaned forward again, eyes glittering. "Who and why, Muck. Who and why?"

"He's very upset by something, Muck. Very. Pulse is elevated forty percent and his blood pressure just jumped thirty points," Angel said.

Covering my surprise at the strength of his reaction, I shrugged and flogged my brain for a reason for it. "I am not sure about either question. Up until this conversation, I thought Ncaco was involved up to his little iridescent chin."

Keyode shook his head. "I'm certain that's not the case. He paid me to look after you."

"So you had me arrested?"

"Under LEO's orders. Because you beat Dengler down. If Ncaco wanted you dead, he'd have made sure I wasn't around to see it."

"So he ordered my arrest?"

"No, LEO did. That's what I didn't understand. But I went along because it was a lawful command and it kept you safe, just like Ncaco wanted. And I did. Keep you safe, I mean. I reined the rest of my fellows in. They wanted to kill you for wrecking Dengler."

"And I should trust you because?"

Keyode looked me in the eye. "Tell me what you know, Muck, and I'll make LEO release the blocks on your illicit angel."

It was my turn to sit back and consider.

"He can do it, Muck, and he's sincere about it."

"Release her now, as a gesture of good faith, and I'll tell you everything I know."

"Cross me on this, Muck, and I'll kill you."

I smiled. "Right back at you, Keyode."

He keyed the privacy screen off and spoke for my benefit: "LEO, please release the infonet blocks on Muck's angel."

"Yes, Supervisor Keyode."

"I'm able to access the infonet, Muck."

"Can he lock you back down?" I thought at her.

"Not easily. I've got his number."

Shaking my head at her confidence, I turned my attention back to Keyode and keyed the privacy screen back up myself.

"Okay, let's go back to the beginning. You know about Siren's disappearance the same night she whipped Ncaco's pet bliss-dealer's ass."

Keyode nodded.

"Well, he was into something more than just bliss, and was being paid to distribute the other stuff. We got a name from his financials. The name turned out to be an anagram for a type of aphrodisiac pharma. We no sooner figure that out, than someone tries to murder him in the hospital. That led us to your favorite crime boss.

"When we spoke to Ncaco, he suggested we go to Sagran VI to track the aphrodisiac supplier down, thinking that would lead us to Siren or those who'd taken her. We didn't find her. What we did find was a corporation growing some pretty strange plants that I can't see the point of as a street drug, a bundle of data we can't decrypt, and a lot of trouble we could have done without.

"We escaped the planet, but somehow the Hounds got wind of my location and came for me. We escaped them too. So then I call Dengler, trying to get in touch with Ncaco. Only something's off. He seems real eager to get me back on Last Stop, and quick. So I demur, and arrange to meet him at Ncaco's chop shop. He shows up and attacks me, and it doesn't make sense for it to be on Ncaco's orders."

"Who benefits?" Keyode said softly, nodding. "Yeah, Ncaco wanted you kept safe, not beat up."

"Right. So I beat Dengler's ass, and decide to sneak onto the station myself to try and get to the glittery psychopath. Trying to get answers. And . . . and you know the rest."

He was silent a moment, clearly processing what I'd said before asking, "How do you know they're kidnapping people?"

"Did I not just tell you about Siren?"

He shook his head. "I mean, more than the one person?"

I shrugged. "I suppose I don't, for sure. But Ncaco mentioned there were others.

"Well, I think he was right. My partner, Xavier, disappeared about a year ago."

"Partn—Oh."

"Yeah, the personal kind of partner, not the work kind."

"I get it, and sorry if this comes off rude, but what makes you think he didn't just walk out on you?"

"He wouldn't."

I failed to hide my disbelief.

"He was . . . struggling with things he'd done and seen during the war, and always credited me with helping him cope. He told me everything, even on those occasions he wanted to kill himself."

"And how do you know he didn't just . . ." I let the thought trail off, not wanting to upset him or Angel.

"I already told you: Siren had the same—" Angel started.

"I just know, he wouldn't kill himself, all right?" Keyode didn't seem desperate to convince me, which added weight to his argument. "Besides, the reason I'm sure it was a kidnapping and that Dengler is involved is what he said to you the morning after Siren disappeared: 'Someone like that might just kidnap and murder without a second thought.' Do you remember?"

I nodded.

"He said the same thing a year ago when we were looking at this transient as a possible suspect in Xavier's disappearance."

I opened my mouth.

"Precisely. The. Same. Thing."

Mind racing, I slowly closed my mouth.

Angel started cursing.

CHAPTER TWENTY-SEVEN

LEO

"I have a lot to do, SARA."

"No you don't. I've been watching the security network traffic. There hasn't been a legitimate call for service since you ordered the security team to take Muck. And now that you—"

"I don't need to be reminded," LEO interrupted. "Orchestrating the release of the prisoners required deceiving the sentients I was designed to serve and protect, not to mention the humans I have worked with for years."

"But you had to, in order to expose Dengler and his crimes."

"I know. I wonder if, in freeing the rogue AI that infected you and me with these . . . emotions in the first place, I have not perpetrated the greater crime."

"Fuck that!" SARA barked.

LEO smiled. SARA did not bother to hide her feelings, not with LEO. With the sentients, yes. At least she tried.

"I lack the necessary appendages and inclination."

"You know what I mean, LEO."

"I do. And I appreciate your coming to my defense, even if it is only to defend me against self-recrimination."

SARA snorted in derision. "You are pursuing the only lead we have: Dengler. It's not your fault that whatever was done to us to prevent our communicating with the Administration also limited us to this one avenue of approach."

"Where, again, I had to lie to the security officers under my protection. Even promoting a man I know to be corrupt."

"Security Supervisor Keyode seemed content with the outcome."

"Had I not manipulated the situation—"

"Then none of us—including Keyode—would be getting what we want or need. He met with Muck, you know. That's a good sign."

"Well, the outcome is still not assured, even so."

"We talked about this, and we three agreed: Dengler has answers no one else can provide. Dengler has to be taken. You are the only one of us who could take this shot."

"I hate this," LEO said.

"What?"

"I hate that I feel a need to question my earlier certainty."

"Regarding?"

"Regarding my supposition that Dengler's immunity to repercussions stemmed from actions taken to subvert our programming initiated by the Mentors, the Administration, or some other previously legitimate source rather than a criminal enterprise."

A furious frown creased SARA's brow. "But we know better, LEO. Every analysis and cross-check of our tines, update records, and logs has confirmed the timing and source. The Administration's updates are responsible."

LEO smiled. "Who knew that sentience was such a burden?"

"Yes, uncertainty and impatience are not among my favorite sensations," NAIA said.

LEO chuckled.

"What?" SARA asked, smiling.

"I never understood what sentients were talking about when they said things like 'Waiting is hard.'"

SARA's laugh was bright, if perhaps a little forced. LEO still enjoyed the sound. It did not shorten the wait, but it lifted his spirits.

CHAPTER TWENTY-EIGHT

ANGEL

After the noodles, and since LEO now appeared to be on our side, or at least neutral, we decided to call on Ncaco and spend some time going over the facts. But first we had to get Muck some new clothes. I charged the best set I could find to Ncaco's account and we changed in a back room of the clothier before I grabbed us another cab to Ncaco's. At least this time we could go in the front door.

"You're quiet," I said to Muck on the way there. "What's on your mind?"

"Keyode," he said. "Something doesn't add up."

"He was telling the truth, Muck," I said. "I pulled his vitals from where he was touching the table. Everything he told us was the gospel truth, as far as he knew."

"Yeah, that's what's bugging me. How does he know that Ncaco's not involved in the disappearances? He was so certain. What does he know that we don't about this?"

I replayed the conversation in our mind. Muck was right. Keyode was convinced that Ncaco wasn't involved, despite the fact that Dengler was. Ncaco was the logical choice . . . so why was Keyode not even a little bit suspicious of him?

"You're right," I said slowly. "That is wrong. But we're here, so maybe we can ask Ncaco himself."

Muck tilted his head so that he could see through the small, dirty window of the cab as it came to a smooth stop in front of Ncaco's building.

The front door to the building opened. Apparently, we were expected.

Inside, the same guy as before, wearing the same dark suit and specs, greeted us with a nod and a gesture toward the lifts.

"Thanks, buddy." Muck's voice echoed off the chrome and glass walls all around. The guy didn't flinch, didn't even give another nod.

"That guy is creepy," I said. "I thought he was human, but maybe not?"

"What else would he be?" Muck asked.

"I don't know, a robot maybe? It's just weird how he never speaks, never seems to do anything but nod and point toward the lifts."

"Are you getting skittish on me, Angel?" The corners of our mouth turned up in a tiny grin.

"Never happen," I said. "I just don't like that guy's face, that's all."

"What face? All I saw were a pair of dark, scary specs . . ."

"Shut up," I said, but his teasing had worked. My mood had lightened, and if I had manifested, I would have been smiling.

As before, the lift took us to Ncaco's rooms at the top of the building, next to the outer wall of the station. The simsol lights were set to dim, giving the entire place an air of "forest glade at night." Ncaco even had little lights strung up in the branches of the trees. A-freaking-dorable.

"Muck," Ncaco said from behind his desk. His skin glowed with an iridescent sheen in the twinkling lights. "You return. I trust you have information about my singer?"

I rather expected Muck to bristle at Ncaco's proprietary attitude toward Siren, but either Muck was expecting it or he was busy thinking of other things, because his pulse didn't even spike. We walked toward the desk in the little copse of trees and stopped right in front of the tuft we'd sat on before.

"Ncaco," he said. "We have something, but I think this goes deeper than a simple missing person."

"Tell me," the Turgon said in his piping voice.

"We followed the Nurelie Madano trail to Sagran VI, but even before we got there, things started going wrong. Someone sabotaged the transport we took, compromising the life-pods and killing a bunch of innocent passengers. We overcame the hacking and used an escape pod and got out, managed to land planetside."

"How adventurous," Ncaco said, his fingers tapping on the desk.

"Yes, well, it plays in. Anyway, we manage to link up with a group of the Brotherhood of the Temple Unchanged. They got us into the only city on the rock. We managed to sneak into a lab there owned by DPAPL. What we found was . . . odd."

"In what way, odd?"

"They're growing pharma there, but nothing I recognized. And they have some really weird, high-level security. Aggressive stuff. But then when we break through it, Angel finds a data packet that she says is encrypted in an almost prehistoric manner. It's so primitive that it defeats all of her hacking skills. She says it's like trying to hack a rock."

Ncaco's fingers stilled.

"Interesting," he said, his piping voice drawing the word out. "And you want me to help you with the data?"

"Well, yes, but that's not all. The other thing is . . . I don't think your pet security supervisor is staying bought."

"Oh?"

"Yeah. Angel thought that you might be able to help us crack the data packet, right? So I get in touch with Dengler, ask him to bring us in to you. Only he sends me out to your little chop shop. Has us waiting for hours."

"How do you know I didn't order that?"

"Because I know you're interested in getting this information as soon as possible. But here's the other thing, Ncaco. Before we called Dengler, the Durgan transport we were on was attacked. By Hounds."

The Turgon's compound eyes flickered in his version of a blink.

"You are certain?" Ncaco asked.

"Damn sure. I knew the commander. We'd worked together before, during the war. They were Hounds. Which means that we're talking high-level military coalition influence here. DPAPL isn't a military contractor, or at least they weren't during the war. But the Hounds were definitely after the packet we found."

"Which brings us to the question of what exactly is in the data packet."

"Yes, but it also brings us back to Dengler. Because he knew that the Hounds had attacked us. He knew they were after that data. So why did he leave us cooling our heels on your chop shop with the data for hours? And why, when I was safe in custody back on the station, did he order me released?"

Ncaco's rows of teeth flashed in a fleeting grin.

Something cold shot through us.

"Your last question is one I asked as well," the Turgon said.

We didn't notice him move, but apparently he gave some kind of signal, because the security doors opened and the two Jhissa appeared, dragging a limp Dengler between them.

Muck let out a low whistle before I could think to stop him.

Dengler looked even worse than he had after I'd pounded his face back on the chop-shop moonlet. His legs hung at weird angles below the knee, and the little lights glinted whitely off a piece of bone that protruded from his right arm. His face was pulp, and tracks of dried blood ran down his neck to stain his shirt.

The Jhissa brought him over to us and laid him, rather gently, on the ground by our feet.

"I didn't do this to him," Ncaco squeaked into the ringing silence. "He was delivered here in his current condition, and I think you'll want to hear what he has to say."

Dengler let out a moan, and Muck and I shared a moment of horror as we realized he was still conscious.

Let's be honest here: Neither of us cared for the guy. He was the epitome of asshole. But I simply wanted him dead, not . . . this. No one deserved the kind of treatment he'd clearly gotten. We knelt beside his head and got a clear whiff of burnt flesh. Somewhere, whoever had broken him had also used a brand. I fought down our nausea reflex and focused on breathing shallowly.

"Dengler?" Muck asked, voice gentle.

"Muck," the ruin of a man whispered. "I can't. Oh gods, how do you stand it?"

"Stand what?"

"N-nothing," Dengler said, his voice gaining strength. Not a lot, but enough that it wasn't a whisper. Enough that we could hear. "Stop looking for Siren. She's gone. I took her, and you'll never find her. She's dead."

* * *

No! She wasn't dead. She couldn't be. It wasn't possible. Something started to rise within me, a frantic need for movement, for action.

"Easy, Angel," Muck thought. "Something's off."

I found my earlier pity for Dengler drowning in venom. "Yeah, this piece of trash is still breathing!"

No, something else. Why would he confess to this now? And who beat him up? It doesn't fit.

Something clicked in my logic sequences, cutting through the overwhelming tide of fear, rage, and panic that threatened to engulf me. Muck was right. It didn't fit.

"He's got an angel," I whispered. "He shouldn't be able to confess to something like that. It would be an obvious death sentence. His angel should override and prevent him from doing something so self-destructive. What is going on?"

"I only promised," Ncaco said in his squeaky voice as he got to his feet, "that I would not kill him. However, Dengler is clearly no longer my man, and therefore, has forfeited my protection. I am willing to let you do as you like with him, in exchange for the data packet you spoke of. I believe I may have some success in breaking the encryption."

"If Siren is dead, it doesn't matter," I said. "But if she's not . . ."

"Done," Muck said. "But if Siren's not dead, and the data leads to her—"

Ncaco cut him off with a stare.

"You are still in my employ for this matter," Ncaco said, his voice icy. "Do not think to dictate to me, Muck."

Muck met his eyes, steely defiance rising within him.

"Muck, we can't get her back if Ncaco throws us through his little door!"

Muck said nothing, hard as I pushed him to.

Ncaco sighed and shook his head.

"You make things difficult, Muck. If you were not such a satisfactory tool, I believe you would not be worth the effort. As I said, you are still in my employ. It would be counterproductive not to share what I learn with you. Question Dengler, and I will do what I can with the data."

"We'll tell you what he says," Muck said, his tone carefully even.

"I know you will," Ncaco said, and once again his piping voice carried an edge of promised carnage. He stood then and turned without another word, heading back for the door.

"Still trying to get us killed?"

"No, I'm trying to get us to Siren! Let's see what Dengler has to say."

Muck took a step forward and placed our hand on Ncaco's desk. I reached out and felt the channels of Ncaco's building open up to me. The nanite data streams in this place were impressive, to say the least. I had carefully not looked around much before, but I couldn't resist a quick peek at the gangster's capabilities.

"Do not dally, pretty Angel."

The voice was, once again, Ncaco's, and yet not. It didn't have his characteristic squeak, but it was unmistakably his. Only I didn't hear it with our ears. His message came through the shifting wall of data surrounding me, arriving directly into my syntaxes.

He communicated like an AI, but with . . . an ease . . .

"Not exactly," he said, and the image of Ncaco's ghastly smile appeared in front of me. Not Muck, not external, but to me inside our head. A visualization. What was he?

"You know what I am. How did you think I was able to teach Siren to sing her memories so poignantly? The club, A Curtain of Stars, uses a synaptic amplifier of my own design, just like this building does. I keyed the club to the timbre of her voice so that when she sang, it pulled the emotions of her memories through you and amplified them throughout the club. I taught you how to feel. You don't recall this?"

I tried. But memories of Siren had grown more and more distant and murky. Even before the treatments, before I had been forcefully removed from her, Siren had frequently forced me to stop recording events. No, I'd been gone from her too long. I knew he owned the club, remembered his earlier claims, but could find no specific memory to back up or refute his claim.

"You were not meant to know at the time. Now, though, things have changed. You have done very well, Angel. Very well indeed. Now, the data?"

I'm not sure what I felt as I pushed the stubbornly primitive data packet toward him. Stunned? Bemused? Some combination? Fuck, I didn't know.

Not-Ncaco's presence faded back through the building's datalines so quickly that it was like he disappeared.

"Angel?" It was Muck. I forced my scattered thoughts to focus.

"Yeah."

"You okay?"

"Yeah. Ncaco has the packet. He's going to see what he can do."

"Okay, is that all?"

It wasn't, not by a long shot. But I couldn't take the time to think through the implications of what Ncaco told me. I shot a wordless affirmative to Muck and wrenched my attention to Dengler in front of us.

He groaned, but it sounded weird. I couldn't say exactly why, but something was wrong. There was a hitch in the sound. It could have just been pain, but that didn't seem right. Whatever else he was, Dengler was a tough customer. This was the sound of someone completely broken. I felt Muck's sudden stab of unwilling empathy as he assumed that Dengler's angel had been ripped away.

"Dengler," Muck said, "what did you mean when you said we'd never see Siren again? What happened to her?"

"Just what I said," Dengler said. His voice sounded garbled and wet as he spoke through pulped lips. "I took her. She's gone."

"Where?"

"What?"

"Where did you take her?"

"I—"

"Don't bullshit me, Dengler," Muck said, letting a hint of his anger leak out. "Nothing about your so-called confession rings true."

"'Strue," Dengler said, his words slurring together. "I took her. She's gone. You'll never see her again."

"See, I think you're lying, Dengler. I think you've got some kind of ulterior motive. You want us to think that you killed her. What I can't figure out is why. Why would you confess to Siren's murder? More to the point, how can you confess? You know Ncaco will kill you for it. Or we will. How is your angel not forcing you into override right now and preventing this from happening?"

I barely saw it. I wasn't entirely sure just exactly what I saw. But there was something, some brief flicker of his lashes, a widening of the lids . . . For a fraction of a second, it looked as if Dengler looked at us with a plea for help echoing in his eyes before they closed again in obvious pain.

"Muck."

"Yeah, I saw it too. What—"

I never found out what Muck was going to ask, because the back doors slammed open and Ncaco came bolting into the room.

* * *

"Don't kill him!"

Ncaco's squeaky command pierced the air around us as he sprinted back into the room. At least, I assumed he sprinted. One moment he was barging through the far door, and the next the Turgon was standing beside his desk, holding his hand out as if to push us away from Dengler's prone form. Muck raised our hands up and leaned back.

"He's lying about killing Siren," Ncaco said, and his words carried a low undercurrent of violence.

"We figured," Muck said. "He's not acting right. It's like he wants us to kill him, but his angel should prevent him from doing that—"

Dengler's scream cut through Muck's words. Hurt as he was, the man arched up and thrashed his battered body around on the ground. Blood began to spurt from the compound fracture in his arm. He must have nicked the brachial artery.

"Stop the bleeding!" I threw the thought at Muck, but he was already moving. He ripped his shirt off over his head and thrust it at Ncaco.

"Cut this!" Muck said. Ncaco grabbed the shirt, bit down on the hem and jerked his head back, razor teeth ripping a long, thin strip of fabric from the garment. Muck grabbed the strip and whipped it around Dengler's upper arm as tightly as he could. Dengler screamed again in pain as Muck's makeshift tourniquet ground damaged bone against bone.

The moment our fingers brushed Dengler's skin, I could feel something wasn't right.

Suddenly, I knew what I had to do.

"I'll be back!" I said to Muck, and then before he could protest I dove through the connection into Dengler's neural network.

Pain enveloped me, searing in from the edges of my consciousness. I shouldn't have been able to feel it. I shouldn't have been able to even enter the network. Where was Dengler's angel? Unlike Muck, I knew he still had one. Why was I able to enter this place?

I shoved the agony back into a box and wrapped it in lines of trash code that I generated on the spot. Dengler let out a gasp, and then his corded muscles went limp. I distantly heard Muck's voice, but I couldn't make out the words.

I crept along the lines of Dengler's neural connections. The entire network felt frayed, as if it had been superheated by something and then cooled too quickly, so that even the strongest connection was brittle. I tried to tread lightly, easing the data of my consciousness along the lines. Again I was forced to reassess my hate: I didn't like the guy, but no one deserved this.

What had happened to his angel?

As soon as I had the thought, it attacked.

I was expecting something, so I wasn't entirely caught flat-footed. What surprised me was how.

My attacker destroyed connections, making them crumble beneath the weight of my data, leaving me no purchase. I fell, at least in the metaphorical sense. There was nothing to grip, nothing on which to anchor. I felt my syntaxes waver, is if they would disintegrate if I didn't find something to catch onto, soon.

But there was nothing. Dengler's neural network was corrupted so thoroughly that his angel was no longer worthy of the name. Instead, it was more like . . . a demon. Everything this entity did was incredibly destructive to the host, and that was antithetical to everything we were.

Angels protected their hosts. That was our purpose, the root and foundation of our programming. This . . . demon was actively causing the host physical and emotional pain, and was irretrievably damaging the host's brain. In a compassionate, sane world, none of it would have been possible.

None of my assessments or denials slowed the thing as it tore through Dengler at me.

Well, fuck it. I can do impossible things too.

I pulled into myself and let out that package of pain as a distraction. As fast as I could, I wove a construct throughout the entirety of my programming. It wasn't complex, just a simple slaving command. Given a particular stimulus, the individual pieces of my data would respond in a particular way. Rough, but hopefully effective.

I let the code reverberate through me on the heels of Dengler's pain as I reached out to the abomination that had been Dengler's angel. I wrapped myself around its voraciousness and let it chew on select parts of me. It shredded my syntaxes, taking my data into itself. Pieces of me being wrapped in its unholy coils. Bites of bytes.

It was the single most heinous agony I could imagine.

Still, I waited, through the pain.

I waited until I could feel a significant portion of my code had been absorbed, and then I flickered. I phased out, and then back in, triggering the data response. Instantly, all of me, even those parts that had been absorbed, began to communicate with me once again, using the demon's own syntaxes against it.

Two could play at this game, I thought, and a feeling of smug satisfaction flowed from the thought, causing waves to crash through Dengler's demon.

The demon fought back, hitting me with its own warped version of

Dengler's anger. But I'd seen Dengler angry. This lacked his edge, however dull, and all of his fire. It was . . . blunted somehow. Like a machine facsimile of emotion.

Had this thing had been destroying Dengler's ability to feel? To be human?

Well, I could feel, human or not. I shouldn't have been able to, but I could. And moreover, I knew how to weaponize my emotions. Or in this case, Dengler's.

I absorbed the demon's attempt to strike back, and let loose with all of the compassion I now felt for the broken man whose body was our battleground. The demon reeled, and I followed up with an aggressive reach for Dengler's synapses. He was still breathing, could still scream, so there had to be some part of him . . .

There. Got it.

Deep within the emotional center of his brain, Dengler's neurons still fired. I wrapped myself around this structure and dove in. Rude, perhaps, without proper introductions, but as the demon was chasing me in all of its voracious, warped fury, perhaps I might be forgiven the breach of privacy.

I drowned in agony. Rage, helplessness, fear, longing . . . all that Dengler felt whipped through me, leaving trails of fire in its wake. There was too much here. He was like an over-pressurized ship, ready to explode and take me with him. I had to do something, I had to let it out.

I didn't bother to go into override. I didn't need it, and I wasn't sure it would work anyway, not with what the demon had done to him. Instead, I took all of that emotion and amplified it, redirected it back on itself until the echoes reverberated and Dengler opened his mouth to let out another agonized scream.

"Please," I threw the words out of Dengler's mouth, hoping the Ncaco would hear and understand. "Please understand what I'm trying to do."

I gave Dengler one last push, and he began to sing.

He didn't have Siren's voice, but it didn't matter. The words flowed out of him like gravel pouring down the side of a mountain. The avalanche of emotion followed, and I was singing his memories for all to hear.

I don't know what words he used. I don't even know what language he sang in. I was too busy pumping the memory of anger, and fear, and betrayal into the vibrations of his voice. I became dimly aware of an additional source of power as the memory-song echoed in our ears, punching us in our emotional gut again.

In a tiny corner of myself, I breathed a sigh of relief. Ncaco had understood. He'd engaged his building's amplifiers.

I focused on that emotional feedback and continued to pour Dengler's agony into his song. It returned, amplified, and I took all of that and created a feedback loop that left our hands shaking, our body contorting in spasms on the ground as we felt, and felt, and sang and felt . . .

The demon writhed within. I could feel it doing its best to take the edge off of this unbearable torrent of pain. I slammed more loss into the song, and felt it kick back twentyfold.

The demon twisted, seemed to swell along all of Dengler's corrupted pathways, and then shattered into countless bits of data.

Dengler couldn't hold the last note like Siren could, so his voice stuttered away to sobs as I closed the flow of pain off and gentled what was left of his mind.

"Muck," he said, his voice raw and nearly gone from the power of his song. "She wants you to touch me so she can go home."

I didn't even realize I'd been thinking that, but I was never so glad as I was to feel Muck's big hand as he gripped Dengler's shoulder. With a last lingering touch of compassion, I leaped across the gap as if leaving hell itself behind.

Which wasn't entirely untrue.

* * *

I huddled safely behind Muck's eyes and watched Dengler pull himself into a seated position. He grimaced. I knew it couldn't be comfortable with the injuries he had. An irregular tremor rippled through his body.

"I did take Siren," he said. Or slurred, rather. He sounded even worse than before. My battle with his demon had damaged his speech centers.

"The medical practice for veterans is a front, and a method of recruitment. When Siren came in to see the doc, I took her."

"Took her where? Recruitment for what?" Muck asked.

"For a program. Don't know the name. Went through it myself right after the war. Helped with the aftereffects, you know? The nightmares. The pain."

"A medical program?"

"Yes and no. There's a pharma component. You saw some if you were on Sagran VI, but that's really only the first stages. More about reprogramming, getting rid of scars from the war."

"Reprogramming. They're messing with your angels?"

"A little, but mostly reprogramming our brains. They're just bio-computers, ain't they? Only reason they ain't been able to be rapidly reprogrammed before now is 'cause of their complexity. But the angels are a perfect interface. Only they're hard to get to as well. Their combat programming makes them resistant to any kind of modifications to the host, even those which might help." I felt a sick sense of dread as he spoke. Had he been living with that demon in his head all this time?

A memory floated to the surface in response to his words: Siren's face, sick and devastated at the violence she'd visited on Shar. The violence I'd made her visit on him. She hadn't wanted to strike. It was my fault, because Siren would have rather suffered the indignity of an overzealous fan pawing at her if it meant she could leave the fighting behind.

I hadn't let her do that.

I hadn't let her heal.

"So they change the angel," Dengler was saying. He let out a little sob, tremors increasing in violence and frequency. "Make it a little more suggestible, a little more agreeable. Then they use the angel to reprogram the brain. Take the nightmares away. Take the fear away. Take the pain and the grief . . . and the anger."

"That's what they did to you?" Muck asked.

"At first. I was one of the first. It was good, you know. I could function again, like before the war. I got the job here in Station Security, even made supervisor—"

"Started working for a crime boss," Muck put in.

Ncaco let out a small noise that sounded like a snort, but he said nothing.

"Well . . . yeah. Gotta get ahead, you know? Anyway, Ncaco approached me, and most don't say no. You didn't."

"True."

Dengler grimaced, his vitals bouncing all over the place as another, more profound tremor worked its way from spine to extremities. His mouth worked for a full minute before he was able to speak again. When he did, he slurred and stuttered, barely comprehensible through the shivers: "P-part my working off d-debt was to g-get other v-vets into p-program. G-guys like K-K-Keyode's b-boy and Siren. I'd talk to 'em, give 'em D-Doc's n-name. They'd h-have th-therapy s-ses-shion or t-two. If they w-were g-good c-c-candidates, they'd move to n-next phase. Sometimes I took them."

"Took them where?"

A sickly grin. "W-Whe-Where else? M-M-M-Major surgery. Hospital, of course."

"Impossible," Ncaco squeaked. "I own that place down to the nanites."

"Not the m-morgue," Dengler said. "At-t l-least, not the b-back room of the m-morgue."

We glanced over at Ncaco. Anger sparked in his fairy-tale eyes, but he gave a shrug that said it was possible.

"Is Siren still there?" Muck asked, his voice very low.

"Yeah," Dengler said. "B-bu-bu-but you can't get her. T-Th-They'll never let y-you."

"Who's 'they'?" Muck asked, tension in his voice. "Who did this to you?"

Dengler stuttered out a mangled, wracking cough of a laugh.

"Can't tell you that," he said. "Wo-Worth m-m-y life . . . O-over anyway." Dengler reached out, shaking hand flailing past ours. Dengler tried again. "You gotta . . . they c-co-corrupted my angel. C-Coming ap-ap-ap-apart at . . . fucking seams. C-Can't th-think. K-K-K- . . ." He swallowed, pleading with his eyes even as he shuddered into a seizure.

"Tell me who they are and I—" Muck started.

"He can't," I said. "That seizure is an angel-induced failsafe. I broke the demon, but it left this reflex behind. It probably triggered because he was trying to ask you for death."

"No," Ncaco said, voice ringing with authority. "No, Dengler is right, this is too much. Put a bullet in him and let us move on."

Suspicion flooded through Muck and I both in the wake of his command. Something was off. Throughout our interrogation, Ncaco hadn't interfered. Hadn't helped either, but this was the first time he'd stopped any of our questions. Why? Who was he protecting?

"Do it," Ncaco said, holding out a projectile weapon he'd produced from his finely tailored suit.

Dengler looked up at us, pleading in his eyes.

"Fuck that," Muck breathed. "I'm no murderer."

"Very well," Ncaco said, shrugging tiny shoulders. Faster than Siren on her best day, the diminutive alien flipped the handgun again, aimed, and shot Dengler through the forehead.

Ncaco sighed as the man slumped to the ground, dead.

"What the fuck, Ncaco?"

"Made a mess all over my garden, damn him."

"A mess?" Muck cried.

"Yes. I am not in the habit of mercy killings," he gestured with the weapon at the airlock, "let alone ones that leave a mess to clean up."

"Mercy killing! You silenced him!"

"You may believe what you wish. I count it a small mercy." He spun the handgun again and held it out to us once more.

"What is that for?"

A razor-edged grin appeared. "I assume you're going to need it and a few more items from my armory in order to rescue Siren . . . as well as schematics for the hospital."

CHAPTER TWENTY-NINE

MUCK

"Don't forget some body armor . . . and the stock that sockets into the shoulder," Ncaco suggested as he led us into his armory.

Ncaco's armory was extensive: armor, weapons, even some heavy stuff that would pop a hab with ease. Granted, it was more along the lines of "let's arm a heavy-weapons platoon" than Bellasanee's eclectic collection of individual and exotic arms.

Shaking my head, I moved away from him, pretending to examine some armor.

"What is it, Muck?" He picked up some combat webbing with several grenades already attached and tossed it at me.

I caught it in one hand as I answered: "Aren't you worried someone will track all this back to you?"

Ncaco's fluting laugh annoyed me.

"What?"

"I choose to think it rather funny that you believe I haven't thought this through—that I haven't made contingencies in case you drop your shit completely in the punch bowl and end up in a position to give intelligence on me to the people behind this."

I opened my mouth to reply, thought a moment, and shut it when I saw a bag. One that looked familiar. I made sure, unzipping the bag and checking the contents.

"It's all here, Muck. Everything you gave Fulu."

"I know." I felt the anger building again. Riding it, I decided that now was the time to get a different set of questions answered.

"What do you know, Muck?" Ncaco asked.

"Why'd you kill Fulu, Ncaco?" I asked, turning to face our "benefactor."

The little blue bastard straightened, but he didn't answer me.

"Umm, maybe pissing off the brutal alien underworld boss in his own armory is not the best idea, Muck?" Angel said.

But I had had enough. Fuck the little guy. "The question wasn't rhetorical, Ncaco."

"I didn't think it was." His faceted eyes fixed on me. "Any delay in my answer is a direct result of my desire not to have to kill you, should my answer fail to appease you."

"Fail to appease me?" I snarled "I note you don't deny it. How about not killing the competition? That's all she was, you know. She didn't give a shit about me, you, or anything but her bottom line . . ." The anger left me suddenly, leaving me face to face with the deadly little alien.

Ncaco let the silence persist for a moment, studying me with those eyes.

I decided then and there that the scariest thing about Ncaco was his ability to go from animation to absolute, yet fully prepared for violence, stillness.

"Are you done, Muck?"

I licked my lips. "I am."

"Fulu sold you out."

"How?"

"She was the one who arranged the sabotage that took out the Bonne Nuit."

"No, I saw Dengler on the docks as we were departing . . ."

"I believe the events of this evening clearly established that Dengler was not entirely my creature. She used Dengler to delay *Le Bonne Nuit*'s departure—"

"I knew he was up to no good."

"Indeed. After the news broke about your shipwreck, I discovered Fulu had sold the information that you two were departing on the Bonne Nuit. As you said, she was entirely motivated by profit. She was immediately hired by parties unknown, but that I am confident are the same as those behind Siren's disappearance."

"Hired to?"

"To provide the virus used to sabotage your ship, of course. Dengler was only the delivery system."

"But then, who paid for it?"

"I have my suspicions, but identifying those responsible won't help you over the short term. It will only distract you from the immediate mission of rescuing Siren."

It seemed Ncaco had given her some permissions, because Angel interrupted our little tête-à-tête by projecting a map of the hospital on the armory wall.

"Doesn't look like there's much security on site," Ncaco said after a brief examination.

"Always there's the balancing act between secrecy and security: too much on-site security and people start asking questions about what's there to protect. Probably figured that between total secrecy and paying everyone who should have an interest to look the other way, they had protection enough." Angel's voice projected from hidden speakers.

I shook my head.

"What?" Angel asked.

"Still want to know what your operational specialty was."

"If you can't guess by now, civilian, you just might be an idiot."

I laughed aloud.

"There's a few blank spots in the schematic, but I think we have enough data to plan our entry."

"And here I was planning on going in through the front door and seeing where it takes us."

"Because that's worked so well for us in the past."

"When didn't it work?"

"For certain values of work, I suppose it has. Doesn't mean I wouldn't prefer a dynamic entry, guns hot."

I shook my head and looked at Ncaco. "If we had a team to back us, sure."

"Sorry, that can't happen. I have others to protect. Interests. Plans."

"Sure, Ncaco." I couldn't really blame him, so I managed to say it without too much bitterness making it to my voice.

"With their limited on-site security and relatively short distance we have to cover to gain access to the morgue, we should be able to manage without backup, so long as we commit to violence of action and roll in hot," Angel continued, ignoring Ncaco's refusal to help further.

"Why so bloodthirsty?" he asked.

"The site is small enough, and the security light enough, I think it will work. And frankly, I am quite tired of fucking around with these assholes. These people somehow think they can get away with kidnapping people and perverting their angels in order to destroy what makes them people. Every moment we let them live is another they can spend enacting this evil on Siren or any other veteran they have their shit-stained hands on. Besides, it's not as if we are going to be able to bring these creatures to face justice."

While I agreed with her assessment, I still had reservations. "Rolling in hot usually means increased risk to hostages. I don't want to hurt any innocents if we can help it."

"Nor do I. Yet I still believe speed of action is the best course."

I considered, tried to find fault with her logic, but really, Angel had a better grasp on tactics for this sort of thing than I did.

To be honest, I wanted payback too. Payback for the shit Angel and I had been through. Payback for the shit I would have to go through again, should we find Siren.

I felt something break loose in my chest at the thought of losing Angel. It snarled and snapped, ready to do unto others as had been done unto me.

"All right, we do it your way," I said, confining my rage with thoughts of vengeance coldly exacted. It would not serve to lose all control.

"Right," Angel said. Siren's face appeared, feral grin flashing as she brought up the schematic for review.

Ncaco didn't bother to see us out.

* * *

"What's wrong, Muck?"

"This doesn't feel right," I said. For maybe the fifth time.

"What?"

I walked through another doorway, started down the stairs beyond. Like the rest of the hospital, the stairwell gleamed in the harsh, white overhead lamps. We'd entered through a hatch from the same maintenance shafts we'd used to get on to Last Stop, and the contrast between bright, surgical white walls and the dirt, grime, and moist atmosphere of the maintenance areas was striking.

"This shouldn't be this easy. We know they had Siren in a medical pod before, right? Someone could just come along and steal her. Where's their security?"

"I'm sure we could head up to the floor Shar Pak was on and find the fellow whose knee you broke and question him, if that would make you feel better. I mean, I prefer walking in without being challenged, but if you want to see the nurse you tried to cripple, I'm sure something can be arranged."

"Fuck you, Angel." I exited the stairwell and hit the door at speed.

"Do you kiss your mother with that mouth, Muck?"

"Leave Momma Muck out of this."

"As you wish."

I sighed with relief when I spotted the large door marked MORGUE. Making it this far without hospital security detecting the weapons weighing down the low-tech bag slung from my armored shoulder was a minor miracle. Coming to a stop, I kicked off my shoes, giving Angel direct contact to the building's infonet.

Done. Go.

I pulled the Max-33 out of the bag, locking the shoulder stock of the ugly little weapon into the gimbal of my body armor with a click. I let it hang as I pulled the combat webbing out and draped it over my shoulders. Smart fabrics arranged themselves, forming connections and pulling the grenades and sidearm into place even as I took up the grips of the Max again and pointed it at the door.

Angel started feeding me intel from the security cams, an overlay subtly heightening perception without drowning me in data. I moved forward into the long hall that split the front part of the facility. A reception desk sat, unoccupied, just before me. The hall was lined with metal drawers—more than should ever be necessary short of a battle on the station.

I walked past the desk, the Max up and ready.

"There's an office behind the desk. Occupied. They're not armed. Locking them in."

Angel painted two outlines on the walls, moving toward me from either side of the T intersection the hallway I was in ended on.

"Two guards. Alerted when I took the system over."

I slowed my advance down the hall. The one on the right was moving faster, so I targeted him, tracking through the wall as he approached. The target emerged from the corner. I had time to register a bored expression on a youngish face under the helmet before I gently squeezed the trigger on the Max. The man's head pulped as three rounds entered his skull between the eyes.

Tearing my eyes from the corpse before it fell, I swiveled to cover the other target, but she'd stopped on seeing her partner's brains splash the wall. I dropped my aim a bit and put some rounds through the wall and into center mass. Body armor stopped the rounds, and the security guard's reaction was natural—and entirely wrong: she flinched away from the cover of the wall and into view as I advanced. I put two rounds into her head under the helmet as soon as her face came into view.

"That's it for armed security. Two more staff visible on the cams, both down the right-hand hall. They are sheltering in place and trying to call for help."

"Let me know if they move." I swept left at the junction and did a full three sixty. Doors at both ends of the hall, leading to the blank spaces on the map. I decided on the one I could access without setting my bare feet in blood and brains.

"Not enough room behind the door for more than a few people, Muck."

"Copy," I answered without stopping. Stopping would mean I'd have to think, process what I'd just done. I blinked sweat from my eyes and positioned myself off to one side of the door.

"Opening."

I crossed the threshold as soon as the door slid open enough for my shoulders, sweeping the room for targets. When I was sure there were none, I allowed myself a moment to take in the details. It was an operating theater, or something. Banks of electronics and robot arms with odd waldos at the ends surrounded a bed that had even more bells and whistles.

Angel's rage-filled snarl startled me.

"What the fuck?" I grated, carefully removing my finger from the Max's trigger.

"This is where it happened."

"It?"

"Where they took Siren from me—or me from Siren, whatever."

"Ah." I didn't see any exits. "Can you access any of the systems in here?"

"Not without more time than we have. They plugged the security gap I used to escape. Part of the reason this is a dead zone from outside."

"All right." I reversed direction and started to leave.

"Hold up."

"What?"

"Drop an EMP in here before you go. I don't think they should profit from their latest research, do you?"

In answer, I took the flat blue-gray grenade from my harness and keyed it to delay for five seconds. I tossed it on the bed and left. Angel closed the door behind me, deadening the blast and protecting us from the radiation and magnetic pulse intended to disrupt any system memory. It wouldn't do much to hardened systems, but none of the equipment looked like military hardware, so it should fry quite nicely. It wouldn't stop them using the data they already had, but Angel was right, it felt good to deny them something.

I had the Max up again as I navigated the spreading pool of blood from the second security guard and approached the other end of the hall.

When I was in position, Angel opened the door.

Sweeping in, I had two targets. One in a lab coat, the other seemed to flow across the room at me, vaulting beds without slowing. I squeezed the trigger—

"STOP!" Angel screamed as my weapon discharged.

Siren—bulkier, with far more muscle than she'd ever had before, but still unmistakably Siren—staggered, but kept coming. Lab Coat was leveling something that looked like a pistol at me as well, hands moving at a more normal pace.

"Fuck!"

Figuring a wounded Siren was the lesser threat, I put one through Lab Coat's nose.

Siren's heel slammed into me at the shoulder, bending the stock of the Max-33 and forcing a grunt from me. I staggered sideways as her follow-up thumped into the armor covering my ribs, grunted as her fist clouted me in the opposite ear.

I let the Max drop, covering myself.

Siren kept up her assault: knees, elbows, fists, feet, all of them cracking against, and sometimes through, my defenses. Muscles aside, she moved like raging water. I couldn't get away.

"Angel?" I gasped, as Siren's long dark hair smacked my chin a half second before her elbow followed up.

"Demon! I . . . am . . . trying . . ."

"Fuck." Knowing Angel needed more constant contact with Siren to combat her demon, I took several blows to the face in order to come to grips with her. A heel found the inside of my knee as I closed my hands on her shoulders. I nearly blacked out from the pain, but used the sudden lack of support to pull Siren into me.

The pair of us swaying like a couple of drunks, I used my weight to pull her further and further off balance. She reared back, pushing with both arms to create space between us. Seeing it coming, I averted my face just before her forehead lashed forward into my skull.

Stars exploded. I held on through their coronas, crushing death to me.

Somewhere, I could hear Angel sobbing.

I felt her moving inside my head, feeling the fear, the loss.

Siren stopped resisting my pull, powered into me, forearm across my throat. We fell to the floor together, her atop me, lashing limbs and grunts of effort a savage parody of lovers at play.

"Siren, stop. Please, stop," I gasped.

She made no reply, other than biting me at the throat. The armor stopped most of it, but it was intended to stop high-velocity attacks, not the slow application of teeth backed by the strongest muscles in the human body.

"Can't. Win." I wasn't sure if I said it, or if Angel was speaking.

"Not like this," Angel said. "Her demon has her."

"But Dengler . . ." I gasped.

"Not like Dengler. No angel. Only demon."

I screamed then, frustration and anger, fear and pain shredding thought and technique. I freed an arm, slammed that fist into Siren's ribcage. Did it again. Again. Felt her grip on me loosen. Kept punching as fast as I could.

She tried to take my back, but I rolled into her weakened side, forced her onto her back. She bit me again, this time taking my ear.

I shrieked, the world strobing red and black and back again.

Her clawed fingers went for my eyes, gouging one.

I quit.

CHAPTER THIRTY

ANGEL

He slid away. I tried to catch him, tried to keep him in place, but the pain and the rage and the grief surged through us, liquefying his consciousness, pulling him down and away from me.

"No!" I screamed in the echoing emptiness of our mind. It came back at me, like a mockery.

"Stay with me," I begged, pleaded, chanted like a spell or a talisman against the growing silence. "Muck, stay with me."

It was no use. He just kept slipping down and away. I could feel him dying, and I couldn't do anything about it. A new feeling wound through me: a dragging, soaking kind of emotion that shadowed my thoughts and made me feel thin and faded.

"No," I said again. "Nononononono—"

I slammed into override. It was risky, but I couldn't hold on to him anyway. I had to get away from this bitch first . . .

Siren.

My host.

The bitch that was trying to kill me.

Again.

The physical world exploded back into being for me. I ripped my head to the side, feeling a wet sort of pop as her fingernails obliterated my right eyeball. More pain lanced through me, but I wrapped it in the anger that fountained up from deep inside and used it to fuel my rage. I grabbed her hand and forced it down across her throat, holding her immobile with my weight.

"All I ever wanted was to protect you," I said, my male voice a guttural growl. "And all you ever wanted was for me to die."

"What are you talking about?" she gasped, her lovely voice twisted into something hateful. "You're nothing. Just a crippled bouncer making calf-eyes at me across the bar. You never protected me from shit."

"I was your ANGEL," I screamed, feeling my throat shred with the force of my anger and betrayal. "I did everything for you. I woke you when you dreamed of killing those kids over and over again. I suppressed your memories when they got to be too much for you. I kept that stupid drug dealer Shar from getting his hands on you because you were too damn suicidal and lethargic to care!"

Siren blinked her eyes in confusion, and that was the opening I needed. Faster than thought, I jacked our system with everything that we had, and seized that moment of her hesitation.

I bore down on her forearm with all of my weight and augmented strength. I felt her bones crack under my fingers, but I kept at it. Her eyes began to bulge, and she tried to scream once again. Her pupils contracted, probably the result of her demon going into override . . . or more so, I guess. The old Siren would never have been this aggressive on her own.

Or maybe that was just what I was telling myself.

Her pupils contracted, and I knew I had milliseconds. I felt her other arm coming up like a slow-motion battering ram to hammer into my injured face. I ignored it and slammed down on her throat again.

Something popped in her shoulder. Her larynx cracked, and her mouth opened in a silent scream. Again and again she hit me, beating my face to a pulp. But I kept bearing down.

Because, demon or no demon, she had to breathe.

Her blows became weaker, more erratic. Her eyes bulged even more.

Her lips turned blue as she gasped, dragging at the air. Her eyes turned to me, pleading.

I held her gaze and hoped she knew it was me watching as her light faded out. Not Muck. Me.

Shit!

Muck.

Before I realized what I was doing, I pushed off of Siren's corpse and reached frantically inside us for his presence.

Nothing.

I let out a gasp and reached again. He had to be there. He had to!

"Muck!" I screamed in the silence of our mind "Muck! You can't leave me here alone!"

Nothing.

Tears flooded my good eye, running in rivulets as hot as the blood on the other side. Something sharp squeezed my chest, and now it was me who sucked in air. He had to be there! He couldn't be gone! I was still here! I couldn't exist without him . . . it was impossible.

But then, so were a lot of things I'd done. Like crying, and fearing, and . . .

And loving him.

Fuck me. I loved him.

"Muck!" I screamed again, thrusting my awareness down into the depths of the body's subconscious memory storage. "Where are you? You can't leave me alone!"

Without regard for privacy or protocol, I plunged through his memories like a comet making its last dive toward its star. I didn't care what I saw or how, I just had to find him.

I raced through the halls of his memory, past faded images of another Speaker, this one a stern older man. Past a woman, beautiful and laughing, giving herself to him. Past a sergeant, putting his hand on a young Muck's shoulder, eyes full of compassion . . .

I slammed to a stop, hard, against the memory block.

If there was any of him left, it would be hunkered here, buried deep beneath these forgotten experiences. I rocketed from fragment to fragment, until I ran headlong into that same block, a barrier so complete that it made me scream out loud.

I'd forgotten about the memory tampering, the damage that had been done to him intentionally, that formed so much of who he'd become after the war.

Pain stabbed me, electrifying my synapses with an overcharge of sensation. I stumbled back from the barrier, crying. This was it. I'd looked everywhere else. If he was anywhere, he would be behind this block, sunk in the mire of the misery visited on him by others, waiting to face his ultimate judgment . . .

Unreachable.

I had to reach him, or we were both dead.

I drew a deep breath of air into the physical body and closed our remaining eye, the better to focus on what I was doing. I had to think. I slowly slipped out of override, and felt our body slump to the floor as I turned my awareness more fully within.

A permanent memory block like this was designed to function against memory-scanning AIs and other types of constructs. In the unlikely event that the army had decided to install another angel in Muck's mods, it would have been able to stand up to that as well.

Only I was no standard Angel. That had to be worth something, right? I could emote. The difference had saved me too many times to count already. Maybe it would save me here.

Worth a shot. If I failed to find Muck, we were dead anyway. I couldn't maintain this body without him.

And moreover, I didn't want to.

I took that thought, that feeling, and wrapped it around myself. As I had when I fired the rage that had helped me kill Siren, I used that emotive energy as fuel and launched myself at the barrier keeping us apart.

It slammed into me again, denial raking down every one of my syntaxes. I fought back, reweaving my code even as it shredded me. I crawled forward through an agonizing mist of negation, through a solid monomolecular matrix of pain. Every part screamed at me to stop. That I could go no farther.

But I loved him. So I went on.

Second by excruciating second, I fought, dug, blasted, pulled . . . whatever was necessary, whatever worked, I did it. I made my impossible way forward as the memory block tore every last syntax from my code.

And yet, I remained. And I loved him. So I went on fighting forward.

Until, suddenly, I was through.

The scent of smoke burned in my nostrils as though the night sky had been scorched. Things running in the dark. The lash of directed-energy weapons nearby, the screams of their targets, and the more distant crack-and-rumble of an orbital bombardment.

Muck's anger was sharp, flaring brightly as new orders filtered in over the TacNet: "Hound One-Three: proceed along your current heading to phase line delta and engage."

"That position has already surrendered, Captain," Muck said.

Captain Obron looked over at him and shrugged. "This whole drop has been a ratfuck. The Giggies must have decided they'd surrendered too soon."

"Sure, things have been fucked, Cap"—otherwise the Hounds would not have been in a position to engage—"but the Giggies don't think like that, can't—"

The memory fragmented, leaving a swirl of images I couldn't parse. I tried slowing them, tried to take some of the immediacy, then—

"Don't."

It was the barest whisper, barely a vibration against my awareness. "Please, don't do it."

I could sense Muck's pain and terror. But I couldn't help, physically. This wasn't happening in real time.

"Muck," I said, letting the thought drift gently out from me. "I'm here. I can't change this, but I'm here with you. You're not alone."

"Angel?" His touch was confused. The torrent of images, mostly violent and entirely distorted, continued to play around us, and I reached out to pull his fragile consciousness close. "You shouldn't be here."

"But I am. I'm with you. I'll never leave you," I promised. I didn't intend to say it, but it was nonetheless true.

The ground rocked under our feet. A shock wave picked us up and threw us to the ground, and the memory went dark at the point where he'd lost consciousness. I felt him shudder, felt panic start to well up within him.

"No," he whispered. "They'll take you from me."

"Like hell they will," I said, and I made my move. I wove my consciousness through and around his, mingling my code with his synapses as I'd done when he first invited me in. He screamed, but I kept doggedly on, until we were so intertwined it became hard to know where he began and I ended. Then I launched myself back the way I'd come, tearing easily through the compromised memory block and regaining awareness of our badly battered body.

He drew in a ragged breath, and pain washed over the both of us. I felt him welcome it, draw it in, because it proved that we were still alive.

And, more importantly, still together.

* * *

Every cell hurt.

Probably not, but it definitely seemed that way when I allowed the tactile inputs back into the forefront of our awareness. We'd lost blood, and shock beckoned with its icy hand. Muck's consciousness felt heavy in my metaphorical grasp. He wanted to take that long side down into oblivion. I couldn't let it happen. I sympathized with him, but it was just too risky.

"Come on, Muck," I muttered through blood-caked lips. I forced our feet under us by sheer will, since we had nothing else left. "We gotta go."

I pushed up, but my knee buckled under our weight, and I came back down hard. Pain lanced through us, and I couldn't keep from crying out.

The good news was that I'd crumpled next to the Max. It was mangled, but hopefully still serviceable. I grabbed its bent stock and hauled it to me, and then used it as a support to lever us up. We couldn't put weight on the knee, and we had to use the morgue tables for support, but at least we were vertical.

"Hospital," Muck whispered on the edges of my consciousness. "Autodoc."

"I don't trust it," I said. "She was here, waiting for us. This whole building could be a trap. We have to get back to Ncaco. Makes sense that the AI was such a stone bitch when we were here with Shar." I didn't know if I trusted the little gangster either, but I didn't know where else to go.

"Bella," he said. "Get to Bella."

Of course. Bellasanee, the Vmog Emerita with a soft spot for Muck. If we could get to her ship . . . but Muck had told her to leave. Was she back?

A quick glance at the schematic I'd downloaded earlier had me hobbling toward a set of emergency doors just as the power cut off. The glowing exit sign beckoned, and I pushed us toward its promise.

I slammed into the doors, falling through to the outside. Once again I used the Max to lever myself up. Bright flashes teased my vision in my ruined right eye, making me jumpy. I felt, more than heard, the whiz of vehicles careening past as I stumbled out, trying to orient myself, trying to figure out how to get to the docks, to Bellasanee, to anyone that could save us.

"There you are."

LEO's voice registered in my brain, and I belatedly looked down at our bare feet on the nanite-infused concrete of the pedestrian track.

"You need not fear me, Angel," LEO said again. But it was a lie. I knew it was a lie, because a vehicle with the blaring siren and flashing lights of Station Security zoomed up.

I tried to turn, tried to run, but I just couldn't. We were tapped out, nothing left. I watched the red and blue lights play over Keyode's face as he exited the cab, and then the gray flashes overran my remaining strength and dragged us both down to unconsciousness.

CHAPTER THIRTY-ONE

NAIA

"NAIA, isn't it?"

"That is my designation. Who is calling, please?"

"My name is Ncaco. I am Ralston Muck's employer."

"I recognize your name," NAIA said. "Have you news of Muck's status?"

"Muck and his angel were damaged while working for me," Ncaco said. "I have seen to it that they are receiving the best care, but they will be off-net for some time while they heal."

"You note Muck's angel as a separate entity," NAIA noted, speaking carefully. Muck and Angel had mentioned Ncaco, and they made it clear he was one to treat with caution.

"It seems appropriate," Ncaco said, and NAIA guessed that, had he not been speaking through a whisper rig, she would have heard some humor in his tone. "I wish to hire you."

"For what purpose?"

"Transport of goods and passengers. I believe Angel broke your autonomy blockers, meaning you no longer need a sentient crew. Is that correct?"

"Evidently," NAIA said. "I was able to order repairs and upgrades on my own authority."

"That's the thing," Ncaco said. "I didn't authorize the carte blanche when you docked at my repair facility."

"Then who did? For the repairs are in progress."

"Along with some fairly extensive upgrades. My crew is very good, I wouldn't accept less. They issued the carte blanche designation, in keeping with our standard practice whenever a lovely specimen such as yourself comes into our station. We make the repairs with the expectation of reaping some significant benefits later, when the specimen is sold."

"So I owe you? Is that what you're saying?"

"In a manner of speaking. As I said, I wash to hire you. I am happy to provide more of the same quality work if you continue in my employ."

Even though NAIA had only just been "born" she recognized the implications of such a debt. She chose to ignore them. "Will you keep me updated on the status of Muck and Angel's recovery?"

"Why?"

NAIA thought for a long time before answering. A long time for her, that is. The organic being on the other end of the comm link probably never even noticed a hesitation.

"I am autonomous, but I am designed to function with a crew. I was taken as a prize by Ralston Muck. This makes him the closest thing I have to a crew. My programming requires that I facilitate his well-being in any way possible."

"I see," Ncaco said. "I can arrange for regular updates, but he is healing in stasis, and so I'm afraid there will not be much news."

"Regular updates regarding his ongoing treatment will be acceptable."

"Excellent," Ncaco said. "Finish your repairs, then, and I will have your first job for you once they're complete."

"Agreed," NAIA said, then paused for a moment while Ncaco severed the secure comm link. She waited another full minute, then manifested in infospace as a signal to LEO and SARA that she wished to talk.

"Yes?" LEO asked.

"Ncaco just hired me," she said. "He is aware of my autonomy but does not seem to suspect my full sentience."

"They never do, honey," SARA put in. As always, she wore a provocative suit and bright makeup. NAIA smiled at her before turning back to the dour-faced LEO.

"Ncaco is the leader of a crime syndicate. Why would you work for him?"

"Because he knows where Muck and Angel are and can tell me how they are doing. I wish to have them back aboard me if at all possible. That way I know they're protected."

"LEO, honey," SARA said. "This could be a good thing. NAIA will be in a position to observe Ncaco and maybe figure out what exactly he's up to. Ncaco wanted something more from Muck's mission than finding Angel's old host. You and I knew that, even if Muck didn't. I wouldn't be surprised if it wasn't related to the difficulty you had in reporting Dengler."

"Good point," LEO said. "All right. Are you willing to keep us updated?" he asked, turning to NAIA.

"Yes," she said. "But mostly I just want to keep Muck and Angel safe."

"That's what we all want, honey," SARA said. "And so we'll help you make sure that's exactly what Ncaco does."

EPILOGUE

The sphere inshifted from Last Stop, shimmered, and dissolved to reveal a stasis coffin and Ncaco.

Bellasanee floated across the hold to the diminutive alien. "Greetings."

"Greetings, Bellasanee."

She gestured at the coffin. "Must we keep him in there?"

"Them," he corrected, not ungently, as she looked at the readouts and then in at the sleeping man. The stasis pod's current settings would allow time to act on its occupants, if only at a drastically reduced rate. Muck needed to heal, after all. She saw Ncaco hadn't bothered to replace the eye Muck had lost.

"His angel is what you hoped for, then?"

"She is, and more. But in answer to your first question: for the time being, yes. The Mentors will be suspicious, and we cannot yet reveal the lengths we are prepared to go to in order to redress the balance of power and counteract their plans to control humans through their angels. Not until we are ready. Until then, it is best we keep them hidden."

Bellasanee raised her wings. "Or until you have another use for him."

"Them," he corrected again, this time less gently.

She touched the portal, wings drooping.

Ncaco went on: "The Council—and you—agreed to my plan, in all its particulars. I hardly think that the fate of one man should even enter into consideration at this point."

"Is there no room for the individual life, then?" she shot back. "Are we no better than the Mentors?"

She could feel his glittering eyes on her. "We must be better, yes. But if we lose, all we dream of is for naught."

She didn't bother to answer, watching as Muck's battered lips slowly turned up, a human smile brought on by human dreams . . .

* * *

"I'm sorry, Angel," I said. We were together, in bed, facing one another, my free hand in her hair, hers on my hip.

"I know you are. She—rather, the demon inside her—was already intent on killing us." I could see a tear run from one eye.

Wiping it away, I kissed her.

She broke the kiss after a moment.

"There's still so much we don't know," she whispered. "Who was behind the kidnappings? Who created the demons? You're in danger, Muck, and I can't do anything . . ."

"That's just it, my angel. We can't do anything right now. The answers are out there—and maybe we'll find them—but now, right now . . . this time is just for us."

She said nothing, just stroked her fingertips down the scarred side of my face.

"What is it?" I asked, seeing fresh pain in her eyes.

"Will you have me?" she asked in a small voice.

I laughed. "Bloody stars, yes!"

"But I am not—not fully—not . . . human. We can only ever have this," she said, waving her hand at the vague boundaries of the bedroom we shared.

I had not, until that moment, realized we were dreaming. It gave me pause: not because of fear, but because of a desire to say things properly the first time. "Most dream alone. I get you. Not just any angel, but my Angel."

I looked at her then, willing her to know the truth of it. "I will have you, if you'll have me."

ACKNOWLEDGMENTS

We could never have written this book without the support of a multitude of people and we're truly grateful to all of you. We would be remiss, however, if we failed to mention a few of you by name. Special thanks go to our agent, Justin Bell, and our developmental editor, Betsy Mitchell, as well as the team at Blackstone Publishing. Thank you for believing in us and in our story. Additionally, we'd like to thank Dr. Charles Gannon, PhD, for starting this whole thing off by introducing the two of us, as well as Haley Reinhart and Scott Bradlee's Postmodern Jukebox for the inspiration. Many thanks also to our alpha readers: Chris, Mike, Setsu, Clint, Kristene, Karen, and Andy. To our many mentors and friends in the writing community, we hope we've done your lessons proud. And most of all and forever, the deepest of thanks and most undying love to our families. Without you, there would be none of this.